...llie said.

She held Case's probing stare. "But most women I know want to take care of themselves."

For the first time, she saw a shadow of cynicism on his face.

Mellie stood abruptly, feeling out of her depth and alarmingly sympathetic toward the man who'd been born and reared with every possible advantage. "I really do have to get busy."

Case unfolded that long, lean body and joined her at the dishwasher, his hands brushing hers as he put his plate alongside her cup. "Is your boss such a slave driver?" he muttered.

They were almost in an embrace, the counter at her back and one big, contrary cowboy planted in front of her. "*I'm* the boss, Case. And I don't need to be spoiled. If I want to fly to Paris this weekend, I'll buy my own damned ticket."

His gaze settled on her lips. For one heart-thumping second she knew he was going to kiss her. "You just told me I'm not your boss. We're here as equals, Mellie. So I guess whatever happens, happens."

* * *

Courting the Cowboy Boss

COURTING THE COWBOY BOSS

BY
JANICE MAYNARD

MILLS & BOON

Published in Great Britain 2015
by Mills & Boon, an imprint of Harlequin (UK) Limited,
Eton House, 18-24 Paradise Road, Richmond, Surrey, TW9 1SR

© 2015 Harlequin Books S.A.

Special thanks and acknowledgment are given to Janice Maynard for her contribution to the Texas Cattleman's Club: Lies and Lullabies series.

ISBN: 978-0-263-25285-9

51-1115

Harlequin (UK) Limited's policy is to use papers that are natural, renewable and recyclable products and made from wood grown in sustainable forests. The logging and manufacturing processes conform to the legal environmental regulations of the country of origin.

Printed and bound in Spain
by CPI, Barcelona

USA TODAY bestselling author **Janice Maynard** knew she loved books and writing by the time she was eight years old. But it took multiple rejections and many years of trying before she sold her first three novels. After teaching kindergarten and second grade for a number of years, Janice turned in her lesson plan book and began writing full-time. Since then she has sold over thirty-five books and novellas. Janice lives in east Tennessee with her husband, Charles. They love hiking, traveling and spending time with family.

Hearing from readers is one of the best perks of the job! You can connect with Janice at twitter.com/janicemaynard, facebook.com/janicemaynardreaderpage, wattpad.com/user/janicemaynard and instagram.com/janicemaynard.

For Jamie and Daniel, who have made Texas
their home...we miss you in Tennessee!

One

"To our new president!"

Three of the four men at the table lifted their glasses in a semicongratulatory toast. Case Baxter, the object of their wry tribute, shook his head and grinned. "Thanks, guys. You're all heart."

Mac McCallum finished off the last bite of his Angus burger and wiped his mouth with a linen napkin. "Seriously, man. What were you thinking? You're like all the rest of us...up to your ears in work. Adding president of the Texas Cattleman's Club to your résumé means more headaches."

Mac was CEO of McCallum Energy...and understood as much as anybody that success was a double-edged sword. Even so, with his big laugh and extrovert ways, he always seemed laid-back and easygoing.

Though the formal dining room at the Texas Cattleman's Club was an elegant venue, the majority of the diners were men like Mac and Case. Tough, honed by physical labor, perpetually tanned by the hot Texas sun. And wealthy… wealthy enough to think they had the world on a string.

Case shrugged. "I know what you're saying. And you're right. But when the committee asked to put my name on the ballot, I could hear my great-grandfather cheering from the grave. It's an honor. And a privilege."

His companions hooted with laughter. Jeff Hartley wiped his eyes. "Of course it is. No denying that. But unless you have some magic formula for adding an extra eight or ten hours to every day, I'm not exactly sure how you're going to manage." Jeff owned and operated the Hartley Cattle Ranch. He knew more than a little about hard work and long days.

Case had an ominous feeling in his gut that said his buddies were right. The truth was, though, Case's family had lived in Royal for generations. They believed in tradition, honor and service. He hadn't been able to bring himself to say no to the nomination. Then again, he hadn't expected to be elected. The other two candidates were older and, as far as Case was concerned, more suited for the position.

But now it was too late for second thoughts. "I'm counting on the three of you to be my unofficial advisors."

Parker Reese leaned back in his chair. "Don't look at me. I'm a doctor, not a rancher. I can get your baby through colic, but all I know about cattle is not to wave a red flag in front of a bull."

In the general laughter that followed, Case spared a moment to marvel at how things had changed. Not long ago, women had finally been admitted into the hallowed halls of the club as full members.

Times, they were a-changin'…

Case looked at Mac with a lifted brow. "I thought Logan was joining us for lunch." Logan Wade was Mac's best friend and one of his key investors.

"He bought three new horses last week," Mac said, "and they're being delivered today. You know how he is."

They all nodded. Horses and women. Logan's two favorite things.

Mac pinned Case with a knowing gaze. "Quit changing the subject. We were talking about you and your soon-to-be-impossible schedule."

"Gil Addison has a son and a wife," Case pointed out. "And he's been a great president. I'm blissfully single."

"True," Mac said. "You're forgetting, however, that Gil is Superman. No offense, buddy, but those are big shoes to fill."

"Your support is duly noted."

Parker, arguably the smartest man in the room, added his two cents' worth. "You've always liked a challenge, Case. Don't let them mess with your head. You've got this."

"Thanks." Case had enormous respect for the dedicated though reserved neonatal specialist. Royal's hospital was lucky to have a doctor of Parker's caliber on staff.

Jeff chimed in, mischief written all over his face. "Parker has more faith in you than I do. I've been in your house, Case. It's such a mess you can't even find the TV remote half the time. I'd suggest burning your place to the ground if we weren't in the middle of a drought."

Case's neck heated. Organization was not his strong suit. Another fact that called his ability to perform his newly acquired duties into question.

"I've already thought about that," he said. "And I have a plan."

Mac gave their waitress a smile as she brought their desserts. "Do tell."

Case stuck a fork in his apple cobbler. "I'm going to hire a housekeeper."

The other three men stared at him.

Mac lifted his spoonful of ice cream and waved it in

the air. "You do know she would have to come inside your house for that to work?"

"Very funny." Case squared his shoulders. "I have the Texas Cattleman's Club to run now. I have to make compromises."

Jeff still seemed shocked. "But what about your rule number one? *Never allow a female into the man cave.*"

"Unless she's a relative." Parker supplied the exception. "Is this new housekeeper a relative?"

Case deserved the inquisition. He was known for his only-half-joking rules for dealing with the female sex. When he was involved in intimate relationships, he preferred to spend the night at the woman's home. So he could leave when he wanted to. "I made the rules," he said, his chin thrust out. "And I can change them. This woman will be a stranger...an employee. She won't be a relative, but she might as well be. I'm not hiring a woman—I'm hiring a housekeeper."

He gave them a warning scowl. "I've learned from my mistakes, believe me." The men at the table knew the unsavory details of Case's not-so-happy marriage. He'd had a fling with his family's accountant, married her and soon found out that she was more interested in spending Case's money than in being a loving wife. It was a salutary lesson.

Jeff turned down a second beer but took a long swig of his water. "Hey, man. A guy's gotta do what a guy's gotta do. And besides, up until the tornado last year, this club-president gig wasn't all that onerous. You'll be fine."

Everyone nodded, but Case saw his own reservations reflected on their faces. Ever since the F4 tornado that had decimated Maverick County and the town of Royal barely over a year ago, the Texas Cattleman's Club had become one of the anchors that held things together.

Coordinating rescue efforts, keeping up morale, apply-

ing for grants, planning reconstruction and renovation—
the club and its president had served the people of Royal
well. Life was mostly back to normal, but there was still
work to be done. So Case couldn't kid himself into thinking that his new job title was ceremonial only.

Jeff interrupted the momentary silence. "If we're finished raking Case over the coals, I have a serious subject to
bring up. Shouldn't we be worried about all the ranches and
other parcels of land that have been sold in Royal lately?
And almost all of it to a single buyer? Does anybody but
me think it's a little odd?"

Mac shrugged. "I'm not really concerned. A number of
people were demoralized by the storm or too strapped for
cash to rebuild. It sounds like they're getting good offers
and the chance to start over somewhere else."

Parker's brow furrowed. "I hadn't heard about this."

Case nodded. "Nolan Dane is back in town and is rep-
resenting a company called Samson Oil in these acquisi-
tions. It doesn't make sense to me, though. Why would
an oil company be interested in the land? The tracts he's
buying up were checked for oil decades ago." Nolan was
raised in Royal, but had been gone for a long time.

"Maybe they're planning to use some of the newer technology and hoping to get lucky," Mac said.

Jeff shook his head. "Nolan seems like a decent guy, but
I'm not a big fan of lawyers, particularly when someone
else is hiding behind that lawyer's legal speak."

"We should give him the benefit of the doubt," Parker
said. "At least as long as the people selling are getting a
fair shake. It seems to me that Case will be in a perfect
position to keep tabs on this kind of thing."

Case glanced at his watch. "Speaking of my upcoming
lifestyle change, I have an appointment in forty-five minutes to interview my new domestic assistant."

"Is that the politically correct term these days?" Jeff seemed dubious.

Parker scrawled his name on the check, charging it to his club account as was their custom. "I think Case is trying to convince himself that a woman won't ruin his carefully preserved chaos."

Mac nodded, his grin broad. "I never met a woman yet who didn't want to domesticate a man. No matter how old she is."

Case lifted an eyebrow. "I am the newly elected president of a venerable organization whose members have run this town for over a century. I think I can handle a housekeeper." He stood, and his friends followed suit.

Mac shook his hand. "You can count on me in the days ahead, sir."

Case grinned. "Bite me."

Parker saluted. "Happy to serve under your command."

Jeff bowed. "*Mi casa es su casa* if you need a place to hide out."

"Everybody's a comedian." As Case said his goodbyes and headed out to the parking lot, he reminded himself what a lucky man he was. He had a ranch and land he loved, a wide circle of friends, and now the respect and a nod of confidence from his peers who had voted for him.

If he could iron out this housekeeper thing, no pun intended, his life would be under control.

Mellie Winslow took in the sights as she made her way down the long driveway leading to the B Hive Ranch. Case Baxter's fields and fences were immaculate, several varieties of placid cattle grazing peacefully as far as the eye could see. She envied him the order and success of his thriving operation.

Though her own small business, the Keep N Clean, was

doing well, it couldn't compare to the prosperity of this massive endeavor. Case must be an extraordinarily busy man—hence his request for a housekeeper.

Mellie knew that a good word from Case Baxter could be a boon to her business. What she didn't know was whether or not Case would accept her proposition.

When at last she pulled up in front of the charming ranch house that had housed generations of Baxter men and their families, she noticed something odd. Apparently, Case's cattle received more attention than did his aging home.

It would be an exaggeration to say the place looked run-down. That wasn't it at all. But the two-story white ranch house with blue shutters seemed tired. Although the wraparound porch was large and appealing, no flowers were planted at its base. No colorful cushions bedecked the porch swing. No toddler bicycles or teen sports equipment lay scattered about the yard.

Although the B Hive Ranch had been in the family for decades, everyone in Royal knew that Case's parents had both died young, and Case was an only child. It would be sad to see the place end up in other hands if Case had no heirs.

It was a possibility, though. Case was in his midthirties and apart from—or perhaps because of—his youthful marriage, which had ended badly, he showed no signs of settling down.

Taking a deep breath to steady her nerves, Mellie reminded herself that this was not her first rodeo. Keep N Clean had just celebrated its eighth anniversary. Mellie herself was a seasoned businesswoman. There was no need to feel intimidated by the power and stature of Case Baxter.

She didn't know him well. Really only in passing.

Hopefully, that was about to change.

Along with her stylish tote that served as purse and catchall, she picked up a navy-and-lime-green folder that she now handed out to all prospective clients. Though the expense of producing the upscale advertising materials had been wince-worthy, she hoped the professional presentation would take her expanding company to the next level.

For some reason, she'd expected someone other than the owner to answer her knock. But only seconds passed before the tall blue-eyed man with dark brown hair opened the door and swung it wide.

He greeted her with a polite smile. "I'm Case Baxter. I'm assuming you're here for the interview?" He filled the doorway, lean and long and wildly handsome.

Mellie shook his hand, feeling his large, warm fingers momentarily squeeze hers. *Wow.* His photograph in the newspaper didn't do him justice. His short hair was neatly cut, though an unshaven chin gave him a rakish air. His clasp was not a second too long. Nothing out of the ordinary.

But her heart beat faster.

He was the perfect specimen of a Texas male. He wore faded jeans that molded to his body in interesting ways… scuffed hand-tooled cowboy boots, a cotton shirt with the sleeves rolled up and an expensive watch that looked as if it could pick up cable channels on Mars.

She found her voice at last. "I'm Mellie Winslow. I own Keep N Clean."

Case frowned slightly. He didn't invite her in. "I thought I was interviewing a prospective housekeeper."

"Well, you are," she said, squirming inwardly. "The truth is, Mr. Baxter, I've been expanding my business. Things are going very well. But when you called asking for help, I decided I wanted to take this job myself."

"Why?"

It was a valid question. She decided that honesty was the way to go. "May I come in so we can talk about it?"

"I supposed so." He led her into the adjoining dining room, where a large formal table groaned beneath the weight of stacks of mail. In the few places not covered by papers, a layer of dust coated the wood.

"Have a seat," he said. "As you can see, I didn't exaggerate my need for assistance."

Mellie sat down, and when he did the same, she slid a Keep N Clean folder across the table. "My rates and services are all listed here. The reason I'd like to do this job myself, Mr. Baxter, is because all of my current staff have taken on as much as they can handle. But I don't want to turn you away. Having the newly elected president of the Texas Cattleman's Club as a client would be invaluable advertising."

"Always assuming you're as good as you say..." He opened the folder and scanned testimonials she'd included from satisfied clients.

Mellie frowned. "I'm a hard worker. I'm meticulous. Also, I don't need anyone to hold my hand every moment. Once you tell me what you require and give me detailed instructions about what I should and should not muck with in your home, I'll be invisible."

Case leaned back in his chair, folded his arms across his chest and stared at her.

She refused to fidget. If this silent showdown was part of his interview strategy, she would pass muster or die trying.

At last he shrugged. "Your rates seem fair. But how do you propose to run your business and at the same time keep my house in order?"

"How do you propose to run *your* business and still keep the TCC in order?"

Sarcasm was one of her failings. Having a smart mouth was not the way to win over prospective clients. Fortunately for her, Case Baxter laughed.

His eyes went from glacial blue to sunshiny skies when he was amused. "Touché." He tapped the fingers of one hand on the table, the small restless gesture indicating some level of dissatisfaction or concern.

Mellie leaned forward, giving him her best reassuring smile. "Have you used another service that wasn't up to par? We could talk about where they fell short."

"No." His jaw tensed for a moment as if some distasteful memory had unsettled him. "I don't tolerate strangers in my home very well. I like my privacy."

"That's understandable. If you prefer, we can arrange for me to clean when you're gone. Or maybe that's the idea you don't like. I could make sure to work while you're here. Whatever it takes, Mr. Baxter. How about a month's trial run? At the end of that time, if you're unhappy with the quality of my work, or if having someone come in to clean bothers you too much, I'll cancel the contract with no penalty."

"I can see why your business is doing well. It's hard to say no to you."

Mellie saw a definite twinkle in his eyes. She flushed. "I'm ambitious. But I think a man like you understands that. You won't regret having me here, Mr. Baxter, I promise. In fact, I swear you'll wonder why you didn't hire Keep N Clean a lot sooner."

"Perhaps I should be absolutely clear. It's more than cleaning. If you come to work for me, I'll want you to take a shot at organizing my home life."

His request wasn't out of the ordinary. Structuring a client's daily environment to maximize family time and personal efficiency was something Mellie enjoyed. But it was hard to imagine Case Baxter allowing anyone, much less Mellie, access to something so personal.

When she hesitated, his eyes narrowed. "Is that a problem?"

"No. Not at all. But you mentioned protecting your privacy, so I would want to be perfectly clear about boundaries."

"Such as?"

She floundered mentally, oddly put off her game by a conversation that shouldn't have seemed the slightest bit provocative and yet drew her thoughts to sex-tossed sheets and whether Case Baxter favored boxers or briefs.

"There are many levels of organization, Mr. Baxter. Everything from creating a well-aligned sock drawer to alphabetizing kitchen spices."

He chuckled, ratcheting up his masculine appeal at least a hundredfold. "I'm sure we can settle somewhere between the two."

"So that's a yes?" She cocked her head, her stomach a swirl of anticipation and feminine interest. Mixing business with pleasure had never been an issue, but with this man, she might have to be on her guard. He had neither said nor done anything to acknowledge the fact that she was a woman and he was a man. But it was kind of a hard thing to miss.

He nodded. "I think it's a workable compromise. We'll see how we get along together. And in the meantime, if you find that one of your other staff members is free to take over here, I'll certainly understand."

"Does that mean you don't want me?"

Sweet holy Hannah. Where had that come from?

Two

His body tightened, on high alert. Though he was almost certain Mellie Winslow hadn't intended anything suggestive by her question, there was enough of a spark in the air to make him react with a man's natural response to a beautiful available woman.

Case hadn't expected the punch of sexual interest. Truth be told, it reinforced his reservations about hiring any housekeeper, much less one who looked like Mellie. He was a sucker for redheads, especially the kind with skin the color of cream and wide emerald eyes reflecting a certain wariness…as if she had been disappointed one too many times in life.

Though she was clearly accustomed to hard physical labor, she was thin but not skinny. The shade of her red curls, spilling from a ponytail that fell past her shoulders, was a combination of fire and sunshine.

He should tell her to go. Right now.

"Are you saying I make you nervous, Ms. Winslow?"

She wrinkled her nose, as if smelling a refrigerator full of rotten eggs. "A little. I suppose. But I'll get over it."

That last sentence was served with a side of feminine defiance designed to put him in his place. She reminded him of a fluffy chicken warning the rooster away from the henhouse.

"Duly noted." He tapped a stack of envelopes. "The trial period works both ways. You may find me such a slob that you'll run screaming for the hills."

Mellie's smile was open and natural. "I doubt that. I've reformed worse offenders than you, believe me."

At that precise moment, he knew he wasn't imagining the sizzle of physical awareness between them. Maybe Mellie didn't notice, but he did. At thirty-six, he surely had more experience than this young woman, who was on the dewy-skinned right side of thirty.

"Don't say I didn't warn you." He glanced at his watch, ruefully aware that he had to put an end to this provocative interview. "I'm afraid I have another appointment in town. So we'll have to wrap this up. Why don't you plan to start Thursday morning? I'll put some thoughts on paper in regard to what I want you to tackle and we can go from there. Does that work for you?"

Mellie stood, smiling. "Absolutely. Thank you, Mr. Baxter. I'll see you soon."

"Call me Case," he said.

"And I'm Mellie."

Case stood at the window, his hand on the lace curtain as he watched his new housekeeper drive away. He knew the time had come to put his house in order—literally—but he had a sinking feeling that he might be making a bad mistake.

The fact that he found Mellie Winslow so appealing

should have put an end to things. He'd fallen for an employee once before and ended up with a broken marriage and a bank account that had taken a severe hit. His track record with long-term relationships was virtually non-existent.

He'd never had sisters. With his mother gone, the only female relatives he had were two cousins in California whom he saw maybe once a decade. He wasn't a good judge of what made women tick. He enjoyed their company in bed. He was even willing to concede that women and men could be friends under certain circumstances.

But as one of the wealthiest ranchers in Maverick County, he'd learned the hard way that a man was not always judged on his own merits. He might marry again one day…maybe. But only if he was damn sure that his prospective bride cared more about his character than his financial bottom line.

As he drove into town, he noted, almost unconsciously, the signs that Royal was flourishing after last fall's F4 tornado. He took in the new storefronts, fresh landscaping and a few empty lots where damaged buildings had been razed in preparation for upcoming construction.

The town had rebounded well, despite tragedy and hardship. Case knew there were still problems to be addressed. Insurance woes remained an issue. Slow payments. Court battles over settlements. The Texas Cattleman's Club had a history of benevolence and community service. Case was determined to use his new position to keep the organization headed in the right direction, particularly in regard to the ongoing tornado cleanup.

For Royal to rebound from tragedy and prosper in the twenty-first century, it would be important to keep all sectors of the local economy alive. Which meant looking out for small businesses. Like the Keep N Clean.

When he pulled up on the side street adjoining the Royal Diner, he saw that the sheriff's squad car was already there. He found Nathan Battle inside, sipping a cup of coffee and flirting with his wife, Amanda, who owned and operated the diner.

Case took off his cowboy hat and tucked it under his left arm. "Sheriff. Amanda. Good to see you both." He shook Nathan's hand and slid into the booth opposite the tall uniformed man he'd come to meet.

Amanda smiled at him. "Congratulations on the election. I just heard the news."

"Thanks." Nathan and Amanda had been high school sweethearts. After a tough breakup as kids, they'd eventually reconnected, fallen in love all over again and married. Case envied the almost palpable intimacy between them. Two people who had known each other for so long didn't have to worry about secrets or betrayals.

Amanda kissed her husband on the cheek. "You boys have fun. I've got to go track down a missing shipment of flour, so Helen will be your waitress today. I'll catch you later."

The server took their order for coffee and dessert, and Case sat back with a sigh. He worked long hours. His daddy had taught him the ranching business from the ground up and drilled into him the notion that in order to be the boss, a man required more than money in the bank. He needed the respect and loyalty of his employees.

Nathan drained his coffee cup and raised a hand for more.

Case shook his head. "Do you live on that stuff?" Nathan was tall and lean and beloved by most of the town. But he rarely had time for leisure.

The sheriff shrugged. "There are worse vices." He smiled at Helen as she gave him a refill, and then he eyed

Case with curiosity. "What's up, Case? You sounded mysterious on the phone."

Case leaned forward. "No mystery. I'm hoping you'll be available to look over the club's security procedures and disaster plans. Last year's tornado taught us all we need to stay on top of emergency preparedness."

"Not a bad idea. I'd be happy to…just email me some dates and times, and I'll block it off on my calendar."

"Thanks. I appreciate it."

They chatted for half an hour, and then almost as an afterthought, Case asked Nathan the question that had been on his mind. "What do you know about Keep N Clean?"

"Mellie Winslow's business?"

"Yes."

"They're a solid outfit. Amanda has used them here at the diner, and I know a lot of people around town who sing their praises. Why?"

"My housekeeper retired eight months ago. Took her pension and headed to Florida. I need help around the house. Especially now that I'm taking on leadership at the club. But I'm out on the ranch a lot of the time, and I don't like the idea of having strangers invade my personal space."

"I'm sure Mellie vets her employees thoroughly. I've never heard a single complaint about anyone on her staff, and I would know if there had been a problem."

"And Mellie herself? She says her staffing situation is stretched to the max, so she would be the one working for me."

The other man obviously knew about Case's short-lived marriage. It was no secret. But it was humiliating nevertheless. Back then, Case had been thinking with a part of his anatomy other than his brain. The resultant debacle had been a tough lesson for a twentysomething.

Nathan raised an eyebrow. "Are you asking as a boss or as a man?"

"What does that mean?" Case hadn't expected to be grilled.

"Well, Melinda Winslow is not only a savvy business-woman, she's a gorgeous unattached redhead who's smart and funny and would be a great companion for any guy."

"Hell, Nathan." Case took a swig of coffee and nearly choked to death when the hot liquid singed his throat. "Why do all of my married friends feel the need to play matchmaker?"

Nathan grinned. "How many times have *you* gotten laid in the last month?"

"Not all marriages are like yours," Case muttered, re-fusing to be jealous of his buddy's good fortune. "Amanda is a peach."

"So is Mellie. Don't let your prejudices get in the way. And to be clear, *now* I'm talking about business again. She can be trusted, Case…if that's what you're asking. You can relax on that score. She's not going to steal the silver or run off with a Picasso."

Case's parents had been art collectors. The ranch house was filled with priceless paintings and sculptures. "Good to know. I liked her during the interview, but it never hurts to get a second opinion. Anything else you want to add to your glowing recommendation?"

Something flickered across Nathan's face…something that gave Case a moment's pause. "What?" Case asked, mildly alarmed.

"Nothing bad about Mellie. But be on your guard if her dad comes around. He's a drunk and a scoundrel. As far as I can tell, fathering Mellie is the only good thing he ever did. I arrest the guy for public intoxication at least several times a year."

"And Mellie supports him?"

"No. He lives off the rents from a handful of properties around town that have been in the Winslow family for generations. In fact, the Texas Cattleman's Club sits on Winslow's land. Mellie helps out with the leasing company now and then, but I think she started her own business in order to keep as far away from him as possible."

"No mother in the picture?"

"She died a long time ago. I imagine she left her daughter some kind of nest egg that allowed Mellie to start her business. The family used to be financially solvent, but Mellie's dad has almost destroyed everything. Booze mostly, but gambling, too."

"Thanks for the heads-up." After taking a bite of pie, Case moved on to another subject. "What do you know about Samson Oil and their connection to Nolan Dane? I hear he's handling a lot of land sales for them."

Nathan nodded. "I've heard it, too. Dane seems a decent sort. And his roots are here. So I assume he's trustworthy. Still, Samson Oil is not a household name. No one seems to know much about them."

"Do me a favor and keep an eye on Dane and the Samson Oil situation. Something about that whole thing seems a little off to me…"

Thursday morning Case found himself pacing the halls of his way-too-big-for-one-man house. At least half a dozen times he'd pulled out his phone to call Mellie Winslow and cancel her services. But he couldn't think of a single explanation that wouldn't make him sound like a paranoid idiot, so he'd resisted the impulse to wave her off.

Relishing his privacy was one thing. But if he continued to keep women out of his house, he'd wind up a withered, curmudgeonly octogenarian with a fortune in the bank and a cold, lonely existence. Still...old habits were hard to break.

Mellie arrived five minutes before their arranged appointment time. He'd have to give her points right off the bat for promptness. When he opened the door at her knock, he blinked momentarily.

It could have been a reaction to the blinding midmorning sun. But more probably, it was the sight of a slender, smiling woman in knee-length navy shorts and a navy knit top piped with lime green. On her feet she wore navy Keds with emerald laces.

The name of her business was embroidered above one breast. A breast that he didn't notice. Not at all.

He cleared his throat. "Come on in. I fixed us some iced tea." Though it was November, the day was extremely hot and muggy.

"Thank you." Mellie carried a large plastic tote loaded with various cleaning supplies.

"Leave that, why don't you? We'll sit down in the kitchen. I hope that's not too informal."

"Of course not."

Mellie seemed at ease when she took a seat. Thankfully, she tucked those long, tanned legs out of sight beneath the table. The back of his neck started to sweat. He wanted to get this over with as quickly as possible and get to work.

He sat down on the opposite side of the table and held out a piece of paper. "Here's a rundown of my priorities. Feel free to add things as you see anything that needs attention."

His newest employee glanced over the list. With her gaze cast downward, he could see how long her lashes were. "This looks good," she said. "I'll start out working full days for a couple of weeks until I get everything deep-cleaned and organized. After that we can talk about how often you'd like me to come."

Case caught himself before his mind raced down a totally inappropriate path. Perhaps Nathan was right. Maybe Case *had* gone too long without sex. Because everything that came out of Mellie Winslow's mouth sounded like an invitation.

Case cleared his throat. "I was at the diner and saw Nathan the other day. The sheriff had good things to say about you and your business…that you were completely trustworthy."

"How did that come up in conversation? Were you investigating me?"

"No, no, no," he said, backpedaling rapidly. "But you can't fault me for asking what he knew about you."

She stood up, her expression going from affronted to glacial in seconds. "In the folder I gave you several days ago there were half a dozen references. Any one of those people could have vouched for me. It wasn't really a *police* matter, Mr. Baxter."

"I've offended you," he said, surprised at her reaction.

She tossed his list at him. "If you're going to constantly keep tabs to make sure I haven't cleaned out your safe or absconded with a priceless painting, then I don't think this is going to work out. Good day, Mr. Baxter."

Before he could react, she spun on her heel and headed for the front door, her ponytail bouncing with each angry step.

"Wait." Belatedly, he sprang to his feet and strode after her, whacking his hip on the corner of the kitchen table. "Wait, Mellie."

He caught up with her in the foyer as she picked up her supplies. "Don't leave," he said. "We agreed to a trial period."

"Shortest one on record," she snapped.

He really had no choice but to grab her arm in a gentle grip. "I'm *sorry*," he said…as forcefully as he knew how. "If you leave, I'll sue for breach of contract." He said it with a smile to let her know he was joking. But Mellie Winslow didn't look the least bit amused.

Wiggling free of his hold, she faced him, her expression turbulent. "I'm proud of my business. It's been built on word of mouth and the quality of the employees I hire. Keep N Clean has never had a single complaint of anything going missing…or of anything being damaged, for that matter."

Case rarely made a misstep, but he knew this was a bad one. "I am sincerely sorry. I shouldn't have asked the sheriff about you."

"Amanda Battle is a friend of mine. Do you understand that I'm embarrassed?"

He did. For the first time, he looked at his actions from Mellie's perspective. To a Texan, honor was everything. She had a right to be upset.

"Let's start over," he said.

She stared at him. "Under one condition. No trial period. You sign the contract today."

The negotiator in him was impressed. But more importantly, as a man, he found her bold confidence arousing. Everything about her was appealing. In other circumstances, he would have made an effort to get to know her more intimately.

Mellie Winslow, however, was here to put his house in order, not warm his bed. "I begin to see why your business is so successful. Very well, Ms. Winslow." He held out his hand. "You've got a deal."

Touching her was his next mistake. Awareness sizzled between them. Her skin was smooth and warm, her hand small and feminine in his grasp. He maintained the contact a few seconds longer than necessary.

When he released her and she stepped back, for the first time, he saw uncertainty in her eyes. "I probably overreacted," she muttered. "I have a temper."

A grin tugged the corners of his mouth. "So the red hair is the real deal?"

"It is. I'm sorry, too. I shouldn't have been so touchy."

They stood there staring at each other, the air rife with things best left unspoken. "I should go," he said. "And let you get started."

She nodded. "If I have any questions, is it okay to text you?"

"Of course."

Her green eyes with a hint of gray warmed slightly. "I'll try not to bother you."

Too late for that. He picked up his keys from the table beside the front door. "See you later, Mellie Winslow. Good luck with my house."

Three

Mellie watched him go with mixed feelings. On the one hand, it was much easier to familiarize herself with a new house if the owner was not underfoot. Still, she wouldn't have minded if her new boss had lingered. She was curious about Case Baxter. Even though he was an arrogant, know-it-all male.

He was an intriguing combination of down-to-earth cowboy and high-powered businessman. It was no secret he was worth millions.

From what she'd heard around town, in addition to running his massive and wildly successful cattle operation, Case liked investing, particularly in small businesses. He believed in supporting the local economy. After the tornado—when the banks were stretched thin giving out loans—Case had floated some cash around the community, as well.

People in Royal liked and respected Case Baxter. Which explained his recent election as president of the Texas

Cattleman's Club. The newspaper had run a bio along with
the article announcing the results. Mellie knew that Case
was thirty-six, which made him seven years her senior.

The age gap wasn't significant, except for the fact that
she still felt as though she was starting out, while Case was
a man in his prime...in every way that counted.

Shrugging off her absorption with the sexy cowboy, she
made herself focus on the job at hand. Case's home was
a stunning example of what could happen when the past
was carefully preserved even amidst modern improve-
ments. Unfortunately, the beauty of the old house was
obscured by clutter.

Judging by the kitchen, Case apparently grabbed only
breakfast and lunch at home. Presumably, he ate dinner
out most nights. She found orange juice and milk in the
fridge and a couple of boxes of cereal in the cabinet. Lunch
items were similarly sparse. Aside from pizzas and a couple of steaks in the freezer, his larder was woefully bare.

There was no reason in the world for her to feel sorry
for Case Baxter. The man had everything he wanted or
needed. He could hire a full-time chef if he liked. But the
thought of him rattling around this big old house on his
own gave her a twinge.

Not many men had the gift of making a home cozy and
warm. Case was a Texas bachelor. Macho. Authoritative.
Accustomed to giving orders and running his ranch. He
wasn't the kind to bake cookies or pick flowers.

That mental image made her chuckle. Time to get to
work.

She started with the dining room, since it seemed the
most straightforward. Case had instructed her to pitch
all the junk mail into the recycle bin and to keep only
the things that looked personal or otherwise important.
Though the stacks of envelopes, catalogs and circulars

were high, anybody with half a brain could sort through this kind of stuff in no time.

When she was done, there were maybe a dozen pieces of *real* mail remaining. She carried them down the hall and put them on Case's desk, a beautiful antique rolltop. His office was curiously impersonal. No knickknacks. No photographs, not even of his parents.

That was the thing about cleaning someone's house. It was an oddly intimate activity. She understood suddenly why a man like Case had been hesitant about hiring help. If the state of his home was any indication, he was a guarded man, one who didn't easily reveal his secrets.

By the time she made it to his bedroom, she had spent most of the day in only three rooms. That was no surprise, really. Decluttering was a slow process, especially when it involved someone else's belongings. But she had been successful. The living room and dining room were now spotless, as was Case's study.

It was past time for her to leave, so his bedroom would have to wait. But she did take a moment to gather discarded clothing and carry the items to the laundry room. Tomorrow that would be her first priority.

She paused in the doorway, lingering a moment, unable to help herself. The man's bed was hedonistic. An enormous carved four-poster that looked Spanish in origin dominated the room. No expense had been spared in the bed linens. The ecru sheets and thick, fluffy coffee-brown comforter were both masculine and luxurious.

The covers were tangled, as if their owner had passed a restless night. In the jumble of clothing she'd picked up off the floor and from a chair and in the bathroom, there were no pajamas. Maybe Case Baxter slept in the nude.

With her face hot and her stomach jumpy, Mellie went back and made the bed quickly before retreating, content to leave this battlefield for another day. Never before had she taken such an intense interest in a client's sleeping arrangements. Her imagination ran rampant, imagining Case's big, tanned body sprawled against those whisper-soft sheets.

She swallowed hard, feeling the unmistakable rush of sexual arousal. This was bad. Very bad. Not only was she too busy for any kind of relationship, sexual or otherwise... but Case was one of Royal's most eligible bachelors. He wasn't likely to be interested in the hired help.

Mellie's family went way back in Royal, maybe as far back as Case's did. Despite that, when she eventually married and started a family, she wanted an ordinary man, one who would have time to be a daddy...a man who was interested in home and hearth.

As far as she could tell, Case had tried marriage and found it lacking. He'd be unlikely to dip his toes into that water again anytime soon, if ever. And since she wasn't the kind of woman who was comfortable having casual sex, there was no point in seeing Case Baxter as anything other than a paycheck and a valuable advertisement for Keep N Clean.

Feeling unaccountably morose, she told herself she was just tired after a long day's work. She gathered her things, let herself out and carefully locked the front door.

After the short drive back to town and a forty-five-minute stop at her office to check mail and phone messages that hadn't been routed to her personal cell, she headed for home. She had a date tonight with a favorite TV show, some leftover spaghetti and her comfy sofa.

But the plan changed when she found her father camped out on her doorstep. It looked as if he had been sitting there for a while, because he had an empty beer bottle at either hip. His eyes were bloodshot. Though he stood when she walked up the path to the small duplex she called home, he was unsteady on his feet.

"You changed your locks," he said, a look of bafflement on his florid face. Harold Winslow was short and round with salt-and-pepper hair and skin weathered by the Texas sun. Once upon a time he had been a successful business-man. But when his beloved wife died, his alcoholic ten-dencies had taken over.

Hugging him briefly, she sighed. "I'm a grown woman, Daddy. I like my privacy. You don't seem to understand that." She had tried her best not to fall into a codependent relationship with her only living parent. But that was eas-ier said than done.

The trouble was, Mellie felt his pain. Ila Winslow had been the center of their lives. When cancer took her away from her husband and sixteen-year-old daughter, their world had caved in. Harold found solace in whiskey. Mel-lie had been forced to grow up far too quickly.

Harold followed her into the house. "Any chance you might fix dinner for your dear old dad?"

She counted to ten beneath her breath, keeping her back to him. "We can order a pizza. I'm beat. I was planning to eat leftovers."

"Pizza works. You got any cash? I left my billfold at home."

It was an old game they played. Harold could live com-fortably off the rents from the properties he still owned. But money slipped through his fingers like water through a sieve. When he ended up broke again and again, he came knocking at Mellie's door...sometimes figuratively, but more often than not, literally...like tonight.

Swallowing her disappointment at having her hopes for a peaceful evening shattered, she managed an even tone. "Go ahead and order what you want. I'm going to change clothes."

By the time she returned to the living room, her father was sprawled in a recliner, the television remote in his hand. He gave her a smile, but behind it she thought she saw despair. His existence was aimless. No matter how hard Mellie tried, she couldn't get him to understand that his life wasn't over. She loved her dad, but once in a while, it would have been nice to lean on him instead of always having to be the grown-up.

Dinner arrived soon after. She paid for the two small, fragrant pizzas and tipped the young man, wondering if the fact that she and her father couldn't even agree on toppings was proof that she would never convince him to see things her way.

They ate in silence, the television filling the void. Finally, she finished her meal and decided it was now or never...a conversation that was long overdue. But she would come at it indirectly.

"I started a new job today, Daddy. I'm going to be cleaning and organizing for Case Baxter."

Harold raised an eyebrow. "The new Texas Cattleman's Club president?"

"Yes. Having him as a client will be a coup, I think."

"I'm proud of you, baby girl."

For once, she thought he meant it. "Thank you." She paused and said a prayer. "I'm doing well, Daddy. Keep N Clean is solvent and growing."

He nodded. "Good for you."

An awkward silence descended, but she forged ahead. "We need to talk about last week."

Immediately, his face closed up. "I'm fine," he muttered. "Quit worrying. I don't drink as much as you think I do."

"Sheriff Battle found you passed out in the street." She

hesitated, dreading his reaction. "I'd like to pay for you to go to rehab before it's too late."

"I hadn't eaten breakfast. My blood sugar was too low. I fainted, that's all."

"Daddy, please. I know you miss Mom. So do I. Every day. But at the rate you're going, I'm likely to lose you, too."

Harold lumbered to his feet and stood with what dignity he could. "There's nothing wrong with me. Surely a man can enjoy a couple of beers without getting a lecture."

It was more than beer. A lot more. And the alcohol abuse was aging him rapidly. "Just think about it," she pleaded. "It won't be so bad. I've read about some beautiful places right here in Texas. I want you to be healthy and strong so you can play with your grandchildren one day."

Her father snorted. "You don't even date. That cleaning company of yours won't keep you warm at night. Maybe you'd better quit worrying about me and find yourself a man."

It was exactly like Harold to go on the attack when she tried to talk to him about his drinking. "I've got plenty of time for that."

For a split second the naked pain in her father's heart was written on his face. "We all think we have plenty of time, Mellie. But love isn't a permanent gift. Losing it hurts. I'm pretty sure that's why you don't let any man get too close. I'll make you a deal, darlin'… When you get your life in order, I'll let you muck around with mine."

She stood at the door and watched him go…his gait slow but relatively steady. He'd had his driver's license revoked time and again. Fortunately, the home where Mellie had grown up and where Harold still lived was centrally located in Royal, making it possible for her father to walk to his destinations for the most part.

As she showered and got ready for bed, she pondered her father's words. It was true that she rarely went out on a date. She'd told herself that getting a business off the ground required determination and hard work. But did it demand the sacrifice of any kind of personal life?

Her pride stung a bit to know that her father had pegged her so well. In her desperate need to get him to admit his failings and seek help, had she overlooked her own response to grief?

Over the years, she hadn't cared enough for any of the men who populated her modest social life to let them get too close. Channeling her energy into Keep N Clean kept her focused. Romance would only get in the way of her life plan.

Ordinarily after a hard day, she was out by the time her head hit the pillow. Tonight, though, she couldn't get settled. Her father seemed increasingly out of control, and she didn't know what to do to help him. He was an adult…with resources. So why did she feel responsible for his actions?

Reaching for a more pleasant subject, she reminded herself that tomorrow she would have the opportunity to spend more time in Case Baxter's beautiful home. It had personality…and history. Bringing it to its full potential would be a pleasure. Not to mention the outside chance she might run into the man himself.

He'd given her a set of keys along with his permission to come and go as she liked during the day. According to Case, he was going to be very busy at the club and also with the ranch. She got the distinct impression he planned to make himself scarce as long as she was working in his house.

Something about that notion made her feel weird and discouraged. Case was exactly the kind of man she found appealing. It hurt that he wanted to avoid her.

Thumping her pillow with her fist, she rearranged the light blanket. The cold would come, but for now, her bedroom was stuffy.

She was finally almost asleep when her phone dinged quietly, signaling a text. Groaning, she reached for her cell and squinted at it in the dark.

Mellie—I hope I'm not disturbing you. I know it's late, but I wanted to tell you thanks. You're a miracle worker. I almost thought I was in the wrong house when I got home tonight. Kudos to Keep N Clean…

Case Baxter. The last person on earth she expected to be texting her at this hour, or any hour, for that matter. Was she supposed to answer? Or simply let him think she was asleep? She hesitated for a moment and then put down the phone.

It was nice of him to take the time to acknowledge her work. Perhaps the message was a peace offering after the argument that had started their day.

With a smile on her face, she snuggled back into the covers, unable to squelch the hope that she would run into Case tomorrow and maybe even see him in her dreams.

Four

Case jammed his Stetson as far down on his head as it would go and hunched his shoulders, trying to bury his chin in the collar of his rain jacket. The weather gods had finally sent Maverick County some moisture, but it wasn't the days-long, soaking rain they needed.

Instead, the precipitation was a miserable, icy-cold drizzle that chilled a man right down to the bone, a dramatic shift from the previous day. Since seven this morning, he'd been out riding the fence line with his foreman, looking for problems. They'd lost two dozen head of cattle in the past few weeks. Everyone suspected rustlers, but before Case involved the authorities, he wanted to make sure the animals hadn't simply wandered away through a hole in the fence.

Now, though he was wet and weary, at least he had the satisfaction of knowing that his fencing was not compromised. Giving the foreman a wave, Case turned his horse and galloped back toward the house. Already this new housekeeper thing was getting in his way.

Ordinarily in a situation like this, he would strip down in the mudroom, walk through his house naked and climb into the hot tub on the sheltered back porch. Unfortunately, that wasn't going to happen today, with Mellie around.

Muttering beneath his breath, he handed off his horse to one of the stable guys in the barn and then strode toward the house. He was grumpy and wet and hungry, and he wanted his castle to himself. His bad mood lasted all the way up until the moment he found Mellie Winslow bending over the side of his bed dusting the base of one of the posts. She was wearing Spandex pants, the navy fabric curved snugly against a firm, shapely butt.

His heart lodged in his throat at about the same time his gut tightened with swift and wicked arousal that swept through his veins. He actually took half a step backward, because he was stunned.

Mellie straightened and smiled, her expression cautious. "Mr. Baxter. Case. I'm sorry. I didn't think you'd be home in the middle of the day. I can move on to another room for now."

He shrugged. "I need a hot shower. Won't be long." Unless maybe he got distracted imagining Mellie in there with him…

"I put fresh towels in your bathroom a few minutes ago. They're probably still warm from the dryer." She paused and seemed hesitant. "Have you had lunch?"

Come to think of it, he hadn't. Which might account for his surly attitude. "No. I'll grab something in a minute."

"Would you like me to fix soup and a sandwich? It's no problem."

His fingers were cold, his skin damp. But inside, he was

burning up. He should have hired a seventy-plus grand-motherly type with a bun and absolutely no sex appeal.

But he hadn't. Oh, no…not at all. He'd brought temptation into his house. Hell, into his bedroom, to be exact. He cleared his throat. "That would be nice. Thanks."

Mellie nodded and walked away.

Case slumped against the wall, his heart thundering in his chest. There was far too much going on in his life right now to get sidetracked by a very inconvenient attraction. He was a grown man. Not a boy. He could control his physical impulses.

In the shower he turned the water hot enough to sting his skin. Maybe the discomfort would take his mind off the fact that he had an erection…a big one. Damn. What was it about Mellie that caught him off guard and made him hungry to strip her naked and take her to bed?

She was beautiful in a girl-next-door kind of way, but Royal had more than its share of attractive women. Case didn't find himself panting after every one of them. Maybe it was the fact that Mellie was in his house.

That was *his* mistake.

He dried off and changed into clean clothes. His others, wet and muddy, lay in a pile on the bathroom floor. Presumably, his new housekeeper would take care of washing them.

Standing in the middle of his bedroom, he acknowledged the truth. He didn't *want* Mellie Winslow washing his clothes. He had far better plans for activities the two of them could enjoy.

It was bad enough that she was cleaning up after him. Maybe he was weird, or maybe his first marriage had ruined him, but he liked relating to women on an even footing. Mellie was talented and capable and she was doing exactly what he had hired her to do. So why was he getting freaked out about everything?

He found her in the kitchen. She hummed as she moved around the room. His oak table, situated in the breakfast nook, was set with a single place mat, a lone plate and glass and a set of silverware.

Mellie waved a hand. "It's all ready, if you want to sit down."

He leaned against the doorframe. "Aren't you joining me?"

Her eyes widened momentarily and a faint pink crept up her neck. "I had a big breakfast. I usually work through lunch."

"At least a cup of coffee, then. You're on the clock, and it's my clock." He smiled to put her at ease, since she was eyeing him dubiously.

"Okay."

He refused to sit at the table and be served as if he were in a restaurant. Instead, he waited until she placed the bowl of tomato soup and the grilled cheese sandwich at his place. "This looks great," he said. "Thank you."

"Coffee to drink?"

"Yes, please. Black."

Mellie poured two cups, added milk and sugar to hers, and then joined him as they both sat down. He hadn't realized how hungry he was until the aroma of freshly prepared food reached him and his stomach growled loudly.

It was Mellie's turn to grin.

They sat in companionable silence for a few moments, Mellie sipping her coffee and Case wolfing down the food she had prepared for him. Though soup and a sandwich wasn't exactly haute cuisine, the comfort food was filling and delicious.

"So tell me, Mellie…what are your ambitions for Keep N Clean?"

If she was surprised by his interest, she didn't show it. "When I'm dreaming big," she said, "I think about franchising and moving into medium-size towns all over Texas."

He raised an eyebrow. "I'm impressed. You must have a knack for numbers."

"I have an associate business degree. But most of the hands-on stuff is self-taught. It's important to discern what a client wants and then be able to provide it. Especially in a service industry like mine. You have to stand out from the pack."

"Very true, I'm sure." He finished his meal and stood to get more coffee. He held out the coffeepot. "More for you?"

Mellie shook her head. "No, thanks. I'd better get back to work."

"Not so fast," he said. The urge to detain her was unsettling. He had plenty to keep him busy. But he didn't want to walk away from Mellie. "Tell me about yourself."

Mellie smiled wryly. "Is that really necessary?"

"Humor me."

"Well…"

He watched her search for words and wondered if she was going to avoid any mention of her father. Fortunately, he was a patient man…so he waited.

She shrugged. "It's not very exciting. I grew up in Royal. My mom died of cancer when I was sixteen. My dad went into a tailspin of grief, meaning I ended up being the parent in our relationship. I knew I wanted to start my own business, so I looked around and tried to find something that filled a niche. Royal had an industrial cleaning company but nothing smaller, other than individuals who worked for themselves."

"And here you are."

She wrinkled her nose. "Working for the brand-new president of the Texas Cattleman's Club."

"Are all your employees as eye-catching in that uniform as you are?"

Her jaw dropped a centimeter. "Um…"

"Sorry. Was that out of line?"

"More like unexpected." She stared at him, gaze narrowed, clearly trying to get inside his head. "Someone told me that you don't like women invading your house."

He winced. Royal's gossipy grapevine was alive and well. "That's not exactly accurate."

"No?" She cocked her head as if to say she knew he was skirting the truth.

"I like my privacy. But since I have neither the time nor the inclination to round up dust bunnies or clean out the fridge, I have to make compromises."

"Ah."

"What does that mean?"

"It means I'm accustomed to wealthy people who barely even acknowledge the presence of a service worker. We're invisible to them. Nonentities."

He frowned. "I can't speak for all the comfortably well-to-do families in Royal, but my friends aren't like that."

"If you say so. And for the record, Case, no one would describe you as only 'comfortably well-to-do.'"

Mellie Winslow had a bit of a chip on her shoulder. He hadn't noticed it before, but she wasn't trying to hide it now. "Does my lifestyle offend you, Mellie?" he asked gently, wondering if she would rise to the bait.

She sat back in her chair, pushing a few stray wisps of hair from her forehead. The set of her jaw was mutinous. "Let's just say that I don't have a single Modigliani hanging in my hallway."

"My parents were art collectors. They traveled the world. But believe me when I tell you I would trade every sculpture and painting in this house to have Mom and Dad back with me for just one day."

Mellie knew she had stepped in it…big-time. She felt hot color roll from her throat to her forehead. The taste of shame was unpleasant. "I am *so* sorry, Case. You're right, of course. Relationships matter more than things. Money doesn't buy happiness."

He grinned at her, his scruffy chin making him dangerously attractive. His hair was still damp from his shower. "Don't get carried away. Money is good for a lot of things."

"Such as?"

He leaned his chair back on two legs, defying gravity, and crossed his arms over his chest. "Flying to Paris for the weekend. Buying a yacht. Scoring Super Bowl tickets. Supporting a charity. Spoiling a woman."

She had a feeling he threw that last one in to get a reaction.

There *was* a reaction. But it happened someplace he couldn't actually see. She cleared her throat. "Being spoiled is nice, but most women I know want to take care of themselves."

For the first time, she saw a shadow of cynicism on his face. "Maybe you know the wrong rich people and I know the wrong women."

Mellie stood abruptly, feeling out of her depth and alarmingly sympathetic toward the man who'd been born and reared with every possible advantage. "There's more soup on the stove, if you're still hungry. I really do have to get busy."

Case unfolded that long, lean body of his from the chair and joined her at the dishwasher, his hands brushing hers as he put his plate alongside her cup. She felt his breath on her cheek when he spoke. "Is your boss such a slave driver?" he muttered.

She turned around to face him. They were almost in an embrace, the counter at her back and one big contrary cowboy planted in front of her. She lifted her chin and propped her hands behind her. "*I'm* the boss, Case. And I don't need to be spoiled. If I want to fly to Paris this weekend, I'll buy my own ticket."

His gaze settled on her lips. For one heart-thumping second, she knew he was going to kiss her. "Don't be so touchy, Mellie. There's nothing wrong with a man doing nice things for a woman."

Things? Oh, Lordy. "Um, no… I guess not." She stopped and looked him straight in the eyes. "Are you flirting with me, Case Baxter?"

He shrugged, a half smile doing interesting things to that enticing mouth. "What happens if I say yes?" His thick eyelashes settled at half-mast. She could smell the soap from his shower and his warm skin.

Her inclination was to tell him. The truth. The shivery, weak-in-the-knees truth. She wanted hot, sweaty, no-holds-barred sex with Case Baxter on his newly made bed.

But sadly, she was known for being smart and responsible. "I suppose if you say yes, I'll have to point out unpleasant things like sexual harassment in the workplace."

"You just told me I'm not your boss. We're here as equals, Mellie. So I guess whatever happens, happens."

Before she could react, he brushed his lips against her forehead, turned on his heel and strode out of the kitchen.

Mellie put her fingers to her lips like a schoolgirl who had just been kissed by the captain of the football team. Case's chaste kiss had not made contact with her mouth at all. But she felt the imprint of his personality all the way to her toes.

Moving cautiously toward the window, she peeked out and saw him striding toward the barn. She hadn't expected him to actually *work* on his ranch. Which made no sense, because if Case had been an entitled, supercilious rich jerk, he'd never have been elected president of the Texas Cattleman's Club. People liked him.

She might like him, too, if she could get past the huge neon sign in her brain that said Off-Limits.

In the meantime, she had things to do and places to be.

The master suite had occupied most of her time today, and not only because she was fascinated with its owner. The bathroom and bedroom were huge. By the time three o'clock rolled around, she had deep-cleaned everything from the grout between the tiles to the wooden slatted venetian blinds.

In addition to an enormous teak armoire, the quarters boasted a roomy walk-in closet. Her fingers itched to tackle the chaos there, but that chore would require a chunk of time, so she would postpone it until tomorrow. No sense in starting something she couldn't finish.

She left earlier than the day before and told herself it wasn't because she was avoiding Case. He was an important client, true, but she still had to run her business.

Back at her office, she popped the top off a bottle of Coke and downed it with a sigh of pleasure. Sure, the sugar and caffeine weren't good for her, but as addictions went, the soda was fairly harmless.

Which was more than could be said for her inability to erase Case from her thoughts. If he was seriously testing the waters with her, she would have more to worry about than a sugar rush. Allowing herself to be lured into a multi-millionaire's bed would be the height of folly.

She knew herself pretty well. Guarded. Suspicious. Independent.

On the flip side, she was hardworking, generous and ambitious. The one thing that she was *not* was a good judge of men's motives. Perhaps because her mother had not been around to share advice, Mellie's father had gone overboard in warning her about guys and sex.

He'd told her sex was all boys wanted from a girl...that it was up to her to make good decisions. Well, here she was. Almost thirty. A modest financial success. A dutiful daughter. And only steps away from missing out on things like romance and motherhood and the chance to meet a man who could make her toes curl with his kisses.

Case might not be her idea of the perfect man for the long haul, but he might be exactly the right guy for the here and now.

Five

Case returned to the house at four thirty, anticipating another round of verbal sparring with the delightfully prickly Mellie. But her car was gone. Was she avoiding him? And didn't she know that the male of the species enjoyed a chase?

He had dinner plans with Nathan Battle tonight. Amanda was out for the evening with her book club. So Case and the sheriff were looking forward to medium-rare steaks, a couple of games of pool and a sampling of sports on Nathan's brand-new big-screen TV.

Nathan had offered to do the cooking. Case brought a case of imported beer and an apple pie he'd picked up at the bakery. The rain had ended several hours ago, so the two men sat outside in the gathering gloom and enjoyed the crisp air.

The scent of beef cooking made Case's stomach growl. Which made him think of the last meal he'd eaten. The one a certain redhead with kind eyes and a stubborn chin had made for him.

Nathan kicked the leg of Case's chair. "I'm the quiet one. You're supposed to entertain me with tales of the rich and famous."

Case slunk farther down in his chair. "I'm not famous."

Nathan laughed out loud. "What's eating you, Baxter? I've had livelier conversations at a morgue. Is the new job title weighing you down?"

"I'm not official for ten more days, so no."

"Then what?"

Case drained his beer and popped the top on a second. "You're imagining things."

Nathan stood, flipped the steaks and sat back down with a sigh. "Then it must be the new housekeeper. Is she making you take off your shoes at the door? Or forbidding you to eat popcorn in the den?"

"Very funny. It's my house. I can do whatever the hell I please. Mellie doesn't run my life."

"Mellie? Wow. First names already?"

"I wasn't going to make her call me Mr. Baxter."

"Fair enough." The other man paused. "Here's the thing, buddy. I have to pass along a warning."

"A warning?"

"Yes. From Amanda. But to be honest, I agree with her."

"Should I be worried?"

"It's not a joke, Case. If you screw around with Mellie Winslow either literally or figuratively, Amanda will come after you. And my wife can be pretty scary when she's on her high horse."

"I don't understand."

"Mellie hasn't had an easy life. You're way out of her league."

"Now, wait a minute." Case felt his temper rise.

"I'm not insulting Mellie. She's great. But you're older than she is, more experienced, and your financial position puts you at an advantage. I'm merely suggesting you not do something you'll regret. I know you, Case. You're not interested in a serious commitment. Admit it."

Case dropped his head against the back of his chair, scowling at the crescent moon above. "You know what it's like to have a failed relationship in your past." Nathan and Amanda had spent years apart. They had been high school sweethearts, but malicious lies had destroyed that bond, and it had been a very long time before they'd reconnected.

"I do. It makes you second-guess yourself. Especially when the reason it happened was that you were young and stupid."

"Are we talking about me or you?"

"Both of us."

Fortunately, Nathan dropped the subject. The steaks were ready, and neither man was the type to spill his guts, even to a friend.

The rest of the evening was lighthearted and comfortable. Sports talk. Good food. But as Case drove back to the ranch later that night, disappointment filled his chest. Mostly because he knew the sheriff was right about Mellie.

She was not the type of woman to indulge in casual sex. And Case wasn't interested in anything else.

Mellie sat at her desk and groaned as she hung up the phone. Two of her employees had called in because their kids had the flu. Which meant a major juggling act on the boss's end. Several houses couldn't be postponed for one reason or another. She called a few clients who weren't tied to a certain schedule and changed their cleaning days, offering a credit toward next month's bill for the kerfuffle.

In half an hour, she had reassigned her workforce and

come to the inescapable realization that she was going to have to put Case off for a couple of days. It wasn't a problem in the grand scheme of things. He didn't have any big social events at his home coming up. He merely wanted her to deep-clean and organize his house.

Postponing the job for forty-eight or even seventy-two hours was not a crisis. But what made her squirm was the fact that Case Baxter would think she was running scared.

She was not completely inexperienced. There had been two serious relationships in her life, both of which she'd thought might turn out to be the real deal. But in the end, the first one had been puppy love, and the second a crush on a man fifteen years her senior.

When she'd finally realized that the older guy was more of a parental figure than a soul mate, she'd broken things off. That was four years ago. She'd been alone ever since. By choice.

She knew when a man wanted her. And she had the confidence to turn a guy down without apology. Her body was hers to give. She was old enough now to understand that true love was rare. Even so, she would not allow herself to be physically intimate with a man on a whim.

Case Baxter tempted her. Her own yearning was what scared her. She liked him and respected him. Even worse, no woman under eighty and in her right mind could be immune to his bold sex appeal.

He was at the height of his physical maturity. Tough, seasoned, completely capable of protecting a woman or giving her pleasure. He was wealthy, classy and intelligent.

Damn it. She was vulnerable around him, and the feeling, although stimulating, was not one she welcomed.

She didn't believe in postponing unpleasant tasks. Pulling out her smartphone, she rapidly composed a text…

Case—I have a couple of employees out today, so I have to cover some shifts. I'll be back at your place in a few days. Will give U a heads-up beforehand. Sorry for the inconvenience. Mellie Winslow

She added her name at the end because she wasn't sure he had entered her contact info into his phone. Before she hit Send, she stared at the words. She was shooting for businesslike and professional.

Would he read her message in that vein, or was her genuine need to postpone the Baxter house going to be seen as a ploy to snag his attention? Oh, good grief. The man probably didn't give a flip about whether or not his cleaning lady showed up. He probably flirted automatically.

She was making a mountain out of a molehill.

The next three days were long and physically taxing. Mellie worked hard, much as she had in the beginning. In her early twenties, by the sweat of her brow, she had turned Keep N Clean into a viable operation. Clearly, she needed to rethink her staffing situation, though. She couldn't continue to work on a shoestring.

She needed enough flexibility to handle unexpected illness on the part of her employees as well as the occasional new customer like Case. The past two weeks were a wake-up call. If she really had dreams for expansion, she would have to take her game up a notch.

The one thing that needled her now was Case's total lack of communication. Given his past behavior, she'd expected some kind of cheeky text from him in return. All she'd gotten was No problem, and that was it. Even this morning when she had messaged him to say she was returning to the B Hive Ranch, there had been no response.

Was he miffed with her for putting him off? Did he

think a man in his position deserved to be kept at the top of the list? Maybe it wasn't egalitarian, but the truth was, he did. The significant fee he was paying her, combined with the cachet of having him on her client list, made keeping Case happy a priority.

It was barely nine when she arrived at the ranch. She saw some activity out in the fields and down at the barn, but the house looked much as it always did. Case had probably been up at first light doing whatever he did when he wasn't tormenting unsuspecting housekeepers.

Though she would have died before admitting it, her heart beat faster than normal as she ascended the front steps. Another weather front had moved in. The morning air was damp and cold, reminding her that Thanksgiving was not far off on the horizon. The date fell early this year.

Hesitating at the front door, she held her key in her hand. Case still hadn't replied to her text saying she was on the way. But he hadn't said *not* to come.

What if he was in bed with a woman? What if he hadn't seen or heard her text? To stumble upon her client in a very personal moment would be humiliating in the extreme.

Muttering beneath her breath, she closed her eyes and wrinkled her nose, berating herself silently for having such a ridiculously over-the-top imagination.

At last, she knocked firmly, listened and finally opened the door. The house seemed empty. Besides, she'd heard the rumors about Case's famous rules. He didn't entertain females at his place.

After hovering in the foyer for several moments, she told herself she was being foolish. Today she was going to tackle Case's kitchen. The sooner she started, the sooner she could escape, and maybe she wouldn't have to deal with the aggravating rancher.

The house was cold, but she didn't adjust the heat. By

the time she'd been working for an hour she would be plenty warm. The windows in the yellow-toned kitchen were designed to let in lots of light, creating a cheery center to the house. But today the skies over Royal were gray and sullen.

November could go either way in Maverick County. At the moment, the weather was depressing and chilly to the bone.

Mellie left her jacket on, shivering in spite of herself. Her usual routine was to clean from the top down. Which meant unloading all the cabinets above the beautiful amber-toned granite countertop. In the utility cabinet she found a stepladder that was just tall enough to give her access all the way to the ceiling.

Cleaning the tops and outer surfaces of the cabinets was not so hard. But when she opened the first one, she grimaced. Dishes and other items were crammed in with no regard for maximizing space. There wasn't even the barest nod toward order.

The best thing would be to empty everything and then come up with a system for replacing items in a manner that would make them easy for anyone to find. The contents of the first couple of cabinets were puzzling. On the very top shelves she found exquisite antique china…lots of it, cream-colored with an intricate pattern of yellow and gold. Farther down were ultramodern dishes in black and white.

She frowned. She was no designer, but the monochrome set looked as if it belonged in a high-end loft in SoHo, not a historic ranch house in Texas. Maybe Case thought the old stuff was not masculine enough for his taste. That was a shame, because there was a good possibility that the stacks of delicate porcelain were something that had been handed down through his family for generations.

Glassware was heavy. By the time she had emptied three

cabinets—three shelves each—her back was aching. The little bottle of ibuprofen she kept in her purse was empty, but she remembered seeing some in Case's bathroom.

In the elegant hallway with its hardwood floor and celadon walls, she stopped dead when she heard a sound. A groan. Not the house creaking as old houses often did, but something human.

She hurried her steps. "Mr. Baxter… Case?"

Another sound, this one muffled.

By the time she reached the open doorway to Case's bedroom, she half expected to find him passed out on the floor, felled by a blow from a burglar. Her imagination ran rampant.

But the truth was equally distressing. Case lay facedown on his bed, wearing nothing except a white button-down shirt and gray boxer briefs.

Thank goodness he was facedown. Her first response was honest and self-revelatory but not pertinent to the situation.

Was he drunk? Surely not on a weekday before noon. She said his name again, approaching the bed with all the caution of a zookeeper entering the cage of a sleeping lion.

When she was close enough to touch him, her brain processed the available info. His head was turned toward her, his face flushed with color. Thick eyelashes lay against his cheeks. His lips were parted, his breathing harsh.

Ever so gently, she laid her hand against his forehead. The man was burning up with fever. Case Baxter had the flu. Or at least something equally serious.

He moaned again as she touched him. When he turned on his side toward her, she stroked his hair before she realized what she was doing. It was the same caress she would have used with a hurting child.

But Case was no child. His big masculine body shook

uncontrollably, though his tanned chest was sheened with sweat. She probably shouldn't have noticed his chest, but with his shirt completely unbuttoned, his flat belly and the dusting of dark hair at his midriff were hard to miss.

Her knees were less than steady, and she felt a bit woozy. Even passed out cold, Case did something to her. Something not entirely comfortable.

Ignoring her inappropriate reactions to the half-naked man, she pushed and pulled at him until she had him covered all the way to the neck. Case's limbs were deadweight. The rest of him was equally heavy.

She sat down at the edge of the bed. On top of the covers. "Case?" she said. "Can you hear me?"

He muttered and stirred restlessly.

"Case." She put a hand on his shoulder, injecting a note of authority, hoping to pierce the layers of illness that shrouded him.

His eyelids fluttered. "What?" The word was slurred.

How long had he been like this? People *died* from the flu. Not that Case was elderly or an infant, but still. "You need a doctor," she said firmly. "Who can I call?"

The patient scrunched up his face. "Head hurts."

Those two words destroyed her defenses entirely. Her newest client might be handsome and rich and arrogant as heck, but right now he was just a man in need of help. "I'll get you some medicine," she said. "But I need to check with your doctor."

"Call Parker." The command was almost inaudible.

She knew who he meant. Parker Reese was a gifted doctor who had saved more than one newborn at Royal Memorial Hospital. Parker and Case were friends. But for the flu?

"Don't you have a regular doctor?"

"Call Parker…"

This time she could barely hear the words. "Sure," she

groused. "I'll call a very busy specialist in the middle of the day to talk about a case of the flu." But she didn't really have much choice. Picking up Case's phone from the bedside table, she sighed when she realized she couldn't access his contacts.

She shook his shoulder again. "I need your code, Case."

"2…2…2…2."

Was he delirious, or did he really have such a ridiculously easy password? Apparently the latter, because it worked. Seconds later she located Parker Reese's info and hit the green button.

She fully expected to get an answering machine, but on the third ring, a deep masculine voice answered. "Hey, Case. I'm about to go into surgery. What's up?"

Mellie flushed. Luckily, the highly educated doctor couldn't see her face. "Dr. Reese, this is Mellie Winslow. I showed up at Case Baxter's house this morning to clean and found him passed out on the bed. I think it's the flu, but I have no idea how long he's been like this."

"Several of us played poker last night. Case left early. Must have been feeling bad. I have a full schedule today, but I'll pop by this evening."

"And in the meantime?"

"Push fluids. Alternate acetaminophen and ibuprofen every two hours. Chicken soup and anything else bland."

"I don't think he's going to be eating anytime soon, but I'll try."

Parker's voice changed. "Do you want me to send out a nurse?"

Mellie hesitated. Two seconds. Three at the most. "Thank you, but no. I can do my work and look in on him from time to time. I don't think he would be happy if we brought a stranger in to look after him."

"Good point."

"I'm sorry I bothered you."

"No worries. I'm glad you did. I'll be by later to check on you both."

Mellie ended the call and stared at the man in the bed. Somehow she had gone from being a paid housekeeper to a volunteer nurse.

What would Case Baxter think of this new development?

Six

Mellie located both medicines and fetched orange juice from the kitchen, as well as a notepad to record the time. She didn't want to be responsible for overmedicating her patient. With a little prayer for patience, she returned to the bedroom.

It was a relief to know that Case hadn't been lying sick and alone in this big house for three days. But that also meant he still had tough hours ahead of him. The flu had hit early this year and with a vengeance. Many people had been caught off guard, thinking they still had time to get a flu shot. Fortunately, Mellie had already gotten hers.

Now she knew why Case hadn't answered her text this morning. He'd been out cold, maybe since he'd stumbled home last night. Poor man. She sat on the edge of the bed again, choosing to ignore the fact that the *poor* man was worth seven or eight figures. Even so, he was human. And at the moment he needed her.

She put a straw in the juice since she wasn't sure she

could coax him into sitting up. "Case…" She spoke in a loud voice, hoping to rouse him. He stirred but didn't open his eyes.

"Case." She touched his arm. While she'd been in the kitchen, he had tossed back the covers. His body was still hidden from the waist down, but a broad masculine chest was on display.

His skin was hot. Too hot. She said his name a third time. Finally, he lifted one eyelid. "Leave me alone."

Grumpy and sick was better than semiconscious. "Dr. Reese—Parker—said you need to drink some juice and take something for your fever."

Case rolled to his side, taking the covers with him. He started shivering again. Big, visible tremors that shook the bed. "Parker c-c-can kiss my a-a-ass."

Exasperated, she glared at the lump of truculent male. "You told me to call him."

"Did not."

"Oh, for goodness' sake." She moved around to the other side of the bed and crouched so she could reach his mouth with the straw. "Drink this. Now." She was only slightly astonished when he opened his lips and sucked down a good portion of the OJ.

The muscles in his throat worked. "Tastes good."

"Of course it does. Now open up one more time. You have to swallow these pills."

She tapped his chin. He cooperated, downing the medicine without protest, but afterward he blinked and focused his fever-glazed eyes on Mellie. "Did you just poison me?" he asked.

"Don't tempt me." She glanced at the clock. Hopefully, his temperature would improve in half an hour or so. She grabbed the extra blanket from the foot of the bed and spread it over Case. "Better?"

His nod was barely perceptible. "Thank you."

Those two words went a long way. He might be sick and ornery, but at least he had enough sense not to alienate the only person helping him. "I'll check on you again in a bit. Sleep, Case. That's all you need to do."

Unexpectedly, he reared up in the bed. "Gotta go to the bathroom." He lurched to his feet before she could stop him. And promptly fell over like a giant redwood. His head caught the edge of the bedside table as he went down. A trickle of blood oozed from the small wound.

Dear God in heaven. Save me from stubborn men. She got down on her knees beside him. "Are you okay?"

He rolled to his back, his face ashen. "I never get sick," he said, a look of puzzlement creasing his brow.

His bafflement would have been funny in another situation. But their predicament erased any humor she felt. How in the heck was she going to put him back in bed?

"Can you get on your hands and knees?" she asked. "I'll help you up."

"Of course I can." Five seconds passed. Then ten. Case didn't move. His eyes were half-open, his attention focused upward. "Please tell me there aren't really snakes on my ceiling."

"Your fever is very high. Those are swirly lines in the paint."

"Thank God." He closed his eyes, and his breathing became heavy.

Mellie rubbed his arm. "You said you needed to visit the bathroom. Let's go." Her heart contracted in sympathy, but she kept the drill-sergeant tone in her voice.

She pushed on his hip, hoping to give him a nudge in the right direction. Finally, muttering and coughing, he rolled over and struggled onto his knees.

"Good," she said. All men responded to praise, right?

Putting her arm around his shoulders, she urged him upward, her back screaming in protest. Fortunately, his brain got the message, and he finally stood all the way upright, albeit with a little stagger.

Slowly, carefully, she maneuvered him toward the open bathroom door. She had cleaned every inch of this luxurious space. It was now as familiar to her as her own. But somehow, with the master of the house sharing it with her, the area shrank.

Case noticed himself in the mirror. His mouth gaped. "I look like hell."

"No argument there." She steered him toward the commode.

Her patient locked his knees suddenly, nearly toppling both of them. "I don't need your help."

She counted to ten. "If you fall in here, you could kill yourself on the ceramic tile."

"I'll hold on to the counter."

"Fine." It wasn't as if she wanted to be privy to a personal moment, no pun intended.

Case leaned on the vanity. Mellie retreated and closed the door. She hovered in the middle of the bedroom, half expecting any minute to hear a crash. Instead, nothing but silence.

At last the commode flushed and water ran in the sink. Finally, she heard something she hadn't expected at all. "Mellie? I could use a hand."

She opened the door cautiously and found him sitting on a bench underneath the window. His face was pasty white. He looked miserable. The fact that he had actually asked for help spoke volumes.

Without comment, she leaned into him and looped her arm beneath his armpit and around his back. "You ready?"

He nodded. It was hard to keep a professional distance

from a guy when pressed hip to hip with his big, muscular body. Fortunately, the brief trip across the bedroom rug passed without incident. She managed with Case's help to get him underneath the covers and settled with his head on a pillow.

Without thinking, she put a palm to his forehead to gauge whether or not his temperature was improving. Though Case was clearly befuddled, he raised one eyelid. "You should go home."

His voice was hoarse and thready. She could barely make out the words. "I marked off my book today to work on your house. I'm cleaning the kitchen. It's no trouble to check on you now and then." It was possible he didn't even hear her response. Already his chest rose and fell with steady, harsh breathing.

There was nothing she could do for him now. Instead, she returned to the kitchen and tackled the mess she had made. She had learned a long time ago that to completely overhaul a closet or a cabinet meant creating chaos in the beginning.

The rest of the day crawled by. Dr. Reese's reference to bland foods was a moot point. It was all she could do to coax Case into drinking water and juice from time to time—that and keep him medicated.

At five o'clock she had a decision to make. She didn't have a child at home or a husband waiting. If she'd been in the middle of something jobwise, she would have stayed an extra half hour to complete the task.

But the kitchen was mostly finished, no mess in sight. And Case's request to put his house in order came with no timeline, no urgency. So there was no reason for her to hang around except for the fact that Case Baxter was sick and alone.

They barely knew each other...at least if you overlooked

the not-so-subtle physical attraction and the way he had almost kissed her earlier in the week. Still, this wasn't about flirting or finding a possible love interest or even indulging in some carnal hanky-panky.

Her current situation was dictated by the need of one human to help another.

Wow, even in her head that sounded like pretentious rationalization.

Finally, she worked out a compromise between her conscience and her sense of self-preservation. She would wait for Dr. Parker Reese to arrive, and then she would head home.

Seven o'clock came and went. Then eight. Then nine. The sun had long since set. Outside, the world was cold and gray. Case's house echoed with silence.

Mellie lived alone, and she was perfectly happy. Why was she so worried about a man who chose to be a bachelor? He liked his freedom and his privacy. It was only because he was sick that she felt sorry for him. Surely that was it.

At nine thirty Case's cell rang, with Parker Reese's number appearing on the caller ID. Mellie had kept Case's phone with hers, not wanting him to be disturbed.

She hit the button. "Hello? Mellie Winslow here."

Parker sounded harried and distracted. "I am so sorry, Ms. Winslow, but we've had two moms check into the hospital in early labor and they're having problems. I'll likely be here most of the night. How is Case?"

"He's sleeping. The fever is down some, but it hasn't broken." She'd found a thermometer in Case's bathroom and had kept tabs on the worrisome numbers.

"You're doing the right things. Don't hesitate to call or text if he seems dramatically worse."

"Oh, but I—"

Parker said something to someone in the background, unwittingly interrupting Mellie's response. "I've got to go," he said, his tone urgent. "Keep me posted."

Mellie hung up and stared at the phone. How had she gotten herself into such a predicament?

She wandered down the hallway and stood in the doorway of Case's bedroom, watching him sleep. Today was Friday. The only things she had planned for the weekend were laundry, paying bills and a movie with a girlfriend on Sunday afternoon. Nothing that couldn't be postponed.

But what would happen if she stayed here? Case might be furious.

Then again, could she live with herself if she went home and something happened to him? He was wretchedly sick, certainly not in any shape to prepare food or even to remember when he had taken his doses of medicine. As long as the fever remained high, he might even pass out again.

Her shoulders lifted and fell on a long sigh. She didn't really have much choice. Only a coldhearted person could walk out of this house and not look back. Even if Case hadn't been handsome and charming and sexier than a man had a right to be, she would have felt the same way.

It was no fun to be ill. Even less so for people who weren't married or otherwise attached. Fate and timing had placed her under the man's roof. She would play Clara Barton until he was back on his feet. When that happened, if he tossed her out on her ear, at least her conscience would be clear.

Her bones ached with exhaustion. Not only had she worked extremely hard today, she'd spent a lot of time and energy on her patient. Suddenly, a hot shower seemed like the most appealing thing in the world. Fortunately, she kept spare clothes in the car for times when she needed to change out of her uniform.

Though it seemed like the worst kind of trespassing, she made use of one of the guest bathrooms and prepared for bed. She found a hair dryer under the sink and a new toothbrush in the drawer. In less than twenty minutes, she had showered and changed into comfy yoga pants and a soft much-washed T-shirt.

Case's king bed was large and roomy, and he was passed out cold. She would get more rest there than if she slept in the guest room and had to be up and down all night checking on him.

That reasoning seemed entirely logical right up until the moment she walked into his bedroom and saw that he had, once again, thrown off the covers. The man might have the flu, but looking at him still made her pulse race.

She would have to set the alarm on her phone for regular intervals, because Case was still racked with fever. When she managed to get the thermometer under his tongue and keep it there for long enough to record a reading, it said 101.2 degrees. And that was with medication.

No telling how high it would go if left untreated.

She gave him one last dose of acetaminophen, coaxed him into drinking half a glass of water and straightened his covers. After turning on a light in the bathroom and leaving the door cracked, she stood by the bed.

When this was all over, he would be back to his bossy, impossible self. But for now, he was helpless as a baby.

Refusing to dwell on how unusual the situation was, she walked around to the other side of the bed and sat down carefully. Case was using two of the pillows, but she snagged the third one for herself. There was no way she was going to climb underneath the covers, so she had brought a light blanket from the other bedroom.

Curling into a comfortable position, she reached out and turned off the light.

* * *

Case frowned in his sleep. He'd been dreaming. A lot. Closer to nightmares, really. His head hurt like hell and every bone in his body ached. Not only that, but his mouth felt like sandpaper.

He had a vague memory of someone talking to him, but even those moments seemed unreal.

Suddenly, the shaking started again. He remembered this feeling...remembered fighting it and losing. Aw, hell...

He huddled and gritted his teeth.

Above his head, a voice—maybe an angel—muttered something.

He listened, focused on the soft, soothing sound. "Oh, damn. I didn't hear the alarm. Case, can you hear me? Hold on, Case."

Even in the midst of his semihallucinatory state, the feminine voice comforted him. "S'kay," he mumbled. "I'm fine."

Vaguely, he was aware of someone sticking something under his tongue, cursing quietly and making him drink and swallow. "You are definitely *not* fine."

The angel was upset. And it was his fault. "Hold me," he said. "I can't get warm. And close the windows, please."

The voice didn't respond. Too bad. He was probably going to die and he'd never know what she looked like. Angels were girls, weren't they? All pink and pretty with fluffy wings and red lips and curvy bodies...

Belatedly, he realized that if he survived whatever living hell had invaded his body, he might get struck dead for his sacrilegious imagination.

Suddenly, his whole world shifted from unmitigated suffering to *if this is a dream, I don't want to wake up*. A body—feminine, judging by the soft breasts pressed up against his back—radiated warmth. He would have whimpered if it hadn't been unmanly. *Thank you, God.*

One slender arm curved around his waist. "You'll feel better in the morning, Case."

The angel said it, so it must be true. Doggedly, he concentrated on the feel of his bedmate. It helped keep the pain away. Soft fingers stroked his brow. Soft arms held him tight.

Maybe he would live after all.

Seven

Case opened one eyelid and groaned when a shard of sunlight pierced his skull. *Dear Jesus*. If this was a hangover, he was never going to drink again. And if this was hell, he was going to beg for another chance to relive his thirty-six years and hope for a better outcome.

He moved restlessly. Even his hair follicles hurt. His chest felt as if someone had deflated his lungs. But his brain was clearer than it had been. Though he didn't want to, he made himself open both eyes at the same time. Sitting in an armchair beside his bed was Parker Reese.

Parker hadn't yet noticed that Case was awake. The other man was checking emails and/or texts, frowning occasionally and clicking his responses.

Case cleared his throat. "Am I at death's door? Have you come to show me the error of my ways?"

His doctor friend sat up straight, his gaze sharpening as he turned toward the bed. "You should be so lucky. No...you're going to be fine." Even so, Parker's expression held enough concern to tell Case that something serious was afoot.

"I didn't know you made house calls." Turned out, it even hurt to talk.

"I don't. Here. Drink something." Parker picked up a glass of ice water and held the straw to Case's lips.

Case lifted his head and downed the liquid slowly, trying not to move more than necessary. "Seriously. Why are you here?"

Parker's eyes widened, expressing incredulity. "Maybe because you're half-dead with the flu?"

"Only half?" Case tried to joke, but it fell flat.

Parker pulled out his stethoscope, ignoring Case's wince when the cold metal touched his skin. Listening intently as he moved the disc from side to side, Parker frowned. "We have to watch out for secondary infections, pneumonia in particular."

"How did you know I was sick? Did I look that bad when I left the poker game last night?"

Parker sat back, his head cocked with a clinician's focus. "Today is Saturday. The poker game was Thursday night."

Case gaped at him. "What happened to Friday?"

This time Parker's grin held a note of mischief that rattled Case. "You tell me. I've only been here twenty minutes."

Case subsided into the warm nest of covers and searched his brain for an explanation. He remembered someone in the bed with him, but that someone definitely hadn't been male. He'd been far too sick for any fooling around, so the woman he remembered must have been a dream.

He wet his chapped lips with his tongue. "No more jokes, Parker. Did I really lose an entire day? Surely you didn't wait on me hand and foot. You're a good friend, but not that good."

Parker chuckled. "I'll take pity on you. Yes, you lost a day. You've been out of it for thirty-six hours. And no. I wasn't here to help, though I'm damned sorry about that. You picked the worst possible time to get sick. We've had baby after baby born at the hospital, some of them in worse shape than you, unfortunately. I haven't even been to bed yet, but I wanted to see how you were doing."

"Then who—?"

Parker held up his hand. "Mellie Winslow showed up to work yesterday morning and found you semiconscious, burning up with fever. She stayed with you all day and all night. To be honest, you might have ended up in the hospital if it weren't for her. You've had it rough."

"Damn." It was the best response Case could summon, and the most articulate. With a sinking feeling in his stomach, he remembered someone helping him into and out of the bathroom. Mellie Winslow? Good Lord. "Where is she now?" he asked hoarsely.

"I sent her home so she could change clothes and get some rest."

"Is she coming back?"

"I'd say that's up to you. Mellie knows you like your privacy."

Case winced. "Yeah, I guess she does." He'd certainly hammered home that lesson when he hired her. "I don't know why she stayed with me. I haven't been exactly cordial." In fact, he'd been a bit of a jerk the last time he saw her.

Parker shrugged. "I can hang around until midday. That gives you some time to think it over."

By the time noon came and went, Case had managed a shower with only a little help, had consumed a modest breakfast and lunch, and had realized with no small dose of humility that he had a lot for which to be thankful. Maybe he could salve his conscience concerning Parker by writing another large check to the hospital. Parker got absolutely giddy when he talked about upgrading technology in the NICU.

But what about Mellie?

Parker was on the way out the door when his phone dinged. Case saw his buddy glance down and then look at him.

"What?" Case asked. "Who is it?"

"Mellie wants to know if she needs to come back. What should I tell her?" There was no judgment in Parker's steady gaze.

"I barely know her," Case muttered. "She's not under any obligation to take care of me."

"She's a nice woman. You could do worse."

"Nathan says Amanda will hunt me down and neuter me if I trifle with her friend."

"Trifle?"

"You know. Play around with her."

Parker shook his head in disgust. "I *know* what the word means. Are you tempted to *trifle*?"

"I don't know. Maybe. She's seen me at my worst."

"Is that a good thing or a bad thing?"

"I'm pretty sure Mellie Winslow isn't interested in my money."

"We were talking about you and the flu. Have you changed the subject?"

Case leaned against the doorframe, his knees the consistency of spaghetti. "I need to get back in bed."

"Yes, you do. Your color is lousy."

"Tell her I'll call her after I take a nap."

"You sure?"

Case nodded. "Yeah. Maybe by then I'll have had an epiphany."

"Sounds painful."

"Very funny." Case held out his hand. "Thank you."

Parker returned the handshake. "Glad I could help. If you get worse, don't hesitate to call. Men make lousy patients. Being a hero in this situation is the worst thing you could do."

"Duly noted."

With Parker gone, the house was quiet again. Case stumbled back to his bedroom and fell facedown on the bed. Parker had made him swear to take medicine on schedule. Case intended to keep that promise, but first he had to sleep.

Mellie paced from one side of her smallish living room to the other. Dr. Reese had said that Case would be in touch. But Reese had contacted her right after lunch, and it was now almost five o'clock.

In the interim, she had put together a dish of homemade lasagna and baked that, along with some oatmeal cookies. The house smelled wonderful, but it looked as if she was going to be eating alone.

She could hardly expect Case to be grateful for her help. Men hated feeling vulnerable. Case probably loathed the realization that Mellie had played nurse. Besides, there was a chance he didn't even remember her being there.

But Mellie remembered. Wow, did she. In the middle of the night when Case had finally stopped shivering and his temperature had moderated, she had relaxed enough to doze with him in her arms. She didn't sleep deeply. But when she roused again and again to check on her patient's condition, it had been a shock to find herself entwined with him in a quasi-intimate position.

Gradually, as the night waned, she'd felt something shift inside her. No matter how much she wanted to maintain boundaries for her own emotional protection, after this weekend she would never be able to look at Case the same way again.

The fact that he hadn't called or even sent her a text this afternoon told her he wanted her to stay away. The loud silence hurt. Even though she thought she understood why he hadn't made contact, her feelings were bruised. In truth, she might have to assign someone else to continue cleaning Case's house. The situation was likely untenable.

Telling herself not to be maudlin and foolish, she wandered into the kitchen and found a paper plate and some plastic utensils. She was too tired to worry about cleaning up after herself, and since she had unloaded the dishwasher only an hour before, she didn't want to make a mess.

She was moments away from scooping out a small serving of pasta when her phone made a quiet noise. Her heart pounding, she wiped her hands and glanced at the screen.

Are you busy?

It was Case.

No. Are you hungry?

She told herself she was only being a Good Samaritan. That she wasn't throwing caution to the wind and launching herself willy-nilly into a situation that was wildly inappropriate. Feeding a neighbor in need was a Texas tradition.

Her phone buzzed again.

I'm starving.

I made lasagna. Would you like me to bring you some?

I don't want to interrupt your evening.

She smiled in spite of herself.

It's no trouble. See you soon.

Working rapidly, she covered the casserole dish and wrapped it in towels to keep it warm. The loaf of fresh bread from the bakery in town could be heated in Case's microwave. Even if Dr. Reese had provided lunch for his friend, that was a long time ago. She didn't want Case to wait any longer than necessary.

On the way out to the ranch, she lectured herself. *Stay calm. Don't let him bait you. Treat him like a brother.*

There were two problems with that last suggestion. Number one—she'd never had a brother. And number two—her reactions to Case Baxter bore no resemblance at all to sibling affection. He disturbed her, provoked her and made her want things.

Unfortunately, the trip was not long enough to gain any real handle on the situation. Before she knew it, she was unloading the car and making her way up the steps of Case's home. With her arms full, she had no choice but to ring the bell.

It was almost a full minute before the door opened. Case stood there staring at her, the planes of his face shadowed in the harsh glare of the porch light. "Please come in," he said.

In the foyer, he insisted on taking most of the load away from her. As she followed him to the kitchen, she couldn't help but notice the way his gray sweatpants rode low on his hips. In the midst of the cheery room she had worked so hard to organize, the lighting was better. Now she could see all of Case. His navy cotton shirt was unbuttoned, revealing a white T-shirt underneath that clung to the contours of his muscled chest.

When she could tear her gaze away from all that male magnificence, she saw—as she'd suspected—that he was definitely not 100 percent. His eyes were sunken and his hair was askew. But he smiled.

"This smells amazing, Mellie."

"I hope you like Italian food. I suppose I should have asked about your preferences before I fixed something."

"I'm not a picky eater."

He set the containers on the table and pulled out her chair. "Let me get you a glass of wine," he said. But she noticed that despite his polite manners, he was weaving on his feet.

"Oh, for heaven's sake." She resisted his attempt to make her take a seat. His skin was clammy and his hands unsteady. "You look like you're about to pass out. Sit down, Case. Now."

Surprisingly, he obeyed, but said, "I don't expect you to wait on me." The statement was a shade on the belligerent side.

She handled him the same way she would a fractious toddler. "You're not well. Sit there and rest while I get things ready."

He didn't argue, but his gaze followed her as she moved around his kitchen. His eyes were dark, his unshaven jaw tight. "I owe you an apology," he said. "For what happened when you were here before."

She shot him a look. "You mean last night?"

His jaw dropped noticeably before he snapped it shut. Dark color slashed his cheekbones. "I don't remember much about last night."

For once, she had the upper hand. He was juggling a healthy dose of discomfiture. It was almost funny to see the suave, self-assured cowboy off his game. "Not much to remember." She set a plate of food in front of him. "Eat it before it gets cold."

He grabbed her wrist, not painfully, but firmly. Enough to stop her in her tracks. "I made inappropriate remarks about your clothing. I kissed you. I'm sorry."

Resting her hand on his shoulder, she let herself lean on him. "Don't be silly. You gave me a compliment. I was flattered. And the truth is, you're *not* my boss. You were right. We're equals. A man and a woman."

"And last night?"

When she slept in his bed, holding him in her arms? "Last night was nothing," she said. "You were sick. I couldn't very well leave you here alone. I'm glad you're on the mend."

When she sat down and took a bite of her lasagna, she almost choked at the look on Case's face. His laser stare made her squirm in her seat. There was no way he could know for sure. He'd been too feverish and addled to understand that she had held him like a lover, doing everything she could to give him comfort.

He finally picked up his fork, but he never took his eyes off her. "Parker told me I lost an entire day…that I had a very high fever. He said I might have ended up in the hospital if you hadn't been here to look after me."

"I think your friend exaggerates. It was no big deal."

Case leaned across the table and put his hand over hers. "It is to me. Thank you, Mellie. For everything."

Eight

Case knew he had shocked her. Hell, he had shocked himself. He wasn't a touchy-feely kind of guy. Beneath his hand, Mellie's fingers were soft and delicate. An impression at direct odds with what he knew to be the truth about the woman. She was strong and independent. She didn't need a man to take care of her. Which made it all the more inexplicable that he had the strongest urge to do that very thing.

He forced himself to release her. "Sorry," he muttered. "I didn't mean to make you uncomfortable." She had the look of a rabbit frozen in the grass, trying to appear invisible.

Mellie shook her head. "I'm not uncomfortable. But I'm trying to figure you out."

When he made himself take a bite, he realized how hungry he was. He chewed and swallowed, weighing her words. "I'm an open book."

She snorted and tried to cover it up as a cough. "Um, no."

"Explain yourself, woman." He waved a fork in the air. When Mellie smiled at him, he felt a tug of desire low in his belly.

"First of all," she said, "you're wealthy and available, but you don't date. At least not in Royal."

"How would you know that?" She had him spot-on, but that was beside the point.

"I have my sources." Now her smile was wry.

"Go on."

"You're a self-professed privacy junkie, but you know everyone in town, and you are so popular and well regarded the powers that be elected you president of the Cattleman's Club."

"Liking privacy is not necessarily the same as being a hermit."

"True."

He circled back to the most promising point. "I'm flattered that you've studied me."

Mellie shook her head. "Don't be. Your ego is too healthy as it is."

"Ouch." He paused, realizing that he was deliberately flirting with Mellie. But his sexual overture wasn't necessarily being reciprocated. "Ego is neither good nor bad. I think it's a matter of degree."

"And where would you fall on that scale? Somewhere near the top, I think."

He stared at her, no longer amused. "You might be surprised." Finishing his meal, he stood and poured himself another glass of wine, cursing the fact that his legs were wobbly. Sadly, it had nothing to do with the modest amount of alcohol he had consumed. How long was this damned flu going to keep him down? He had places to go, people to see.

At his best, he would have enjoyed sparring with Mellie

Winslow. But he was definitely not at his best. He brought the bottle with him to the table and collapsed into his chair, trying not to let on that he was light-headed.

Mellie studied him. "You need to be in bed," she said.

"Will you join me?" The words popped out of his mouth uncensored. His subconscious was an uncivilized beast.

His dinner companion gaped. Her mouth snapped shut as hot color reddened her cheeks. "What is it about men?" she muttered, the question apparently rhetorical.

Now he had her measure. If he wanted to keep Mellie off balance and not the other way around, all he had to do was give her the unvarnished truth about what he wanted from her. "What do you mean?"

She shrugged. "You're barely able to stand, and still you obsess about sex."

"It's in our DNA. We can't help it. Especially when a beautiful woman brings us dinner and plays nurse."

"I wasn't playing last night. You were sick."

"I'm only sorry I wasn't able to enjoy it."

"Case!"

Now it was out in the open. He wanted her. And he was almost certain she wanted him, too. But he needed confirmation before he went any further. He would never pursue a woman who wasn't interested.

"There's a strong spark between us. But tell me you don't feel it, and I'll leave you alone. Am I wrong?"

He saw the muscles in her throat work as she sputtered and looked anywhere but at him. "You're not wrong."

Three words. Three damn words, and he was hard as granite. He studied her, unable to come up with a response. She wasn't wearing her uniform. Instead, soft denim jeans outlined long legs and a narrow waist. In deference to the weather, she wore a pale green pullover sweater. The

V-neck exposed a long porcelain-skinned throat and fragile collarbone.

A man could get lost nibbling his way across that territory.

Under other circumstances, he would have stripped her naked and taken her on this kitchen table. Tonight, however, he had to accept his limitations. "Sadly, I don't have the stamina at the moment to follow up on that interesting admission."

"There's no reason you should." She appeared entirely, frustratingly calm...until one noticed the way her lips trembled the tiniest bit.

"We're dancing around this, aren't we?" The woman who almost certainly didn't have casual sex and the man who wanted more than he was able to give at the moment.

Mellie stood, resting her hands on the back of her chair. "I'll come back tomorrow...with more food."

"Don't be afraid of me, Mellie." He meant it. He couldn't bear the notion she might think he was blasé about this. The level of his fascination with her, the depth of his hunger, made no sense. But he wasn't a man to walk away from something he wanted. Even when having her and protecting her seemed to be two diametrically opposed behaviors.

And that wasn't even considering the fact that his actions might spark the wrath of Amanda Battle...or worse, her sheriff husband.

"I'm not afraid of you," Mellie said, her beautiful eyes grave. "Or even afraid of the possibility of us. But I've never started a physical relationship with a man, knowing up front that it had an expiration date."

Her words made sense. He even understood her caution. The feminine hesitation, though, only made his libido fight all the more to be heard. "It's not necessary to plan every turn in the road in advance...is it?"

Temper sparked in her expressive eyes. "Do me the favor of not pretending, Case. If I have sex with you, we both know it will be a physical thing only. No hearts and flowers. No pledges of undying love."

"That's pretty cynical."

"But accurate."

He wanted to argue, but he didn't have a leg to stand on. Mellie had pegged him pretty well. "So that's a no?" Never in a million years would he admit that her harsh assessment of his motives stung. Most women in this situation would be all over him.

But he was rapidly learning that Mellie Winslow was not *most* women.

She shrugged. "Let's take it a day at a time. This flu isn't going to go away overnight. Maybe you'll have the opportunity to rethink your invitation."

"Don't go," he said gruffly. He wanted her here...under his roof. In a way he hadn't wanted anything in a very long time. "It's not like I can seduce you. I can barely hold my head up."

Mellie shivered, though the kitchen was warm. He was doing it again. Winnowing away her good intentions. Trying to pretend that he wasn't the Big Bad Wolf and Mellie a wretchedly willing Red Riding Hood.

"I can't stay the night." That was a lie. She *could*. But she wouldn't.

"A movie, then. I'm sick of lying in bed."

"Such a touching offer. I'm better than boredom."

"You have a smart mouth."

She took pity on him. Beneath his masculine swagger, he was the color of milk. "I'll stay for a while."

"Good."

When he got to his feet, she moved closer and slipped

an arm around his waist, inhaling the smell of warm male. "I don't want to scrape you off the floor again."

He chuckled, the low sound making her catch her breath. "Is that how I got the knot on my skull?"

"Let's just say that you were not the best patient last night."

He kissed the top of her head casually, as if they were an old married couple wandering down the hall to watch a favorite TV program. "You're more than I deserve."

"Damn straight." Making Case Baxter laugh was fast becoming her life's work. But it was either that or give in to the urge to join the handsome, bad-to-the-bone cowboy in his bed.

They had their next argument in the den. Case collapsed on the expensive leather sofa and crooked an arrogant finger. "Come sit with me, Mellie."

"I'll be fine right here." She snagged a spot on the matching love seat, a safe distance away from the heavy-eyed male. "Have you taken your medicine?"

He scowled at her. "Is that all you can talk about? You're a broken record."

"I'll get it," she said wryly. Clearly, he was feeling like roadkill and didn't want to admit it.

When she returned after gathering what she needed from his bedroom and the bathroom, Case was holding the remote, his expression moody as he channel surfed. She put a hand on his forehead, not surprised to find it ferociously hot.

"Take these." She shook a couple of caplets into her palm and held out a glass of water.

"I feel fine."

His big body radiated tension. They had entered dangerous territory. Case was physically frustrated, not only from sexual arousal but because his brain was writing a check his body couldn't cash. As far as she could tell, he was holding himself upright by sheer stubbornness.

She nudged his knee, keeping her tone light and gentle. "Be reasonable, and I'll sit with you. You can put your head in my lap."

It was the perfect opening for some of his sharp-edged sexual innuendo. The fact that he said nothing worried her. He must feel worse than she realized.

When he finished the glass of water—and in the process downed his meds—he stretched full-length on the sofa. Mellie sat down as promised, stroking the hair from his forehead. "Do you really want to watch a movie?" she asked.

He shook his head without opening his eyes. "No. I feel like hell."

"Okay, then…"

After a few seconds, Case's breathing deepened, and she knew he had fallen asleep. The old house creaked and popped as it settled for the night. On the mantel, a beautiful clock ticked away the minutes.

The moment was surreal. How had she and Case transcended so many social barriers so quickly? She was the hired help. He was the rich cowboy. He had one failed marriage behind him. She'd always been too afraid of loss to give marriage a try.

Yet here they were. As intimate together as if they had already become lovers.

With nothing else to command her attention, she traced the shell of his ear with her fingertip, trying to imagine what he would be like in bed. Healthy. Vigorous. Demanding.

She pressed her legs together, her insides shaking with what could only be described as lust. Delicious, quivery, melting need. Heaven help her when Case was back to his old self.

Right now he was like some brilliant sun dimmed by a dust storm. The essence of the arrogant cowboy was still there but muted. The reduced kilowatts made it possible for her to keep up her guard. Maybe it was his vulnerability that stripped away her defenses and misgivings. Perhaps Case Baxter had seduced her without even trying.

The evening waned along with her need to hold him at bay. Would she end up sharing his bed? Why shouldn't she? Becoming Case's lover might well turn out to be the highlight of her adult life.

She knew most of the available men in Royal. Not one of them had sparked more than a fleeting interest in her over the years. So maybe she was destined to be happily single, a focused businesswoman, a dutiful daughter and a generous friend.

Living alone was not a dreadful thought. She understood Case in that respect. There was something to be said for peace and quiet and the chance to spend time with your thoughts. Case valued his privacy. Mellie valued her independence. It was a match made in heaven.

Temporary. Wildly enjoyable. Mutually satisfying.

Regretfully, the two of them were not going to get intimate tonight.

At nine o'clock she eased out from under her not-unwelcome burden and stood to stretch the kinks out of her muscles. Case never made a sound. He was deeply asleep.

His chin was shadowed with the beginnings of a dark beard. Even though she had seen him numerous times with his customary scruffy facial hair, now he looked far less civilized.

She felt guilty for leaving him like this. Still, he was a grown man and she was under no obligation, ethically or otherwise, to stay. Parker Reese would check on him eventually.

After tidying the kitchen and gathering her things, she slipped out the front door and locked it behind her. Unfortunately, when she arrived at home, she found her father sitting on the doorstep again.

Nine

She greeted him with a grimace. "It's late, Dad. What do you want?"

He didn't even offer to help her carry anything into the house. Which, unfortunately, was typical. Harold Winslow spent most of his time worrying about Harold Winslow.

"I need to borrow fifty bucks, baby girl. Just until Monday. I'm good for it."

She'd long since given up keeping track of her father's IOUs. His requests were always modest amounts. Fifty here, a hundred there. Even when she gently reminded him he owed her money, he was all smiles and apologies. But the repayment never took place.

It was her own fault. All she had to do was cut him off, and he would get the message...eventually. But regardless of his failings, Harold was her father. He'd helped raise her, and he'd been the one she'd clung to when her mother died. He was her own flesh and blood.

"Why do you need the money, Daddy?" She dumped everything on the kitchen counter and confronted him.

Harold gaped, his expression both astonished and cagey. She'd never before pressed him about where the cash went. She hadn't wanted to know.

His bloodshot eyes stared back at her. "I had a lot of bills this month," he muttered.

"Is that why you don't have enough left for drinking tonight and tomorrow?"

"I don't appreciate your tone," he snapped.

She had definitely ruffled his feathers. But at the moment, she was so tired and dispirited she didn't care. "I'm not an ATM. I have expenses of my own and a business to support."

"Where have you been tonight?"

The change of topic caught her off guard. After a split second's hesitation, she saw no reason to dissemble. "I took dinner to Case Baxter. He has the flu."

"Well, ain't that sweet."

Her father's colloquial sarcasm nicked her patience. "I'm tired, Daddy. And it's late. Why don't you go home and have a rum and Coke...without the rum."

Harold's face turned red. "What's gotten into you, girl? If you think hangin' out with that fancy-ass richer-than-God cowboy makes you something special, you're wrong. Big-shot ranchers don't marry women who clean their toilets."

His deliberate crudeness broke her heart a little bit. Was this what they had come to? She refused him one time and he attacked?

Her chest aching with emotion, she reached for her purse, opened it and took out a handful of bills. When she held out her hand, Harold grabbed the money as if he was afraid she might change her mind.

Suddenly, her father was all smiles. "You're good to your old dad. I won't forget it." He folded the money clumsily and stuffed it in his shirt pocket.

She dug her teeth into her bottom lip, trying not to cry. "I'm done, Daddy. This is the last time. I want you to get help."

"I told you…I'm fine. Don't know why you're kicking up such a fuss about a little bit of cash."

"I've been looking at the rental income. You could be living like a king." She helped out with the Winslow Properties business, and though she wasn't in that office very often, she knew enough to realize the incoming cash was substantial. And she also knew that Harold wasn't pouring any of that money back into upkeep and development.

"You worried about your inheritance? Is that it?"

The insult barely registered. She had figured out a long time ago that her father would be lucky not to end up a pauper. "I'm worried about *you*," she said quietly. "And though you may not believe me, I'm done. No more handouts."

He backed toward the door, his posture hunted. "I may sell the Courtyard," he said defiantly. "I've had inquiries from a company called Samson Oil."

The Courtyard was an old renovated ranch several miles west of town. It included a large barn and a collection of buildings that housed a growing and thriving arts community, consisting of both studios and retail shops. The land on which the Courtyard sat increased in value day by day.

"You know selling would be a big mistake." He was threatening her. Manipulating her. Classic addict behavior.

Harold shrugged. "That's your opinion. I gotta go. See you later."

Before she could react, he disappeared. Moments later she heard the front door slam.

She sank into a kitchen chair and buried her face in her

hands. If she had stayed at Case's house, she could have avoided her father tonight.

Scarcely five minutes had passed when her doorbell rang again. *Damn it.* If Harold had come back, she was going to have a little hissy fit. She wiped her eyes with the back of her hand and stood up, grabbing a paper napkin to use as a makeshift tissue.

Rarely did she let her father get to her. But as she blew her nose, she conceded inwardly that his barbs had hit the mark. He was often a mean drunk, and tonight was no exception.

It was a distinct relief to find Amanda Battle on the other side of the door. "Come in," Mellie said.

"I won't stay long. I know it's late." Amanda slipped past her, shivering dramatically. "What happened to the warm days?" The sheriff's wife was tall and slim and full of energy.

"We're headed toward the holidays. It was bound to happen. What's up, Amanda? I doubt you came to see me for a discussion about the weather."

Amanda chuckled. "The guys are playing poker at our house. I had to get out of there for a few minutes. Besides, I need a firsthand report. Nathan called Case a little while ago to see how he's doing, but you know how men are. Case said he was fine."

"You don't believe him?"

"Parker told us Case was in bad shape. He said if you hadn't shown up at the ranch to clean yesterday and found Case, he might have ended up in the hospital."

"Well, I don't know about that. I'm glad I happened to be there. I did take dinner to him this evening. He was grumpy but overall seemed somewhat better." Better enough to flirt, anyway. Not that she was about to tell Amanda that.

"You're definitely a Good Samaritan. But don't worry. Several of his friends and their wives and girlfriends have put together a meal schedule. We won't let him starve. You're off the hook with a clear conscience. And Parker is going to keep tabs on Case's flu symptoms."

"That's great."

Mellie knew Amanda didn't mean to sound dismissive… or as if she were kicking Mellie to the curb. Even so, the unintentional message was clear. Mellie was not part of that tight-knit circle of friends. It was ridiculous to let her feelings be bruised. Maybe because she had recently gone several rounds with her father, she was feeling fragile.

Amanda glanced at her watch and sighed. "I'd better get back. I promised Nathan I'd throw together some nachos."

Mellie raised an eyebrow. "At this hour?"

"When this crew convenes, they like to pretend they're all eighteen again."

"You wouldn't have it any other way. I hear it in your voice."

Amanda shrugged, her expression sheepish. "Yeah. You know me—I love to cook for people. And these guys work so hard it's fun to see them unwind."

"Nathan is lucky to have you."

Amanda's grin was smug. "Yes, he is."

Mellie walked her friend outside, feeling unmistakably envious of Amanda's good fortune. What would it be like to be loved in such a way that you knew the other person would never let you down or disappoint you, at least not in any significant way?

Ila Winslow had been that person for Mellie. But once she was gone, Mellie had been forced to face a few cold, hard truths. Love, true love, whether familial or romantic, was rare and wonderful.

* * *

The next day dawned bright and sunny, which seemed a shame given Mellie's mood. She would have much preferred gray and gloomy so she could blame her low spirits on something other than the fact she was not going to see Case Baxter today.

She attended church and brunch with a friend, then popped by the gym for her regular yoga class. In the locker room afterward as she showered, washed her hair and changed, she felt much better. Case was a blip on her radar. No need to get all hot and bothered about a guy who wasn't even her type.

Yeah, right. Her sarcastic inner woman-child sassed her.

As was her custom, Mellie had left her cell phone in the car. No one ever needed her on Sunday, and she always relaxed more knowing that she was unplugged from the electronic world, even if only for an hour and a half.

It was a shock to return to her vehicle in the parking lot and find that her cell phone had exploded with texts.

My cleaning lady has gone missing.

Twenty minutes after that: I pay double time on Sundays. Are you interested?

Mellie stared at the screen. Interested in what? The shiver that snaked down her spine had less to do with cold air hitting her damp hair than it did the prospect of deliberately placing herself beneath Case's roof during nonbusiness hours.

Then a third text: You've already been exposed. Why not keep me company?

Why not, indeed? She slid into the driver's seat, uncertain how to answer. She decided to go with bland and professional and see what happened. I don't work on Sundays, she texted. Hope you're feeling better. I thought I would stay out of your way for now. Once you're well, I can pick up where I left off.

She made it a habit not to text and drive, so on the way home she ignored the series of dings indicating she had new messages. It wasn't until she pulled into her garage that she let herself read Case's responses...one right after another.

I don't give a damn right now if my house is clean and organized.

I'm bored.

Give a guy a break.

How humiliating was it that her hands shook as she used her phone? Case was telling the truth. He was bored, and he thought Mellie was available. She should ignore him... pretend her cell was turned off...or invent a very important function she simply couldn't miss.

Gnawing her lip, she walked a fine line between cordial and suggestive. You sound grumpy.

Of course I'm grumpy, he shot back. I'm in solitary confinement.

You probably deserve it. Oops. That definitely sounded flirtatious. JK, she added rapidly.

Her phone stayed silent for a full two minutes. She'd offended him. Yikes.

Finally, he wrote back.

Please come see me, Mellie. I'll be on my best behavior. And you don't need to cook for me. I've got enough food here to feed an army regiment.

Well, shoot. She was a strong person, but not strong enough to say no to something she really wanted. She tapped the screen.

Okay...give me an hour. Do you need me to bring anything?

Just you.

As a woman, she was generally low maintenance. An hour should have been enough time to get ready and drive out to the ranch. But she dithered over what to wear. Finally, she chose a charcoal-gray wool skirt with knee-high black leather boots and a scoop-necked black sweater with a gray chevron pattern across the chest. Silver hoop earrings and a silver necklace with a key charm completed her look.

The outfit was probably too dressy. But she could always let him think she had worn this to church. Her mother's voice echoed in her head. *Never pretend to be something you're not, Mellie. Tell the truth, even if it hurts.*

Mellie stared in the mirror, tucking a stray fiery strand behind her ear. For a moment, she contemplated leaving her long hair loose. But that might send the wrong message. Since she wasn't exactly sure what it was that she wanted to communicate to Case Baxter, it was probably smarter not to be quite so...flamboyant.

Her hair was hard to miss. Which was why she often kept it confined to a knot on top of her head or in a ponytail. Neither style seemed appropriate for tonight. She pulled the thick mass of red and gold to the side of her neck, secured it with a hairband and let it fall over one shoulder.

As she examined her reflection in the mirror, she saw

much more than a young woman dressed up for an evening that was definitely not a date. She saw uncertainty. Maybe a slice of anxiety. Most visible, however, was the undercurrent of excitement.

Grimacing, she turned and fled before she could change her mind again about what to wear. She grabbed her coat from the closet by the front door, slid her arms into it, freed her hair and scooped up her car keys.

The early evening had turned foggy. Case's house appeared out of the gathering gloom like a regal old lady, sure of her place in the community. Lonely, perhaps, but unapologetic. A light beside the front door offered a welcoming glow.

Mellie felt her pulse wobble as she climbed the steps to the porch.

Case met her at the top of the stairs, the door half-open behind him. "It's about time," he said. When he grinned, she knew he was teasing.

"You shouldn't be outside," she said. "It's freezing."

He put an arm around her shoulders and steered her into the house. "I had to get some fresh air. It's like a tomb in here."

As he took her coat, she smiled wryly. "Nicest tomb I've ever seen."

He shrugged. "I'm still running a fever. You can't trust anything I say."

And wasn't that the crux of the matter?

She laughed because he wanted her to. Still, the irony was not lost on her. "Do you really have a temperature?"

Case stopped short and bent his head. Taking her hand, he placed it on his forehead. "See."

He wasn't kidding. "How long since you've had medicine?"

"I don't know. Four hours? Five? It's probably time."

"Case…"

"Don't scold me," he said. "It makes me hot, and I'm too weak to ravish you." He urged her along the hallway and into the den. A roaring fire in the fireplace added warmth and color to a room that was sophisticated but comfy. A silver tray laden with an assortment of decadent treats was set up on the coffee table in front of the sofa.

After surveying the chocolate-dipped strawberries, champagne and candied fruits, she shot Case an incredulous glance. "Where on earth did this come from? Your friends have outdone themselves."

He sat down rather suddenly, his face an alarming shade of white. "My friends brought fried chicken and green beans. I ordered this stuff online from a specialty shop in town."

"Ah." The small luxuries seemed an odd choice for a man recovering from the flu. But then again, her personal experience with wealthy men was practically nonexistent. Perhaps for Case, this was the equivalent of buttered popcorn and jujubes at the movie theater.

"Sit down," he said gruffly, his eyes closed. "I'll be okay in a minute."

"Did you actually eat any of the fried chicken?" she asked.

"Not yet. I took a shower."

The unspoken inference was that getting his hand-delivered meal onto a plate was more than he could handle. Poor man. "Rest for a few minutes and I'll bring your meal in here."

"Thanks."

He was trying so hard to act tough, but the flu was no respecter of persons. Even a broad-shouldered, macho, athletic guy like Case Baxter could fight back only so far before admitting defeat.

In the kitchen she saw that Case had piled a few dirty dishes in the sink. On the granite-topped island she found a large disposable aluminum pan filled with an enormous amount of fried chicken. And it wasn't from the chain restaurant in town. This was the real deal.

Her mouth watered. So much for the yoga class. Ignoring her better judgment, she fixed two plates with crisp chicken breasts, home-canned green beans and fluffy yeast rolls with butter. Who knew what her host wanted to drink? But the truth was, he should have plenty of water.

Balancing two bottles she plucked from the fridge, she picked up the plates and carried them back to the den. Her host had fallen asleep again.

She stood there looking at him for long minutes, wishing she could put a name to the yearning that tightened her throat and forced her to blink moisture from her lashes. For years she had kept an eye out, always wondering if there was some special guy out there for her. But Prince Charming never showed up.

Now…here…in the most unlikely of places, she found herself tumbling headlong into an infatuation that was sure to break her heart.

Ten

Case came awake with a start, jerking upright and wondering if he had dreamed Mellie. No…there she was. Sitting across from him. Looking young and sexy and prim, her knees pressed together and her hands folded in her lap.

"Sorry," he grimaced. "I keep doing that."

Mellie lifted a shoulder. "That's the drill. Lots of rest and plenty of fluids."

He ran a hand through his hair, wincing when the restrained motion made his head throb. "How long have I been out?"

"Only forty-five minutes."

Damn it. "And you've probably been sitting here starving."

"If I was that hungry, I wouldn't have waited for you. Give me a minute and I'll put everything in the microwave to warm it up."

"No." Once Mellie left the room, he'd probably crash again. "I'm not that picky. Let's do this."

"If you're sure…"

It occurred to him that sitting up long enough to eat was a daunting proposition, even though he was ravenous. Still, he washed the Tylenol down with the bottle of water and then started in on his chicken.

Mellie ate quietly. She was a restful woman. At least when she wasn't arguing with him. He managed half of the chicken breast, the roll and a few of the green beans before he admitted defeat. Pushing his plate away, he leaned back in the embrace of the sofa and rested his head, telling himself he was on the mend. Mind over matter. That was his mantra.

His companion looked askance at him. "You need the protein," she said.

"I had a mother. I don't need another one."

Mellie blinked, set down her fork and stood. "I'll come back when you're in a better mood."

The careful rebuke hit its mark.

"I'm sorry," he muttered. "Don't go."

She crossed her arms at her waist. "I'm getting mixed signals, Case."

"I know." It was true. He wanted to be alone to wallow in his misery, but at the same time, he was intrigued by Mellie Winslow and charmed by her matter-of-fact caring.

Her hair glowed tonight, the long strands catching light from the fixture overhead. The sweater she wore was fitted but not tight. Even so, he was well aware of her ample breasts.

"Sit down. Please. I have a proposition for you."

The expression on her face told him she was evaluating all meanings of that statement. "Um…"

"Oh, hell, Mellie. I can't even finish dinner. Do you really think I'm going to lure you into my bed?"

"Of course not," she muttered, looking anywhere but

at his face. She sat down hard on the sofa, not so much an act of will as a necessary evil, as if her legs had given out. He knew the feeling.

It was a sure bet she didn't trust him. But he had a plan to win her over. "I'd like to become a silent partner in the Keep N Clean. With my investment, you wouldn't have to wait to expand."

Mellie opened and closed her mouth like a fish gasping for oxygen. She shook her head. "No, thank you."

He stared at her, his pulse far too rapid. "Maybe you didn't understand. I'd like to give you fifty thousand dollars. It's the least I can do to repay you for playing nurse."

Now his dinner guest looked murderous. "The milk of human kindness is not for sale, Mr. Baxter. Some things in life are free."

"Has anyone ever told you that you're incredibly over-sensitive?" Aggravation made his head ache like the devil.

She stared him down, her green eyes chilled to the shade of moss. "You hired me to clean and organize your house. An ordinary business arrangement. I neither want nor need your investment money."

Though it took every ounce of energy he could muster, he levered his body off the sofa and joined her on the love seat. Her spine was so straight it was a wonder it didn't crack under the weight of her disapproval.

He rested his arm behind her shoulders. "Don't make a hasty decision, Mellie. This is what I do. I find it very rewarding to help local businesses grow."

"You don't get it."

They were so close he could see the faint, almost imperceptible veins beneath her fair skin. At her temple… in the dip above her collarbone. "So explain it to me," he urged. "I'm listening." He was trying to listen, though all he really wanted to do was kiss her.

Mellie's head was bent, her profile as simple and sweet as a Madonna's. The feelings she invoked in him, however, were a far cry from religious. More like the temptations of the damned.

She inhaled and exhaled, sliding him a sideways glance that begged for understanding. "The Keep N Clean is *mine*. I've sweated and worried and planned and strategized… every mile of the way. I could have stepped into the family business and worked alongside my father, but I needed something that belonged to me…something he couldn't ruin."

"That's pretty harsh."

"You don't know him." Her smile was bleak. "He's an alcoholic…with not the slightest interest in recovery. People in town make jokes about him. The sheriff has a cell with Harold's name on it. I didn't want to be a part of that, but…"

She ground to a halt, biting her lip, her distress almost palpable.

"But what?" He smoothed a strand of hair away from her cheek, tucking it behind her ear. Her skin was softer than a Texas sunrise, all pink and pretty and sweet.

"I can't bear to see him go completely down the abyss. So I keep giving him money. Which is stupid, because his business pulls in twice what mine does."

Her voice broke as a single tear rolled down her cheek. Mellie seemed oblivious. Case felt something twist inside his chest. He couldn't tell if it was a good feeling or a bad one…maybe just damned scary.

Pulling her head to his shoulder, he stroked her hair, releasing the band that held it and using his fingers to winnow through the fragrant mass. "Sometimes doing the right thing is really hard."

"How would you know?" The question was tart.

He rested his chin on top of her head. "My college

roommate had a drug problem, but he hid it from me for almost a year. I was constantly bailing him out of jail and making excuses for him. Until the night I came home from a date with my current girlfriend and found Toby on the floor of our apartment. Dead. From an overdose."

He recited the tale simply, even though the recounting jabbed at a spot in his heart that had never quite healed.

Mellie pulled back to look at him, her eyes wide and distraught. "Oh, Case. I'm so sorry." She put her hands on his cheeks. "You must have been devastated."

Her simple empathy reached down inside the hard shell he'd worn since his divorce and found purchase in a tiny crack. Emotions roiled in his chest, feelings he hated. It was much simpler when he saw Mellie Winslow as simply a potential bed partner. He didn't want to know her inner-most secrets. He didn't want to care.

But he was lost...defeated. Almost before the battle had begun. "I want to kiss you," he said raggedly, "but I can't. I'm sick."

Her smile was both wicked and reassuring. "Then I'll kiss *you*," she whispered.

Never in his life had he let a woman take the initiative. Though he didn't mind an aggressive woman in bed if the mood was right, he liked to lead the dance. Even so, it was damned arousing to submit, even momentarily, to Mellie's slightly awkward affections.

She started with his stubbly jaw, her tongue damp against his hot skin. The feminine purr of pleasure sent every drop of blood to his sex, leaving him hard and breathless.

"Mellie?"

She ignored him. Leaning into his embrace, she nuzzled his ear, kissed his brow, traced his nose with a fingertip. When her mouth hovered over his, he protested. "No." It might have been more convincing if he hadn't been dragging her against his chest. "I don't need your pity."

"But you want to kiss me."

It was a statement, not a question. He shuddered, his arousal viciously demanding, relentlessly insistent. *Take, take, take.* "Of course I want to kiss you," he said, the words sandpaper in his throat. Any living, breathing heterosexual male would want to kiss her.

Carefully, telling himself he was still in control, he slid a hand beneath the edge of her sweater and found the plane of her belly with his fingertips. Mellie's sharp intake of breath spurred him on. When she didn't move, not even a millimeter, he found her breast and palmed it.

Hell. Her curves were all woman. Beneath a layer of silky stuff and lace, he felt her heat, her life force. Wanting turned him inside out.

Moving slowly so as to not alarm her, he eased them into a reclining position, Mellie on her back, Case on his side—against the couch—his upper body sheltering hers.

She stared up at him, wide-eyed. "We can't do this."

He unfastened the button on the side of her skirt... lowered the zipper...exposed her practical cotton undies. "I know."

"Wait." She put a hand on his wrist. "Weren't you supposed to woo me with champagne and strawberries?"

He was shaking. Either his fever was back or he was out of control. "Dessert," he said, the words barely audible. "In a little while."

His hand moved of its own accord, breaching the inconsequential narrow barrier of elastic on her bikini underpants and sliding lower.

Mellie whimpered. There was no other word for it. In that raw, needy sound, he heard every last one of his scruples and reservations spelled out. This was insane. *He* was insane.

He swallowed hard. "Shall I stop?" She would never know what the question cost him.

She held his hand against her body, gripping his wrist until her fingernails dug into his skin. The spark of pain drove his lust a notch higher. "Don't you dare."

When he found the moist cleft of her sex, they both groaned. As he stroked her gently, he felt her lift against his hand.

He was dizzy...hungover...and he hadn't even popped the cork on the bubbly. "Close your eyes, Mellie."

Mellie panted, her chest rising and falling rapidly. Why hadn't he removed her sweater? Hell, he couldn't stop now. It wouldn't be fair.

"I want to see you naked," he said urgently.

"Please, don't stop..." The three words were raspy, but ended on a sharp cry.

Watching and feeling Mellie find satisfaction was humbling. No pretenses. No big show. Just a woman experiencing pleasure—deep, raw gratification.

When she could breathe again, he rested his forehead on hers. "I want you."

She licked her lips, her expression befuddled. "You've been desperately ill. Maybe your heart's not healthy enough for sex." She dared to tease him.

"My heart's fine," he groused, not amused by her joking allusion to a television commercial. "And I don't appreciate the reference. I have the flu, not ED."

She curled her arms around his neck, smiling drowsily. "You're gorgeous even when you're sick. It's not fair. And PS, I've never done it with a cowboy."

"You *still* haven't done it," he pointed out, his disgruntlement tempered only by the fact that he felt like hell.

"They say anticipation is half the pleasure."

"I'd like a chance to find out."

"The first day you're well, I swear. We'll drink that champagne and go for it."

"Cheap advice from a woman who just—"

She clapped her hand over his mouth. "Don't be grouchy. Your time will come. In fact, if you think you're up to it, I'm right here. Carpe diem and all that."

He thought about it. Seriously. For about ten seconds. But a quick assessment of his head-to-toe misery settled the argument. "No," he sighed. "I want to impress you with my carnal prowess."

"Is that really a thing?"

"You'll have to wait and see, now, won't you?"

She frowned, examining his face, no doubt spotting the damp forehead and the sudden lack of color. "You need to be in bed," she said firmly. "Alone."

He wanted to argue. He *really* wanted to argue. But damn it, Mellie was right. "I don't want you to leave," he said. "You keep me occupied."

"That's one word for it." She sat up, forcing him to, as well. When they were hip to hip, she took his hand. "I think it's best if I put cleaning your house on hold…give you a week to recover without anyone underfoot. If you're better by the end of the week, we'll talk about resuming our original schedule."

"I *have* to be better by the weekend," he said.

"Why?"

"The club is throwing a big party Saturday night to honor me as the new president."

"Ah."

"That's all you have to say…*ah*?"

She cocked her head. "What do you want me to say?"

"You could at least act interested."

"I don't follow."

"Oh, for God's sake, Mellie. You know I want you to go with me."

She stood abruptly. "I most certainly do not. We're barely acquaintances."

"Aren't you forgetting what just happened? When I rocked your world?" He smiled to let her know he was kidding about the world-rocking thing.

Mellie actually winced. "Aside from your Texas-sized ego, what you and I have been dancing around is the possibility of a fling, *not* any kind of official status. That's crazy."

"Why won't you go with me? It's a single social occasion, not a relationship."

Her reluctance dinged his pride. It wasn't boasting to say that any one of a large number of women in Royal would be pleased to attend the upcoming party as his guest. Mellie looked as if he had offered to take her to a funeral.

"I like my life just fine, Case. Other than the occasional run-in with my dad, I'm pretty happy with the way things have turned out for me. I own a business I love… I have a lot of interesting friends. I'm not interested in finding a man to take care of me."

His temper started a slow boil. "We're talking about a *party*, Ms. Winslow. It's hardly a basis for what you're thinking about."

"True. But if we end up in bed together, I'd rather no one else know about it. That way when we're done, there won't be any messy explanations to deal with."

When we're done… Maybe if he hadn't felt so rotten, he might have been able to understand why her blithe prediction about their future bothered him so much.

"Fine," he said, his jaw clenched. "I won't ask again. If you want me, you'll have to say so. I'm done here."

Eleven

If you want me, you'll have to say so. Mellie replayed those words in her head a thousand times over the next four days. Her departure from Case's house Sunday evening was not her finest hour. He had stormed out of the room, and she had left without saying goodbye.

She was ashamed of her behavior. Her only excuse was that, even sick, Case Baxter made her jittery and uncertain about things she had always seen as rock solid in her life. For one, her assumption that having an intimate relationship with a man was something she didn't have time for.

Honestly, she worked so hard and kept so busy, she rarely thought about what she was missing. She dated now and then, but with only a couple of exceptions over the years, she'd never felt an inescapable urge to have sex just for the sake of having sex.

She thought about it. Alone at night. In the privacy of her bedroom. But her fantasy lovers were compliant and undemanding…exactly the opposite of Case Baxter.

What did he want with her?

By the time she closed the office for a late lunch on Thursday afternoon, she had brought her books up to date, signed contracts with three new clients and worked herself into a mental frenzy of uncertainty. Instead of heading home, she pointed her car in the direction of the diner.

She had to talk to someone, or she'd explode. Amanda was the logical choice.

Fortunately, the sheriff's wife was in her usual spot, smiling and swapping jokes with her regular customers. Mellie had purposely waited until almost two o'clock, hoping that the noon rush would be over and Amanda would have time for a chat. Because of the subject matter, Mellie snagged the booth in the far back corner, hoping to talk quietly without being overheard.

When the other woman headed her way, Mellie waved a hand at the opposite side of the booth. "Do you have time to take a break? I need some advice."

Amanda said a word to her second in command and slid onto the bench seat with a sigh. "Success is killing me," she said. But the smug pride on her face told a different story.

"You love it," Mellie said.

"True. What's up, girlfriend? It's not like you to drop by in the middle of the day."

Mellie played with the saltshaker, feeling the tops of her ears warm. This was embarrassing. "I may have done something stupid."

Amanda leaned in, her elbows on the table, hands clasped under her chin. "Do tell. Are we talking five-hundred-dollar-shoes stupid or forgot-to-thaw-the-chicken-for-dinner stupid?"

"It's more of a personal matter."

"Oh. My. Gosh. You've had sex."

"*No.* Well, sort of. But not really. You're missing the point."

Amanda raised an eyebrow. "Do I need to give you a lesson about the birds and the bees? Was there nudity involved? Skin-to-skin contact? At your age, I'd think you'd be pretty clear about the definition."

Mellie glanced around wildly, making sure no one was in earshot. "Lower your voice, please," she hissed. "I'd rather this not end up on the evening news."

"Who is it?" Amanda demanded. "The new wrangler over at Hartley Ranch? Or, no, it's the dentist…right? He's asked you out a half dozen times and you finally said yes."

Mellie smiled, despite her turmoil. "It's not the dentist. He kept wanting to whiten my teeth…not at all romantic."

"Then who?"

"Back up," Mellie said. "I didn't have sex. Or at least not all the way. More like teenagers in the back of a car."

Amanda appeared to be struck dumb, her eyes wide with astonishment. "It's like I don't even know you," she said.

Mellie wondered suddenly if she should have kept things to herself. But she couldn't move forward without at least an amateur second opinion. She decided to come at the situation from another angle. "I've been invited to the party at the Cattleman's Club Saturday night."

"Okayyyy… So what's the stupid thing you did?"

"I said no."

"Ah. And now you want to change your mind."

"Maybe. But what if he's already asked someone else?"

"Is that likely?"

"I'm not sure. He was mad when I turned him down. Said he wasn't going to ask again. That I would have to tell him if I wanted to go." She fudged a bit. That wasn't exactly how Case had phrased it. He'd said Mellie would have to say she wanted *him.*

"I still haven't heard a name." Amanda's brow creased.

"The *who* isn't important. Because even if I decide to contact him, I don't have a dress to wear."

"That part's easy." Amanda sat back and took a sip of the iced tea she'd brought with her to the table. "Last year when Nathan and I were invited to the governor's mansion for a law enforcement ball, I bought a dress I never wore. I decided the color didn't work for me and the skirt was way too long and too hard to hem. But the dress was on clearance, so I couldn't return it. You and I are about the same size. Plus, you're taller, so I think it will work. Why don't I bring it by your house this evening?"

"That would be great." Except that Mellie had been counting on a lack of wardrobe choices as her reason not to go to the party.

Amanda glanced at her watch. "I've gotta get back to work. I'll text you when I'm on my way…okay?"

"Sure."

Amanda stood and tapped the table with her finger. "You can't keep his name a secret forever. If the dress works, the price for my fashion donation is full disclosure."

"I don't know why you're making such a big deal about this. If I end up going, you'll find out who it is. You and Nathan will be at the party…right?"

"Of course…but I hate surprises. So you might as well tell me tonight."

By 6:00 p.m. Mellie chickened out and sent a text to Amanda.

Changed my mind about the party. Thanks anyway.

Amanda was not so easily dissuaded. She showed up at Mellie's house half an hour later, garment bag in hand.

When Mellie answered the door, Amanda frowned at her. "I never figured you for a coward."

Mellie stepped back, shrugging helplessly. "I'm not a coward. But it's complicated."

"Isn't it always?" Amanda placed the long black bag on Mellie's coffee table and sat down on the sofa.

Mellie took the chair opposite. "I've waited too long to say yes. It's a moot point now. Sorry you came for nothing."

Amanda stared at her. "Tell me who it is."

"Case." Even saying his name out loud made Mellie shiver with a combination of anticipation and dread.

"Case who? Your boss?"

Apparently, Mellie was right. The idea that Case Baxter might invite his housekeeper to the most important event of the year was inconceivable. "Yes."

At last Amanda grasped the enormity of the situation. Her jaw dropped. "Case Baxter invited you to be his date for the party honoring him as the new president of the Texas Cattleman's Club and you turned him down?" That last part ended on a screech.

Mellie winced. "Yes."

Silence reigned for long minutes. Amanda looked at Mellie as if she were some kind of alien being. "I didn't think you even knew Case until you started cleaning his house."

"I didn't. But when he got sick and I helped him out a bit, we…um…"

"Fell madly in lust with each other?"

Mellie couldn't decide if Amanda was scandalized or delighted. "I didn't even like him at first," Mellie said. "He's arrogant and bossy and opinionated…"

"In other words, a Texas male. It's in their DNA, Mellie."

"Maybe."

"But you got past that first impression, obviously."

"I still think he's all of those things, but when he was so sick, I saw another side of him. A human side. A vulnerable side."

"Oh, dear."

"What?"

"You're falling for the guy."

"Don't be silly. He's handsome, and when you get to know him, not so bad, but this isn't about anything long-term."

"So why did you turn him down?"

A very good question. "He's the guest of honor Saturday night. He'll be in the spotlight. I'm not a center-of-attention kind of girl."

"So?"

"I shouldn't even have mentioned this to you. I'm not going, so it doesn't matter."

"Try on the dress. And don't argue." Amanda could be like a dog with a bone when she wanted something.

"Fine. But only because you won't leave me alone until I do." Mellie snatched up the dress in its protective covering and hurried down the hall to her bedroom, trying to ignore Amanda's mischievous smile.

When she unzipped the garment bag, she sucked in a breath. The gown was amazing. It was halter necked and backless. The chiffon-and-silk fabric almost glowed. The color started out as sea-foam green at the bodice, edged into a slightly darker hue at the hips and continued the length of the dress, sliding from one shade into the next as the mermaid-style skirt fell in a dozen layers of tiny ruffles.

No woman could resist trying it on. With a few contortions, Mellie managed the zipper on her own and slid her feet into strappy high heels. One look in the mirror told her the gown was made for her.

Amanda called out from the living room. "I want to see it. Come model for me."

"Give me a minute." Mellie stared in the mirror, trying to imagine the expression in Case's eyes if he saw her in this dress. She didn't suffer from false modesty. Her body was nice…average. But in this confection of multishaded green, she felt like a princess.

Amanda actually stood up and clapped when Mellie walked into the living room. "You look amazing. And I was right. The length is perfect."

"I can't wear a bra." Her shoulders and back were bare.

"You don't need one. I'm so excited you're going to the party."

Mellie held up a hand. "I haven't even tried to contact Case, and if I do, he's probably asked someone else already."

Amanda chuckled. "Why don't we find out?"

"Now?"

"Of course now. The event is less than forty-eight hours away."

"I'll text him later tonight. Let me change out of this and we can grab some dinner. Didn't you say Nathan was working tonight?"

"Yes. But I think my stomach can wait five minutes for a meal. Quit stalling."

"Be honest, Amanda. Don't you see that this could be a disaster? Gossip spreads faster than wildfire around here."

Amanda hugged her, careful not to muss the dress. "It's a very simple question. If he enjoys your company and you like being with him, all that matters is whether or not you can keep from getting hurt."

"It won't last long. He's not interested in anything serious."

"That's all the more reason to enjoy it now. You work hard, Mellie. And you deserve an exciting evening with one of Royal's premier eligible ranchers."

"Sounds like a B-grade reality show."

"I'm serious. Do the Cinderella thing for one night. And come Monday, everything can go back to normal."

"You make it sound so easy."

Amanda picked up Mellie's cell phone. "Here." She held it out. "Do it before you get cold feet."

"I already have cold feet," Mellie complained. But she took the phone and pulled up Case's contact info. Hastily, without overthinking it, she clicked out a message.

If the invitation is still open, I would like 2 go with you to the party Saturday nt.

Suddenly, she felt like throwing up. It was going to be so embarrassing when he told her it was too late…that he had invited someone else. Every passing second made her want to climb into a hole and hide.

Even Amanda seemed abashed, her romantic soul shriveling in the loud silence.

Suddenly, Mellie's phone dinged.

I'll pick you up at 6:30. Glad you changed your mind.

Heart pounding, Mellie replied.

Only about the party. Just so we're clear.

Chicken?

No. Practical. How R U feeling?

100%. Good enough to rock your world. ☺

"What's going on over there?" Amanda asked when Mellie giggled.

Who knew a man like Case Baxter would use an emoticon?

Mellie sat down on the sofa, her legs suddenly too weak to hold her up. "Um, nothing special. He says he's glad I changed my mind."

"Well, there you go. You were worried for nothing."

Maybe. Or maybe her worries were only beginning.

Twelve

Friday flew by in a blur. Mellie subbed for one of her ladies, worked on her scheduling for three weeks out and at the end of the day went for a mani-pedi at her favorite salon.

That night she fell into bed, too exhausted to worry about her upcoming date with Case. But Saturday morning, the day of reckoning arrived. She and Amanda met after lunch to get their hair done.

They had booked simultaneous appointments. Amanda requested that her hair be arranged in a soft knot on top of her head with tendrils framing her face. She would look adorable.

The salon owner and Amanda ganged up on Mellie when Mellie asked for a similar style. "Yours needs to be down and wavy," Amanda insisted. "That gorgeous color will pop against the green of the gown."

"And who says I want to *pop*?"

The other women ignored her, their plan already in progress.

An hour later it was done.

Mellie had asked for a trim, but her hair still swung softly against her shoulders. She paid for her session and waited as Amanda did the same. The truth was, she *did* feel a little bit glamorous.

They saw several other women in the shop, as well— ranchers' wives mostly, with a few girlfriends thrown in. Tonight these would be the people observing Case and his date.

On the sidewalk, Mellie parted company with Amanda. "Promise you'll rescue me at the party if things get weird."

Amanda laughed, her cheeks pink from the heat inside. "Nothing is going to get weird, but yes… Nathan and I will look out for you."

After that somewhat reassuring promise, Mellie went home and second-guessed her decision a thousand times. When she was stressed, she liked to clean, so that's what she did. After a couple of hours, her house was spotless. But she was still jittery.

When Case arrived to pick her up, Mellie felt as awk- ward as a preteen on her first date. She opened the door and managed not to swoon. He stood there filling the entryway…tall, incredibly handsome, king of his domain in the conservative tux that fit his long, lean body to per- fection. Clearly, he was on the mend.

His lazy grin lit a spark deep inside her. She wanted to gobble him up but at the same time had the urge to run away.

He must have nicked himself shaving. She could see the tiny red spot where he had managed to staunch the trickle of blood.

As she stepped back so that he could come in, his warm

gaze raked her from head to toe. "Hello, Mellie." His tone was low and intimate. "You look stunning." The words held a level of intensity she hadn't anticipated.

"Thank you," she muttered. "I'm ready. All I need to do is grab my wrap."

Case was fully recovered from the flu, but he still felt a little unsteady on his feet. Mostly from lying around all week. Inactivity wasn't his usual style.

The fact that Mellie had changed her mind about being his date tonight gave him great hope for the culmination of the evening. Now that he was well, he wasn't about to let her get away a second time. All he'd been able to think about as the days dragged by this week was how amazing it had been to hold Mellie and kiss her and how desperately he wanted to do so much more.

If it had been up to him, the club wouldn't be throwing a party in his honor this evening. But he understood that his new title came with certain social obligations. Having Mellie at his side would go a long way toward making the evening's festivities palatable. Despite her reservations about being seen in public with him, he was going to be proud to have her on his arm tonight.

Thank God he was finally well. Everything was going according to plan.

As she disappeared down the hallway, he watched her go, taking note of the way her dress dipped low in the back. His breath came faster and his forehead was damp, but his symptoms had nothing at all to do with the flu. Mellie Winslow was a smart, gorgeous, funny woman.

And for tonight she was his.

By the time he had tucked her into his vintage sports car, he realized two things. One, he should have brought the larger Mercedes. He and Mellie were so close in this small space he could have leaned over and kissed her with no trouble at all. Given the fact that he was already hard just from looking at her and inhaling her light scent, he was in trouble.

Secondly, Mellie was as nervous as a long-tailed cat in a room full of rocking chairs. She seemed pale, but maybe that was a trick of the light. "Relax," he said. "We're going to a party. I want you to have fun."

Mellie half turned in her seat. "I don't know why I let you talk me into this." Her eyes were huge. The pulse at the base of her throat beat rapidly.

He smiled, ruefully aware that he was in far deeper than he wanted to admit. What he was about to do would make them late, but it would be worth it. Leaning across the gearshift, he held her chin in one hand and slid his other hand beneath her masses of golden-red hair to cup her nape. "I can't wait all night to taste you."

He kissed her slowly, even though he wanted to do the opposite. Her lip gloss would have to be repaired, but that was a minor inconvenience. She responded instantly, moving toward him and sighing as his tongue mated with hers. Her skin was soft and warm, her kiss feminine and eager.

Damn. His memories hadn't been exaggerated by his illness at all. Here he was, stone-cold sober, fever-free and wildly out of control already. He inhaled sharply and released her, pausing only to run his thumb along her trembling lower lip. "Say something," he demanded.

Her faux-fur wrap had fallen away. Mellie retrieved it and huddled into the warmth. "Like what?"

Now that her bare shoulders were covered, maybe he could manage a coherent conversation. "I want to strip that dress from your body and drag you into the backseat."

So much for conversation.

Mellie managed a smile. "I'd invite you inside, but I

think it's probably a terrible faux pas for the newly elected president of the Texas Cattleman's Club to miss his own party."

He gripped the steering wheel, needing to refute her statement but knowing she was right. "Afterward. Tonight. I want to stay over."

The silence lasted several beats too long for his peace of mind. Mellie wrinkled her nose. "I'd rather you not. My neighbors are nosy."

Hell. "Be honest with me, Mellie. Are you objecting to the venue or to the idea of you and me?"

This time her answer was even slower in coming. "The venue only, I suppose. I'd like to think I could say no to you, but I won't lie to myself. I want you, Case. But we seem to be at an impasse, because I know you don't have women spend the night out at the ranch."

A knot inside his chest relaxed. "For you, I'll make an exception." He meant his response to be light and teasing, but the six words came out sounding like a vow.

Mellie nodded slowly. "Okay, then. We can swing by here later, and I'll pack a bag. If you're sure."

He wasn't sure at all…about anything…except that before midnight, Mellie Winslow was going to be in his bed.

Mellie felt as if she had fallen down the rabbit hole. Suddenly, her career seemed far less important than her love life. Since when did she calmly make plans to spend the night with a man? She hadn't had sex in over two years. Maybe she should warn Case that she was rusty. Or maybe he knew enough for the both of them.

As they pulled up in front of the imposing Texas Cattleman's Club, a uniformed parking valet hurried forward, ready to take the keys and whisk the car away. Case helped

Mellie out of the low-slung vehicle, both of them taking care not catch her dress on anything.

When she stood at his side, her stomach full of butterflies, he slipped an arm around her waist. "You ready?"

She nodded, but her heart plummeted. Out at the ranch, Case had simply been a sick male who needed her help. Now…here…it was going to be impossible to ignore who he really was.

That truth was hammered home with a vengeance as they stepped through the doors of the club. Camera flashes went off in chorus. Reporters shouted questions. Case gave the press crew an easy smile and a good sound bite, even as he kept his arm curled protectively around Mellie and steered them toward the ballroom, stopping only to drop off Mellie's wrap and clutch purse at the coat-check counter.

Another doorway, another entrance.

This time there were no cameras, but instead a surge of well-wishers who wanted to congratulate Case. It was inevitable that he and Mellie would end up separated. She smiled and wiggled her fingers at him to let him know she was okay. It was actually kind of sweet to see how many people gathered around him to say hello.

As she waited for the crush to subside, Mellie looked around the room with curiosity. This was only the third time in her life she'd ever been inside the club, and the other two occasions had been long ago.

The building was a century old and had been cared for well over the years. Tradition mingled with luxury seamlessly. It was fun to see so many people dressed to the nines and ready to party.

Mellie smoothed her skirt and kept a smile on her face. Just as she was planning to go in search of an out-of-the-way corner, strong fingers gripped her elbow. "You're not getting rid of me that easily."

"Case." She was startled to find him at her side. A moment ago he'd been surrounded by a small crowd of people.

"I want you to meet Mac McCallum," he said. "And his sister Violet. Mac is an energy technology whiz. Violet keeps their family ranch running smoothly."

Mellie shook hands with each of the attractive McCallum siblings. "Lovely to meet you both."

Violet grinned. "I think this is going to be a short-lived conversation. They're motioning for the two of you to lead out the first dance of the evening."

Mellie's mouth went dry. She looked up at Case as they made their way to the center of the room. "Do you even know how to dance?" she whispered. "'Cause I'm not exactly a professional."

"My mother and grandmother were old school. Young men had an obligation to learn the ways of gentlemen. Dancing was at the top of the list."

"I'm impressed."

The orchestra stuck up a dreamy tune as Case swept Mellie into his arms. At some level she was aware that she and Case were alone in the middle of the floor. Overhead, a priceless chandelier sparkled, showering them with small rainbow flashes of light. The crowd was four- and five-people deep, pressed back around the edges of the room.

But in Case's arms she forgot to be either nervous or self-conscious. He held her confidently, steering her easily in a waltz. His hand was warm on her back. "Thank you for coming with me tonight," he said, his smile a flash of white in his tanned face. "You've made this a lot more fun for me."

"You didn't really need a date," she pointed out. "There

are all sorts of women in this room who would love to dance with you."

He dipped her skillfully and laughed when she couldn't stifle a small gasp. "I didn't want any of them," he said. "I only want you."

After that, the song ended and everyone took the floor as the next song began.

Case bent to whisper in her ear. "Let's get something to eat."

She nodded, even as he extricated them from the mass of bodies nearby. Fortunately, the air was cooler and the people fewer as they approached the buffet tables. Mellie filled her plate with boiled shrimp, beautiful canapés and various hors d'oeuvres. "This looks amazing."

Case served himself three times as much, but then again, he was a big man who needed a lot of fuel. He found a table for two. "Eat fast," he joked. "More of my friends want to meet you."

Mellie knew the moment alone wouldn't last long. It seemed as if every eye in the room was on them. Her earlier reservations about being seen in public with Case Baxter came flooding back. "It's easy to see why you were elected," she said. "You're very popular."

He lifted an eyebrow as he wolfed down a spicy meat-ball. "It would be the same for anyone who holds this posi-tion. People like knowing they have access to influence."

"That's a pretty cynical statement."

"But true. I learned a long time ago not to believe my own press. When a man has money and power, people flock around like bees to honey. Underneath it all, I'm just a Texas cowboy."

"If you say so." Maybe he was being modest and maybe he really believed what he said. Either way, he wasn't see-ing clearly. There was something special about Case...

something that made her want to be with him for more than a single night. Something elemental. Something real.

She didn't particularly enjoy the barrage of eyes trained on their table at the moment. The avid interest made her worry about finding food in her teeth or spilling wine on her beautiful dress. Still, it was a relief to know that she didn't feel as out of place as she had expected.

When they finished eating, Case began to introduce her to an endless stream of his friends, including Jeff Hartley, a local rancher who appeared to be without a date for the party, and Drew and Beth Farrell, to name a few. Some of them—such as Dr. Reese—Mellie knew already, at least in passing.

Royal wasn't all that big. Families tended to own the same land for generations. Drew and Beth shared the story of how they had been not-so-friendly neighbors until the wicked F4 tornado stranded them together in a storm cellar.

All of Case's circle of friends were interesting people. Beneath the social chitchat, though, Mellie knew what Case was thinking. Because she was thinking about it, too. Sex. Naked, wild, exploratory sex. Two people attracted to each other without much else in common.

When Case was pulled into a conversation that seemed to be more business than pleasure, Mellie hung back on the far edges of the room, listening to the band and chatting with Amanda and Nathan. Unfortunately, her support team was heading out early.

Amanda hugged Mellie. "It's been a fun evening, but Nathan was up at five this morning. We're going home."

Mellie returned the hug. "Thank you again for the dress. I think Case likes it."

Nathan snorted. "Every man in the room likes it. You're a knockout, Mellie Winslow."

"Hey." Amanda pinched her husband's arm. "I'm standing right here."

He scooped her up and gave her a thorough kiss, one that left Amanda pink cheeked and starry-eyed. "Mellie knows I only have eyes for you, sweetheart. Don't you, Mellie?"

"I do. And she feels the same way about you. Now go home before you get arrested for public indecency."

Their laughter was equal parts smug and rueful.

Watching the Battles walk across the dance floor to the exit gave Mellie a funny twinge in her chest. Amanda and Nathan had known each other forever. Their relationship was rock solid, and they were more in love today than they had ever been.

What would it be like to have that kind of security and trust in a relationship?

She was still rattling that question around in her head when a young cowboy came up to her and asked for a dance. He couldn't have been more than twenty-one or twenty-two. Mellie felt ancient in comparison, but his earnest invitation was sweet.

They moved around the dance floor in silence. The young cowhand seemed nervous, because he glanced in Case's direction now and then. "Mr. Baxter is giving me the evil eye," he said.

"Don't mind him. You and I are having a nice dance. Nothing wrong with that."

"Your dad is Harold Winslow, right?"

Mellie stumbled slightly. "Um, yes. Why do you ask?"

Now the invitation made more sense.

The kid cleared his throat. "My cousin owns one of the shops out at the Courtyard. Word got around this week that your dad is thinking of selling the place. It's made folks nervous about their businesses. When I saw you here tonight, I thought I'd get an answer straight from the horse's mouth."

"You might want to rethink that comparison," Mellie said drily.

The cowhand blushed. "You know what I mean. Is it true?"

Mellie mulled over her answer. "It may be true that my father has been talking big and throwing his weight around. But I'm part owner of the company, too, and as far as I know, there are no plans to sell. Who is your cousin, anyway?"

"Raina Patterson. She owns the antiques store Priceless."

"Oh, yes… I know her. Please tell Raina I'll be out to see her in the next couple of weeks to set things straight. And tell her she has a sweet cousin."

Now the wrangler's neck and ears were as red as the stripe in his Western shirt. "Thank you, ma'am. Nice dancing with you."

Mellie had no sooner grabbed a glass of punch than Case appeared at her side again. For a big man, he surely was quiet and fast when he wanted to be. "Should I bow or salute?" she asked. "Now that you're officially the president and all?"

He snagged her glass and took a sip, his lips landing exactly where hers had been. "I saw the young pup encroaching on my territory. Don't you know you're supposed to throw the small ones back in the water?"

"Very funny. He's a sweetheart."

"I'll bet. He was one of the brave ones. Every unattached guy in this room is thinking about doing what he did."

"You do know how to flatter a girl." She smiled, her confidence buoyed by Case's wry observations.

Case lifted an eyebrow when a tall man with shaggy brown hair and green eyes approached them. The man gave Mellie an appreciative glance. "I don't know how you ended up dancing with Case," the man said, "but I'd be love to take a turn on the dance floor with you, pretty lady."

"Well, I—"

"This one's taken," Case said, glowering. He glanced at Mellie. "Meet my buddy Logan Wade. He likes fast horses and fast women, not necessarily in that order."

Mellie laughed. "Nice to meet you, Logan."

Logan shook her hand, his grip warm and firm. "Don't listen to him. I'm harmless. Case is the ladies' man in our group. At least I'm not opposed to marriage on principle."

From the look on Case's face, he wasn't amused by his friend's ribbing.

Case glanced at his watch. "I've done my time," he muttered. "Mellie and I are going to get out of here. This crowd will party for several more hours."

Logan kissed Mellie's hand theatrically. "When you get tired of this guy, give me a call."

Thirteen

Case's mood soured. Was Mellie tempted by Logan Wade's offer? Surely not. But the other man was definitely popular with women. They loved his easy-going personality.

Case shoved aside the unwelcome realization that Mellie might be looking for something more than Case wanted to offer. He had enjoyed the evening more than he'd thought he would. But right now he was focused on the after-party.

He hoped Mellie was on the same page, because he was wired and hungry. For a brief moment he thought about heading straight to the ranch. It was possible once they got to Mellie's house, she would change her mind.

At a stop sign, in the glare of a streetlight, he studied her profile. "Penny for your thoughts," he said lightly. Surely she wasn't actually thinking about Logan's smooth flirtation. The other rancher was only trying to needle Case.

When she gave Case her full attention, her luminous,

deep eyes drew him in. For a moment, he thought she wasn't going to answer. Then she drew a visible breath. "Will you tell me about your wife?"

The question was way down on the list of things he'd expected her to say. "Is that a prerequisite for tonight?"

"I didn't mean to make you angry."

"I'm not angry," he said, gripping the steering wheel. "But it's old news."

"I'd still like to know. Please…"

He shrugged, wishing he had loosened his bow tie. "I was young and stupid. Leslie worked for my dad. She saw me as a meal ticket, I guess. Dad tried to warn me… suggested a prenup. But I refused. We'd been married for six months when Leslie cleaned out two of my bank accounts and skipped the country."

"I am so sorry. You must have been devastated."

"She didn't break my heart, if that's what you're thinking. But she sure as hell damaged my pride and my self-respect."

"Because you couldn't see through her?"

"Yeah. I guess I wanted to believe I was irresistible."

"You are, as far as I'm concerned. I'm not in the habit of having *sleepovers* with men I've known all of about ten minutes."

In her voice he heard an echo of the same reservations that plagued him. He pulled up in front of her house and put the car in Park. "This isn't the norm for me, either, Mellie. And I might point out that I offered you fifty grand as an investment, but you turned it down. So I'm hoping it's my charm and wit that won you over."

As an attempt at humor, it fell flat.

Mellie's small white teeth worried her lower lip. "Maybe that was a ploy on my part to get you to trust me."

"Go get your toothbrush," he urged, his voice hoarse. "I can't wait much longer."

She stared at him, her hands plucking restlessly at the tiny ruffles on her skirt. Despite their current locale, she reminded him of a mermaid, luring a man into the deep.

"Is this a one-night stand, Case?"

"It's not anything yet." He sighed. "I can't imagine letting you go after only one night."

"But you agree that the two of us are temporary."

His temper boiled over, exacerbated by lust and uncertainty. "Damn it, Mellie. Do you want this or not?"

She swallowed, and he saw her chest rise and fall. "Wait here," she said. "I'll be back."

Twelve minutes and thirty-seven seconds. That was how long it took. When he saw the door to her house open, he jumped out of the car and met her, taking the small overnight bag and tossing it in the trunk.

She was still wearing her mermaid gown, which was a good thing, because he had fantasies of all the ways he wanted to peel the silky fabric away from her creamy-skinned body. He helped her into the car, waited until she tucked her skirt inside and closed the door.

The drive out to the ranch was silent. The miles ticked by rapidly. His brain was a jumble of wants and needs and more angst than was warranted in advance of a simple sexual encounter.

When he pulled up in front of his house, he realized he'd forgotten to leave a single light on. Through the windshield, he saw the night sky punctuated with a million stars. One of the many things he loved about living in Texas was the immensity of the universe overhead.

Every male instinct he possessed urged him to drag Mellie up the stairs and into his bed ASAP. But he wanted to woo her, to win her trust, to make her comfortable with him.

"Can you walk in those shoes?" he asked.

She nodded. "As long as we're not talking a marathon."

"I want to show you something."

Once they were out of the car, he took her hand in his and led her toward the small corral to the left of the house. Though it was often empty, tonight a single horse stood sentinel.

"This is Misty," he said. "I bought her recently. I thought you and I might ride together sometime."

The small mare whinnied and cantered toward them, her tale swishing in the cool night air.

Mellie leaned on the fence rail, her expression animated. "She's beautiful. But I don't know how to ride."

Case raised an eyebrow. "A Texas woman who can't handle a horse? Shame on you." He lifted her by the waist and set her on the railing. Her skirt fluttered around his arms like a swarm of butterflies. "I'd love to teach you... if you're willing."

His guest's smile was demure. "I'm sure you could teach me all sorts of things."

And just like that, he reached his limit. Moving between her legs, he dragged her head down for a kiss. Hot and hard and deep. The mare lost interest and wandered away. Case lost his head and wandered into dangerous territory.

Mellie in the shimmer of the moonlight was just about the prettiest thing he'd ever seen. Her hair was more pale gold than red in this moment. And her skin glowed like pearls.

"Inside," he groaned. "Where there's a bed."

Her husky laugh inflamed him. "I thought you'd never ask."

As he lifted her down from her perch, he couldn't bear to let her go. Instead, he scooped her into his arms and carried her toward the stairs that led to the porch.

Mellie curled one arm around his neck. He smelled her, felt her, tasted her on his tongue. Everything about the night turned mystical and enchanting. And he'd never once seen himself as a whimsical man.

He caught his toe on the second step and nearly sent them both to disaster. But he managed to find his balance. "Sorry," he muttered.

She put a hand on his cheek, her fingertips cool against his hot skin. "I'm not complaining. This is my very first experience with being swept off my feet. I think you're doing just fine."

Managing the final few stairs with only a little hitch in his breathing, he set her down long enough to fish the house key out of his pocket. "*Fine* is a sucky adjective."

He pulled her into the house and flipped the lock, backing his lovely guest up against the barrier that separated them from the outside world. Taking one of her delicate wrists in each of his big hands, he raised her arms over her head and pinned her to the door. "I don't know where to start," he said, utterly serious. "I've dreamed about you every night for a week."

"I hope the reality isn't a disappointment. I haven't done this in a very long time."

His lips quirked. "I'm told it's like riding a bike."

"Or a big, strong cowboy?" The deliberately naughty challenge nearly broke him.

"It's a long night," he said. "I don't want us to peak too early."

"*Peak*? Interesting choice of words."

"Shut up and let me kiss you," he groaned. He wasn't holding her all that tightly. One wiggle or protest from

Mellie and she would be free. But to his everlasting relief, she didn't seem to mind being his captive.

He pressed the weight of his lower body against hers. Still holding her arms over her head, he kissed the side of her neck, nuzzled the spot just below her ear. "You put something in my food last week," he complained. "Some drug that makes me want you incessantly."

She nipped his chin with sharp teeth. "I'm no femme fatale. Maybe you've been on a celibate streak. Maybe I'm available. Maybe you're grateful that I didn't leave you alone to suffer that first night."

He had to let her go so he could touch her. Reverently, he covered her breasts with his hands. Clearly she wasn't wearing a bra. And just as clearly, her firm, young flesh was made for his caress. Her nipple budded beneath the silky fabric as he brushed his thumb back and forth.

"I don't know what it is," he admitted. "And I don't care. But I need you tonight, Mellie. More than you know."

Again he picked her up, and again her head came to rest over his heart. He traversed the halls of his quiet dark house by memory, avoiding furniture and other pitfalls. In his bedroom, he paused. Mellie hadn't said a word. Was she shy? Having second thoughts?

"Talk to me," he said. "Tell me what you want."

The drapes at the windows were open wide. In the ambient light he saw enough of her smile to be reassured that she wanted the same things he did, though she didn't obey his demand for her to speak.

Gently, he set her on her feet and spun her around until he could reach the single fastening at the nape of her neck. He slipped the beaded button free of the buttonhole and eased the entire bodice of the dress to her waist.

The room was hushed, every molecule of air quivering with anticipation. Opposite them, the mirror over his dresser reflected a ghostly tableau. When he embraced her from behind and dragged her back against his pelvis, they both groaned.

It was torture to shape her bare breasts with his hands. He wanted to see her fully, but there was something wickedly sensual about their dim, shadowy figures in the glass.

At last he turned her to face him. A few inches of zipper at the base of her spine gave way beneath his questing fingers, and then he held her hand as she stepped out of the dress.

She tapped his throat with a fingertip. "Your turn."

He had to wait, chest heaving as she fumbled with his bow tie and unfastened the studs down his front. When that was done, he shrugged out of his jacket and shirt and tossed them aside far more recklessly than he had her soft gown.

With Mellie standing in front of him clad in nothing but stilettos and undies, he was a wreck. "Time out," he croaked.

At this particular moment he didn't have either the patience or the fortitude to make it through a slow undressing. He kicked off his shoes, ripped off his socks, and shucked his pants and boxers in short order.

Totally nude, he snagged her wrist and drew her back into his embrace. "Leave the shoes on," he begged.

"Whatever you want, cowboy." Her voice was warm as honey on a summer day. He heard arousal and humor in equal measures.

His erection bobbed eagerly against her belly, but she didn't seem to mind. He ran his hands over her satin-covered butt, imagining all the ways he was going to take her. "This first round might be fast and furious, but we've got all night." It was a promise and a reminder to himself. He could afford to be patient...maybe.

One last time, he indulged in the pleasure of carrying her, this time to the king-size bed. He flipped back the covers and deposited her on the mattress. After striking a match to the small candle on the bedside table, he lowered himself at her side and splayed a hand against her flat belly. "I have condoms," he said flatly. "I would never take chances with you."

He wanted her to know she could trust him.

Mellie wasn't shy. At least not anymore. One hand closed around his shaft and stroked lazily.

He sucked in a sharp breath, mortifyingly close to embarrassing himself. "Let's save that part for later, darlin', when I'm not so trigger-happy."

She released him. "If you say so."

The only reason he'd been at all able to hold himself in check was that he'd let her keep her last item of clothing. But now it was time for the panties to go. When he slid them down her legs, the nylon snagged on the sharp heel of one shoe. "I'll buy you more," he swore. "A dozen pairs in every color of the rainbow."

Without warning, she rolled to her stomach, arms cradling her head. "You could massage my back," she said, her voice muffled. "All that standing and dancing in heels isn't easy." She bent her knees and crossed her ankles in the air, taunting him with the sexy pose.

At least he thought that was what she was doing. Maybe she didn't understand how damned sexy she looked. Telling himself he was no rookie kid in the bedroom, he straddled her waist and settled his thumbs on either side of her spine. With firm pressure, he moved from her bottom to her shoulders in steady increments.

Mellie's hands fisted in the sheets. "Damn, you're good," she mumbled. "This is better than sex."

He caressed every inch of her back. Up and down. Back and forth. "Not even close."

When her body was lax and warm, he reached for the handful of small foil packets he'd put in easy reach. He sheathed himself rapidly, then flipped her to her back and positioned himself between her legs.

Mellie watched him, eyelids drooping, cheekbones flushed with color, arms over her head. "You're a very beautiful man," she said quietly, her gaze raking him from chest to groin.

Gripping her hips, he shoved deep in one forceful thrust. He didn't realize he had closed his eyes until he saw tiny yellow spots of light that pulsed in time with his heartbeat. The fit was perfect.

In retrospect, perhaps he should have started with something more original than missionary position sex. But honestly, his brain circuits were shot to hell and back. Already he needed to come. Needed it more than air and water and food. But he battled the urge.

He wanted Mellie as hungry as he was…and as desperate for the pleasure that hovered just out of reach. His hands were dark against her white skin. He liked touching her…liked the notion that she had come to his home… to his bed.

Later, perhaps, he would remember his rules. And wonder why he'd broken them for someone he'd met only a few weeks ago. But now it didn't matter.

Now she was everything he wanted and needed.

He moved in her slowly, controlling the joining of their bodies with a firm grip, loving the way her eyelids fluttered shut as her breathing quickened. "This is only the beginning," he muttered.

Mellie arched her back, her rose-tipped breasts quivering as he picked up the pace. "Promises, promises."

How could she make him smile in the midst of blind lust? He changed the angle slightly and felt the moment she caught her breath. Knowing she was with him, teetering on the brink, he let go, shuddered and collapsed into the storm.

Fourteen

Mellie couldn't breathe. The problem originated in one of two sources. Either her condition was the aftermath of a wildly lush and powerful orgasm, or it was due to the fact that a large, heavy man lay on top of her, apparently comatose.

She allowed herself a smug smile. For a woman who was out of practice in the bedroom, she hadn't done half-badly. Of course, in all honesty, most of the credit had to go to Case. Alpha males might be stubborn and aggravating and impossibly bossy, but in certain situations, it was nice to have a man with confidence. A man who could play a woman's body as if only he knew the tune.

In the quiet of the bedroom, she cataloged the situation. She needed to go pee, but she didn't want to move. She took in Case's bed…Case's bedroom…Case's big warm frame sprawled in her arms. If she were a cat, she'd be purring right now.

A river of feelings moved through her veins. Relaxation. Joy. Quiet amazement. For once, she had ignored her cautious instincts and let nature take its course. Most of the time, she ran a tight ship. Work. Home. Work and more work. Losing her mother as a teenager had left her with a need for security. And Harold was never going to be any help there.

But holding things together all the time was difficult. She'd become a grown-up before she had a chance to make teenage mistakes. Maybe she was regressing. Maybe Case Baxter was her adolescent blunder. Sleeping with a client wasn't exactly the most professional move she'd ever made...

Suddenly, her lover groaned and rolled onto his back. She held her breath until he settled back to sleep. When his breathing was even and deep again, she slipped from the bed and tiptoed naked into his bathroom, then eased the door shut behind her.

After taking care of business, she found a thick navy robe on the back of the door and slid her arms into it. She had to roll up the sleeves and belt the waist tightly, but it at least gave her some protection from the vulnerability of prancing around stark naked.

Her reflection in the mirror made her wince. Wild hair, mascara smudges, whisker burns on her neck. Her thighs tightened at the memory of Case nibbling his way from her ear to shoulder.

In hindsight, it might have been prudent to actually bring her overnight case *inside*. Fat lot of good it was doing her out in Case's car. But then again, she and Case had been too busy cavorting in the romantic moonlight to worry about pedestrian realities like toothbrushes and nighties.

When she turned out the bathroom light and prepared to

slip back into bed, her stomach growled loudly. She'd been too nervous to eat much at the party, and lunch today had been slim, as well. Fortunately, she knew her way around Case's kitchen. And she knew how much food his friends had brought over while he was sick.

As she reached into the fridge for a container of cold chicken, two big hands grabbed her butt. She yelped and spun around. "Case!"

He gave her a mock scowl. "I woke up and you were gone." Then his eyes narrowed. "Is that my robe you're wearing?"

She flushed. Case had on nothing but a pair of cotton pajama pants. His big bare feet were sexy, which meant she was in real trouble. Because she'd never been turned on by feet before. "My overnight bag is still in the car."

Case grabbed the ends of the terrycloth belt and drew her against him. "My robe never looked so good." He lowered his head and kissed her, long and sweet, making her toes curl against the cold ceramic-tile kitchen floor.

She twined her arms around his neck. Without shoes, the difference in their height was magnified. He made her feel fragile and cherished. She'd always been proud of her self-sufficiency. But it turned out there was something to be said for the notion of allowing a big, strong man to take charge once in a while.

She buried her nose in his bare shoulder. He smelled of soap and warm male skin and sex. "I was raiding your leftovers," she said.

He chuckled, the sound reverberating through her when he kissed the top of her head. "You don't really want cold chicken, do you…"

It was more a statement than a question. She raked her fingernail across his flat copper-colored nipple. "Is there a better offer on the table?"

"Maybe." He inhaled sharply. "If I feed you popcorn, will you come back to bed afterward?"

"I could be persuaded."

He picked her up by the waist and set her on top of the butcher-block island. Moments later he had the microwave humming. The scent of hot popcorn filled the air.

When it was done, Case opened a bottle of wine, poured two glasses and hopped up to sit beside her, handing her the bowl of popcorn. "It doesn't take much to make you happy, does it?"

Mellie shrugged. "We all have our weaknesses. But I like to think I'm a realist. The most important things in life are free."

He was quiet for a long time. What was he thinking?

This huge, wonderful house was a lonely cave for a man to rattle around in. He should have a wife and several children to keep him company. Then again, some guys liked being bachelors.

"May I ask you a personal question?" she asked.

Case drained his wineglass and set it aside. "Sure. Fire away."

"With your parents gone, how do you celebrate Thanksgiving?" The holiday was less than a week away.

"I don't really." Case shrugged. "I have an aunt and uncle in Austin. They always invite me, and sometimes I accept. Other years I go skiing with friends in Colorado."

"Have you celebrated any holiday in this house since your parents died?"

"No."

When he didn't elaborate, she knew she had hit a nerve. "Would you let me cook for you next week? Nothing fancy…just turkey and dressing and maybe a pie or two."

"You don't have to feel sorry for me, Mellie. I've been thinking about Thanksgiving, too. But I thought we could head down to Key West for the long weekend. Rent a boat. Sail around the islands. Eat fresh seafood and dance under the stars."

"Sounds like a movie. Way too good to be true." Did he feel the need to impress her? Or was the idea of having a woman cook for him too domestic...too *familiar*? "Never mind," she said lightly. "It was just a thought."

When he put a hand on her bare knee, she jumped. The sides of her robe had gaped, allowing him a glimpse of her legs covered in gooseflesh.

"We need to get you back in bed," he said. "Before you catch pneumonia."

The change of subject was awkward, but she let it slide. "Bed sounds nice." And maybe round number two. Her snack had revived her. Leaving the door open for other hungers to be sated.

They walked hand in hand to the bedroom. A yawn caught her unawares.

Case laughed. "I'll let you sleep first."

"First?"

"Before round two."

Scrambling onto the mattress, she shed his robe and held out her arms. "I can sleep when I'm dead."

This time she took the initiative. She pulled Case by the wrist. "Lie down on your back," she said. "It's my turn to play tour guide."

"Whatever the lady wants."

The words were playful, but the fierce light in his eyes was anything but. His hard body quivered, poised for action. When Mellie reclined beside him and delicately licked the head of his shaft, he cursed and groaned. It was heady stuff to make the mighty Case Baxter weak and needy.

She stroked him with two hands. He was a big man everywhere.

Moments later he grabbed her wrist in an iron hold. "Enough." The glazed expression in his eyes told her what he wanted.

With only a second or two to decide if she was feeling sexually adventurous tonight, she moved over him and sat on his upper thighs. "I like having you at my mercy," she whispered. The sense of being in control was false. She knew that. Case Baxter might be a Texas gentleman, but in certain situations, the veneer of civilization wore thin.

His chest rose and fell rapidly. His cheekbones carried a flush of color, and his eyes were so dark the pupils were barely discernible. "I'll let you call the shots on this one, Mellie. Be my guest."

The words were lazy and compliant, but his hands fisted at his hips and cords of muscles flexed in his arms. The lion wasn't sleeping...merely biding his time.

After she reached for a condom, she opened it and rolled it over Case's erection. Then rising onto her knees, she lowered herself and took him deep. He'd given her one outstanding orgasm already, but she was greedy. She wanted more.

Case cursed and grabbed her ass in a bruising grip. "Don't move," he begged.

Was he really so susceptible to her charms? It seemed unlikely. Mellie possessed a healthy self-esteem, but she knew Case had access to more women than was good for him. Money, good looks, Texas cowboy charm...the trifecta wasn't really fair to the female sex.

She had to question his ex-wife's intelligence.

Mellie rested her hands, palms flat, on her lover's chest, feeling the heat of him, the light dusting of hair, the tough, muscled breadth of him. She'd told herself a hundred times that she could play this game and not get hurt. But suddenly, a knot lodged in her throat.

When had she let him become so human? When had he
ceased to be the wealthy, powerful president of the Texas
Cattleman's Club? When had she forgotten he could buy
and sell the Keep N Clean a hundred times over and never
miss the cash?

Her enjoyment of the intimate moment wavered.

Case—damn him—noticed instantly. "What's wrong?"
he demanded.

"Nothing."

He grimaced. "The universal female response. And you
don't sell it any better than the next woman. Talk to me,
Mellie."

Unexpectedly, a wave of bittersweet regret rolled over
her. Hot tears stung the backs of her eyes, but she'd have
died before letting him see. "I'm fine," she whispered.
"Great, in fact. Just tired."

"I'll let you sleep soon," he swore. "But first, my turn…"

Case knew this time was different. Earlier, he and Mellie had come together in the heat of a mutual passion.
Reckless. Unabashed. Grabbing for what they wanted…
wringing every drop of physical sensation from the experience. The sex was some of the best of his life.

And yet now he felt a shift in the force. A ragged tear
in the veil of pleasure.

He moved on top, taking Mellie with him by the simple expedient of clamping his arms around her waist as
he rolled over and maintaining the connection that made
their bodies one. Maybe she *was* tired. But he had the sinking feeling that she had slipped away from him mentally.

He'd never asked about other men in her past. She'd
told him it had been a long time since she'd been intimate
with anyone, and he had believed her. Now he wished he

had pressed for more details. After all, Mellie had wanted to know about Leslie.

Despite his mental turmoil, his body seized control. Desperately he entered her, again and again, trying to force her into coming with him, but even as he found his release, he knew he was alone in that moment.

Mellie was unnaturally still. He moved to the side and slung an arm over his eyes, feeling ashamed for no good reason he could understand. Why did women have to be so damned complicated?

Was she asleep? Was she hurt?

"Mellie?" He wasn't even touching her hip to hip.

The candle had long since burned out. Her voice in the darkness was small and shaky. "Will you take me home, please?"

Stunned and angry, he reached for the lamp and turned it on. Mellie winced and turned away, but not before he saw her damp eyes. "God, honey, what is it? What's wrong?"

She had the sheet clenched in her fingers, the soft cotton covering her bare breasts. Though she managed to look at him, it was only a fleeting glance. He saw her throat move as she swallowed. "I thought I could be one of those women who has sex as a lark. You know, just for fun. But I don't think I can. I like you, Case. And I respect you. But I really, really don't want to fall in love with you."

The last sentence was flat. He felt much as he had the time a horse kicked him in the chest. No air in his lungs at all. Coupled with a jolt of pain that would have brought him to his knees had he been standing.

What the hell did she want him to say? The days were long gone when he said the *L* word with no thought of the consequences. Hell, he didn't want to fall in love either. Did he?

He was angry and confused and dangerously close to taking her again just to prove how good they were together.

Perhaps he should have talked to her quietly, explained all the reasons she was panicking for nothing. But his limbs still trembled. He'd come hard, out of control, needing everything she had to give.

And now this.

"Fine," he said, the word like glass in his throat. "Put on your dress and I'll drive you home."

He grabbed up his things and carried them across the hall, leaving Mellie the privacy of his room. Alternating between fury and despair, he dressed rapidly and went to stand in the front foyer. He was afraid if he lingered in the hallway, he would bust through the door and drag her into bed again.

Part of him wanted to make promises…anything to get her to stay. But he'd made a fool of himself once over a woman. Any man who let himself be manipulated by female emotions deserved to fall on his ass. That was a young man's lesson.

Case Baxter was older and wiser now.

He had his keys in his hand when Mellie appeared. Her face was pale, her expression composed. But her posture was somehow broken, as if she were leaving the field of battle. Her beautiful dress was rumpled. She carried nothing, not even a purse. He'd been in such a hurry to make love to her they'd left everything in the car when they came in earlier.

"I'm ready," she said.

He opened the door and stepped aside for her to precede him down the steps. Only then did he realize that Mellie's fur wrap lay in a heap on the porch. Neither of them had noticed it fall. They had been too focused on each other to care about inconsequential things.

Mellie bent and picked up the stole, pausing only long enough to drape it around her shoulders and hold it tight. The temperature had plummeted after dark. With her bare toes and all that bare skin, she must be freezing.

"The car heats up quickly," he muttered.

His companion didn't answer. She moved rapidly down the steps, slipped into the passenger seat and closed her own door before he could help. Earlier, the interior of the small sports car had created intimacy. Now it only magnified the gulf between the two adults who had started the evening with such enthusiasm.

In front of Mellie's house he reconsidered. "Do you want to tell me what's really going on?"

Her hands twisted in her lap. "I'm not playing games. Merely having second thoughts. I think tonight scared me a little bit. We've moved so fast I'm feeling wobbly on my feet."

"Are you saying I pressured you?" That thought left a nasty taste in his mouth.

Mellie turned toward him. "Oh, no…no…no… This is about me, not you. It was sweet of you to ask me to the party, and I enjoyed every moment of tonight."

"But you're done."

"Can we call it a strategic time-out?"

"If this is a ploy to secure my interest by playing hard to get, I should tell you it won't work."

Fifteen

Silence fell like a hammer in the wake of his stupid, belligerent remark. Mellie unlocked her door, picked up her tiny purse from the console between the front seats and got out. "I'd like my bag, please." He'd felt winters in the Rockies that were warmer than her icy request.

"Damn it, Mellie. You know I didn't mean that. You're making me crazy."

"My suitcase, please." She stood there like a queen waiting for a peon to do her bidding.

Gritting his teeth, he reached into the backseat and extricated the bag. He pulled up the handle and passed it to her. "It's three a.m. Nothing makes any sense at this hour. Let's talk tomorrow. Dinner. I'll fly us to Dallas in the chopper. You'll love seeing the city from that viewpoint."

She raked a hand through her hair, looking like a weary angel doing battle with a recalcitrant sinner. "I appreciate the invitation, but I can't. And I think it would be best if I assign another one of my ladies to clean your house. You run with the big dogs, Case. I'm just an ordinary woman who never really believed in the Cinderella story."

"What in the hell does that even mean?"

"I was supposed to clean and organize your house. You got sick. I felt sorry for you. We bonded over chicken soup, and both of us were a little curious. So now we know. To-night was fun."

"And?" He couldn't believe she was giving him the brush-off. Particularly after the incredible sex they had shared. Didn't she know how rare it was to have that kind of physical connection right off the bat? He'd felt comfort-able with her and at the same time eager for more.

"And I think it's best if we stop before things get too intense. You don't even know me, Case. Not really. And I don't know you."

He was too proud to argue. And too self-aware to deny she was telling the truth. When Leslie trashed his life, he had stopped letting so much of himself be vulnerable.

"I'll walk you to the door," he said quietly.

Mellie's brief nod ended the conversation.

Her little house was neatly kept. The front door was recessed at the back of a narrow concrete stoop. In the dark, neither of them saw the obstacle. Mellie stumbled and would have fallen if Case hadn't grabbed her arm.

"What the hell?" His protective instincts kicked into high gear.

Mellie groaned. "Oh, no. It's my father."

The pile of dark clothing on the tiny porch rumbled and moved. Harold Winslow sat up, reeking of whiskey and some other less definable odor. "'Bout time you got home, my girl. Leaving your old pop out in the cold isn't nice."

"Why are you here, Daddy?"

Case noted the total lack of inflection in Mellie's voice.

Harold made it to his feet with Case's assistance. "Came to see you. You weren't here. Didn't have any cash for cab fare to make it home."

"Let's get him inside," Case said in a low voice. "You said your neighbors gossip. Maybe we should keep this quiet before we wake up the whole street."

Once they'd all made it into Mellie's living room and turned on the lights, Case stifled a groan of pained amusement. They were a sad-looking trio. After walking Harold to the sofa and helping him sit down, Case shrugged out of his tux jacket and tossed it on a chair. His shirt was open down the front because he hadn't taken the time to refasten the studs.

Mellie was definitely bedraggled. Her hair was tangled in a just-out-of-bed style that was actually damned appealing. When she looked across the room at him, he had no choice but to go to her and put an arm around her waist. When he touched her, he could feel the trembling she couldn't control.

She lowered her voice. "May I speak with you in private, Case?"

"Of course."

Harold seemed oblivious to any byplay, so Case and Mellie left him to his own devices. In the glare of the fluorescent overhead light in the kitchen, Mellie appeared distraught. "I am so embarrassed," she whispered.

Case shrugged. "Alcoholism is a terrible disease. Have you ever gotten him to an AA meeting?"

"Again and again. But when he's sober, he's the most sensible man in the world. And can argue a person blind. I can't tell you how many times he's convinced me he's absolutely stopped drinking. I'm his daughter. I know him better than anyone. But that's how good he is."

"He's probably able to be convincing because he believes it himself. He believes he can stop anytime he wants to."

"I suppose."

"Would you like me to take him home for you?"

She shook her head slowly. "No. He's my parent. My problem. But thank you for offering. I'm sorry our evening ended this way."

Case leaned against the counter, yawning. "Turns out you had already kind of jacked it up anyway, so no harm done."

Mellie gaped at him and then burst out laughing, which was exactly the response he'd been hoping for. Anything to get that look of sick defeat off her face.

"I can't believe you said that to me, Case Baxter."

"I've been told I have a dark sense of humor." Her smile affected him to an uncomfortable degree. He grimaced. "Will you be okay with him?"

"Yes. He'll sleep it off on the sofa. Maybe tomorrow morning I'll find out why he's here."

"Will you loan him more money?"

Her expression was hunted. "I said I wouldn't."

"It's hard. I know it is." Case brushed her cheek with his thumb. "I don't want to leave you. Hell, I didn't want you to leave my house. You make it feel like a home."

"That's just the furniture polish I use. It probably reminds you of your grandmother."

For a moment he thought she was serious. Then he saw the tiny spark of mischief in her eyes. "Trust me, Mellie. *Nothing* about you reminds me of my grandmother."

He kissed her cheek and hugged her briefly. Nothing more. He didn't want to pressure her, particularly not after the encounter with her father.

By unspoken consent they returned to the living room. Harold was hunched over the remote, squinting at the numbers, trying to find a channel he wanted. He looked up when they appeared. "You staying the night?" He addressed his question to Case.

Mellie winced, but Case took the old man's query in stride. "No, sir. I'll say goodbye now."

He took Mellie's hand and dragged her with him to the front door and outside onto the dark stoop. "I'd like to kiss you good-night, Mellie."

"You kissed me in the kitchen."

"Not like that. Like this." Sliding a hand on either side of her neck, he used his thumbs to lift her chin. He brushed her mouth with his...pressed his lips to hers...breathed the air she breathed.

Mellie sighed and went lax in his embrace. Case kept an iron rein on his libido. Now was the time for tenderness. For understanding.

"I do care about you, Case," she whispered, sending his stomach into a free fall. "But we aren't right for each other."

It was not the occasion to argue the point. She met him kiss for kiss, the embrace lasting far longer than he had planned. So long, in fact, that he now had a painful erection with no hope of appeasing his need for her.

It took everything he had to pull away. "Good night, Mellie."

"Good night, Case." She waved as he strode out to his car.

Mellie would rather have done just about anything than walk back inside her house. Harold was a millstone around her neck. As she gave inner voice to that thought for the hundredth time, she felt like a lousy person. Other people's parents had cancer or even worse challenges to face.

At least Harold was healthy. Of course, there was no telling how long his liver would hold out.

Her intention was to walk past her father with a brief good-night. She wanted a hot shower and her own bed. In that order. Harold had pulled this stunt too many times. Even so, she fetched pillows and blankets so he wouldn't have to sleep on the bare sofa.

As she leaned down to pick up her small evening purse, she saw something that made her stomach curl with dread. A billfold. A familiar billfold, half-hidden beneath her father's leg.

"Oh, Daddy. What have you done?"

Her father tried to stare at her haughtily, but the effect was ruined by the fact that his eyes were glazed over. "I don't know what you mean."

Perhaps she might not have recognized the wallet in other circumstances. Many men's wallets were similar. But she had seen this particular one earlier tonight when Case took it out of his pocket to retrieve the coat-check ticket for Mellie's wrap and purse at the club.

"Give me that," she cried. Hands shaking, she flipped open the expensive leather. "How much did you take?"

Harold stood and nearly fell over. "Are you calling your own flesh and blood a thief?" He was wearing a leather jacket that Mellie's mother had given him twenty years ago. The coat no longer buttoned around his expanding waist, but he refused to give it up.

Gritting her teeth, Mellie reached into the nearest pocket of her father's jacket and wanted to bawl like a baby when her hand came back out with a couple of hundred-dollar bills. "Oh, God, Daddy. How could you?"

At that very moment, a knock sounded at her front door. Given the hour, it was a safe bet she knew who it was. She shoved the bills back in Case's wallet and glared at Harold. "Is there any more?"

She wasn't even sure he heard her. He had dropped back onto the sofa and was sprawled facedown, snoring like a grizzly bear.

Mellie took a deep breath and told herself no harm had been done. She opened the door and managed a smile. "I bet you're looking for this."

Case nodded, his expression relieved. "It must have fallen out of my jacket pocket."

She didn't say a word, and Case didn't seem to notice. He looked past her to the noisy houseguest on her couch. "You sure you don't want me to take him home?"

"We're good," she said, her throat tight.

"Okay. I don't suppose this qualifies for another kiss?"

She shook her head, wanting him to leave so she could fall apart in private. "You've had your quota. Good night, Case."

He sketched a salute and walked away from her a second time, taking part of her heart with him. She closed the door and leaned against it, tears already dripping from her chin.

Tonight was the worst thing she had ever seen her father do. Stealing? Was it a thoughtless crime of opportunity, or was Harold more lost than she realized?

Bracing herself, she searched every pocket on his person. He never even woke up. Thankfully, there was no more money to be found. Maybe this could be chalked up to a near disaster.

In her bedroom, she locked her door for no other reason than that she needed to feel the world was at bay for a few hours. She took a shower and tried not to imagine Case's big gentle hands caressing her body. How could one twenty-four-hour period hold so much joy and heartache in equal measures?

When she tumbled onto her bed and climbed beneath the covers, she clutched the extra pillow to her chest and told herself she didn't have a broken heart.

Not even the pitiful lie could keep her awake anymore.

Sixteen

Case was in a bitch of a mood. Mellie was avoiding him. By phone and in person. It was as if she had up and vanished off the streets of Royal. Four days had passed since the night of the party. On Monday another Keep N Clean employee had shown up bright and early to do the second story of his house. The lady was a pleasant middle-aged woman with a no-nonsense attitude.

He showed her around and gave her carte blanche to carry out the careful list of chores her boss had spelled out. Then he saddled his favorite horse and spent the rest of the day riding his property and brooding about how one ornery redhead had made his life miserable.

Fortunately, he did have a number of things to do at the club. Because of his illness, he was behind in learning his new duties. Gil Addison had blocked off some time on Tuesday to show Case files and paperwork and to introduce him to the young assistant who held court inside the imposing club offices.

Tami knew who got in to see the president and who didn't. She also was extremely efficient and very good at her job. "I'll look forward to working with you," Case said. She smiled politely, already turning back to her desk to resume her work.

Gil nodded. "She'll be the continuity you need, especially if I'm not around to answer questions. But you'll get the rhythm of things pretty quickly."

"I hope I can do the job as well as you have." Gil was a straight-arrow kind of guy, and Case respected the hell out of him.

Gil's careful smile took years off his age. "I'm looking forward to spending some extra time with my family. You'll do a great job as president, Case. Everyone is delighted to have you at the helm."

By midmorning on the Wednesday before Thanksgiving, the club was virtually empty. A lot of people traveled for the holiday, and the ones still in Royal were busy baking and entertaining out-of-town company. Case decided to put in a few hours on the computer and then head home.

He'd have football to watch and movies to enjoy. Lots of men would envy him.

Around eleven o'clock Tami's voice came over the old-fashioned intercom. "Mr. Baxter? There's a Harold Winslow here to see you. He doesn't have an appointment."

Case rubbed the center of his forehead. Surely he owed Mellie this much. "Will you show him in, Tami? I'll give Winslow fifteen minutes. As soon as we're done, you and I can both lock up everything and leave." The club would be shut down from noon today until Friday morning to give employees time to spend with their families.

A couple of minutes later, Tami escorted Harold into Case's small office and excused herself. Case stood and held out his hand, not at all sure Harold would remember Saturday night's fiasco.

Harold grimaced as he shook Case's hand. "Thank you for seeing me on such short notice, Mr. Baxter."

"Please call me Case. And have a seat."

Harold was dressed impeccably today in a sport coat, crisp slacks, and a shirt and tie. The metamorphosis was astonishing. The older man leaned forward, elbows on his knees. "I hope you'll accept an apology for my behavior the last time you saw me. Not my finest hour. But I'm working on it."

Case shrugged. "We all have our issues. What can I do for you today?"

Harold sat back in his chair and crossed his legs. "I've had inquiries from an investor about purchasing this property. So I think it's in your and my best interests to discuss the current lease payments."

"Wait a minute." Case did some quick mental backflips and remembered Nathan telling him that the club sat on land belonging to Winslow Properties. But Case hadn't thought anything about it at the time. He'd assumed there would be legal papers on file somewhere outlining the agreement. Since he didn't know that for sure, he decided to tread carefully. "You're talking about Samson Oil, right?"

Harold's genial smile never faltered. "You've heard of them, I see. Their offer is very generous. But on the other hand, I'd hate to see the club have to move."

Case flinched inwardly. The other man clearly thought he had the upper hand. "I've only just taken over as president," Case said. "I'm still in the process of learning the ins and outs of the club's operations. I wasn't aware that it was time for contract negotiations."

"My great-grandfather offered this property to the club years ago for a nominal fee. But we've never had more than a gentleman's agreement. This might help." Harold extracted a folded spreadsheet from his inside breast pocket. "Here's the info from my files. The rent over the years has been very reasonable, as you can see. But we're deep into a new century now, and I can't let sentiment overrun my need to turn a profit."

Case studied the figures, his expression impassive. In his chest, his heart pounded a warning rhythm. If there was no written agreement, Harold Winslow had the legal right to increase the lease payments anytime he saw fit.

"According to this schedule," Case said slowly, giving himself time to think, "the rent has seen modest increases every two years. What did you have in mind?"

Harold named a figure that was twenty times the current lease payment. "I realize that's a big jump, and I don't want to make trouble. Still, think about what could happen. If I sell to Samson Oil, they might tear down this building entirely. All that history…gone in a flash."

The threat was not even veiled. Harold Winslow had resorted to blackmail. And Case, who had been the new club president for all of ten minutes, was completely caught off guard.

"I'd have to convene my board," Case said. "To talk this over."

Harold smiled. But the calculating gleam in his eyes told Case this was not a friendly conversation.

"Not much to talk over," Harold said. "Either you accept my terms, or you start looking for a new location to build the club."

"Why would an oil company want land that was checked for oil over a century ago and found dry?"

Harold shrugged. "Don't know. Don't care. I'm a businessman. Money talks."

"And it doesn't bother you that the community might see you as greedy and unsympathetic and run you out of town?"

"Afraid not."

"Royal would never let a new owner move the club from its present location. Have you talked to your daughter about all of this?"

Harold looked him straight in the eye. "Of course I have. Mellie wants money to expand her business. This was her idea."

Direct hit. *Goddamn it.* "How do I know you're telling the truth about that?"

"Women lie all the time. They manipulate you and make you believe what they want you to believe. Ask her how you happened to leave without your wallet the other night. See what she says. I think you'll be surprised."

Case drove back out to the ranch in a daze. Though Nathan had been the one to tell him that Mellie's family owned the land on which the Texas Cattleman's Club sat, Mellie herself had never actually mentioned it. The omission seemed painfully suspicious in light of today's revelations.

And he got even more suspicious when he pulled up in front of his house and found Mellie sitting on the top step.

He got out of the car slowly, his mind racing. Memories of Leslie's lies and machinations filled his throat with bile.

Mellie didn't move. Instead, she waited for him to walk up the staircase. When she patted the seat beside her, he shook his head. "I'll stand. Why are you here, Mellie?"

Her smile faltered. "I was feeling bad about the way we argued the other night. Tomorrow is Thanksgiving. I'm renewing my offer to cook for you."

"No, thanks." He didn't dress up his refusal.

"Am I missing something?" she asked.

"Why didn't you tell me your family owned the land where the TCC sits?"

She had the gall to look puzzled instead of guilty. "It's not a secret. I guess it never came up. Or I thought you already knew."

"And one more question. It wasn't an accident that I lost my billfold at your house Saturday night, was it?"

This time the guilt on her face was clear. His heart shriveled in his chest, even as pain choked him. How could she look so open and sweet and plan to blackmail him?

"My father took it," she said, "while you and I were in the kitchen. When I realized what he had done...after you left, I made him put the money back. That's when you showed up at the door."

"So, to be clear, you chose to protect your father rather than tell me the truth." The incident wasn't such a big thing by itself. But combined with Harold's demand for an exorbitant rental increase, Case had to wonder what other things Mellie had been hiding from him.

Mellie went white, her expression agitated. "It all happened so fast. No harm was done. He does such stupid stuff when he's drinking. I'm really sorry, Case."

"My hat's off to you, Mellie," he said. The pain was gone now, replaced by a raging need to hurt her as much as she had hurt him. "You even told me what you were doing. Winning my trust little by little so you could blackmail me and line your pockets. It makes perfect sense that you turned down my fifty-thousand-dollar offer. You had bigger plans...much bigger."

She stood shakily. Since Case was a few steps below her, they faced each other eye to eye. "You've got this all wrong, Case. I don't want your money."

"Not mine, it seems. But your father just stood in my office and demanded a new Cattleman's Club lease at twenty times the price. Threatened to sell the property out from under us if I don't agree to his terms. You *do* want money. But far more than I was offering. And you don't mind dragging my reputation through the mud to get what you want."

"I'll talk to him," she swore. Ashen and trembling, she was very convincing.

"No more theater," he said. "I know it was your idea. He told me so. The thing is, Mellie, if you hadn't overplayed your hand, you could have ended up with a ring on your finger. I was falling for you. Hard. But I had a narrow escape. You and your dad have a nice little scam going. Maybe you even arranged for him to be on your front porch when I brought you home. I actually felt sorry for you."

She reached for him. "I've been falling for you, too, Case. Please don't let my father ruin what we have."

Her touch burned his arm. Jerking away, he tried not to think about how it felt to rest in her arms. "What we have is *nothing*, Mellie. Nothing at all. You gambled and you lost. Now it's over."

Mellie drove back to town and later didn't remember doing so. She was in shock. In denial. Case had looked at her with such cold fury and contempt she felt dirty.

Her first instinct was to hole up in her little house and hide. Thanksgiving came and went. Her father neither called nor came by. He was avoiding her, no doubt. Only on Friday did she find the strength to do what had to be done.

She went to her father's office and found it empty. But everything she needed was on the computer and written on notepads in her father's messy scrawl. Rapidly, she made a list of all the property to which the Winslows still held title. At one time, Harold had been one of the largest landowners in downtown Royal.

But in the past two years, he had sold off more and more, leaving him with only a dozen small tracts and two significant parcels of land—the one on which the TCC sat and the slightly larger one outside of town where the Courtyard was located.

After locking up the office, she went to her father's house, where she found him passed out on the sofa. His condition was a reminder that she was doing the right thing. Though she had been prepared to have a knock-down, drag-out confrontation, she left without disturbing him.

Nathan Battle and one very cranky judge were next on her list. Judge Plimpton didn't like being disturbed on the golf course.

Fortunately, Mellie had legal rights. Mellie's mother had left her portion of Winslow Properties to Mellie and not Harold. So although Harold ran the company, Mellie was an equal partner.

By bedtime that night, all her plans had been set in motion.

Case was already regretting his election as club president. What was supposed to be a largely ceremonial title had landed him in a hell of a mess. It was the Tuesday after Thanksgiving, and here he sat in a room with two lawyers and the nine-member board.

One of the lawyers was speaking, shaking his head. "Sadly, Mr. Winslow is on firm ground in this instance as far as I can tell. As he told you, Mr. Baxter, the original lease arrangement from years ago was a gentleman's agreement with Winslow's ancestor. Unfortunately, subsequent generations saw no reason to add more official parameters. Gil Addison remembers a conversation with Harold Winslow at the beginning of his tenure, but at that time there was only a two percent increase in rent."

One of the board members chimed in. "What if we were to offer to buy the land from Winslow?"

"With what?" Case had already combed through the ledgers. "The club has spent quite a bit of capital in the last few years, first on renovations and more recently to repair tornado damage. The financial bottom line is healthy but certainly not adequate to purchase a piece of property this size."

The second lawyer checked his notes. "So what do we know about this Samson Oil company? Are we sure they would evict you immediately?"

Case ran a hand inside the back of his collar, feeling the walls closing in. "We don't know much, unfortunately. Only that they have been quietly buying up property in and around Royal…and giving fair prices as far as I can tell. The thing is, though, a new landowner could choose to present us with even worse terms than those Winslow is offering."

Everyone in the room fell silent. Though no one would blame Case for the current situation, in his gut, he felt guilty. If he hadn't gotten involved with Melinda Winslow, she and Harold might never have concocted this scheme that might possibly cost the club its identity.

The first lawyer reinforced Case's worst fears. "Mr. Baxter is right. Even if the entire town were to rise up in protest, there would be nothing to stop a legal landowner from doing anything and everything with this property. Without a written lease covenant, we're in murky waters."

Case pressed his temples, a pounding headache building. To move the club intact was impossible. The history within these walls was the history of Royal itself. It made him sick to think of how much they stood to lose.

"Let's break for lunch," he said. "We'll reconvene at one." In the meantime, he had no choice but to confront Mellie again and persuade her to reconsider.

He was too angry and upset to eat anything at all. So he locked himself in his office and dialed Mellie's cell number. Time after time, his call went to voice mail. Hearing her speak was a knife to the heart.

But she never answered.

When he finally gave up, he rested his head in his hands and tried to think clearly. Mellie knew her father was an alcoholic. Why would she collude with him in such a distasteful maneuver?

Unless he was completely mistaken, and maybe he was, this scheme didn't sound like Mellie at all.

When the lawyers and board members returned, Case was no closer than ever to a solution. He could live with embarrassment. He could even live with the fact that once again a woman had used him for financial gain. What he couldn't bear was knowing that his community had placed their faith in him, and the club might lose everything on Case's watch.

Discussion raged helplessly for three more hours, circling back again and again to the fact that Harold Winslow held all the cards. One by one, each man and woman in the room came to the same conclusion. The Texas Cattleman's Club was facing a crisis as stark and painful in its own way as last year's killer storm.

Suddenly, a knock on the door drew Case to his feet. Tami's smile was apologetic. "I'm so sorry, Mr. Baxter. But this registered letter was just delivered, and it's marked Urgent."

"Thanks, Tami."

Case turned to find the group progressing without him. He had no problem with that. It gave him a chance to tamp down dread before he opened the very official-looking envelope.

He read the brief message once, twice...a third time. All of his instincts went on high alert, looking for a further threat. The document made no sense.

Without explanation, he handed it over to one of the lawyers. Conversation ceased as everyone around the table sensed something of import going on.

The lawyer scanned the contents and showed it to his colleague. Both of them studied the letter before finally looking up wearing smiles. Lawyer number one shook his head. "It seems your problems are over, ladies and gentlemen. According to this, Winslow Properties has agreed— in writing— to keep the current lease price in place for the next five years. And they have no intention of selling the land to Samson Oil or anyone else."

"But why?" One of the board members voiced the bafflement they were all feeling.

The second lawyer folded the letter and handed it back to Case. "Who knows? Maybe there was never really an offer at all. But the point is, the crisis has been averted."

Case frowned. "Why would Harold threaten me and then back down? It doesn't make sense."

Gil Addison shrugged. "Maybe he had second thoughts. Maybe he was drunk when he came up with his plan to gouge the club. Who knows? But that's his signature. So why look a gift horse in the mouth?"

And maybe Mellie had been telling the truth. Maybe she'd had nothing to do with Harold's ploy. Case nodded, but inside, his stomach churned.

The room cleared out quickly after that. Case spoke

briefly with the two legal professionals, making sure there wasn't anything more Case needed to do at the moment. Soon Case was the only one left.

He stood by the window, looking out at the crisp autumn day. Across the street, city workers stood on ladders beginning to hang this year's Christmas decorations on the lampposts.

The momentum of the holiday season was in full swing. Even with all the activity going on up and down the busy thoroughfare, Case saw none of it. The only image burned in his brain was the memory of Mellie's face when he tossed accusations at her.

Good God. What had he done?

He snatched up his keys and strode outside to his car, determined to see Harold Winslow face-to-face and demand the truth. The Winslow Properties offices were open, but inside, no Harold. Only a pleasant thirtysomething receptionist.

"Hello," Case said, giving the woman his most non-threatening smile. "I'm here to see Harold Winslow."

"He's not here," the woman said. "May I take a message?"

"Do you know when he'll be back?"

"Not for some time, sir. Miss Melinda will be running the business in her father's absence."

"I see."

"Are you by any chance a friend of the family?"

"You could say that."

"Shall I give you her phone number?"

Case swallowed. "I have it. Thanks."

He wandered outside and leaned against the brick facade of the building, his heart in his boots. The enormity of his arrogant blunder stood before him…irredeemable… unforgivable. It was entirely possible he had ruined the best thing to ever happen to him. And all because he'd been hung up on the fact that his first wife had never really loved him...that when people looked at him, they saw dollar signs and not the man he was.

If the topic of his downfall had been any less personal and painful, he might have been tempted to ask one of his married buddies for advice. But this situation was deeply intimate, and he knew in his heart that Mellie wouldn't want her name and the nature of her relationship with Case bandied about. She was a very private person.

In a few days, it would be December. The nights would grow longer and the days shorter. Christmas cheer would fill the streets of Royal, Texas. But for Case, this holiday season loomed bleak and empty. He'd been given the most precious gift of all...a woman's trust.

And he had thrown it away.

Seventeen

Mellie was exhausted. Running two businesses at the same time required her utmost attention. During the day she bounced back and forth between both offices. At night she fell into bed too wiped out to do more than say her prayers. At the top of the list was an urgent plea that her father was not going to hate her for what she had done.

It had required a concerted effort by a number of people, but Mellie had managed to more or less kidnap her father and check him into a wickedly expensive but highly successful rehab facility about a hundred and fifty miles from Royal.

Her father had been sober and shaky when she left him there. She'd given him an ultimatum. Either dry out and learn how to make a change, or resign himself to the fact that Mellie was going to run the family business and there would be no more handouts for Harold.

The rules at the facility were very strict. For the first

thirty days, Mellie would have no contact at all with her father. It wasn't until later that she realized those rules meant she would be spending Christmas alone.

She had many friends, of course, but she would not intrude during family time. She was a grown woman, and she could get along on her own.

Today was Friday. The letter from her lawyer had been delivered to the Texas Cattleman's Club on Tuesday. Case had to have seen it by now. And yet nothing. Seventy-two hours, with not a peep out of him.

The total lack of communication indicated more clearly than anything else that Case Baxter had no intention of either forgiving Mellie or continuing their relationship. She should have told him right away that her father had taken the wallet. Her lie of omission had caused Case to question her motives…to doubt her sincerity. And he already had trust issues when it came to women.

Mellie's first instinct had been to protect her father, even though he didn't deserve it. But her misstep had cost her dearly.

Gradually, though, as the hours and days passed, her regret changed to anger. Case *should* have trusted her. It had been far too easy for her father to drag her into his little blackmail scheme. If Case had really cared about her, he wouldn't have been so quick to believe Harold's lie. She had given Case her body and her heart and yet it hadn't been enough.

Because he didn't love her.

At the moment, despite her own personal heartache, she was driving out to the Courtyard because Raina Patterson had sent an agitated email asking for a meeting. Apparently, Mellie's indirect reassurances via Raina's cousin had not been enough.

When Mellie pulled up and parked, she was struck again by how charming and appealing this little cluster of studios and shops had turned out to be. Mellie found Raina inside the big red barn, frowning over a cash register receipt.

Raina looked up when the bell over the door tinkled. "Miss Winslow," she said. "Thank you so much for coming to see me."

"It's a beautiful day," Mellie said lightly. "No hardship at all. What can I do for you? In your email you sounded upset."

Raina grimaced. "I don't know quite how to say this because I thought the matter was settled. But I received a letter from your father saying that our rents were going to quadruple. I think it must have come last week, because I found it in a stack of mail on my desk that I had overlooked. He said he had a good offer for this property, but he'd be willing not to sell if we all agreed to the new terms."

Mellie held on to her smile grimly, disguising her utter disgust with her father's methods. "I think I can relieve you on that score. That letter would have been mailed before I checked him into rehab. I'm running the business now, and we have no plans to increase the rent. In fact, you and all the other tenants will receive a registered letter to that effect on Monday from *me*, stating the new terms. I'm sorry my father caused you sleepless nights."

Raina's relief was almost palpable. "Thank you, Miss Winslow. I'm very sorry about your father, but you don't know how much this means." She handed Mellie a small clay pot glazed in shades of ochre and midnight blue. "Please accept this as a thank-you. I think I speak for all the artists here when I say it's hard to make a living via a creative endeavor. With a stable rent, we'll be able to keep our books in the black."

"The Courtyard shops and the farmers' market are helping make Royal a center for tourism and the arts. What you do is very important. I hope your business will continue to grow."

Though Mellie chatted with Raina for several more minutes, her heart wasn't in the conversation. Eventually, she said her goodbyes and returned to her car.

Though she had reassured the shop owner, it was little consolation for her own situation. She felt as if her whole world had caved in. Even though she had convinced herself that she and Case weren't suited, his lack of faith hurt more than she could have imagined.

Until now she had never understood that heartache could be an actual physical ailment. Remembering the hours she had spent in Case's bed was nothing less than torture. He'd been so gentle with her and at the same time hungry and demanding, drawing a response that stunned her. Until Case she hadn't understood the human body's capacity for pleasure. Sex with Case had opened her eyes to how narrow she had made her life.

It would be a long time before she got over this. A very long time. But perhaps one day she would be given another chance at happiness with a man who was worthy of her heart and her trust.

Grabbing up her purse and briefcase, she got out of the car and stopped dead when she saw Case sitting on her doorstep.

He held up a hand, his expression impassive. "Don't worry. I parked the car two streets over at the grocery store. I know how much you dislike gossip."

She realized he wasn't kidding. Good grief.

It seemed prudent to halt a good six feet away. Her decision-making skills always took a hit when she got too near Case Baxter.

His jaw was shadowed, his eyes sunken with exhaustion. Stress lines she hadn't noticed before bracketed his mouth. "I need to talk to you, Mellie."

She folded her arms across her waist. "So talk."

"Privately. Please."

It seemed dangerous and stupidly hopeful to let him into her house, but she couldn't help it. "Very well."

In her living room it was impossible to forget what had happened in this spot just two weeks before. Humiliation washed over her, reddening her throat and face.

Case must have been affected strongly, as well, because he frowned. "I'd rather not do this here. I have some snacks and a picnic blanket in the car. Will you go for a drive with me?"

"It's chilly outside." She teetered on the edge of uncertainty. Even if Case forgave her and she forgave him, they still weren't suited as a couple. Wouldn't she simply be inviting more heartache if she dragged this out?

Case had his hands shoved in his pockets. His jeans were soft and worn and conformed to his hips and legs like a second skin. His yellow cotton shirt was a button-down with the sleeves rolled up above his broad wrists. "Please, Mellie," he said. "It's important."

"If it's so important, why didn't you talk to me on Tuesday? You did get the letter...right?"

He nodded slowly. "I did. And I went to find your father and demand an explanation."

"But he was gone. My assistant told me you came around asking questions. You didn't try to find *me*, though."

"That's true. I wanted to think about things before I saw you again."

"I checked my father into rehab. And gave him an ultimatum. He blows through money when he drinks, and apparently, he'll stoop to anything to scrape up cash. Including blackmailing good tenants who have never done him any wrong."

"You didn't know what he was doing…"

"No." She grimaced. "And unfortunately, it wasn't only you he targeted."

"So will you come with me so we can talk?"

"If it's that important. But I'd like to change first."

She switched outfits rapidly, going by Case's appearance as a guide and changing into jeans of her own. She grabbed up a scoop-necked sweater in a shade of teal that flattered her pale skin and then slipped her feet into black flats.

A quick check of her face in the mirror, and she was done, though her pulse raced with uncertainty and fear.

When she returned to the living room, Case was standing where she had left him. He didn't smile, even now. In fact, his sober demeanor rattled her quite a bit.

Without speaking, they exited the house and walked for fifteen minutes until they came in sight of an old dusty Land Rover parked at the curb. "This is Betsy," Case said. "She can go anywhere, anytime."

Mellie was glad he hadn't brought the sports car. She'd managed to maintain her composure up until now, but she needed to keep some physical distance between her and Case.

She didn't ask where they were going. That would involve conversation, and apparently, Case was fresh out of that. They drove out toward his ranch, leaving her to wonder if that wasn't their destination. But Case flew right past the B Hive gate and kept on going.

At last he turned onto a narrow rutted lane. Now it was clear why he'd brought the Rover. Though the tire tracks were deep and well defined, wild grasses growing in the middle dragged at the bottom of the vehicle.

Finally, the car came to a stop. Nearby, a small stream rippled and gurgled. Across the creek, a gentle rise, likely one of the highest places in Royal, drew attention to a single large oak, its branches flung wide in what would be wonderful shade in the summertime.

While Case grabbed up a few items from the back of the vehicle, Mellie shaded her eyes and scanned the area. She couldn't see another soul for miles around. The sense of peace and isolation was stunning.

Case looked her way. "Come on," he said. "I want to show you something."

She followed him toward the creek and across a small bridge. Even then Case didn't take her hand. It was as if he was afraid to touch her.

When they approached the rise, she could see two small tombstones at the top beneath the tree. She and Case climbed the hill, and he spread out the blanket. He indicated the small stone markers. "My mom and dad are buried here. I used to come out and talk to them a lot. Haven't done that much lately. But I wanted you to see this place."

"It's beautiful," she said. "Absolutely perfect." She bit her lip, shivering slightly, though not so much from the cold as from her jangled emotions.

"Mellie…" He stopped, his jaw working.

'What?"

"I am so damn sorry. I never should have believed him. You even told me how convincing he could be. But when he said that raising the lease price was your idea, I was furious and hurt and—"

"And you thought I had betrayed you."

"Yes." His face reflected grief and sorrow.

"You jumped to that conclusion pretty quickly...almost as if you were expecting me to hurt you."

"It doesn't reflect well on me, but I've had a hard time with women since Leslie. No, that's not exactly it. I've had a hard time with *me*. I have a tendency to be arrogant and in charge, so back then when I let myself be blinded by Leslie's come-ons, it made me doubt myself."

"Your marriage was over a long time ago."

"Yes. But I've never really wanted to be close to another woman until I met you. Suddenly, there you were in my house and in my bed and I couldn't help falling in love with you."

She blinked. "What did you just say?"

"I'm in love with you, Mellie." His smile was lopsided.

"Love doesn't happen so quickly."

Finally, he took her hands in his. "Maybe not for you. But I'm willing to wait."

She wiggled free of his hold, mostly because she wanted so badly to nestle against his chest and feel his heart beating beneath her cheek. She wrapped her arms around her waist, feeling as if she might fly into a million pieces like dandelion seeds dancing on the wind.

"You and I both live in Royal," she said. "Always have... probably always will. And now you're the president of the Cattleman's Club in addition to being one of the wealthiest ranchers in the state. My father will always be my father. He's in rehab, that's true, but you and I both know that the statistics for full recovery aren't stellar."

"What are you saying, Mellie, my love?"

Hearing him say the words brought tears to her eyes and a painful lump to her throat. "I *can't* be in love with you," she said, the words hoarse. "You may not ever be able to trust me completely. And my father may come between us down the road."

Case took Mellie by the wrist and reeled her in. "I'll never doubt you again," he said, utter certainty in his voice. "When we made love to each other, *that* was the real us… no masks, no barriers. We were the only people in that bed. And that's the way it's going to be. You and I against the world. Forever. If you say yes, of course."

His expression let her know that he was not completely sure of her response. Her knees wobbled. "Sex doesn't solve all the problems," she muttered, even as her stomach pitched and rolled.

Case held her close, tipping up her chin so he could settle his lips over hers. "I need you, Mellie," he whispered, his breath warm on her cheek. "Like I need air and food and a place to lay my head at night. I need your wonderful entrepreneurial spirit and your gifts of organization. I need your independence and your work ethic and the way you go above and beyond the call of duty. I need your compassion and your kindness. But most of all, I need your love."

"Oh, Case." He wasn't being fair.

"Oh, Mellie." He mocked her gently as he pulled her down onto the sun-warmed quilt. "Forgive me for doubting you. Make love to me. Let me show you how the world stops when we're together, flesh to flesh, heart to heart."

He waited an eternity for her answer.

"I don't want to rush into anything," she said. "I need us to be sure."

"But do you love me?"

The vulnerability on the face of this big, strong man

broke her heart a little bit. He'd opened himself up to her, had been the first one to speak words of love. It was a pretty good apology…a very nice way of making amends.

"You're everything I've ever looked for in a man, Case," she said. "You're the other half of me."

Eighteen

They undressed each other slowly, shoes first and then the important stuff. The afternoon was chilly, but the heat between them was sufficient. Case shivered when he felt her hands on his bare chest. He'd come so close to killing something wonderful, so close to losing the one person who could make him want more than a bachelor's existence in a big empty house.

With steady hands, he lifted her sweater over her head and then unfastened her bra. Soft, firm breasts filled his hands. "You're beautiful, Mellie."

Big green eyes looked up at him, searching his face as if she expected to find something she didn't like. "Please be sure about this, Case. I can't change who I am… I can't change my father."

He eased her onto her back and undid the snap on her jeans. "You're perfect just the way you are. And Harold will be the only grandparent our children have, so you and

I will just have to keep him on the straight and narrow and make sure he has plenty of little ones to spoil. I want you, Mellie. Now and always."

Her jaw dropped. "Children?"

"Children. Marriage. The whole package. That's what I want. What I need."

He slid his hands inside her pants, dragging them and her underwear down her legs. When she lifted her hips, he eased the tangled clothing away.

Mellie's skin was covered in gooseflesh. He stood and stripped, vowing to warm her up or die trying. He'd be lying if he said he didn't enjoy the way Mellie's eyes widened as she took in the evidence of how much he wanted her.

Seconds later he moved between her thighs and then cursed when he realized he'd forgotten the condom. Mellie laughed softly while he scrambled for his discarded pants and found the item he needed.

And then the waiting was over. He moved in her with his heart burning and his brain marveling that a man could be so clueless about what was important in life.

Mellie wrapped her legs around his waist, taking him deeper, kissing him wildly until neither of them could breathe. Her skin was soft and warm. He felt as if nothing he said or did was enough. He was helpless to make her see what a miracle she had wrought inside him.

He fought for control, even as his body drove mindlessly to a pinnacle that promised physical bliss.

But beneath it all, some tiny rational still-functioning part of his brain noted an important omission. Mellie hadn't said she loved him.

Shoving the thought aside, he concentrated on the feel of her sex as it squeezed him. When he felt the tiny ripples that told him she had reached the end, Case let himself go, giving a muffled shout and burying his face in her shoulder.

* * *

Mellie felt out of control. The contrast to her usual state of mind was sobering. She could barely cobble together a coherent thought, much less a mature, informed opinion about whether or not Case was in his right mind.

She wanted to believe him. She really did. She wanted to plunge headlong into the fairy tale where the girl who sweeps up the cinders meets her prince.

Idly, she stroked Case's hair. It was thick and silky and warm from the sun. His weight was a welcome burden. His body was the only thing tethering her to the ground at the moment.

Case loves me. She said it again inside her head, rolling the three words around and around until she made herself dizzy.

Finally, he moved, rolling over onto one elbow. "I told myself I was going to withhold sex until I got the answer I wanted."

Mellie laughed out loud at the disgruntlement on his handsome face. "Show me a man who can withhold sex, and I'll call Guinness World Records. Besides, what answer are you talking about? I didn't hear any question."

His smile made her stomach curl. "I don't need you to say anything you don't mean, but strictly as a matter of information, do you think you might fall in love with me eventually? Despite the fact that I acted like a giant horse's ass?"

"No." Mellie didn't have to think about it.

Case flinched. "I see."

"You don't see anything, but that's okay, because I like this abjectly groveling version of Case Baxter."

The man growled. He actually growled. "Explain yourself, woman."

His narrow-eyed glare made her shiver. In the best possible way. She put a hand on his cheek, trying not to fixate on the fact that Case was spectacularly nude. "I won't be *falling* in love with you, because I'm already there. How could I resist a sweet-talking cowboy like you?"

"Say it the right way," he demanded. "Now."

"I. Love. You."

His chest rose and fell. "Well, all right, then." He twisted a lock of her hair around his finger. "We could build out here. A woman should have her own place."

"I love the ranch house, Case. But you keep skipping parts of the script. Either that or I'm getting sunstroke."

"Nobody gets sunstroke in November." He teased her nipple with his fingernail.

Oh, wow. She wet her lips with her tongue. "Was there something else you wanted to ask me?"

"Hmm?" He seemed easily distracted.

"Case? I don't think the president of the Texas Cattleman's Club should live in sin. It sets a bad example."

"Whatever you say, my love."

"Case!"

He flopped over onto his back and spread his arms wide, his big masculine body a thing of beauty under the hot Texas sun. Shielding his eyes with one hand, he gave her the smile that had been her undoing. "Melinda Abigail Winslow…will you marry me?"

"You know my middle name?"

He grabbed her wrist and pulled her down on top of him. "I do…"

She felt him against her, chest to chest, thigh to thigh. "Do you also know that I'm partial to engagement rings?"

"Patience, my love. I have a plan."

She nibbled his ear. "Do tell."

"Tomorrow is December 1," he groaned. The pained

sound evidently had something to do with the way she was rubbing against him.

"Go on."

"I want to spend the entire month making you happy. And I thought we'd start by flying to Paris and picking out an obscenely large solitaire for your left hand."

Mellie reared up in shock? "Paris, France? But you have work to do...and a brand-new position. And I have two businesses to run."

He rubbed her bottom in lazy circles. "Don't say *position*. It gives me ideas."

She scooted away from him and started dragging her clothes on, despite Case's muttered protests. "I think you've had a relapse. We need to get you home. You and I are responsible members of the community. We can't fly off to Paris on a moment's notice."

"You're such a spoilsport."

"One of us has to be practical." When she was decent again, she stood up and stretched, shaking her head to make sure she wasn't dreaming.

Case put his arms around her from behind, a small red leather box in his right hand. "Well, in that case, I guess you'll have to settle for this."

She spun to face him, frowning. "What is that?"

"A ring."

She took the box but refused to open it. "How did you know I'd nix the Paris idea?"

Case shrugged, his smug patronizing smile making her want to smack him or kiss him or both. "I *know* you, Mellie Winslow. And I love every inch of your sensible, hard-working, down-to-earth self."

"You make me sound boring as hell."

"Au contraire, my sexy, beautiful housekeeper. Open the box and you'll see what I think of you."

Mellie was scared. But she opened the box anyway. "Oh, Case…"

"I love how you say that." He kissed her softly and pulled the ring out of its velvet nest. "Give me your hand."

Mellie trembled visibly as Case slid an enormous square-cut emerald onto the appropriate finger. The ring was amazing and exotic. "But this is…" She swallowed hard.

He cradled her in his arms, resting his chin on top of her head. "It's how I see you, Mellie. Stunning. Unique. Incredibly feminine. As precious and rare as the earth itself."

She wiped her nose on his sleeve. "You're a poet," she whispered. "And I never knew. I thought you were bossy and arrogant and—"

He put his hand over her mouth. "We'll work on how to give compliments later."

Without warning, he stepped back and went down on one knee. "I'm going to do this again, just to make sure. Mellie, will you be my wife and make babies with me and create new holiday memories to replace our sad ones? Will you work by my side and warm my bed at night and grow old with me?"

Her face was wet and her heart was bursting. "Yes, Case. All that and more. I love you. Now get up and take me home."

* * * * *

A delicious warmth spread throughout Jessie's body when he deepened the kiss.

"I think we'd better…stop this before I do something that's sure to…get me into big trouble," Nate said, sounding as short of breath as she felt. "Right now, I want you more than I want my next breath, and as bad as I hate to say this, it might be best for you to sleep across the hall tonight."

The warmth inside her increased and her pulse raced. "Is that what you want me to do?"

"Hell, no!" He laughed as he shook his head. "What I'd like to do is to take you upstairs right now, remove every stitch of your clothes and spend the entire night making love to every inch of your delightful body."

Her heart skipped a beat and she had to remind herself to breathe. "Then why don't you?" she asked before she could stop herself.

A deep groan rumbled up from his chest. "Jessie, I'm not in any shape right now to be a gentleman. If you don't mean what you just said, then it would be a real good idea to put some distance between us right about now."

Reaching up, she cupped his lean cheeks with her hands. "I don't want to move away from you, Nate."

* * *

Pregnant with the Rancher's Baby
is part of The Good, the Bad and the Texan series—
Running with these billionaires will be one wild ride!

PREGNANT WITH THE RANCHER'S BABY

BY
KATHIE DENOSKY

MILLS
BOON

Published in Great Britain 2015
by Mills & Boon, an imprint of Harlequin (UK) Limited,
Eton House, 18-24 Paradise Road, Richmond, Surrey, TW9 1SR

© 2015 by Kathy DeNosky

ISBN: 978-0-263-25285-9

51-1115

Harlequin (UK) Limited's policy is to use papers that are natural, renewable and recyclable products and made from wood grown in sustainable forests. The logging and manufacturing processes conform to the legal environmental regulations of the country of origin.

Printed and bound in Spain
by CPI, Barcelona

Kathie DeNosky lives in her native southern Illinois on the land her family settled in 1839. She writes highly sensual stories with a generous amount of humor. Her books have appeared on the *USA TODAY* bestseller list and received numerous awards, including two National Readers' Choice Awards. Kathie enjoys going to rodeos, traveling to research settings for her books and listening to country music. Readers may contact her by emailing kathie@kathiedenosky.com. They can also visit her website, www.kathiedenosky.com, or find her on Facebook.

This book is dedicated to my beautiful daughter,
Angela DeNosky Blumenstock.
Thank you for the research help
and for being the sweetest daughter
a mother could ever ask for.

One

Nate Rafferty couldn't help but smile as he looked around the big, open area in one of his newly constructed barns. From the minute he'd mentioned having a party to celebrate his buying and renovating the Twin Oaks Ranch, his brothers' wives had decided it needed to be a theme party. He'd been fine with that and told his sisters-in-law they were in charge of making it happen.

He'd even left the decision up to the women on what the theme would be, and they had outdone themselves, turning what was going to be his hay barn into a kid-friendly haunted house and full-on Halloween party. The monsters, scarecrows and ghosts were cute rather than scary, and his niece and nephews were going to love all the pumpkins, happy jack-o'-lanterns and garlands of colorful fall leaves that had been hung around the dance floor and bandstand.

Trying to decide if he wanted to go as the Lone Ranger or John Wayne, Nate walked out of the barn and started across the ranch yard toward the house. He'd gone only a few feet when he stopped dead in his tracks. A petite blond-haired woman was just getting out of the gray compact SUV she'd parked close to the garage.

How in the name of Sam Hill had she found him? And why?

He'd purposely avoided mentioning anything about buying the Twin Oaks Ranch to Jessica Farrell. He'd planned to wait until he finished renovating it, so he could surprise her and invite her to spend a weekend with him. Of course, the last time he'd seen her had been about four and a half months back—when she had still been speaking to him.

Not that he'd been all that worried about it. He had never had a problem charming his way back into her good graces and he had no reason to believe he couldn't do so again, even though she'd been pretty determined that their on-again, off-again relationship was permanently off.

It had been that way between them for the past couple of years and whenever it seemed like things were getting a little too serious, he always found a reason to break things off between them. But the last time she'd told him not to bother calling her again and to forget where she lived.

Of course, it wasn't the first time she'd told him to

lose her phone number. They went through something similar about every three or four months. He'd give her time to simmer down, call and sweet-talk her into seeing him again. Then, after spending several weeks of being real cozy with her, he could feel himself start to get in a little deeper than he intended. That's when he'd cut and run.

He knew it wasn't fair to Jessie. She was a wonderful woman and deserved better than the likes of him. But where she was concerned, he didn't seem to have a choice. He simply couldn't stay away from her.

But this was the first time she'd sought *him* out and he couldn't for the life of him figure out why, especially not after the way they'd ended things the last time. When they'd parted several months ago, it had been different than before. He'd told her that he thought they should take a break and stop seeing each other for a while. That's when he had seen a finality in her violet eyes that hadn't been there before. But she was here now, so it must not have been all that final.

"Jessie, it's good to see you again," he said, walking toward her. Dressed in jeans and an oversized pink sweatshirt, she somehow managed to make the baggy fleece look sexy. Real sexy. "It's been a while, darlin'. How have you been?"

When she turned to face him, she didn't look all that happy to see him. "Do you have a few minutes?" she asked, her tone serious. "I need to talk to you."

"Sure." He couldn't imagine what she wanted to talk about, but at the moment, he didn't care. He wasn't going to tell her, but the truth was, he had missed her—

missed the sound of her soft voice and her sweet smile. "Why don't we go inside and catch up?"

Her long ponytail swayed back and forth as she shook her head. "I won't be here that long."

Placing his arm around her slender shoulders, he turned her toward the house. "You didn't drive all the way from Waco just to turn around and go back," he said as he ushered her across the patio to the French doors. "I'll tell my housekeeper you'll be staying for supper."

When they entered the family room, she surprised him when she ducked from beneath his arm and turned to face him. "Don't bother, Nate. I worked the late shift last night and as soon as we talk, I need to get back home and get some sleep." She was a registered professional nurse he'd met when she had taken care of his brother a couple of years ago after Sam had been injured in a rodeo accident.

"You can always sleep here," he said, grinning.

If looks could kill, he would have been a dead man in two seconds flat. "You have a housekeeper?" she asked. When he nodded, she frowned as she looked around. "Is there somewhere a little more private where we can talk?"

Nate stared at her. He'd never seen her as determined as she appeared to be at that moment. "Let's go into my office," he finally said, motioning toward the arched doorway leading out into the foyer. "We can talk privately in there."

Guiding her along, he waited until they were seated in his office with the door closed. "What was it you needed to talk to me about?" he asked, looking across the desk at her sitting in the leather armchair in front of him.

She nibbled on her lower lip as she stared down at her tightly clasped hands resting in her lap. "I want you to know that it's taken me over four months to come to the decision to tell you." When she looked directly at him, her pretty violet eyes were filled with resignation. "My first inclination was not to bother. But I didn't think that would be fair to you."

Nate sat up straight in his desk chair as his scalp started to tingle. He wasn't sure what she was talking about, but his gut was telling him that whatever she had to say would be life changing. Had she met someone else? Was she telling him that she had committed herself to another man and it wasn't fair not to tell him? Or was she talking about something else?

"Why don't you stop beating around the bush and just tell me what you think I need to hear?" he asked.

She took a deep breath and met his questioning gaze head on. "I'm almost five months pregnant."

"You're pregnant," he repeated. His gaze flew to her stomach as her words began to sink in and it felt like the air had suddenly been sucked out of the room. His heart raced and his knees threatened to buckle as he stood up and came around the desk to stand in front of her. "You're going to have a baby?"

"That's what pregnant means."

"How did that happen?" he asked before he could stop himself.

The look she gave him stated louder than words that

she had some serious doubts about the level of his intelligence. "If you don't know about the birds and bees by now, Nate, you never will."

Taking a deep breath, he shook his head in an effort to clear the ringing in his ears. "You know what I mean." He rubbed the sudden tension building at the base of his neck. "We were always careful about protection."

"There could have been a microscopic tear in one of the condoms or some other kind of defect." She shrugged one slender shoulder. "Whatever happened, I'm pregnant and you're the daddy. But I don't want anything from you," she added hurriedly. "I make more than enough to support myself and the baby, and I'm perfectly capable of raising a child on my own. I just thought it was only fair to let you know about the baby and find out if you want to be part of his or her life. If not, I want you to sign all of your rights over to me and we'll both be out of your life for good."

"Like hell," he said emphatically. "If I have a kid, I'm going to be involved in every aspect of its life."

She gave him a short nod, then stood up. "That's all I wanted to know. I'll have my attorney get in touch with yours. They can work out a fair custody agreement and a suitable visitation schedule."

"Where are you going?" he asked, reaching out to place his hands on her shoulders to stop her. "You can't just waltz in here, tell me that you're having my baby and then leave."

"Yes, I can," she said. There was a defiance in her voice that warned him not to argue with her. "If I didn't have a conscience, I wouldn't even be here. But I happen to believe that a man has a right to know when he's fathered a child, even if he's not dependable. For now, that's really all you need to know."

A strong sense of guilt settled across his shoulders. Given their past and the way he'd treated her and their relationship, he should probably be grateful that she had bothered telling him at all. But he couldn't let her leave without discussing things further. There were things he wanted—needed—to know.

"Jessie, I'm sorry for the way things have been between us in the past," he said, meaning it. "I take full responsibility for that and if I could go back and change it, I would. Unfortunately, I can't do that. But from here on out it's important that we work together."

She backed away from him. "I told you I won't keep you from seeing the baby. The lawyers will—"

"Yeah, I got that," he interrupted. He took a deep breath. "Look, I realize that I'm not exactly your favorite person right now and I can't say I blame you. But there are things I want to discuss with you and a whole hell of a lot more that we need to decide."

She stared at him for a moment before she spoke again. "I'm sure this came as a shock. Believe me, I wasn't expecting it either. But it doesn't have to be complicated. We can let the lawyers take care of sorting all of this out."

"Darlin', I don't see how this can be anything but complicated," he said, noticing for the first time how tired she looked. A sudden idea began to take shape as he stared into her pretty violet eyes. "You're exhausted. Why don't we table this for the time being?"

"Don't worry about me," she said, shrugging. "I'll be fine as soon as I go home and get some sleep."

"I don't like the idea of you driving all the way back to Waco as tired as you are," he said. "It isn't safe."

"I'll be okay." She frowned. "Besides, my welfare isn't any of your concern."

"Yes, it is," he insisted. "Do you have to work tonight?"

She shook her head. "I have the weekend off. Why?"

"My family is having a Halloween party here tomorrow night and I'd really like for you to join us. I've got five guest bedrooms upstairs and you can have your pick of any of them." He used his index finger to brush a strand of blond hair that had escaped her ponytail from her smooth cheek as an excuse to touch her. His finger tingled from the contact and he was heartened by the slight widening of her pretty eyes, indicating that she felt it, too. "It will also give us time to talk and make a few decisions after you've had time to rest."

He'd wisely avoided mentioning that she could share the master suite with him. He might not be the brightest bulb in the chandelier, but he wasn't fool enough to think she would be receptive to picking up their relationship where they left it almost five months ago.

She tried to hide a yawn behind her small, delicate hand. "I told you the law—"

"I know. But don't you think it would save a lot of time and be easier for all concerned if we had everything worked out in advance?" he asked.

"Nate, I'm really too tired to discuss this right now," she said, yawning. "All I want is to get home and go to bed."

"At least take a nap before you start back to Waco," he stalled. If he could get her to stay for a while, it would give him time to come to grips with the unbelievable fact that he was going to be a daddy. At the moment he was completely numb. But he needed to pull it together so he could think. He had to come up with a better argument for her staying, at least for the party. Now that he knew she was carrying his baby, it was even more important that they work things out. And damned quick.

"Maybe just a short power nap would help," she conceded.

Without hesitation, he put his arm around her shoulders to guide her out into the foyer and up the stairs. He wasn't going to give her time to change her mind.

When he walked her down the upstairs hall, Nate opened the door to the bedroom across from his. "Will this room be all right?"

"I'm leaving as soon as I wake up," she warned.

"Just get some sleep now," he said, leading her over to the bed. Pulling back the colorful quilt, he waited until she kicked off her tennis shoes and got into bed before he bent down to kiss her forehead. "If you need anything, I'll be in my office."

She had already fallen asleep.

Standing beside the bed, he stared down at the only woman he hadn't been able to stay away from. Jessie was smart, funny and as sweet as she was pretty. So why hadn't he been able to commit to her?

Nate knew his foster brother Lane Donaldson would probably have a field day using his master's degree in psychology to analyze Nate's motives. But Nate didn't want to delve too deeply into his reasons for avoiding commitments. It all tied into his past and it wasn't something he could change, nor was he eager to think about that dark time in his life.

The only thing he could do now was what his foster father Hank Calvert would expect of any of the boys he finished raising. Hank had preached to them over and over that when a man makes the decision to sleep with a woman, he'd better be ready to accept his responsibilities if he made her pregnant. And that was just what Nate intended to do.

His aversion to commitment was about to undergo a dramatic change. Jessie had shown up to tell him he was going to be a daddy and he fully intended to do right by her and his kid. Sometime within the next week, he was going to kiss his blissful bachelorhood goodbye and make her his wife.

When Jessie woke up, bright sunlight peeked through a part in the yellow calico curtains and it took a moment for her to realize where she was.

After working all night in the traumatic brain injury ICU, she had called Nate's brother Sam to ask where she could find Nate. She hated having to involve Sam in her quest to get hold of Nate, but Nate had moved recently. The last time he had broken things off between them, she had deleted his number from her cell. Sam had been very nice and given her directions to the Twin Oaks Ranch. She supposed she could have asked for Nate's number and called, but news like hers was something that needed to be delivered in person.

After going to her prenatal checkup, she had driven directly to the ranch to tell Nate he was the father of her baby. In hindsight, she probably should have gotten some sleep before she confronted him with the news. But if she had put it off any longer, she couldn't be certain she wouldn't have talked herself out of telling him at all.

For the past few months, she'd been torn over what to do and she still wasn't certain she had made the right choice in telling him about the baby. For one thing, she was beyond tired of being Nate's puppet. In the past, he would give her a call and talk her into rekindling their relationship, then when everything seemed to be going great between them, he'd find a reason they should stop seeing each other for a while. And for another, she wasn't sure he deserved to have equal custody of the baby. How good of a father would he be, given his inclination for coming and going the way he'd done in the past?

The last time he decided to pull his vanishing act, she'd told him not to bother getting in touch with her again. It had broken her heart, but she refused to allow him to control the course of their relationship any longer. Shortly after that she had discovered she was pregnant. And even though she felt it was only right to let a man know he had fathered a child, her main concern was whether or not Nate would always be there for the baby. It was one thing to disappoint her. It was something else entirely if he disappointed their child.

Unsettled by the thought, she threw back the covers to sit up on the side of the bed. That's when she realized just how exhausted she'd been. She had not only slept the rest of yesterday and last night, she was still fully dressed.

Jessie quickly made the bed and headed downstairs. She had the next two nights off and she needed to get home. There were several things she needed to get done this weekend and she still had an hour's drive just to get back to Waco.

As she reached the bottom of the stairs, she sighed heavily when Nate came out of the office. So much for avoiding him on her way out.

"Good morning, sleepyhead," he said cheerfully.

Why did the man have to look so darned good to her? She didn't want to notice how his straight light brown hair stylishly brushed the collar of his chambray shirt or the way his blue eyes twinkled when he smiled at her. She was still angry with him and resented the way he thought he could come and go in her life without a second thought to the effect it had on her—how much it hurt her emotionally.

"You should have awakened me," she said, noticing the grandfather clock in the foyer indicated it was already midmorning.

"You were tired." His smile turned to a grin. "Besides, I thought you'd probably want to be fully rested for the party tonight."

"I'm not attending your party," she said, stepping down onto the cream-colored marble tile floor of the foyer. "I told you that yesterday."

He shook his head as he walked over to her. "No, you didn't."

"It was implied and you know it," she stated. "When you insisted that I had to get some sleep before I drove home, I told you I intended to leave as soon as I woke up from a nap. That was a strong indication that I had no intention of attending your family gathering."

He reached out to lightly run his finger along her jaw, causing her skin to tingle where he touched her. "Now that you've had some rest, would you like a cup of coffee or something to eat?" he asked, ignoring her argument against staying for his party. "I don't know all that much about pregnancy, but when they were expecting, all of my sisters-in-law ate like ranch hands once they got past being sick."

"I cut out caffeine when I discovered I was pregnant, but a muffin or bagel and a glass of milk would be appreciated," she answered, knowing just what the women had gone through.

In the early weeks of her pregnancy, just the thought of food was enough to make her sick. But now that the morning sickness had cleared up, it seemed she was hungry all of the time.

"Why don't you have a seat in my office and I'll go tell my housekeeper to fix a tray for you," he said, placing his hand to her back to guide her toward the doorway.

"Why don't I eat in the kitchen and then just go out

the back door to my car when I'm done?" she countered, starting to turn in the opposite direction of the office.

"We have to talk," he insisted, bringing his arm up to wrap around her shoulders and steer her back toward his office.

"Nate, it would be better to let the lawyers—"

"Do you really want strangers calling the shots on how we go about raising our kid?" he interrupted.

Jessie stared at him as she tried to decide what to do. He had a point about attorneys sitting across a conference table making the important decisions about their child. It really did seem impersonal and detached from the situation. But she had wanted to avoid spending any more time with him than she had to. For the past two and a half years Nate Rafferty had been her biggest weakness and she needed to stay strong in order to resist his charming appeal.

"I only have two nights off and I have things I want to accomplish," she hedged. She had intended to start cleaning out the second bedroom in her apartment to turn it into a nursery.

"This is the future of our baby, Jessie." The earnest expression on his handsome face made her feel guilty and she found herself nodding in agreement in spite of her need to put distance between them.

Fifteen minutes later, Jessie stared at the small bowl of fresh fruit, a honey-wheat bagel with cream cheese, scrambled eggs, crispy bacon, a glass of orange juice and a tall glass of milk sitting on a tray on the edge of Nate's desk. "Whose army were you intending to feed?" she asked. "I can't eat all of this."

"Rosemary said you needed the protein and fruit as well as the calcium in the milk and vitamin C from the orange juice," he said, shrugging as he lowered himself into the armchair beside her. "She said it would be good for both you and the baby."

Jessie's eyes widened. "You told your housekeeper I'm pregnant?"

He nodded. "She has six kids and fifteen grandkids. They're all healthy and I figured if anyone would know what your nutritional needs are now that you're pregnant, she would."

While she appreciated his thoughtfulness, Jessie wasn't entirely certain she was comfortable with him telling others about the baby until they had worked out an agreement they could both live with. But she wasn't going to argue with him about it now. They had bigger issues to settle.

"You said you wanted to work out custody and visitation?" she asked, picking up the fork on the tray to take a bite of the fluffy scrambled eggs.

He shook his head, then took a deep breath as if what he was about to say was extremely difficult for him. "None of that will be necessary once we're married."

She stopped with the fork halfway to her mouth. "Excuse me?"

"We'll do the right thing and get married," he repeated as if it was the answer to all of their problems.

Her appetite deserting her, Jessie slowly placed the

fork full of eggs back on the plate and shook her head. "No, we won't."

"Sure we will," he said, reaching to take her hand in his. "I've already qualified for the National Finals. I'll skip the rodeo this coming weekend and we can have the wedding here. Or if you prefer, we can fly to Vegas and have a reception for family and friends at a later date."

Jerking her hand from his, she stood up to pace the length of the room. "Have you lost your ever-loving mind? I'm not going to marry you."

He rose to his feet and, walking over to her, placed his hands on her shoulders to stare down at her from his much taller height. "I didn't mean to upset you, darlin'. I'm pretty sure it's not good for you or the baby."

"How would you know?" she demanded, glaring up into his incredible blue eyes. "How many times have you been pregnant?"

He gave her a sheepish grin. "This is a first for both of us."

"Never mind. It doesn't matter. You wouldn't get the point, even if I explained it to you." She shook her head. "I didn't come here to tell you that I'm having a baby because I wanted you to marry me. I simply thought you should know that you'd fathered a child. Period. If you want to be part of the baby's life, I won't try to stop you. But I'm not part of the deal, Nate. We can work something out so that we're both involved with raising this baby, but that doesn't mean we'll be involved with each other."

He took a deep breath. "I realize that's what we could do, Jessie. But making you my wife is what I want."

"No, it's not, Nate." She had hoped to hear him say those words for over two years, but she knew better than to believe he really wanted to get married. He'd broken up with her too many times for her to believe any such thing. "You might think that now. But we both know you'll lose interest within a few weeks and then you'd not only resent me and the baby for trapping you into doing something you didn't want to do, we'd be facing the heartbreak of a divorce."

"That's not going to happen, Jessie. When I make that commitment, it's for life." He ran his hand through his thick, straight hair. "I know I've let you down before, but—"

"Stop right there," she said, holding up her hand. "That's something else we need to get straight right here and now. I'm a big girl and I have no one else to blame but myself for allowing you to come and go in my life the way you've done. But the stakes are higher now, Nate. Disappointing me is one thing, but I refuse to allow you to upset our son or daughter. This is our child—my child—we're discussing and I swear I'll fight you with everything that's in me if you don't grow up and be there when he or she needs you. Being a parent isn't a game or something you run from whenever you get tired of playing the devoted daddy. It means you're there twenty-four/seven, no matter how tough it gets. If you can't handle that, then I'd rather you don't even bother."

"Jessie, I give you my word that from now on, you

and the baby are my top priority," he said, sounding sincere. He slid his hands from her shoulders down her arms to catch her hands in his. "I want us to get married and be a family. And I swear I will never cause you another minute of heartache."

"Then why did you make it sound as if you were going to be accepting responsibility for a crime instead of asking me to marry you?" she asked bluntly. "Did you even listen to yourself?"

"What do you mean?" he asked, looking bewildered.

"No woman wants to enter into a marriage with a man knowing that she was 'the right thing' for him to do," she said, shaking her head. "Besides, you had to take a deep breath before you could even get out that you want to make me your wife."

He stared at her for several long seconds before he finally spoke again. "Just give us a chance—give *me* a chance—darlin'. This is all new to me."

"Nate, I've already given you more chances than you deserve," she said, refusing to believe that this time would be any different than the others. He was only offering marriage because of the baby, not because he loved her and wanted them to build a life together.

"Do you have some vacation time you can take?" he asked suddenly.

"Yes, but I'm saving it for after the baby is born so that I can extend my maternity leave," she explained, wondering why he wanted to know.

"When is your next doctor's appointment?" he continued to question her.

"I have an ultrasound scheduled in two weeks," she answered. "Why are you asking about all of this?"

"I'd like for you to be here for the party tonight, then stay with me for the next couple of weeks," he said. He paused for a moment as if catching his breath. "Let me prove to you that getting married *is* what I want."

"I don't see how that's going to work," she pointed out. "You normally take a few more weeks than that to lose interest. Besides, you had to take a deep breath before you could tell me you wanted to prove how much you want us to get married. That doesn't instill a lot of confidence for the case you're trying to make. And all I'm hearing is what you want. Have you even considered what I want?"

He gave her a short nod before he asked, "What do you want, Jessie?"

"I want you to be a good father and love our child," she said slowly. "That's more important to me than anything else."

"I already love the baby and I give you my word that I'll be the best daddy I can possibly be."

She noticed that he failed to include her with his declaration. If she hadn't known before that the only reason he was offering marriage was because of the baby, she certainly did now.

"That's all I want from you," she said, when he continued to look at her expectantly.

"All I'm asking is to let me prove to you that being a good dad isn't the only thing I want. Stay with me until after Thanksgiving," he countered.

"Nate, I don't see how my staying here for a month

or even two weeks will prove anything," she said, shaking her head. He didn't love her and that was that. There was no sense wasting her vacation time on something that, in the end, wouldn't change that fact.

"What do you have to lose?" he asked.

"The vacation I intended to take after the baby is born," she answered. *As well as what's left of my heart after you broke it the last time.*

"If I can't convince you that I'm completely sincere about our being a family, then we'll call the lawyers and let them work out an agreement," he said, oblivious to her inner turmoil.

"I can't go to the party," she stalled. "I don't have anything to wear."

If she went along with his request and stayed for any length of time, she was afraid she would be tempted to fall back into their old pattern of him charming her into his bed. That was the last thing she wanted to happen. There was simply too much at stake now. The baby was counting on her to stay strong and resist the temptation Nate posed.

"I've already taken care of something for you to wear to the party," he said, looking quite pleased with himself. "I called Sam's wife, Bria. She and her sister, Mariah, were going to pick up their outfits at the costume shop up in Fort Worth. I asked her to pick out something for you and stop by one of the women's shops to get you a full change of clothes for tomorrow."

"Please tell me you didn't let her know about my pregnancy," she said, reaching up to rub at the sudden pounding in her temples.

"No, I thought we could tell everyone together to-night at the party," he said. "I just told Bria that you're about the size of our other sister-in-law Summer and that you liked your clothes nice and loose." He glanced down at her stomach. "I figured you might need a little extra room for the baby."

"I haven't said I would go to the party," she reminded him.

"You haven't said you wouldn't." His sexy grin told her he knew he was wearing her down.

She supposed that if she did stay, it would be as good a time as any to tell his family about the baby. And if she was present she would have a little more control over *what* he told them. As persistent as he was about convincing her to marry him, he'd probably tell his family that they were planning a trip down the aisle as well as about her pregnancy.

Being there to stop him from misleading his family would be the wisest choice. She wasn't going to marry him and set herself and the baby up for the heartbreak of watching him leave when he got bored.

"If I stay for the party, that doesn't mean I would be here for an extended period of time," she reminded him.

He stared at her for several long seconds before he cupped her face with his hands. "Jessie, you've experienced all of this from the moment you learned you were pregnant. But I've missed out on a lot these last four and a half months and I really don't want to miss any more. I promise that if you'll stay with me for the next month, I won't push for anything more than you're willing to give. This time will not only give us the opportunity to explore every option and be sure we're making the right decisions, it will give me the chance to feel like I'm really a part of this and get used to the idea of being a dad."

The sincerity in his voice and the heartfelt look on his face produced the results she was certain he had been going for. Now if she didn't stay, she'd feel so guilty about it she'd probably never be able to sleep again.

She'd had almost five months to get used to the idea of becoming a mother. Nate had had less than twenty-four hours to come to terms with being a father and she was sure it was still pretty unreal for him. And he did have a point about making decisions concerning how they raised their child. Their baby deserved to have its parents making the choices instead of stuffy lawyers spouting out legalese. She was going to have to figure out how to deal with Nate for the next eighteen or so years anyway. She might as well start now.

"I would have to go back home to get some clothes," she warned. Between now and the trip back to her apartment, she would hopefully be able to harden her resolve and shore up her defenses against his charismatic charm. In the past, she'd had about as much backbone as a jellyfish when it came to resisting Nate, and spending a month with him would be a true test of her willpower. But she could understand his wanting to take an active role in the pregnancy. It would be a good start to his bonding with the baby and that was something she wanted for her child.

"We can go to your place tomorrow and get whatever you need." His expression turned serious. "I really want this opportunity for us, Jessie. Please say you'll stay."

She might have had a chance if he had been demanding or insistent. But the sincere tone of his voice and the hopeful look in his eyes were impossible to resist. Maybe she needed this test to prove to herself that they could raise their child together without her falling into bed with him again.

"All right, I'll arrange to take the time off and stay until the weekend after Thanksgiving," she heard herself say. "But only on one condition."

"What's that, darlin'?" he asked, lowering his head to brush her lips with his.

"I don't want any pressure from you about getting married," she stated flatly as she backed away from him.

"I promise."

"I'm only here for you to prove to me that you're sincere about wanting this baby as much as I do and to work out custody and visitation." As an afterthought, she added, "And just for the record, at night I'll be staying in one room and you'll be staying in another."

Two

Standing with his brothers at the makeshift bar his hired men had constructed for the party, Nate was only half listening to the conversation about his brother's rodeo stock company and the bucking bulls he owned that had been selected for the National Finals Rodeo. He was too busy watching Jessie. She was as cute as a button in the girl garden-gnome costume that Bria had picked up for her to wear to the party. She'd had to leave the vest off because it was too formfitting, but the white apron over her full red skirt hid her rounded stomach just fine.

Seated on a bale of hay, Jessie was listening attentively to his two nephews Seth and little Hank jabber about their new ponies. He could tell by the way she smiled at the little boys going on about riding their "horsies" that she loved kids. When his niece Katie toddled over to her, Jessie picked up the baby girl to sit on her lap without a moment's hesitation. She was going to be a great mom, and he could only hope to be half as good of a dad.

His heart stuttered and he had to take a deep breath to chase away the fear tightening his chest. Just the thought of being a daddy scared the living spit out of him. What if he couldn't live up to the responsibility? He was a fantastic uncle to his niece and nephews. But that role didn't carry nearly as much responsibility as being a father. What kind of dad would he be?

His biggest fear had always been that he would turn out to be as negligent and undependable as his and Sam's father had been. That's why he'd never really thought about having kids. Hell, he hadn't even thought about having a wife because of it. But it was all he'd been able to think about for the past twenty-four hours. Could he live up to his responsibilities?

Of the six men he called his brothers, Sam was his only biological sibling and had turned out to be as solid as a rock. He was the exact opposite of their old man, and it gave Nate hope that he would be just as reliable as Sam. But how would he know for sure?

"So what's up with you, Nate?" T. J. Malloy asked, interrupting Nate's disturbing thoughts.

"Yeah, this is the first time you've asked the little blond to join one of our family get-togethers," Ryder McClain added, grinning from ear to ear.

"Maybe now that he owns the Twin Oaks Ranch, Nate is finally ready to settle down," Lane Donaldson speculated as he cradled his infant son in the crook of his arm.

"I've got a hundred bucks that says he and Jessie are married by spring," Sam said, glancing from Nate to Jessie and back. "Yesterday when she called to ask me where she could find you, she sounded pretty determined."

"Jessie called you and you didn't tell me?" Nate demanded, glaring at his older brother.

Sam shrugged. "She asked me not to and I told her I wouldn't. And you know as well as the rest of us about Hank's number-one rule."

"Yeah," Nate said, his irritation fading at the mention of their foster father and the personal code of ethics he had taught the boys in his care. "Break a bone if you have to before you break your word."

His brothers all nodded in agreement.

Jaron Lambert pulled his wallet from the hip pocket of his jeans, got out a hundred-dollar bill and plunked it down on the top of the bar. "I say Nate and Jessie will be hitched by the middle of this coming summer."

"I've got Christmas," T.J. said, adding his money to the pool.

"I'll take Valentine's Day," Lane spoke up, putting his hundred with the rest.

Ryder pulled his wallet from the hip pocket of his jeans, then looked him up and down before he slapped Nate on the shoulder. "I'm betting they'll be married by Thanksgiving."

Nate shook his head as he listened to his brothers bet on when he and Jessie took a trip down the aisle. It had always been this way with the brothers. From the time they were all placed into the care of their foster father, Hank Calvert on the Last Chance Ranch, the six of them had a betting pool going on just about everything. Of course back then they had all been dirt poor and had nothing better to do than speculate on the next time it rained or which one of them would be the first to win a buckle at one of the junior rodeos they all competed in.

Now that they were all self-made millionaires, instead of betting fifty cents or a dollar, the stakes were a lot higher. These days it was nothing for them to bet a hundred dollars or more on who would be the next one to tie the knot or add to the family with the birth of a baby. But up until yesterday, he hadn't even considered the possibility that he would be the next one they speculated on or that they would all be right in doing so.

Every time one of them mentioned him getting hitched he felt a twitch at the corner of his left eye. He still couldn't believe that he was finally willing to take the plunge and get married. It scared the living hell out of him that he might let Jessie and their baby down. But he had a responsibility to both of them and he was going to do everything in his power to live up to what a good husband and father should be.

Focusing on the pile of money on the bar to keep himself from dwelling on all of the what-ifs, Nate shook his head. "While you all waste your time and money, I'm going to ask Jessie to dance." The kids had abandoned her in favor of playing with a cardboard box someone had left over by the refreshment table, and he decided now might be a good time to find out when she wanted to tell his family about the baby.

He threw his empty beer bottle in the recycling bin at the end of the bar and walked away. He was in enough trouble with her. He didn't want to add more by telling the guys about her pregnancy before she was ready. And if he stuck around much longer, there was a real possibility of him accidently tipping them off that something was up. If that happened, they would needle him until hell froze over trying to get him to tell them what was going on.

Hiding things from the people who knew you best wasn't all that easy. That was the only downside he could see about being so close and knowing each other so well. But he wouldn't have it any other way. He knew he could count on his brothers being there for him no matter what, just as he would be there for them.

"Are you having a good time, darlin'?" he asked, walking up to where Jessie still sat on the bale of straw.

With her attention on the kids, she smiled. "I'm having a wonderful time. But I'm apparently not nearly as interesting as a cardboard box."

Nate took her hands in his to pull her to her feet. "Just wait until you see the kids at Christmas. They get all kinds of excited and can't wait for us to remove the toys from the boxes. Then they toss the toy aside and sit down to play with the box."

Her light laughter made his insides vibrate with a tension he knew all too well. He wanted her. Hell, even during the times when he'd broken things off with her and gone his own way, he'd still wanted her. Maybe that was the reason he hadn't been able to stay away from her. He had a feeling the reasons went much deeper, but he wasn't going to think about that now. He wanted to hold her in his arms without having her remind him that she wasn't there to rekindle their romance.

"Would you like to dance, darlin'?" She loved kicking up her heels on the dance floor and he wanted her to enjoy herself. If she had a good time, it might remind her of what they had shared in the past.

"I think I would, sheriff," she said, referring to the tin badge he had pinned to his shirt.

He nodded to the frontman in the band he'd hired and, right on cue, they ended the song they had been playing and immediately launched into a popular slow country song. When the group had first arrived, he'd told the man the title of the song he wanted them to play and to be watching for his signal. It was the song he and Jessie had danced to the first time he'd taken her out for a night on the town.

"You had that planned," she accused.

Grinning, he took her into his arms and swept her out onto the dance floor. "Yup." He leaned close to whisper in her ear. "You didn't tell me I wasn't allowed to remind you of the first date we went on or how good we are together." He wisely refrained from mentioning that was true for other things besides dancing.

He felt her tremble against him a moment before she put a little space between them. "Nate, the first thing we're going to do after this party is to set down some ground rules. Otherwise, I'll be going home tomorrow and I won't be back."

"Sure thing, darlin'," he said agreeably as they swayed in time with the music.

She could lay down all the rules she wanted, but that little shiver was all the indication he needed to know that she wasn't impervious to him. And he had every intention of reminding her of that fact every chance he got.

He waited until the song ended before he asked, "When do you want to make the announcement about the baby?"

She sighed. "I suppose now is as good of a time as any. But don't you dare mislead your family into believing that we're getting married because we're not."

"I give you my word," he said, nodding. He wasn't about to do anything that would send her running back to Waco before the end of the month they had agreed on. And that was exactly what would happen if he so much as hinted to his family that marriage was a possibility. Besides, he had until just after Thanksgiving to figure out how he was going to accomplish that goal. He was determined not to fail. He wanted her to agree to be his wife and for them to be married before the baby was born.

Putting his arm around her shoulders to guide her, they walked over to Bria and her sister, Mariah, chatting with some of their friends by the refreshment table. "Bria, could you get the family together and meet Jessie and I outside for a few minutes? We have something we'd like to tell everyone."

"Of course, Nate." Smiling, his sister-in-law turned

to Mariah. "Go tell the men to meet us outside while I find Summer, Taylor and Heather."

Within a few minutes Nate and Jessie stood just outside of the big barn doors, surrounded by his family. He knew his sisters-in-law would be excited by their news and would start making plans for baby showers and whatever else women did to welcome a new baby into the family. But his brothers were going to give him hell when they learned that marriage wasn't a sure thing.

Their foster father had raised them with a clear sense of what was right and wrong. From the time they had been old enough to start dating, Hank Calvert had told them it was their responsibility to protect a woman. And in the case of an accidental pregnancy, a man had a moral obligation to do what was right and give the woman and child his name.

Nate knew that in this day and time, that way of thinking might be considered antiquated, but there was no man he respected more than his late foster father. Hank's teachings had served him and his brothers well over the years and turned them from rebellious young hell-raisers into honest, upstanding adults. As far as he was concerned, that kind of guidance shouldn't be ignored. Besides, the thought of having Jessie at his side every day and in his bed every night was a very appealing aspect of marriage, even if it did scare the hell out of him.

"So what's up, bro?" Jaron asked with one of his rare smiles. The quiet, brooding one of his brothers, Jaron was the only one that Nate knew for certain hadn't completely rid himself of the ghosts of his past. They all had had a few residual hang-ups from their lives before being sent to the Last Chance Ranch. But Jaron's ran deeper than the rest of them.

"Yeah, spill the beans, hotshot," T.J. chimed in.

Nate glanced at Jessie as he reached for her hand. "We just wanted to let you know that we'll be adding another member to the family in a few months. We're going to have a baby."

There was a stunned silence that followed his announcement and one look at the expression on Sam's face let Nate know his failure to mention a wedding had not gone unnoticed. With a slight shake of his head, he let his brothers know not to ask about it until later. He knew they would respect his wishes and remain silent—for now. But as soon as the opportunity presented itself, he was going to have some explaining to do.

"That's wonderful," Bria said, breaking the silence as she stepped forward to hug him and Jessie. God bless her, Bria could read a situation faster than anyone he knew and always seemed to know exactly what to say to ease the tension.

"I'm so excited for you," Summer McClain added happily, shifting her daughter to her hip in order to reach out and hug Jessie.

"We've got another baby shower to plan," Lane's wife, Taylor, spoke up enthusiastically. "I've got some new appetizers in mind that will be perfect for the refreshments." A personal chef, Taylor was always looking for reasons to try new recipes on the family.

"When is the baby due?" T.J.'s wife, Heather, asked.

"In late March or early April," Jessie answered. Nate

could tell by the tone in her voice she was relieved that no one had asked about a wedding.

"Do you know if you're having a boy or a girl?" Mariah asked, giving Jaron a pointed look. Every time one of the sisters-in-law became pregnant, Mariah and Jaron argued about what gender they thought the baby would be. It appeared this time was going to be no different.

Jessie smiled as she shook her head. "I'm having an ultrasound in a couple of weeks to find out."

"Congratulations," Sam finally said, stepping forward to give Jessie a brotherly hug. He stared hard at Nate. "I think this calls for a beer, don't you?"

"Great news," Ryder said, wrapping Jessie in a bear hug. When he put his hand on Nate's shoulder, Nate could tell by Ryder's iron grip that he was about to be escorted to the bar for his brothers' interrogation.

"Jessie, if you don't mind, we'd like to take this bonehead back to the bar to toast your good news," Lane explained, handing his baby son over to his wife, Taylor.

"I don't mind," she said, smiling. "It will give me a chance to ask your wives what I can expect with a newborn and what baby products they've found to be the most useful."

As his brothers walked him back into the barn, Nate heard the excited voices of the women as they offered their suggestions on what they thought Jessie might need to get ready for the baby. He wasn't the least bit surprised. Whether she realized it or not, she and the baby were already considered members of his family and everyone would do whatever they could to help her and make her feel welcome.

"Okay, what's the story, bro?" Sam demanded when they reached the bar.

"And why didn't we hear that the two of you are making plans to get hitched?" T.J. asked as he motioned for the bartender to get them all a bottle of beer.

"You all know about as much as I do," Nate admitted as they walked over to a more private area away from a group of their friends. "Jessie showed up yesterday to tell me she's about four and a half months pregnant, I'm the daddy and when I told her we'd get married as soon as possible, she flat-out refused."

"You *told* her you'd marry her instead of asking her to be your wife?" Lane asked, his expression incredulous.

"Way to sweet-talk a woman, bro," Jaron said, shaking his head. "Even I know better than to do that."

"For a ladies' man, you sure screwed that up," Ryder stated disgustedly.

"And you tried to give me advice on how to talk to a woman when Heather and I first started seeing each other." T.J. took a swig of beer from the bottle in his hand. "I'm glad I had the good sense not to listen to you."

Sam folded his arms across his chest and glared at him. "How do you intend to straighten this out with her, Nate?"

"I've already come up with a plan," he answered, watching the women and kids reenter the barn. They all looked as if they were having a lot better time than he was at the moment.

"You want to run this scheme of yours past us and get our input before you try to execute it?" Lane asked.

"Yeah, the way you messed up that proposal, it sounds to me like you need all the help you can get," Jaron added.

As much as he had riding on the outcome, Nate figured he could use some advice from his brothers and especially from Lane. Having the opinion of a licensed psychologist definitely couldn't hurt and might just give him the edge he needed to convince Jessie of his sincerity.

"I got her to agree to stay with me until after Thanksgiving so we can work out joint custody and how we're going to raise the baby," Nate answered. He stared across the dance floor at Jessie and the rest of the women. "And while I'm at it, I'm going to pull out all the stops and show her that I really do want to get married."

"The way things have gone down with you two in the past, you've got your work cut out for you." T.J. stated what Nate was certain all of his brothers were thinking.

"It for damned sure isn't going to be easy," Ryder added.

"And there's no margin for error," Lane warned. "If you don't get it right this time, they'll be passing out ice water in hell before you get a second chance."

Nate nodded. No matter how scary it was to commit himself to one woman, especially knowing that he'd have to reveal everything about his past, he had too much to lose not to do everything in his power to make things right between them. "I'm going to get Jessie to agree to marry me or die trying."

As Jessie listened to Nate's sisters-in-law discuss possible themes for the baby shower they were planning for her and the refreshments they might serve, she couldn't help but feel envious of the strong family bond the women and their husbands shared. Over the past couple of years, Nate had told her a little about his blended family, and how he and Sam met the other four men they called brothers when they were placed in the foster care system.

Sent to the Last Chance Ranch as teenagers, the six boys had found their salvation as well as each other, thanks to a kindhearted man named Hank Calvert and his unique set of rules to live by. The boys he fostered had stayed tight throughout the ensuing years and from what she could see, the women they married had become just as close.

"When you find out the baby's gender do you intend to tell everyone or let it be a surprise?" Heather asked.

"I thought I'd let everyone know the gender, but keep the name secret until the baby is born," Jessie said, resting her hand on her stomach. "I know it sounds strange, but I'd like to introduce him or her to everyone by name."

"If you don't mind, could you let us know what you're having as soon as you have the ultrasound, Jessie?"

Summer asked, smiling. "That way we'll know what colors to use for decorations."

"And if you've chosen the colors for the nursery, that might be useful as well," Heather added as her little boy, Seth, ran up to hand her a bouquet of dried weeds he'd obviously picked out of a hay bale. After she thanked him and gave him a kiss, he rejoined the other two toddlers. "T.J. gave me a bouquet of flowers the other day and Seth tries to mimic everything his daddy does."

"That's so sweet." Jessie found the little boy's gesture very touching and she knew for certain she would be just as happy having a boy as she would having a girl.

"It would also be helpful if you register at one of the baby boutiques in Waco as soon as you can so we can put that on the invitations," Bria suggested, bringing the conversation back to the shower they were planning.

"They're using some of the most unusual combinations of colors these days," Taylor commented as she shifted her baby son to her shoulder for a burp after he finished the bottle she had been giving him. "I hadn't even considered the colors I used until I saw them in one of the baby boutiques."

"I hope you get to decorate with a lot of pink and purple for a little princess," Mariah stated as she got up from the bale of straw she was sitting on to walk over to the three toddlers playing with the box again.

"That's only because she wants another excuse to argue with Jaron," Taylor confided. She got up and picked up a diaper bag. "Time to get this little man changed and settled down for the night."

As Taylor walked out of the barn toward the house to get her son ready for bed, Bria explained the ongoing disagreement between Mariah and Jaron. "Whenever one of us announces that a new baby will be joining the family, Mariah insists it will be a girl and Jaron is just as determined it will be a boy." Shaking her head, she sighed. "It's their way of dancing around the real issue between them."

Jessie nodded. "Nate mentioned that Jaron and your sister have been attracted to each other for years, but he thinks he's too old for her."

"When she was eighteen, a nine-year gap in their ages did make a difference in maturity and experience," Bria said. "But now that she's twenty-five and he's thirty-four, Jaron is the only one who thinks it still matters."

"I'm twenty-six and Nate's thirty-three. Neither of us have given the seven-year age difference a second thought. I wonder why he's so insistent that it's a problem?" Jessie asked, frowning.

"If you can answer that, you will have solved one of the mysteries of the universe," Summer stated as she hurried over to keep her daughter from trying to stand on a pumpkin.

An hour later as she helped the women clear the refreshment table, Jessie was more envious than ever of the love and devotion they all shared. They might be a blended family, but they were closer than some people she'd seen who were related by blood.

She sighed heavily as she thought about her own family. For whatever reason, her parents had never seemed to care if she and her older brother had a close relationship. Of course, her brother had been a junior in high school when she was born and as with most teenage boys, he thought he had better things to do than to pay attention to his baby sister.

Unfortunately, she wasn't really all that close to her parents either. Her mother and father were real estate brokers and when they weren't busy selling mansions to the überrich residents of Houston, they were attending a social function at the country club to make more contacts for their agency. About the only time she could remember them paying all that much attention to her was when she told them she was going to become a registered nurse instead of earning a business degree in college. They had both been extremely disappointed with her decision and couldn't understand why she didn't want to follow in their footsteps like her brother had done.

That hadn't changed since she graduated and started her career. Sadly, she didn't hold out a lot of hope they would react any differently when she finally told them about the baby either. They were simply too caught up in brokering real estate deals to be bothered with family. And the only reason they had more to do with her brother was because he was just as driven by the almighty dollar as they were and had joined the family business.

"Do you have plans for Thanksgiving, Jessie?" Bria

asked, bringing her back to the present. "If not, we'd love to have you spend the day with us."

"I usually work most of the holidays," Jessie answered, omitting the fact that she volunteered for those days. Spending time at the hospital was preferable to the periods of awkward silence that always seemed to develop whenever she visited her parents. "Could I let you know a bit later?"

"Of course," Bria said. Her voice barely above a whisper, she added, "I'm sure you and Nate have a lot of things you need to work out. But I want you to know that whatever happens, you and the baby are always welcome anytime we have a get-together."

Touched by the gesture, Jessie blinked away tears. "Thank you. That means a lot."

Several minutes later, Nate's brothers and their wives hugged Jessie and told her how happy they were that she'd joined them for the evening and how thrilled they were about the baby. As she watched them depart, she had to fight the wistfulness building inside her. She had always longed to be part of a family like Nate's—to have that kind of unconditional support and acceptance.

But as tempting as it was, she couldn't allow the lure of a close, loving family to influence her decision when it came to Nate's offer of marriage. When she made that commitment, she refused to settle for anything less than love from her husband. However, it gave her immeasurable comfort knowing her baby was already anticipated and welcomed into such a wonderful family.

"Did you have a good time, darlin'?" Nate asked as they started walking toward the house.

Jessie nodded. "It was good to see your brothers and Bria again. I hadn't seen them since Sam was in the hospital a few years ago. And I'm glad I got to meet your other sisters-in-law and Mariah. They're all very nice."

"My brothers can be real pains in the ass sometimes," he said, giving her a grin that never failed to take her breath away. "But I wouldn't trade them for anything. They have my back and I have theirs. And their wives are real sweethearts. They all go out of their way to make sure the family stays close by having dinners and throwing parties like we had tonight."

As they entered the house, she did her best to ignore Nate's charming expression and focus on the fact that he hadn't invited her to any of his family gatherings in the past. She had a feeling she knew why. It had been his attempt to keep their relationship casual and to discourage her from thinking that what they had between them was more serious. But as much as that fact bothered her, she couldn't really hold his reluctance for her to be around his family against him.

She *had* avoided introducing him to her family as well. While he'd been determined to keep things light, she had been trying to spare him a cold reception and an uncomfortable interrogation about the size of his net worth. But he hadn't seemed to notice that she hadn't introduced him to her parents and she wasn't going to call attention to it.

"Is something wrong?" he asked when they started up the stairs.

Startled out of her musing by his question, she shook her head. "No. I'm just a bit tired." She wasn't about to tell him the real reason behind her pensive mood. That was something two people who were in a relationship would share and she wasn't about to go there. That might give him the idea she was getting closer to resuming their relationship, which she wasn't.

When they walked down the hall and stopped in front of her bedroom door, he didn't try to put his arms around her as she thought he might. Instead, he smiled as he cupped her cheek with his palm. "I'll be right back," he said, crossing the hall to disappear into the master suite. When he returned, he handed her a white T-shirt. "Since I failed to have Bria pick up something for you to sleep in, I thought this would be more comfortable than sleeping in your clothes."

"Thank you," she said, accepting the garment. Until he mentioned it, she hadn't given what she would sleep in a second thought.

"I'm glad you had a good time. Sleep well, darlin'." Leaning forward, he kissed her forehead, then reaching around her, opened the bedroom door for her to enter. "I'll see you in the morning."

Staring up into his blue eyes, she swallowed hard. Why was she disappointed that Nate hadn't really kissed her? This was the way she wanted it to be between them.

"Good night, Nate," she said, escaping into the room and closing the door firmly behind her.

What was wrong with her? She didn't want *that* kind of attention from Nate Rafferty. He'd proven that she couldn't put her faith and trust in him not to hurt her. She had done so over and over, and each time he'd left her to pick up the pieces of her broken heart.

Now that they were having a baby and their lives would always be tied together, it was even more important to protect herself from heartbreak. It would be so much easier raising the baby if they could at least be friends.

Sighing, Jessie took off the gnome costume and slipped into the T-shirt Nate had given her to sleep in. She was immediately assailed by Nate's clean masculine scent and a shiver of longing slid up her spine. Chiding herself for her reaction, she climbed into bed and it crossed her mind that when she went back home tomorrow, it would definitely be in her best interest to stay there. But she had told Nate she would stay with him until after Thanksgiving so they could make decisions and to give him a chance to feel as if he was a part of the pregnancy.

Jessie turned to her side and tried to stop thinking about how he had originally asked her to stay in order to convince her he wanted to get married. She had no doubt that Nate had convinced himself that was what he wanted. But she wasn't foolish enough to think he could change his mind that fast about something he wouldn't even consider a remote possibility until she announced she was pregnant.

He'd only suggested it because of the baby. It had nothing to do with loving her. As far as she was concerned, love was the only reason a couple should consider entering into a marriage.

She closed her eyes tight against her threatening tears. She had stopped wondering why Nate couldn't love her and resigned herself to the fact that he never would. But that didn't stop her from remembering how gently he touched her or from longing for the safety she always felt when she was wrapped securely in his strong arms.

Three

Late the following afternoon, after driving to Waco to get Jessie's clothes and stopping by the hospital for her to make arrangements to take off work for the next month, Nate couldn't help but smile as he carried Jessie's luggage into the ranch house and up the stairs to the room across from the master suite. How could one petite woman need so many clothes? He'd carried in two large suitcases that were so stuffed he was surprised the zippers hadn't given way, a smaller one that was just as full and a good-sized tote bag. And all the way back to Twin Oaks she'd worried that she might have forgotten something. He chuckled. As long as he had access to a washer and dryer, he could get by indefinitely with whatever he could fit into a gym bag and a boot carrier for his dress boots.

While Jessie went to work hanging things in the closet and filling dresser drawers, Nate looked around the room. "You know, this bedroom would be the obvious choice to turn into a nursery."

"Why would you need a nursery?" she asked, stopping to look at him. "You won't be having the baby overnight until he or she is older."

"And why won't I?" He shook his head. "When I told you I wanted to be part of the baby's life, I meant starting from the day he's born."

She took a deep breath and finished putting several pairs of socks into the dresser drawer before she turned to face him. "While I'm glad to hear you want to be a hands-on dad, you having the baby by yourself for more than a few hours won't be possible."

"Why not?" he asked, folding his arms across his chest. "Don't you think I can handle it?"

"Not unless you grow a pair of breasts and start producing milk," she shot back, laughing.

"Oh," he said, rubbing the back of his neck with his hand. "I, uh, hadn't thought about that."

Her smile was indulgent when she walked over to place her hand on his arm. "I'm not saying you won't be part of the baby's life while he or she is an infant. I'm just trying to tell you that for a few months it would be impractical for you to have the baby for any length of time."

The feel of her hand on his arm through his chambray shirt sent a shaft of longing from the top of his head to the soles of his feet. It had been months since he'd lost himself in her softness and the slight widen-

ing of her pretty violet eyes was a good indication that
he wasn't the only one remembering that fact. It was
all he could do to keep from reaching for her. But he'd
given his word he wouldn't push things.

Forcing himself to concentrate on what she'd said,
he had to admit Jessie had a valid point. But he wasn't
going to give up that easily.

"Then how are you going to handle going back to
work if you breast-feed?" he asked, frowning.

"With maternity leave and the vacation days that
I've saved, I'll be off until the baby is three or four
months old," she answered. "I'm sure I'll be able to
work something out after that."

He covered her hand with his. "It looks like that's
the first issue we need to put on the list of things we'll
have to work out."

"I suppose so," she murmured, slipping her hand
from beneath his and turning back to the bag she had
been unpacking.

As he stood there wishing he could take her in his
arms, Nate did his best to shore up his patience. He had
told his brothers he would pull out all the stops to get
her to marry him. But he had to take his time if he had
any chance of convincing her that he really wanted to
make her his wife. Rushing her would only send Jessie
running back to Waco faster than a New York minute.

"After you get your things put away, I thought we'd
drive over to Beaver Dam for supper at the Broken
Spoke," he said, deciding it was time to put his plan
into action. "Today is my housekeeper's day off and I'll
be the first to admit I'm not much of a cook."

"I could make something for us if you'd rather stay in this evening," she offered, reaching into the tote bag to remove what looked to be some kind of wedge-shaped pillow.

Nate briefly wondered what it was, but just as quickly dismissed it as he shook his head. "The day's been pretty busy already and I'm sure you're more than ready to relax and enjoy the rest of the evening."

He purposely omitted that the Broken Spoke Bar and Grill had a nice little dance floor and a jukebox filled with slow country love songs. Many a cowboy had used that dance floor and songs on that old jukebox as an excuse to hold his woman close while they swayed in time to the music. Nate fully intended to continue the tradition with Jessie.

"All right," she finally said, emptying the last suitcase. She glanced down at the clothes she had on. "Will what I'm wearing be appropriate or should I change into something less casual?"

"The food is pretty good, but the Broken Spoke isn't fancy." He glanced at her jeans and loose mint-green shirt. "What you're wearing is just fine."

"Then I guess I'm ready whenever you are," she said, picking up her shoulder bag.

As he stepped back for her to precede him from the room, Nate swallowed hard. He hadn't really paid a lot of attention to the size of Jessie's belly until now. But her gauzy shirt highlighted the small bulge more than concealed it, unlike her sweatshirt and the gnome costume's apron had done the day before.

He took a deep breath as they left the house and he

helped her into the passenger side of his truck. He had never given much thought to a pregnant woman's figure and the effect it had on her sex appeal. But there was no other way to describe Jessie other than sexy as hell. Even though she wore loose clothing, he could tell that her breasts were larger and her smooth complexion seemed to have a glow about it that begged for his touch. And for reasons he didn't even want to think about, just the thought that she was carrying his child made him want her.

Shaking his head, he rounded the front of the truck and climbed in behind the steering wheel. Had he lost his mind? He'd never in his entire life given a pregnant woman, and whether or not she was attractive, a second thought.

As he started the truck and steered it down the lane to the main road, Nate decided not to think too much about the reasons behind his finding Jessie so alluring. He had always desired her and that was something that would never change. Of course, he would feel different about her now than other women. She was the mother of his child. The woman he was going to make his wife, even if he wasn't sure he could live up to expectations.

When a knot formed in the pit of his stomach and his palms started to sweat, he tried to focus on something—anything else. Even if he didn't know how to go about it, he was going to give it everything he had in him, and be the best husband and father he could possibly be.

Jessie looked around when she and Nate entered the Broken Spoke Bar and Grill. It was typical of a lot of small-town Texas watering holes in big ranch country. The red vinyl seats on the chrome chairs and booths had a few repaired cracks and the Formica tabletops had seen so much use they had faded from shiny to a dull, flat black. But as dated and well used as the decor was, everything appeared to be neat and clean.

"Will this be all right?" Nate asked as he guided her to a table toward the back of the room.

"It's fine," she said as she continued to look around.

Several men dressed in worn jeans, work shirts and denim jackets sat on stools at the bar talking to a couple of women, while a few others played pool. They all wore wide-brimmed hats and scuffed boots, indicating they most likely worked on some of the many ranches in the area.

"There aren't very many women," Jessie commented when Nate held her chair for her.

He shrugged and lowered himself into the chair beside her. "There are quite a few more on Friday and Saturday nights, but even then the men outnumber the women."

"What can I get for you folks this evenin'?" a young ponytailed waitress asked, walking up to the table.

Jessie looked at Nate. "What are you having?"

"My usual," he said, grinning. "Steak, home fries, coleslaw and a beer."

"I'll have the same," she decided. "But instead of the beer, I'd like a glass of milk, please."

"You got it." Nodding, the waitress snapped her chewing gum as she wrote down their orders. "How do y'all want those steaks cooked?"

After telling the girl how they liked their steaks, they made small talk for a few minutes before Nate reached over to cover Jessie's hand with his. "Jessie, I think I've come up with a way that we can both be with the baby during his first year."

"Or her first year," she corrected as she removed her hand from beneath his. His calloused palm on her skin was a distraction she didn't need. "The baby might be a girl."

His smile when he nodded made her feel warm all over. "Either way, I don't want to miss out on all the things that other dads get to experience. That's why I think you should move to the ranch."

She could understand and was even encouraged by his desire to be part of their baby's most formative year, but she wasn't going to marry him. "Nate, I told you I don't want to be pressured. I'm not going to do something that we both know would end in disaster."

"Hear me out, darlin'," he said, his expression turning serious. "I'm not going to lie to you. I do want us to get married and I'm not going to give up on that. But that isn't what I'm talking about right now. I'm suggesting that you move to the ranch and let me be part of the rest of your pregnancy as well as the baby's first year."

Before she could answer, the waitress brought their dinner and Jessie waited until the girl walked over to another table before she commented on his outrageous proposal. "I can understand you wanting to be there to see all of the baby's firsts, but I can't move to your ranch, Nate. My job is in Waco."

"You can take a leave of absence," he said as if it

would be the easiest thing in the world to do. He picked up his knife and fork to cut into his steak. "Or if you want to continue working, you could get a job at the hospital or one of the doctor's offices around Stephenville. It's not nearly as big as the hospital where you work in Waco, but small hospitals have sick people, too."

"I realize that. But why would I want to trade a five-minute commute for a half-hour drive?" she asked, sitting back from the table to stare at him. "You could always move to Waco."

He shrugged. "I have a lot more room at Twin Oaks than you have in your apartment. Besides, there's one big advantage if you moved to the ranch."

"And what would that be?" she asked, picking up her fork to spear one of the potato wedges on her plate.

"You would have help with the baby and wouldn't have to worry about finding someone to babysit while you're working," he said, reaching for his beer.

"That would be great during the week, but what about the weekends? You're normally competing in a rodeo somewhere out of state and even if it's here in Texas, it would require that you find a place to stay for a night or two." She shook her head. "The chances of me having weekends off if I worked at a hospital are extremely slim. Who would keep the baby then?"

"I'm pretty sure we can work it out," he said, smiling. "But we've got plenty of time. It's just one option to consider."

They fell silent while they ate and by the time they finished, Jessie had pushed his suggestion to the back of her mind. He might think it was a viable solution, but she knew better. It was going to be a true test of her willpower living at the ranch for a month. There was no way she could be with him for over a year without falling victim to his charismatic charm again.

"I think I'll check out what songs they have on the jukebox," Nate said, rising from the table.

As she watched him walk across the small dance area, Jessie caught her lower lip between her teeth. Nate's shoulders were impressively wide and filled out his chambray shirt to perfection. A shiver of longing slid up her spine when she thought about how it felt to be surrounded by all that masculinity as he made love to her.

If just watching him caused that kind of reaction, she was in serious trouble. How on earth was she going to resist his allure for the next month?

Lost in thought, she jumped when Nate walked up beside her and reached down to take her hand in his. "I think that's our song, darlin'. Would you like to dance?"

Before she could protest, he pulled her to her feet and ushered her out onto the dance floor. "Nate, this isn't a good idea."

"Why? Are you too tired?" he asked, wrapping his arms around her.

"N-no." It hadn't even occurred to her to use the excuse he'd handed her.

"It's just a dance, Jessie," he whispered close to her ear.

With his body aligned fully with hers and his warm breath feathering over her sensitive skin, she couldn't remember her own name, let alone come up with a good reason why they shouldn't be dancing. But as his body moved against hers, Jessie gave in to the impulse to lean closer and the longing that rushed through her body was almost overwhelming.

As Nate moved them in time to the music, the feel of his rapidly hardening body sent a wave of heat coursing from the top of her head to the soles of her feet. Her knees wobbled and she had no choice but to cling to him to keep from melting into a puddle at his big, booted feet.

When the song ended, she drew on every ounce of strength she had left and pulled from his arms. "I—I must be more tired than I thought," she lied as she faked a yawn. "We should probably leave."

He stared down at her for a moment before he grinned. "Whatever you say, darlin'."

They both knew she was fibbing, but to her relief, Nate didn't call her on the ruse and after tossing money on the table for their dinner along with a generous tip, he placed his hand to the small of her back to guide her to the exit. Neither spoke as he helped her up into the truck and the ride back to his ranch was just as silent.

"Would you like to watch a movie?" he asked, when he parked the truck between his Mercedes sports car and her SUV in the three-car garage. He got out of the truck and came around to open the passenger door for her. "I noticed the newest Melissa McCarthy comedy is on pay-per-view."

He knew the actress was one of her favorites and she was tempted, but on the ride home she realized that she really was tired. "Could we take a rain check on that? There's a good chance I would fall asleep in the middle of it."

"Sure," he said, lifting her down from the truck seat. "We can watch it tomorrow night and I'll get Rosemary to make us some popcorn." As they walked into the house, he asked, "Or would you prefer to drive up to Stephenville for dinner and a movie?"

Although going out was tempting, it sounded too much like a date. That wasn't what she was there for and she certainly didn't want to give Nate the false impression that she was falling under his spell yet again.

"Staying here for a movie is fine with me," she answered decisively as they climbed the stairs. "I'll be able to turn in right after it's over."

When they reached her room, he stopped her when she started to open the door. "Do you think you'll feel up to going with me to the rodeo up in Amarillo this coming weekend?" he asked.

"Why wouldn't I?" she asked, frowning. "I'm not ill, I'm pregnant."

"I wasn't sure if you thought it would be too tiring," he said, reaching up to rub the back of his neck with his hand. "I'll be the first to admit that I don't know all that much about how a pregnant woman feels or what she should or shouldn't do."

Unable to stop herself, she placed her hand on his arm. "Other than becoming seriously addicted to naps, I feel good," she said, smiling. "So good in fact, I plan on working right up until the baby is born."

"Okay. Let me go back and rephrase my question. Would you go with me to the rodeo this weekend?"

She knew she should tell him no and be content with a little alone time so that she could think. But she just couldn't resist the chance to finally see how good of a rodeo rider he was. In the two and a half years they'd known each other, Nate had never asked her to watch him compete, and she wasn't about to miss the opportunity. Between her work schedule and the fact that she was on duty most weekends, it had made sense. But it would have been nice if he had at least asked her to go with him when they'd been seeing each other, even if she would have had to turn him down.

"I'd like that." Knowing they would need to be there for two or three nights, she felt compelled to add, "As long as we have separate rooms."

"Of course." Tracing his index finger along her jaw, he leaned forward to kiss her forehead. "Sweet dreams, darlin'."

The feel of his lips on her skin and the look of longing in his eyes stole her breath and it took everything she had in her to turn, walk into the bedroom and shut the door. Releasing the breath she'd been holding, Jessie changed into her nightshirt and grabbed her wedge pillow before climbing into bed. Once she'd turned to her side and arranged the pillow to support her stomach and one of the bed pillows to support her back, she found herself staring at the closed door, wondering if Nate was going to have as much trouble going to sleep as she knew she would.

As a deep sadness began to fill her, a lone tear trickled down her cheek. She impatiently swiped it away with the back of her hand. What was wrong with her? Why did she feel such a keen sense of disappointment?

He was doing exactly as she had asked him to do. Although he had admitted over dinner that he hadn't given up on wanting them to get married, he wasn't pressing the issue. And other than a couple of chaste kisses to the forehead and holding her when they danced, he hadn't made a move toward a more intimate caress.

The baby chose that moment to move and placing her hand on her stomach, Jessie bit her lip as she tried to fight the wave of emotion threatening to swamp her. She missed Nate holding her, loving her. In all of her twenty-six years, she'd never felt as safe and secure as when she was in his arms. But she couldn't let her emotions sway her.

This was the way she wanted it—the way it had to be. She couldn't afford to let down her guard and fall for him again. It wasn't just her welfare she had to think about anymore. Her child was counting on her to make responsible decisions and she wasn't about to let her son or daughter down.

She was going to protect them both from the heartbreak that she feared would accompany her becoming involved with Nate again. It would be better for their child to never know what it was like for his or her parents to be together, rather than go through the upset when they eventually broke up.

Jessie took a deep, shuddering breath. She just hoped she could remain strong and not give in to the temptation of starting something again with Nate that she knew he either couldn't or wouldn't commit to.

The following evening, Nate yawned as he carried a tray with a big bowl of popcorn, a bottle of water for Jessie and a soft drink for him into the media room. He'd spent the entire night lying awake, thinking about the woman in the bedroom across the hall from the master suite. Holding her while they danced at the Broken Spoke, feeling the slight bulge of her rounded stomach rubbing against his lower belly and knowing it was his baby she was carrying had revved his engine faster than he could slap his own ass with both hands.

It was an entirely new experience for him to get turned on by a pregnant woman. That fact alone had caused him to question his sanity more than once. But it was the memory of the lovemaking that had created their child that sent him into the master bathroom for a cold shower in the middle of the night and again early that morning.

Jessie was the most exciting woman he had ever known and having her with him was heaven and hell rolled up into one very enticing little package. He wanted to hold her and show her how good life could be for them. But how was he supposed to convince her that he could be what she wanted him to be if she kept him at arm's length and didn't tell him what it was she wanted?

That afternoon he'd ridden to the south pasture with his men on the pretense of moving a herd of heifers, but the entire time he'd been thinking about what he had to do. At some point, he was going to have to tell her about what he had done to land himself and Sam at the Last Chance Ranch. Then if she could get past that, he needed to find a way to convince her to let him do what was right and marry her.

"Rosemary told me the two of you had a nice little talk this afternoon," he said, setting the tray on the coffee table in front of the leather sofa.

Jessie nodded. "While you and your men were moving your cattle into another pasture, Rosemary and I talked about how different things are now for new mothers than when she had her babies."

"Oh, yeah?" Lowering himself onto the couch beside her, he shook his head. "I wouldn't think there were too many variations on something like being a new mom."

"You'd be surprised," she said, laughing.

The delightful sound sent a wave of heat straight to the region south of his belt buckle. But more than that it gave him hope. Jessie had apparently started to relax and he took it as a good sign that her guard was coming down.

Whether it was that knowledge or the lighthearted mood, Nate grinned. "Are you going to tell me how it's different or are you going to make me guess?"

"I should make you guess." The twinkle in her violet eyes caused the heat inside him to increase. "Your answers might be very interesting."

"You want to shoot me a break here, darlin'?" He laughed. "You know as well as I do that I don't know beans from buckshot about this stuff."

She smiled. "Rosemary and I discussed some of the things that have been developed over the past thirty years to make things easier to care for a baby."

He scooped a handful of popcorn from the bowl to keep from reaching for her. "Let me guess. She compared the way she did it in the good old days to what women are doing today and found the new way lacking."

"Not at all. Rosemary said she wished she'd had all the items available that new mothers have today when she had her first child," Jessie answered as she reached for some popcorn.

"Wow! Whatever these things are, they must be pretty impressive," he said, picking up the remote control. "We'll have to make a trip to one of the baby stores so you can show me all these new gadgets."

"Why do you think they have to be something special?" Jessie asked as she opened the water.

When she put the bottle to her mouth to take a drink, Nate had to stifle a groan. The memory of how those soft, perfect lips felt on his skin caused his heart to race and made it feel like the temperature in the room had gone up at least ten degrees.

"Nate, are you all right?" she asked, her expression concerned.

"Uh, yeah," he lied, popping the top on the soft drink can to take a big gulp. "I'm fine. Why?"

"Aside from the fact that you looked like you might be in pain, you didn't answer my question," she explained.

Oh, he was in pain all right. But it wasn't the kind

she was thinking about. Having her with him and not being able to hold her, kiss her, was about to kill him. He had always thought she was pretty, sexy and a lot of fun to be with, but he had to admit that they hadn't spent a lot of time together that hadn't involved making love. Now that they were spending time where he had to concentrate on more than mind-blowing sex, he was starting to pay more attention to how perceptive she was and how much he enjoyed her intellect.

When she continued to stare at him, he forced himself to focus on what she'd said. "I was just trying to imagine what could have made that big of an impression on Rosemary. She doesn't put her stamp of approval on just anything."

"Well, she seemed to like the convenience of the forehead digital thermometers and the video baby monitors." Jessie smiled. "And she especially liked the idea of electric breast pumps."

"A breast pump?" he asked, sounding like a damned parrot. He wasn't sure he even wanted to know how those things worked. "I'm sorry I speculated."

"Don't tell me you find talking about breast pumps embarrassing," she teased.

"To tell the truth, I really never gave something like that a second thought." Nor was he sure he wanted to.

It wasn't exactly the subject that made him uncomfortable, it was the fact that he just flat didn't know anything about taking care of an infant. As he started the movie and they settled back against the soft brown leather couch cushions, he decided it might not be a bad idea to start a list of things he needed to research on the internet before the baby was born. He'd taken his turn babysitting his niece and nephews on occasion, but they had been several months old and it had only been for a few hours at a time. If he was going to do this "dad" thing right, it appeared that he needed to learn a whole lot more about newborns and their care. Unlike his biological father, he wasn't going to mess things up and fail at something this important.

About halfway through the fast-paced comedy, he noticed Jessie start to yawn and without a second thought, he put his arm around her. When she leaned back to stare up at him, he thought she might pull away, but to his relief she drowsily rested her head against his shoulder and in no time he could tell by her shallow breathing that she was sound asleep.

He smiled. It was further proof that she was definitely letting down her guard with him. Now all he had to do was make sure he didn't become impatient and push for more before she was ready. Considering all he could think about was how sweet her kisses were and how responsive she was when they made love, that was going to be damned hard to do. But he had too much riding on the outcome of her month with him to screw up things with Jessie this time around.

When the movie ended, Nate was reluctant to let her go. Instead of waking her to go upstairs to bed as he should have, he turned the television to the late-night news and continued to hold her. As he sat there pretending to watch what the meteorologist predicted for the next few days, he thought about the woman in his arms and the baby she carried. Wondering if he could feel the baby move, he placed his hand on her stomach and waited.

"It's not unheard of, but I think it's a bit too soon for you to be able to feel movement," Jessie murmured.

"But you can feel him?" he asked, leaving his hand on her stomach. At least he was touching her, even if it was several inches below where he'd like his hand to be resting.

She nodded as she sat up straight. "At first I wasn't sure because it was just a light fluttery feeling."

Nate had never wondered when a pregnant woman felt a baby move. But he was finding there were a lot of things he had never thought about before that had become very important since Jessie had announced he was going to be a daddy.

"How long ago was that?"

"I first noticed it about three weeks ago and then it gradually became stronger and more frequent." She smiled. "Now it's starting to feel a little more like she's gently nudging me."

"And that doesn't hurt or make you feel sick?" If he had something moving around inside of him, he was pretty sure he would be as sick as a five-year-old kid after eating a full bag of Halloween candy.

Instead of answering his question, she used her index finger to poke him just above his navel. He immediately started laughing and caught her to him to keep her from doing it again.

"Not fair." He grinned. "You know that's the one place I'm ticklish."

"You wanted to know how it felt," she answered, her laughter joining his. "I just thought I'd show you."

As he held her close and their eyes met, their smiles faded. "I want to kiss you, Jessie."

"That wouldn't be a good idea," she said, her voice soft and not at all discouraging.

"Do you want me to kiss you, darlin'?" he asked, cupping her cheek with his palm.

"No."

He kissed her cheek and the tip of her nose. "I've never known you to lie before."

She stared at him for what seemed like an eternity before she answered. "Nate, there are times when what we want and what's best for us are two different things."

If there had been any question that she was afraid he would hurt her again, it had just been answered. He could have kicked himself for causing Jessie so much heartache, but he couldn't change that now. All he could do now was move forward and make sure that it didn't happen again.

"Darlin', I know that I've been a thoughtless bastard and you have every right not to want anything to do with me," he said, choosing his words carefully. "Believe me, if I could go back and do things different, I would. But all that's in the past now and besides, circumstances have changed. All I can do is give you my word that it will never happen again."

"Because of the baby," she said slowly.

When he nodded, Nate watched her catch her lower lip between her teeth to keep it from trembling and knew she was fighting to keep her tears in check. It tore him apart to think he was the reason behind all of her turmoil. It reminded him of the times before her death that he had witnessed his mother cry over something his father had said or done. He might not know what a lifetime commitment was all about, but he knew for damned sure it shouldn't be filled with stress and uncertainty. Nate silently made a vow to do everything in his power to never cause Jessie that kind of emotional pain again.

"N-Nate, we went over this before," she said, her voice shaky.

When a lone tear slid down her cheek, he wiped it away with the pad of his thumb, then gently kissed where it had been. "I know we covered this the other day and I asked you then to let me prove to you that I can change. But I can't do that if you won't let me hold you or kiss you. I need to be able to show you, Jessie."

She closed her eyes as she murmured, "N-Nate, I'm tired of your on- and off-again games."

"I know, darlin'," he said, pulling her more fully against him. She was wary and he couldn't blame her. He held her for several long seconds as he tried to find the words to get her to take a leap of faith. "I'm sorry for the way I treated you in the past and I'll be the first to admit that I should be shot for doing that. But I'm in unfamiliar territory here and trying to do what I think is right. All I can do now is ask that you forgive and trust me."

"That's asking a lot," she said, opening her eyes to stare up at him.

He nodded as he leaned forward to kiss her cheek. "I know it's going to take a lot of courage, Jessie. But you'll never know for sure if you don't take the chance. Give me that much and I swear you won't be sorry you did."

The look in her eyes told him she was still frightened, but to his relief, when he slowly began to lower his head, she didn't pull away. Lightly brushing her perfect mouth with his, Nate wondered how he had been able to stay away from her for the past several months.

He felt that way every time he went back to ask her to give him another chance and he briefly wondered if he would get antsy again when things started getting more serious than he intended. But he was going to have to push that concern aside. He was determined to do the right thing and marry her, just as his foster father would expect him to do. But he couldn't help but worry about the next step. What if she pushed *him* aside once she learned what had landed him and his brother in foster care when they were kids and the reason behind it?

Soft and sweet, her lips clung to his and he forgot all about his reservations. When he deepened the kiss to explore her tender inner recesses and reacquaint himself with the taste of her passion, she brought her arms up to circle his shoulders. It caused his heart to beat double time and his breath to lodge in his lungs when she kissed him back. Savoring her like a fine wine, he leisurely stroked her tongue with his as he imitated a more intimate union.

His body began to tighten predictably. Deciding it would be best to end the caress before he took things too far, he started to ease away from the kiss. It appeared she was going to give him another chance and he wasn't going to blow it. Besides, he was only adding more tension to his already frustrated libido.

But apparently Jessie had other ideas and, suddenly taking control, she did a little exploring of her own. Nate's body hardened so fast it caused him to feel lightheaded and, groaning, he had to shift to keep his jeans from emasculating him.

"I think it's about time for me to walk you upstairs to your room," he said as he tried to force air back into his lungs.

Everything in him urged him to kiss her again and with a lot more passion. But he couldn't risk doing something stupid now. Not when one wrong move could give her reason to end things between them for good.

When they climbed the stairs and walked to her bedroom, he kissed her cheek, stepped back and started back downstairs. "Sweet dreams, darlin'."

"Aren't you going to bed now?" she asked.

Turning back, he shook his head. "I've got a rodeo coming up and I need to put in some time in my workout room."

"Thank you for inviting me to go with you this coming weekend." She gave him a smile that set his pulse to racing as she opened the door. "I'm looking forward to seeing you ride."

He nodded. "I'm looking forward to having you there with me."

As she went into the room and closed the door, he realized it was true. He was anticipating having her watch him ride. It was something he had avoided because he had wanted to keep things light between them and not make her think they were becoming a couple.

But at the moment, that was the last thing on his mind. He had a fire in his blood that only Jessie could put out. And since making love to her wasn't an option just yet, he fully intended to exhaust himself. Maybe then he would be able to get some sleep.

Heading back downstairs, Nate went straight to the workout room and, taking off his shirt, picked up a twenty-five pound weight and started doing bicep curls at a furious pace. He had enough adrenaline flowing through his veins to bench-press a tractor and considering all he could think about was the woman upstairs, it was going to take a minor miracle to work off that kind of rush.

A half hour later, when he climbed the stairs and walked down the hall to his room, Nate stopped to stare at the closed door across the hall. He knew for certain he was destined for another fitful night. All he could think about was having Jessie in his bed, holding her and loving her until the break of dawn. His body immediately began to tighten and burn with a need that was all too familiar.

"Son of a bitch," he muttered, resigned to the fact that he was once again going to suffer through a shower cold enough to freeze the balls off a pool table.

Four

As Jessie and Nate started up the steps of the grand-
stand at the rodeo in Amarillo, he reached out to take
her hand in his and the warmth that flowed through
her from the contact was breathtaking. Since their talk
a few nights ago, he had taken every opportunity to
remind her of how things could be between them with
tender touches and kisses that left her weak and trembling. But she hadn't had to stop him from going too
far. She could tell he wanted more, but true to his promise, he wasn't pushing her further. The only problem
was, it was becoming a true test of her resolve not to
ask him to. This was the longest they had gone without making love and she missed the intimacy between
them.

When they reached the seating area where the families of the contestants and rodeo personnel sat, Jessie was happy to see Summer and Bria waving to her and Nate to get their attention. At least she would have someone she knew to sit with and talk to while she waited for Nate to compete in the bull and bareback riding events.

"I didn't know your brothers and their wives would be here," she commented as they reached the row of seats where the women sat with their children.

"Ryder is one of the bullfighters and Sam is the stock contractor," Nate answered as he pushed his wide-brimmed Resistol back on his head. Putting his arms around her, he gave her a quick kiss. "I hate to just walk you up here and leave, but I've got to register and see what my draws are."

She frowned. "Your draws?"

"The bull and horse I'll be riding today," he said, grinning.

"I think I need a crash course in rodeo terminology." Knowing he needed to register for the events he would be competing in, she smiled. "Go ahead and do what you have to do. I'll be fine here with Bria and Summer," she assured him. "I'm looking forward to talking to them again."

"I'll see you after the bull riding," he said, giving her another kiss.

As Nate turned to go back down the bleacher steps to find the registration office, Jessie made her way to the empty seat beside Summer and her little girl, Katie. "It's good to see I've got you two to explain what's going on," she said when she sat down.

"Is this the first time you've seen Nate ride?" Bria asked.

Jessie nodded. "I usually have to work weekends."

She didn't want to explain that this was the first time Nate had asked her to watch him in the two and a half years they had been seeing each other. For some reason it just seemed a little embarrassing to admit she obviously hadn't meant that much to him.

"Have you already taken your maternity leave?" Summer asked, shifting her sleeping daughter from her shoulder to her lap.

"No, I took some vacation time to stay with Nate until Thanksgiving," she admitted. Explaining his requests, she added, "Given our past history, I'm still not sure I'm doing the right thing."

"I can understand your reservations," Bria said, her tone sympathetic. "He's been extremely inconsiderate in the past and you have every right not to trust him. But I don't think you have to worry. Deep down Nate really is a good guy and he'll be great with the baby." Grinning, Bria added, "However, when it comes to your relationship with him, you're in charge now. Don't hesitate to make him grovel a few times. He definitely deserves it."

"Bria's right," Summer agreed. "He does deserve a hard time. But I've never known any of the six brothers to go back on their word. If Nate says he wants to marry you and make a life for the baby, I can guarantee he means it."

Jessie had no doubt that Nate would be a good father. He was great with his niece and nephews, and she was confident that he would love their baby. But it was the way he felt about her that kept her awake at night. Had she set herself up for another fall?

He had a track record when it came to their relationship and it wasn't a good one. And even though she had agreed to let him show her how it could be between them, she didn't hold out a lot of hope that he wouldn't lose interest in her as he'd done before.

That was why while staying out of his bed might be extremely difficult for her, it was for the best. If they made love, she knew she'd fall for him all over again and that's something she just couldn't allow herself to do. It was her job to protect the baby, but she also needed to protect her heart as well. Unfortunately, when it came to Nate, she didn't seem to have a lot of choice in the matter. From the moment they met, he had been her biggest weakness and it appeared that he always would be.

"Jaron's competing today as well as Nate," Bria commented when the announcer acknowledged the cowboys competing in the day's events who had already qualified for the National Finals in Las Vegas.

"Is Mariah going to be here to watch him?" Jessie asked.

Bria shook her head. "He's never asked her and she wouldn't even if he did. She refuses to watch Jaron ride—especially the bulls. She's afraid he might be injured and she can't stand the thought of seeing that happen."

"I can understand how she feels," Jessie admitted. "I'm nervous about watching Nate climb on the back of any animal with nothing more on its mind than throwing him off so it can stomp on him."

Summer sighed. "I know what you mean. Even though he doesn't ride and I've seen him save cowboys from being injured more times than I can count, I still hold my breath whenever Ryder jumps in front of a bull to distract it."

"How much longer is Ryder going to work as a bullfighter?" Bria asked. "I know he's cut back a lot since Katie was born and only works the rodeos Nate and Jaron compete in."

"He says he'll give it up completely once they stop riding." Summer gave Jessie a reassuring smile. "Even though it makes me nervous, my husband really is one of the best at what he does. He'll move heaven and earth if he has to in order to make sure Nate and Jaron don't get hurt. And if that means risking his own safety, that's what he'll do."

Bria nodded. "Sam told me that all of the bull riders breathe a little easier when they know Ryder is working the event."

Nate had told her several times that his brother Ryder was one of the bravest men he'd ever known and had a protective streak a mile wide when it came to those he loved. Knowing that he was in charge of keeping the men safe did make her feel a little more relaxed about the bull riding. But as a nurse, Jessie had seen some of the damage those animals could do to the human body and the thought of something like that happening to Nate or any of the brothers scared her as little else could.

When the rodeo began Jessie did her best to relax and enjoy the timed events. She couldn't believe how fast some of the cowboys were at roping and tying a calf or how quickly cowgirls could race their horses around barrels without falling off.

"The bareback event is next," Bria said, glancing at the program. "Nate and Jaron will both be riding in this one."

"The horses aren't as dangerous as the bulls are they?" Jessie asked, hoping that was the case.

Bria shook her head. "If a cowboy is thrown before the eight-second horn goes off, the horse doesn't turn back and try to hurt him."

Several contestants attempted to ride the horses they had drawn for the event—some of them even successfully—before Nate was announced as the next rider. From their seats in the grandstand they had an excellent view of the riders climbing onto the backs of the animals, and Jessie found herself sitting on the edge of her seat when the light gray horse Nate was attempting to mount reared up in the chute.

"Does that happen often?" she asked, alarmed. As she watched, the chute crew helped Nate reposition himself on the horse's back as if it was no big deal.

"There are some horses that have a bad habit of doing that in the bucking chute and the gate men know to put a rope on the horse to keep it from rearing up and injuring itself or the rider," Bria said, frowning. "But this is the first time I've seen Silver Streak do that. Normally he waits until he gets out into the arena to cut loose and go wild."

Jessie had forgotten that Sam was the stock contractor providing the livestock for the different events. Of course, Bria would be familiar with all the animals and their particular habits.

Once Nate was settled on the back of the animal, he nodded his head and a man on the outside of the bucking chute swung the gate open. The horse jumped straight up, then seemed to explode out into the arena kicking and pitching sideways as it tried to throw Nate from its back.

"Silver Streak is outdoing himself," Bria said excitedly. "If Nate can hang on for the full eight seconds, he's going to get one of the highest scores of the day."

"How do you know?" Jessie asked, breathing a little easier when the horn signaled that eight seconds were up and two cowboys on saddled horses rode up beside the bucking animal for Nate to dismount safely.

"Fifty percent of the score is based on how well the horse bucks and the other fifty is based on how well the cowboy rides it," Summer explained. "Silver Streak did everything he could to buck Nate off. But Nate did an excellent job of riding the horse for the full eight seconds."

Summer had just finished her explanation of the scoring system when Nate's score was announced over the loudspeaker. Compared to the scores of previous riders, his was by far the highest.

"That's going to be hard to beat," Bria said, smiling.

"I'm sure the cowboy who's about to ride will try," Summer said, laughing when Jaron's name was announced.

"Is there a big rivalry between Nate and Jaron?" Jessie asked, feeling a sense of pride at Nate's accomplishment.

"All of the guys are very competitive," Bria answered. "But they're all proud of the others' accomplishments as well."

Summer nodded. "If Nate wins, Jaron will be the first one to congratulate him, the same as Nate will do if Jaron wins."

"I love the way they're all so supportive of each other," Jessie said, meaning it. Coming from a family that had never encouraged a strong bond, she envied them.

"They've all been through a lot together and I vowed when I married Sam to help them stay close," Bria admitted. "That's why we have so many parties and family dinners. It's a good way for them to maintain the bond they formed as teenagers."

"I love that Katie and I are part of it all," Summer stated, smiling. "I went from having no siblings to having this wonderful, loving family that made me feel like I'd always been part of them." She reached down to squeeze Jessie's hand. "You and your baby are part of that now, too."

"Thank you," Jessie said, blinking back tears as they watched the rest of the rodeo.

She really didn't see how she could be considered one of them if she and Nate weren't going to be together. But it was a real comfort knowing that her child would have the love and acceptance of such a wonderful extended family.

By the time the bull-riding event started, Jessie had relaxed a little more. But as Nate climbed onto the back of the big, mean-looking bull he'd drawn, her body tensed involuntarily. Unable to watch, she closed her eyes to keep from seeing him be hurt.

She opened her eyes in time to see Nate dismount and fall to his knees. Thankfully the animal proved to be fairly docile. Instead of seeking revenge, the bull trotted out of the arena without even bothering to look Nate's way. That eased her mind a little; now all he had to do was ride two more bulls over the next couple of days without being injured and she would be able to relax completely.

After a nice dinner with his brothers and their wives, Nate carried his and Jessie's bags into the hotel lobby and stopped at the front desk. They were late checking in and he hoped they could get squared away without too much hassle. The drive up to Amarillo had taken a lot longer than he had anticipated because of traffic tie-ups on the interstate due to construction, and they hadn't had time to stop by and check into their rooms before he had to be at the rodeo arena to register for his events.

"I have two rooms reserved for the next three nights," he said, approaching the front desk. When the desk clerk looked up, Nate gave the man his name and waited while he keyed in the information on his computer.

"I'm sorry, Mr. Rafferty, we only have you down

for one suite for the three nights," the guy said, shaking his head.

"Is something wrong?" Jessie asked, walking up beside him.

"They only have one room reserved for us," he said, barely resisting the urge to cuss a blue streak. She was never going to believe that it was the hotel's screw-up and not him trying to pull a fast one on her. It wouldn't be the first time he'd arrived at a hotel to find there had been some kind of computer mix-up. Of course, because of his VIP status with the hotel, they usually bent over backward to accommodate him. But he'd just as soon not deal with any kind of issues if at all possible.

"But you told me you were getting two rooms," she insisted, her tone a little suspicious.

"I did." He reached into the hip pocket of his jeans to fish out his wallet. Removing his identification and the hotel's VIP card, he pushed them across the counter toward the man squinting at the computer like it held the secrets of the universe. "Please check your files again. I booked one suite online over three months ago and I called at the beginning of this week to book another."

Without comment the man keyed the information into the computer, then after clicking the mouse a couple of times and keying in more information, he looked up. "I think I know what happened. Whoever you talked to when you called to make your reservation for the second room put you into the system as wanting one suite with two beds, instead of two suites with one bed."

Nate shook his head. "Whatever. I need two suites."

The guy shrugged as if he didn't know what else to do. "I'm sorry, but I can't give you another room because we're booked solid. The rodeo is in town."

Nate rolled his eyes and pointed to the fringed leather chaps draped over his arm. "I know the rodeo is in town." He looked at the man's name tag. "But that doesn't solve our problem now, does it, Ralph? I'd really hate having to stay elsewhere from now on because you aren't able to accommodate my request."

Ralph quickly shook his head. "That won't be necessary, Mr. Rafferty. I'll see what I can do, but because of the rodeo being in town…"

"Yeah, I got that, Ralph. The rodeo is in town." Nate took a deep breath as he tried to hold on to his patience. "Just check to see if there's any way you can accommodate my request."

"Nate, let's just take the suite he has reserved for you," Jessie said, surprising him.

"Are you sure?" he asked.

Since their talk a few nights ago, things had been going along pretty well between them and he'd like to keep it that way. But staying in the same room with Jessie, even if it was a suite, sleeping so close to her and not being able to make love to her would be like playing with a stick of dynamite. It was bound to get him into trouble and damned quick.

"I'm tired and I'm sure you are, too," she said, nodding. "As long as there are two beds, it shouldn't be an issue."

A sudden wave of heat surged through his body and he gritted his teeth as he turned back to the desk clerk.

Sharing a room might not be a problem for her, but it sure as hell would be for him. Unfortunately, staying in the same suite seemed to be their only option.

"We'll take what you have," he finally said, knowing he would be completely insane by morning.

"Would you like help with your luggage?" Ralph asked as he handed Nate a couple of key cards.

"No, I'll take care of our bags," Nate answered as he signed for the room.

A few minutes later, as he and Jessie rode the elevator to the fourth floor, Nate couldn't help but wonder if having to sleep in such close proximity to Jessie instead of with her was his penance for the way he'd handled their relationship over the past two and a half years. If he thought he'd gone through hell the past several days with her in the room across the hall from his, he couldn't imagine what it was going to be like sleeping just a few feet away from her. He was pretty sure he already had frostbite from freezing his ass off every night in a cold shower. How on God's green earth was he going to make it through the next few nights without turning into an icicle?

"This is nice," Jessie said, oblivious of his inner turmoil when he opened the door to their room. "These are amazing." She touched the expensive silk comforter on one of the beds. "Which one do you want?"

The one you're going to be in. "It doesn't matter to me," he answered. Setting their luggage on the floor in the bedroom, he hung his chaps on the valet stand, then turned to watch her walk around the room. She stopped at the balcony doors to look out at the brightly lit Amarillo skyline. "This room has a great view."

"It's a nice city," Nate agreed, continuing to watch her. He could tell she was a little nervous about the arrangement and trying to put her at ease, he pointed to the minibar. "Would you like something to eat or drink?"

"We just had dinner with your brothers and their wives."

"I heard you tell Bria and Summer that you're always hungry," he said, grinning. "I just thought you might need a snack before we turn in."

"I think I'm going to shower, then go on to sleep," she said, unzipping one of her two bags.

He picked up the huge television's remote control. "I think I'll watch a little TV. Will that bother you?"

As she dug through the bag to find whatever she was looking for, she shook her head. "No, but go ahead and watch whatever you like. It won't disturb me." She laughed as she straightened with a hot-pink nightshirt in one hand and a zebra-striped toiletry bag in the other. "I think I proved the other night when we were watching the movie that I can sleep through whatever is on the TV, even if it's something I want to see."

He barely managed a smile as she turned to go into the bathroom. All he could think about was her taking off her clothes to get into the shower and him joining her. His body tightened to an almost painful state when he remembered the times they had showered together over the past couple of years.

Clenching his jaw so tight it would take a crowbar to

pry it open, he sat down on the end of one of the beds and took off his boots. How the hell was he going to get through one night of being in the same room and not being able to make love to her, let alone three?

"Nate, could you please check to see if there are extra pillows on the closet shelf?" Jessie asked as she came out of the bathroom several minutes later.

He did his best not to stare as she walked over to the bed to put the clothes she'd been wearing before her shower into her suitcase. The hot-pink nightshirt she wore wasn't even remotely sexy under normal circumstances. It hung all the way to her knees, was completely opaque and couldn't have been more shapeless. But that didn't seem to matter. Just knowing that she probably didn't have anything on under it besides her panties had him feeling like a range-raised stud seeing his first filly.

"Are you all right?" she asked when he continued to stare.

"Just peachy," he muttered, swallowing back a groan.

"Could you check the closet?" she asked again.

"Uh, right. Pillows." Focusing on her request, he looked inside the closet and shook his head. "No extras. Why do you need them?"

"I forgot to bring the wedge pillow," she said, frowning. "I always put that under the side of my stomach and another pillow against my back."

"You can use one of mine," he offered, knowing it wouldn't matter how many he had. He wasn't going to get any sleep anyway.

"Or you could call the front desk and have one sent up to the room," she suggested.

He shook his head. "I only need one anyway."

"Are you sure you don't mind?" She continued to rearrange her clothes in the suitcase. "You need your rest if you're going to compete tomorrow."

If he hadn't found the situation so dismal, he might have laughed at her erroneous assumption that he'd be able to relax enough to sleep. But there wasn't anything funny about being aroused for a week. He had finally broken down and found his own relief, but that was always hollow and only relieved his physical discomfort. It did absolutely nothing to alleviate the emptiness he felt not having Jessie in his arms.

"I think I'm going to take a shower now," he said, unsure of how many more cold showers his traumatized body could endure. Grabbing a change of underwear from his duffel bag, he motioned toward the bed he knew for certain he would lie awake in for the entire night. "Go ahead and take both pillows if you need to."

He hoped by the time he got out of the shower, Jessie was in bed, covered up to her ears and sound asleep. When he came back into the room ten minutes later with his teeth chattering like a set of fake choppers from a novelty shop, he shoved his clothes into his duffel bag and turned to find her snuggled up in a nest of bed pillows. Unfortunately, she was still wide awake.

"Can't...sleep?" he asked, trying not to shiver.

"I can't get comfortable," she said, sitting up.

He frowned. "Is something wrong with the bed?"

She shook her head as she punched the pillow she'd

had at her back. "No, the bed is fine. It's the pillows. They're too soft. They flatten out when I lean back against them."

"Is this a pregnancy thing?" he asked, wondering if it was for her comfort or had something to do with the health of the baby.

"Yes," she said, punching the pillow again before she gave up and tossed it back onto his bed. "Since I'm on my feet so much when I'm working at the hospital, I'm trying to make sure I protect and rest my back muscles as much as possible."

"Is that because your stomach is getting bigger?" he asked, figuring the bigger a woman got the more extra strain it put on her back.

Nodding, she pushed her silky blond hair out of her eyes. "And I've already started wearing a maternity support belt when I work."

He wasn't even going to speculate on how that little jewel was worn or what it did. Just the name of it suggested that something was uncomfortable. The thought that he was responsible for Jessie experiencing any discomfort made him feel guilty.

"I'm sorry, darlin'," he said, sitting down on the side of her bed.

She looked confused. "What are you apologizing for?"

"If I hadn't made you pregnant, you wouldn't be having all these problems with your back," he said, feeling a lot like a fish out of water. He really needed to research what she was going through and what he could do to help make things easier.

Instead of accepting his heartfelt gesture, she laughed. "Nate, I'm not having back issues. Yet. What I'm doing now is preventive." Smiling, she placed her hand on his forearm, sending a shockwave coursing throughout his body. "And even if I do start having backaches in the last few months of my pregnancy, it will all be worth it once I hold the baby."

The realization that she was looking forward to having his baby, instead of viewing the unplanned pregnancy as a mistake, caused a warm feeling to spread throughout his chest. "You really mean that, don't you?"

"Of course," she said, placing her hand on her rounded stomach. "Why wouldn't I?"

He shrugged. "Since I wasn't exactly your favorite person when you discovered you were pregnant, I wasn't sure how you'd feel."

"No matter what happened in the past or will happen in the future, it doesn't change the way I feel about our baby," she said, her tone serious. "I might not have planned this, but I've loved this child since the moment I learned I was carrying her."

"Or him," he said, grinning. "We won't know the gender for another week."

"As long as he or she is healthy, I really don't care," she said firmly.

Staring at her, he surprised both of them when he motioned toward the middle of the bed. "Move over."

"Nate—"

"I'm going to be your back support," he said, easily lifting her to the center of the mattress.

All things considered, he was probably out of his mind to think that he could hold her all night without losing what little sense he had left. But she needed her rest and he was going to see that she got it, no matter what kind of hell he had to go through.

When he stretched out beside her, Nate turned onto his side, then pulled her back against his bare chest. "Is that comfortable?" he asked as she arranged one of the pillows under the side of her belly.

"Yes, thank you." She suddenly went perfectly still. "Why are you so cold?"

"I had to take a shower," he said truthfully.

"A cold one." Her tone indicated she knew exactly why. "Maybe you supporting my back isn't such a good idea." She sounded sleepy and not all that convincing.

"It feels good, doesn't it?" he asked, nuzzling the side of her neck. Her silky hair against his face felt like heaven and he didn't think twice about leaning over to kiss her cheek.

"Mmm-hmm," she murmured, snuggling into him.

"Then don't worry about it, darlin'," he said, feeling his body start to react. He took a deep breath and tried to relax. "Nothing is going to happen unless it's what you want, too."

"Even though it frightened me, I liked…watching you ride…today," she whispered sleepily. "You're very… good."

Before he could tell her that he was sorry he hadn't asked her to watch him before and that just knowing she was in the stands was all the incentive he needed to make a better ride, Nate could tell by her even breathing that she had fallen asleep. Kissing the side of her head, he closed his eyes and willed himself to relax.

Even though he wanted her more than he wanted his next breath, he could feel himself start to get sleepy and briefly wondered if he was just that exhausted or if it was due to the fact that he had her in his arms. But as he lay there enjoying her soft body against his, an unfamiliar protectiveness settled over him. And his last thought as he finally drifted off into the first peaceful sleep he'd had in a week, was that he would move heaven and earth to keep this woman in his life and in his bed, even if he was scared spitless that he was going to screw things up.

Five

On Sunday afternoon, Jessie sat in the rodeo grand-stand with Bria, Summer and their children, watching the bulls being loaded into the bucking chutes for the bull-riding event. Nate had made it through the past couple of days unscathed and won the right to compete in the final round. Now if he could just get through this ride without being hurt, she could breathe a little easier—at least until the next time he climbed onto the back of one of the ill-tempered beasts.

As she continued to watch the activity around the bucking chutes, Nate walked into view and her breath caught. He was without a doubt the sexiest cowboy she'd ever seen. Wearing a Western-cut red plaid shirt with the long sleeve rolled up to the biceps on his rid-ing arm to keep it from getting caught in the bull rope, her heart skipped a beat. His muscles were strong, well-defined and felt absolutely wonderful wrapped around her as they slept.

Thinking about the past two nights, her chest tightened with emotion at how solicitous he had been. Each night he had let her rest her back against his chest and snuggle close to him. And she knew what a sacrifice that had been on his part. She'd felt his arousal several times against the back of her upper thighs, but he'd been a perfect gentleman and hadn't tried to coerce her into making love. He'd told her nothing would happen unless she wanted it to and he had been true to his word. The only problem was, she had struggled both nights to keep from turning to him, to once again feel the strength of his lovemaking.

It was so tempting to throw caution to the wind and give in to what she knew they both wanted. But she had to stay strong, and not just for her or the baby's sake. She had to consider the effect it would have on Nate as well. She could tell he was trying so hard to make this work between them—something that he'd never done before. If they made love again and he discovered that he couldn't commit to anything long-term, she knew for certain he would end up hating himself for hurting her again. Rather than allow that to happen, it was better for all concerned if they didn't go there at all.

"Nate's up next," Bria said, bringing Jessie out of her musings.

"What kind of temperament does the bull have that he'll be riding?" she asked, hoping the animal wasn't as mean as some of the others she'd seen.

Bria winced. "I'm afraid the bull he's riding is known for wanting to hook a rider with his horns."

Jessie gasped. "Please tell me you're joking."

"Don't worry, Jessie," Summer said, grabbing her hand to give it a gentle squeeze. "Ryder will be there to turn the bull when it's time for Nate to dismount safely."

Unable to take her eyes off Nate climbing over the side of the chute to ease himself down onto the back of the bull, Jessie could only nod as she continued to hold Summer's hand. Her gaze riveted on him, she held her breath when he leaned back slightly, gave a short nod of his head to signal he was ready and the gate to the chute swung open wide.

The bull immediately jumped straight up, then bumped into the chute as it bucked its way out into the arena. Lurching and twisting, the animal seemed to pull out all the stops to get the man off its back before it settled into a dizzying spin as if chasing its own tail. When Nate started to slip sideways, Jessie was certain her heart quit beating until he managed to straighten himself back onto the middle of the animal's broad back.

When the horn blared, signaling the eight seconds were up, everything seemed to move in agonizingly slow motion. Ryder ran forward to gain the bull's attention so that Nate could dismount, but she knew instantly that something was wrong. He continued to hold on to the bull rope as he slid to the bull's side.

Jumping to her feet, she covered her mouth with her hand to hold back her scream. Terror like she'd never known flowed through every vein in her body at the sight of Nate being dragged like a rag doll while the bull continued to buck. She wanted to do something to get Nate away from the furious animal, but all she could do was watch helplessly as Ryder ran along on the opposite side of the bull, trying to free Nate's hand from the rope.

"Nate's gone down in the well," Bria said, her expression worried. "He's hung up in the bull rope and can't get to his feet."

Both Bria and Summer were used to seeing all kinds of things go wrong during the rough-stock events and if the women were upset, Jessie knew it had to be bad.

Another bullfighter did his best to distract the beast as Ryder worked to untangle Nate's hand, but when it finally slipped free and he slumped to his knees on the dirt floor of the arena, Nate didn't get up and sprint to the fence like he'd done after his other rides. While the other bullfighter managed to entice the bull away from Nate, she watched Ryder kneel down beside him and Jaron run over from the chutes to see what was wrong. Her heart sank when Ryder and Jaron both motioned for the Justin Heelers to enter the arena.

Knowing the medical team would get him out of the arena and take him to a triage area to assess his injury, Jessie turned to Summer. "Where will they take him?"

"Follow me," Summer said, picking up her daughter's diaper bag and starting down the steps of the grandstand. As a former public relations director for the rodeo association, she led them to the area behind the chutes where several officials stood. "Where's the training room?"

"Sorry ma'am, but y'all can't go back there," one of the older men said, shaking his head. "It's authorized personnel only."

"Try and stop me," Jessie stated determinedly.

"If you need authorization, talk to Sam Rafferty about his wife and sisters-in-law going into the training room to check on his injured brother," Bria said, stepping forward. "I'm sure he'll tell you that it would be highly inadvisable to try to stop us. Now get out of the way."

The man looked at the two women holding sleeping babies, then at Jessie, who was obviously pregnant. He immediately stepped out of their path, having decided it wasn't worth the fight. "It's the second door to the right, Ms. Rafferty," he called after them as they hurried down the corridor.

When they reached the training room, Summer motioned toward an open door down the hall. "We'll wait for you in the press room."

"Thank you," Jessie said before hurrying in.

Entering the training room, Jessie was relieved to see Nate sitting up on a cot with his legs stretched out in front of him. One of the medical staff was using a pair of scissors to cut the right leg of his jeans from the hem up to the knee. When the man peeled back the blood-soaked denim, she could see that Nate had a deep laceration on his calf, but otherwise looked to be all right.

"I'm fine, Jessie," Nate said quickly when he looked up and saw her.

"What happened?" she asked as her gaze traveled from his head to his feet to make sure the cut was his only injury.

"My leg got caught between Whiplash and the latch on the gate when he left the chute." He shrugged. "It isn't the first time I've needed stitches after a ride."

If she could have gotten closer to him, she would have bopped him on top of the head. She had been worried to death about his welfare and he was dismissing the incident as no big deal.

"How does your arm feel?" she asked, knowing that it had been under a major strain when he was hung up in the rope.

"It'll be okay." He winced when he tried, but failed to lift it above his head. "It's sore, but nothing that an ice pack won't fix."

"You're lucky it wasn't dislocated at the shoulder." She made it over to a chair in the corner to sit down when her knees began to wobble. Now that she'd seen Nate was going to be all right, the adrenaline started to wear off and she was as weak as a newborn kitten. "And don't you dare say it wouldn't be the first time you had a shoulder injury," she warned. "It's the first time I've ever seen you get hurt and it's a very big deal for me."

He stared at her for a moment before asking the man cleaning the wound on his leg to give them a moment. "Come here, darlin'." When she walked over to him, he pulled her down next to him. "Jessie, I'm sorry. I forgot that this weekend was the first time you've seen me ride. Are you all right? You aren't so upset that it's causing you problems, are you?"

"I think I was frightened out of at least a year or two of my life, but other than that, I'm okay," she assured him.

He used his index finger to lift her chin until their eyes met. "I'm going to be just fine. A few stitches or a dislocation are just part of being a rodeo rider."

Before she could tell him how glad she was that he hadn't been seriously injured, he leaned in close and the moment his mouth covered hers, she forgot all about the rodeo, bulls or where they were. All she could do was feel the warmth flowing through her from being held by him again.

When he deepened the kiss she put her arms around his neck and, kissing him back, instantly felt a need begin to build inside her that only Nate could ease. She wanted to once again feel his strength surround her and feel the gentle power of his lovemaking.

"Well, I see that you can't be too bad off," Ryder said, laughing.

At the sound of Nate's brother's voice, Jessie tried to pull away from him, but he tightened his arms around her to hold her to him. "Thanks for saving my bacon out there, bro. I owe you one."

"All in a day's work," Ryder said, walking over to get a chemical ice pack from one of the shelves. "They don't call me Dances With Bulls for nothing. But you're wrong about owing me one. It's more like you owe me a dozen or so."

"Who won the round?" Nate asked.

"Jaron took first and you got second," Ryder said, activating the ice pack to place it on his knee. After wrapping an Ace bandage around it to hold it in place, he started toward the door. "He and Sam will be coming to see about you as soon as Sam makes sure his wranglers get the livestock loaded up and Jaron collects your and his winnings from the pay window."

When the doctor walked back into the room, Jessie stepped away from the cot. "I'm going to go find Bria and Summer while the doctor finishes cleaning your leg and sutures the laceration." It was a good excuse to escape and regain her equilibrium. Turning back, she advised the doctor, "While you're at it, you might want to check his shoulder. I think it might be partially separated."

"She's a registered nurse down in Waco," Nate said when the doctor raised an eyebrow. "If she says to check it out, you'd probably better do it."

The doctor nodded. "An observant nurse is worth her weight in gold."

"I'll see you in a little bit, darlin'," he said, giving her a look that made her insides feel as if they had turned to warm pudding.

As she walked down the hall to the media room where Summer and Bria waited, Jessie knew that she was quickly approaching the point with Nate where she was going to have to make a decision. She was either going to have to trust that Nate wouldn't lose interest in her this time and resume their relationship, or end things between them for good before she lost her heart to him completely. And no matter how many times she told herself to stay strong, she knew it wasn't going to do any good.

Unfortunately, she was afraid the die had already been cast. If she wasn't already head over heels in love with him again, she didn't have far to fall.

"Jessie, I swear I've got this," Nate said, refusing to allow a woman to carry her own luggage. Especially one who was five months pregnant. His foster father would roll over in his grave if Hank knew one of the boys he finished raising wasn't sticking to the Cowboy Code, even if it was because of an injured shoulder and a gimpy leg.

"Nate, you didn't want me driving the three hundred miles from Amarillo after you took pain medication, but I managed that." She gave him a pointed look. "Trust me, I'm perfectly capable of carrying at least one of the two small overnight cases."

Dropping both of their bags, Nate wrapped his good arm around her and kissed her until they both gasped for breath. "Give it up, darlin'. I'm getting the luggage. You just open the door for me."

She stared at him for several seconds before she sighed. "All right. But when we get into the house, I want you in bed with that leg elevated and ice on your shoulder. You don't want to make things worse by ignoring doctor's orders."

"Is this Jessie the bossy nurse talking?" he asked, grinning as he bent down to pick up both bags with his good arm.

"Yes." She opened the door leading from the garage into the mudroom. "And you're going to find out just how mean and bossy I can be if you don't do what I tell you."

"Do you want to play nurse and patient after we go to bed?" he teased as they walked into the kitchen. "I can let you adjust my arm sling and check my stitches right after you give me a bed bath."

Rolling her eyes she shook her head. "You're incorrigible."

"You can't blame a guy for trying," he said, laughing.

"Nate, being injured is serious," she said, turning to frown at him. "If you don't take care of your shoulder, you could cause permanent damage to the tendons and ligaments."

"Shh. You'll wake Rosemary," he said, knowing that a bomb could go off outside her bedroom and the woman would snore her way right through it.

He had hoped to divert Jessie's attention. The tactic failed.

"I still don't see why we couldn't have spent the night in Amarillo and come back here in the morning as we'd planned to do," she whispered as they walked down the hall and started up the stairs.

"I have approximately three weeks to get this shoulder straightened out before National Finals in Las Vegas," he explained when they reached their rooms. "I've got a physical therapist on retainer and he can be here tomorrow morning to start my rehab exercises. I want to get the jump on this because if I don't I might as well skip Vegas and stay home."

"You've been hurt so many times you have a concierge physical therapist?" she asked, her expression disbelieving as she opened the bedroom door. "How did I not know that?"

"I guess I just got hurt during the times when we weren't seeing each other," he said evasively, carrying her bag over to set it on the bed. He didn't want to tell her that several of the times he had been injured it had been right after he broke things off with her and he'd had his mind on her instead of being focused on his riding.

She started to dig through her suitcase, presumably for her nightshirt. "Well, don't forget to prop your leg up and put ice on your shoulder for about twenty minutes before you go to sleep."

Setting his duffel bag on the floor, he reached for her. "I'm going to need your help," he said, pulling her to him.

"What on earth for?" she asked, sounding delightfully breathless.

"I have a registered nurse staying with me and you expect me to do all this medical stuff on my own?" he asked, kissing the satiny skin along the side of her neck. He nibbled at the hollow behind her ear. "I think you should sleep with me in my bed tonight so you can take care of me and make sure I'm all right."

"Really? You're going to use that excuse?" she asked, shivering against him.

He nodded. "I might not get the pillow in the right position when I prop up my leg. Or the ice pack might slip off my shoulder and I wouldn't be able to put it back in the right spot."

She leaned back to look up at him. "Nate, I don't think—"

"I served as your backrest for the past two nights," he reminded her.

"That's not fair," she said, her expression not nearly as disapproving as he was sure she meant it to be. "Those pancakes the hotel was passing off as pillows were too flat to serve as any kind of support."

"I can't help it if I got used to holding you while we sleep," he said, tracing his finger down her delicate cheek. "Besides, darlin', I hate to admit it, but I'm hurting too bad right now to do anything anyway. And once I take another pain pill, I'll be zonked out in no time." When she began to nibble on her lower lip, he knew she was going to give in. "Come on, Jessie. Didn't you like being snuggle buddies?" He used his thumb to stop her from worrying her lip, then gave her a gentle kiss. "I know I sure liked it."

She closed her eyes and nodded. "All right. But just for tonight."

"Why don't we just take it one day at a time and see how long I need you with me?" he suggested, knowing that once he got her in his bed he intended to make sure she stayed there.

"Nate, where is your arm sling?" Jessie asked when she sat down on the couch and noticed that he wasn't wearing the stabilizer.

"I've graduated to Kinesio tape," he answered

proudly. He stopped watching the crime show on the big-screen TV in his media room to lift the sleeve of his T-shirt. Two strips of the brightly colored support tape used by a lot of athletes ran from his shoulder down to his biceps. He was fortunate that it had only been a partial separation and not a complete dislocation or a break. And she was certain the injection the doctor had given him to reduce inflammation had helped tremendously.

"I've always been amazed by how fast a good physical therapist is able to get results," she said, happy to hear Nate was progressing so quickly. It had only been five days since Max, his physical therapist, had showed up to start working with Nate on his rehab exercises. "Does he think you'll be ready to take part in the National Finals next month?"

Nate smiled. "Yup. Max says I'll be ready a few days before I have to be in Vegas. That will give me a chance to ride a couple of Sam's practice bulls to get back in the swing of things."

Jessie forced a smile. "That's nice. You'll have to tell me all about the finals when you get back." It was a complete lie. She didn't want to think about him riding another ornery animal—not even for practice— or that he might get hurt again while he was doing it.

"I won't have to tell you about it," he said, smiling as he shook his head. "You'll be right there with me."

She stared at him for endless seconds and tried to stay calm. "I really don't think I can do that, Nate," she said, choosing her words carefully.

He frowned. "Why not, darlin'?"

"I'll be working at the hospital in Waco by then," she said, thinking quickly. "And I can't use any more of my vacation days or else I won't have any extra time to take off when the baby is born."

"Don't worry about time off without a paycheck," Nate replied as if it didn't matter that she wouldn't have money to pay her rent. "I'll take care of whatever you and the baby need."

"Excuse me?" She wasn't sure she had heard him correctly. "You're absolutely not going to pay my bills." It would make her feel like a kept woman to have him taking care of her expenses.

"Calm down, Jessie." He took her hands in his. "I'm just telling you that I want to make sure you have as much time with the baby as you'd like before you go back to work. I know how important that is to you and I'm going to make sure that it happens."

It was true that she was determined to keep her financial independence, but there was more to her reaction than that. The main reason she was so upset had nothing whatsoever to do with her going back to work or him paying for her to stay home with the baby. It was all about his week and a half at the rodeo National Finals in Las Vegas and the danger he would face on the meanest bulls the stock contractors had to offer. Not to mention that she was overly tense from the frustration of spending every night lying in bed with him snuggled against her. Since their night in Amarillo the longing had built inside her and she felt as tightly wound as a coiled spring.

"Can we discuss this later?" she asked suddenly.

If they continued to talk about it, she was afraid she would end up telling him the real reason she wouldn't be going to watch him ride—that she was scared to death she'd see the man she was falling for get hurt again or worse.

Nate continued to stare at her for a moment before he finally nodded and put his arms around her. "I don't want you to worry, Jessie—not about having extra time with the baby or about me getting hurt when I'm riding the bulls. Stress isn't good for you or the baby."

She didn't even try to correct him about his assumption that she was frightened he would be injured again. They'd both know she would be lying if she did.

"That's easy for you to say. You aren't the one having to watch and know that there's nothing you can do to stop the disaster happening right before your eyes," she said, giving up all pretense about what the real issue was that had her so upset. "You weigh about a hundred and seventy pounds. Those bulls weigh two thousand. When it comes right down to it, who do you think will be the first to break?"

He leaned back to look at her. "Are you telling me you want me to quit?"

Upset and unable to sit still, she rose to her feet to pace the room. What did she want? Nothing would please her more than to know he was never going to risk his life on the back of another one of the vile animals. But just because she wanted that, didn't mean it was right for him. That was his decision to make, not hers.

She took a deep, steadying breath. "I would never

ask you to do that, Nate. You're a bull rider. It's what you do. It's who you are. And I know you're good at it."

He continued to sit on the couch, staring at her. "You've always known I ride the rough stock, Jessie. I told you that up front the day we met."

She stopped pacing to look directly at him. "Knowing what you do is one thing. Watching you do it is something else entirely."

"I understand you're concerned that I might get hurt," he said calmly. "But I know what I'm doing, darlin'. I've been riding bulls for almost twenty years and I'll admit that I've had a few close calls. But in all that time I've only been seriously injured once."

As far as she was concerned that was one time too many. But she refrained from telling him that. She still wasn't sure where things were going with them and didn't feel she had the right to ask him to give up riding, even though her heart was telling her that was exactly what she wanted. If he quit, it had to be because it was what he wanted. Not because it was something she wanted him to do.

"I understand that, Nate." She shook her head. "I'm just telling you I can't watch you."

He got up from the couch to walk over and put his arms around her. "Why does the possibility of seeing me get hurt bother you so much, Jessie?"

His deep baritone and the feel of being wrapped in his strong arms caused tears to fill her eyes. Unwilling for him to see how emotional she was about the subject, she laid her head against his broad chest.

"I don't like seeing anyone hurt, Nate," she hedged.

"Being a nurse, I've seen how truly fragile the human body can be."

"You didn't answer my question, darlin'," he persisted, kissing the top of her head. "What bothers you so much about the idea of me being hurt?"

She knew what he wanted her to say—knew that he wanted her to reveal how she truly felt about him. But she wasn't ready for that. She wasn't ready to admit, even to herself, just how much he really meant to her. If she did that and he didn't feel the same way about her, she would only be opening the door for more heartbreak. She had done that too many times before and each time she had been devastated when it didn't work out between them. The last time, she hadn't been sure she would make it until she discovered she was pregnant. And as crazy as it sounded even to her, she had taken comfort in the fact that if she couldn't have Nate in her life, she would at least have his child.

"I think I'm going to go upstairs," she said pulling from his arms. She needed time to come to terms with the fact that she was so very close to falling in love with him again—if she hadn't already. "I'm really tired and I'd like to be rested up for the drive down to Waco tomorrow to have the ultrasound."

Walking from the media room without looking back, Jessie knew Nate watched her leave. She was grateful that he hadn't tried to stop her, even if a small part of her was disappointed that he hadn't.

Six

Sitting in the waiting room next to Jessie, Nate watched several pregnant women and their partners being called back to the examination rooms and wondered if the guys felt as clueless about all this as he did. He'd done a little research on the internet about what a woman went through as the baby grew inside her and how her body changed, but he couldn't say it felt all that real to him.

Maybe he hadn't come to terms with the fact that he was going to be a daddy. He still couldn't feel the baby move when Jessie told him to put his hand on her rounded stomach. When was a man supposed to feel a deep emotional connection with his baby? Was he the only guy to feel like he was part of something that he couldn't quite get a handle on? Or was he destined to be like his biological father—a man who was incapable of feeling anything that didn't benefit him in some way or hadn't come out of a whiskey-soaked haze?

The thought that he might turn out to be cut from the same cloth as his worthless father was Nate's worst nightmare. Joe Rafferty had been an abject failure at being a husband and father, and the day he walked out to leave his two sons on their own after their mother died had been the luckiest day of their lives.

They'd had to resort to armed robbery just to survive. But even that had turned out to be a lucky break for them. After getting caught, they had been placed in the care of Hank Calvert and during their stay at the Last Chance Ranch, they'd learned what it meant to be honest, law-abiding men.

His brother Sam had turned out to be a great husband and father despite the early example their father had set for them. But Nate had yet to prove himself. Could he live up to the standard his brother had set? Could he be the man he'd always hoped he would be?

"Jessica Farrell?" a woman in a white lab coat called from the door leading back to the examination rooms.

Brought back to the present, Nate rose to his feet and took Jessie's hand in his as they walked down a hall to the room where the ultrasound would be done. He had no idea what he was supposed to do, but he figured holding her hand for moral support was a good start.

"I'm Dr. Evans," the woman said, introducing herself to Nate.

"Nate Rafferty, ma'am," he said, removing his Resistol and extending his hand.

The doctor smiled as she shook his hand. "Are you two ready to find out if you're having a boy or girl?"

"I've been waiting for this day since I discovered I was pregnant," Jessie answered, sounding excited as they entered a small room.

When the doctor looked at Nate expectantly, he didn't know what else to do but nod. He wasn't about to explain that he had only learned about the baby a couple of weeks ago or that he hadn't quite wrapped his mind around the idea that he'd fathered a child.

"If you'll help Jessica up on the table, we'll get started and take the first pictures of your baby," the doctor said, closing the door and seating herself on a stool beside a machine with a small television screen. "Dad, you can stand on the other side of the table in order to get a better view of the screen."

Helping Jessie up onto the small bed, he took his place where the doctor had indicated as he tried to take in the woman's use of the term *dad*. But before he had the chance to let that sink in, Jessie raised her red maternity top and eased her slacks down to reveal her stomach. He had felt the firm bump when he held her against him and the few times he'd put his hand on it when he'd try to feel the baby move, but she hadn't actually shown her stomach to him. He'd seen her beautiful body many times before, but that had been before she'd become pregnant. Was she self-conscious now about the changes in her body?

She had no reason to be. She was more beautiful now than he'd ever seen her.

When Dr. Evans squeezed some clear jellylike stuff

from a tube onto Jessie's stomach, then picked up something that looked like a microphone, Nate reached down to take hold of Jessie's hand. He wasn't sure if it was for her moral support or his. All he knew was that it felt as if he was about to witness something very profound and something that would change his life forever.

With the first touch of the instrument to the clear gel on Jessie's stomach, the screen displayed a shadowy image. For the life of him, Nate had no idea what he was supposed to be looking at.

As the doctor continued to slide it around on Jessie's abdomen, she pointed to the machine. "There's your baby's profile," she said, smiling.

His gaze riveted to the screen, Nate's breath lodged in his lungs when he recognized a little head and an arm and leg. The world suddenly seemed to stand stock-still and reality hit him right square between the eyes. That was his baby he was watching—the child he had made with Jessie.

He glanced down at her lying on the table. Tears had filled her violet eyes and the most beautiful smile he'd ever seen curved her perfect lips. At that moment, he wasn't entirely sure he didn't have a tear or two trying to escape his own eyes.

"Does everything look all right?" Jessie asked.

"Everything looks just fine," Dr. Evans assured her, nodding. "It appears that your baby is right on target for a twenty-week-old fetus, both in size and development."

"That's wonderful," Jessie said as one of her tears slowly trickled down her lightly flushed cheek. He gently wiped it away with his index finger, earning a smile from her. "Is the baby turned so that you can see the gender?" she asked.

Dr. Evans moved the probe around a moment before she grinned. "Well, it looks like you're going to be buying a lot of pink and purple. There's no doubt about it, this baby is most definitely a little girl."

"I'm having a girl," Jessie murmured like she couldn't quite believe it.

When she looked up at him with such excitement and wonder on her face, he didn't think twice about lowering his head to kiss her with all the emotion he was feeling but couldn't put a name to. At that moment, Nate felt like beating his chest and doing the Tarzan yell. He was going to be a daddy and it suddenly became more important than ever to make sure Jessie and the baby stayed with him—not just for the rest of the month or the first year of the baby's life. He wanted them with him from now on.

He had to get past his concern of turning out like his miserable old man and be there for them through thick and thin—to protect them and take care of them.

"I'll get some pictures ready for you," Dr. Evans said quietly as she handed Jessie some tissues to wipe away the remaining gel. She clearly knew how special the moment was and didn't want to intrude.

Once Jessie had cleaned away the last traces of the gel and rearranged her clothes, Nate helped her off the table. "Is there anything else we need to do?" he asked.

"No. I'll see you in a couple of weeks for your regular appointment," the doctor answered as she handed Jessie the pictures and opened the door to precede them out into the hall. "And you know if you have any problems, I want you to call my office or go straight to the ER."

"What did she mean by that?" Nate asked. He didn't remember Jessie mentioning anything other than morning sickness in the early weeks of her pregnancy. "Is something wrong? Have you been having problems? Is there something we haven't been doing that we should?"

"Calm down," Jessie said as they walked out the doors of the clinic to his truck. "I haven't had any issues, nor do I expect any. And for that matter, neither does Dr. Evans. She frequently reminds all of her patients to seek medical attention if they do experience something out of the ordinary or that they're concerned about."

Nate breathed a little easier after Jessie's explanation, but it appeared he needed to put in a lot more time on the computer. There was a whole hell of a lot more he needed to learn about what a woman went through during pregnancy, not to mention what was happening with the baby. And the sooner he got started the better.

"Did you get finished doing whatever you needed to do on the computer?" Jessie asked Nate when they walked into the media room after dinner. From the time they returned from having the ultrasound in Waco until just before dinner, he had been sequestered in his office, working on what she assumed to be ranch business.

"Not quite," he said, picking up the remote from the coffee table.

"Is there anything I can help you with?" she offered as she sat down on the couch.

Turning on the television, he shook his head. "I've only got a few more things I need to read up on." He sat down beside her and put his arms around her. "Have I told you lately how beautiful you are?"

"Where did that come from?" she asked, laughing self-consciously. "How did we go from talking about what you're doing on your computer to how you think I look?"

His sexy grin made her feel warm all over. "I turned the computer off, darlin'." He kissed her forehead, cheek and the tip of her nose. "But seeing you sitting here looking so damned irresistible turns *me* on."

"It doesn't take much for that to happen," she teased, loving the look of appreciation in his dark blue eyes.

"You've always had that effect on me," he said, his expression turning serious. He brought his hand up to cup her cheek. "From the first time I met you, I wanted you." He lightly brushed her lips with his. "You excite me in ways that I could have never imagined."

The sincerity in his tone and the desire in his eyes stole her breath. Over the past week she had lain in his strong arms each night, felt the evidence of his need and known the toll it had to be taking on him. For that matter, it had become exceedingly more difficult for her as well. She longed to once again have him join their bodies, to feel the exquisite power of his lovemaking and bask in the intimacy of being one with the man who meant so much to her.

When Nate lowered his head to cover her mouth with his, it didn't occur to her to resist. She wanted his kiss, wanted to lose herself in his gentle caress. As his lips moved over hers, she lifted her arms to thread her fingers in the light brown hair at the nape of his neck and gave herself up to the feelings only he could awaken in her.

A delicious warmth spread throughout her body when he deepened the kiss to stroke her inner recesses with such tenderness it made her feel as if she might melt into a puddle. She had always responded to his mastery, but each time he kissed her, the need inside of her became more intense than anything she could ever remember.

Tightening his arms around her, he took her with him when he stretched out on the couch and, partially lying on top of him, she immediately felt his arousal as it strengthened with every beat of his heart. Her own body answered with an empty ache deep in the most feminine part of her. Whether it was due to the fact that they had shared a very poignant moment during the ultrasound or due to her crazy pregnancy hormones, she wanted nothing more than for him to make her his once again.

She knew she would have to put aside all of the things that had been holding her back and that she might very well end up getting her heart broken again. But as one of her coworkers always said, the heart wants what it wants. And her heart wanted Nate.

"I think we'd better…stop this before I do something that's sure to…get me into big trouble," Nate said, sounding as short of breath as she felt. He moved her to his side and turned to face her. "Right now, I want you more than I want my next breath and as bad as I hate to say this, it might be best for you to sleep across the hall tonight."

The warmth inside her increased and her pulse raced. "Is that what you want me to do?"

"Hell, no!" He laughed as he shook his head. "What I'd like to do is to take you upstairs right now, remove every stitch of your clothes and spend the entire night making love to every inch of your delightful body."

Her heart skipped a beat and she had to remind herself to breathe. "Then why don't you?" she asked before she could stop herself.

A deep groan rumbled up from his chest a moment before he leaned back to look at her. "Jessie, I'm not in any shape right now to be a gentleman. The past week has done a real number on my nobility and willpower. If you don't mean what you just said, then it would be a real good idea to put some distance between us right about now."

Reaching up, she cupped his lean cheeks with her hands. "I don't want to move away from you, Nate. I want to be so close to you that our hearts beat as one."

He closed his eyes for a moment and she watched a nerve jerk along his jaw. "Are you sure about this?"

"Yes," she said decisively. She would face whatever consequences her actions caused later. At the moment, being in Nate's arms, having him love her as only he could was all that mattered.

"Let's go upstairs, darlin'," he said, getting up to help her from the couch.

Neither spoke as they walked out of the media room, across the foyer and up the stairs. Words were unnecessary. They both knew what they were about to do was the next step in resuming their relationship and whether it worked out for them or not, Jessie knew in her heart she would regret it for the rest of her life if she didn't give them the chance to find out.

He put his arm around her shoulders as they went down the hall to the master suite and once the door was closed behind them, he took her in his arms for a kiss that left her weak in the knees. When she sagged against him, Nate swung her up in his arms to carry her across the sitting area to the king-size bed.

"From what I've read, it should be safe for us to make love," he said, setting her on her feet. He reached up to trace her jaw with his index finger. "But I want to make sure, darlin'. Did Dr. Evans mention anything that might indicate we shouldn't?"

"No." His concern was touching. "As long as we aren't rough, everything should be fine."

He chuckled as he lifted her maternity top up and over her head. "No wild, swing-from-the-rafters-like-a-monkey kind of sex, huh?"

She smiled. "I don't recall you and I ever engaging in anything like that before."

Shaking his head, he kissed her collarbone as he unfastened the clasp of her bra. "That's never been my style, darlin'. I've always preferred taking my time and loving every inch of you."

A shiver of anticipation coursed through her as he slid the lacy straps from her shoulders and tossed it aside. "I've always thought your body was beautiful," he said, his tone husky as he cupped her breasts in his calloused palms.

She knew her body looked vastly different than it had the last time he'd seen it and although she felt sexy and took pride in her impending motherhood, she had heard that some men found it to be a turnoff. "A lot of things have changed because of the pregnancy," she said, feeling a little self-conscious.

"I noticed that at the doctor's office today," he said, nodding. When he kissed each of her breasts, then raised his head, the look in his eyes made her feel like the most cherished woman alive. "Maybe it's because it's my baby you're carrying, but I've never seen you look more beautiful than you do right now."

His heartfelt compliment caused a lump of emotion to clog her throat and she raised up on tiptoes to press a kiss to the steady pulse at the base of his neck. "You look pretty good yourself, cowboy," she said, loving the look of sincere appreciation in his dark blue eyes.

She had always thought Nate was the sexiest, best-looking man she'd ever met and no matter how many problems they'd had in the past couple of years, that hadn't changed. Something told her it never would.

Kneeling in front of her, he removed her slippers, then his gaze captured hers as he hooked his thumbs in the waistband of her maternity jeans to slowly, carefully lower them and her panties. Jessie braced her hands on his wide shoulders as she stepped out of the garments and watched him toss them on top of the rest of her clothes.

Her breath caught when he placed his hands on either side of her stomach and leaned forward to kiss the taut skin. "You've always been the sexiest woman I've ever known." There was a reverence in his voice that left no doubt in her mind he meant every word he said.

Rising to his full height, he reached for the lapels on his chambray shirt, but stepping forward, Jessie brushed his hands away to stop him. "Let me."

He nodded. "I'm all yours, darlin'."

She unfastened the snap closures to press her lips to the newly exposed skin. "I love your body," she said as she continued kissing her way down his chest. By the time she reached the well-defined muscles of his abdomen, his breathing sounded extremely labored. Glancing up, she asked, "Are you all right?"

His charming grin sent a wave of heat flowing through her veins. "If I was any better, I'm not all that sure I could stand it."

When she tugged his shirt from his jeans and pushed it off his shoulders, she placed her hands on his broad chest. "I love how hard your muscles are," she said, touching the thick pads of his pecs.

He shuddered when she used her index finger to trace each flat male nipple. "Keep that up and the show will be over before we ever get started," he said, capturing her hands in his. "I promise that next time you can take off all of my clothes," he said, stepping back to unfasten the button at the waistband of his jeans. He quickly removed his boots and, carefully unzipping his fly, shoved the denim and his boxer briefs to his ankles. Stepping out of them, he kicked them toward the pile of clothes on the floor. "It's just been too damned long since I made love to you, darlin',” he said, reaching for her.

The feel of his hair-roughened male flesh meeting her softer feminine skin sent a wave of need from the top of her head all the way to the tips of her toes. It seemed as if it had been an eternity since Nate had held her body to his without the encumbrance of clothing and she longed for an even closer connection.

“Please, Nate,” she said, trembling with desire to be one with him. “I...need you. Now.”

“Where?” he asked, brushing his lips over hers.

“Inside,” she whispered.

Without another word he lifted her to the middle of the bed then stretched out beside her. Taking her in his arms, he gave her a kiss that made her feel as if she might burn to a cinder.

“We may have to be a little creative with the position,” she whispered, hoping he understood. The changes in her body also dictated a change in the way they made love.

“That’s why you’re going to be on top this time,” he said, nibbling kisses along her collarbone a moment before he turned to his back. When he lifted her over him, the promise in his blue gaze caused her heart to beat double time. “We’ll figure out more positions later. Right now, I need to be inside you, darlin’.”

As she took him in, Jessie closed her eyes at the overwhelming feelings of joy spreading throughout her body from their coming together once again. She never felt as complete as she did when she and Nate made love, and she'd missed being part of something that felt so perfect, so right.

When she opened her eyes, he was looking at her with such tenderness that she teared up. "I've missed you, Jessie," he said, his voice hoarse with need as he cupped her face with his palms. "Take me with you, darlin'."

Unable to remain passive any longer, she began to move in a slow rhythmic motion against him. All too soon, the pleasurable tension holding them captive began to build toward the peak of fulfillment and Jessie tightened her body around him to prolong the enchantment.

Nate moved his hands to her hips and she could tell by the look on his handsome face that he was fighting the same battle she was. They both wanted their joining to last, but the lure of mutual satisfaction was too strong a force to resist.

All too soon the tight coil of need within her let go its grip and, crying his name, Jessie gave herself up to the waves of pleasure coursing through her. Her gratification must have triggered Nate's because she felt him surge into her one final time then hold her to him as he filled her with his essence.

When she collapsed on top of him, Nate gently lifted her to his side to wrap her in his strong arms. As he cradled her to him, she knew in her heart that she loved him—had never stopped loving him.

But as she floated back to reality, the uncertainty of their circumstances returned full force. Had she further complicated an already complex situation?

After watching the wonder on his face when they saw their baby for the first time on the ultrasound, she had no doubt that he would be a good father and always be there for their daughter. Unfortunately, she still had her doubts about him losing interest in his relationship with her. Everything was fine for now. But they had been down this road before. Things would be going great between them and he'd suddenly decide that they needed to take a break.

There was so much she was risking that it was overwhelming. She had laid her heart on the line again. What if Nate wasn't able to work out whatever issues he had about commitment? He had said he was ready to take that step and wanted them to get married, but of all the times he mentioned loving the baby, she couldn't remember a single time that he had mentioned loving her. Could she take that leap of faith, knowing that he might never give her his heart as fully as she gave hers to him?

And then there was the risk of his job. She wasn't sure her nerves could take watching him ride bulls, knowing what the price of a single mistake could be. She would never ask him to give up such a big part of who he was just because she was frightened of what might happen to him. But she wasn't sure she could live with the risk of him being seriously injured or worse.

"What's wrong, Jessie?" he asked gently, tipping her chin until their gazes met. "I didn't hurt you, did I?"

"No," she said, shaking her head.

"Then why are you crying?" he asked, wiping the moisture from her cheek.

"Th-that was beautiful," she said, thinking quickly. She hadn't even realized she was crying.

She wasn't exactly lying. Their lovemaking had always been meaningful. But she wasn't going to tell him that it wasn't the reason for her tears.

"You're beautiful," he said, smiling. He kissed her with a tenderness that caused a fresh wave of emotion to fill her eyes. When he raised his head, he frowned. "*Now* why are you crying?"

"P-pregnancy hormones," she stammered, not entirely sure they weren't partially responsible for her unsettled feelings.

He surprised her when he nodded. "I've heard they can cause mood swings."

"Where did you hear that?" she asked, grateful for the distraction from her earlier thoughts.

He chuckled as he tucked her to his side and reached to turn off the bedside lamp. "When my sisters-in-law were pregnant, my brothers all stashed tissues in their pockets like a miser stashes away cash."

Yawning, she nodded. "That was probably a good idea."

"I think I'll get a few of those pocket packs to carry with me the next time I go to town," Nate said, grinning.

"Another...good idea," she agreed as sleep began to overtake her.

Nate listened to Jessie's even breathing for several minutes to make sure she was asleep before he arranged a pillow behind her back for support and eased himself out of bed. Gathering his discarded clothes from the floor, he tossed them into the hamper before entering the bathroom for a quick shower.

Ten minutes later, he pulled on fresh jeans and a T-shirt, checked to make sure Jessie was still asleep and headed back downstairs to his office. He had spent the entire afternoon reading everything he could find online about pregnancy and a baby's development. There were a few more things he needed to check out before he felt like he might have a grasp of what he could do to make things easier for Jessie through the next several months as well as what he could expect during the baby's birth.

Picking up the pictures on his desk that the doctor had printed from the ultrasound, Nate stared at the image of his daughter. *His daughter.*

He swallowed hard. He was going to have a little girl. Just the thought caused his stomach to ache and his head to pound. When she got old enough to date, how in the hell was he going to keep teenage boys like he had been away from her?

A protectiveness suddenly came over him that he'd never experienced before. Now he understood what Ryder had meant about making sure he was cleaning his guns whenever Katie started dating and some pimple-faced boy came around the Blue Canyon Ranch to pay her a visit. Ryder was hoping just the sight of a couple of rifles and a shotgun or two would scare the kid into being a gentleman. Nate decided right then and there to file that idea away for future reference when his daughter got old enough for boys to start hanging around the Twin Oaks Ranch.

Turning on the computer, he took one last look at the image of his baby girl before propping it up against the monitor and opening the internet browser. He might be scared half out of his mind of all the things he would face being the father of a daughter, but he was going to protect Jessie and his little girl in every way he could. They were counting on him and he wasn't going to let them down. He was going to get his act together this time and do things the right way or die trying.

Seven

When Jaron dropped by the following afternoon, Nate took him to see the new herd of Black Angus cattle he and his men had moved to the south pasture a couple of weeks ago. "I'll be adding a herd of working horses after the first of the year." Nate propped his forearms on the gate as they watched the stock graze on the thick Bermuda grass.

"You'll need them," Jaron said, nodding. "When we were helping you stretch new fence last spring, I noticed you have a couple of places on the eastern side of the ranch that are so grown up with scrub and downed trees they're only accessible on horseback."

"Yeah, over the years storms have taken down a lot of trees and the previous owner wasn't all that interested in cleaning them up," Nate explained. "I've got clearing those areas on the to-do list for next spring and summer." He shrugged. "That's if there's enough time to get to them between cutting and putting up hay in the barn for next winter and everything else that we'll have to do."

"You know who to call if you need some extra hands to get it all done," Jaron stated. It didn't surprise Nate that Jaron had volunteered himself and the rest of their brothers to help out. All any of them had to do was pick up the phone and they would be there in a heart-beat to lend a hand.

"What about rodeo?" Nate asked. "The summer schedule is the busiest time on the circuit. How are you going to juggle competing and helping me get all this stuff done?"

"I'm going to cut way back on the number of events I enter this next year—if I compete at all." Shrugging one shoulder, Jaron gave a half smile. "The competi-tion is getting younger, the bulls are meaner and I'm looking at getting out before I get hurt too bad to enjoy my retirement."

Nate knew what his brother meant. He was thirty-three and Jaron was thirty-four. Once a rough stock rider turned thirty, the clock started to tick. Between the inevitable injuries, and the wear and tear of compe-tition taking a toll on a rider's body, he had five or so years left that he would be healthy enough to compete at the world-championship level. As with any other highly physical professional sport there were excep-tions to the rule. But not all that many.

"I've been giving it some serious thought the past

week or so myself and I'm thinking about hanging up my chaps and spurs after the finals this year," Nate said, staring out across the pasture. "I figure I'd rather go out a winner than a has-been."

Jaron nodded. "That's what I've been thinking. I'll bet Jessie's happy about your decision. I know she was pretty upset when you got roughed up in Amarillo."

"I haven't told her yet," Nate said, shaking his head. "But I don't think she'll be sorry to hear it." They were silent for a time before Nate admitted, "Finding out that I'm going to be a daddy has been a game changer for me. Jessie and the baby are going to need me and I'm determined I'm not going to let them down. I can't be there for them if I'm too gimped up to get around."

"I was wondering if that might not have played a big part in your decision," Jaron admitted.

Nate knew his brother would understand. Like Nate and Sam's, Jaron's father had been anything but a positive role model for his son.

"I know a lot of other riders have wives and kids and don't think twice about competing in the rough-stock events." Nate shook his head. "But you and I have watched a couple of friends die in past years because of wrecks in the arena and I want to make sure I don't put Jessie and our daughter through that."

"The baby is a girl?" Jaron asked, sounding incredulous. When Nate nodded, his brother threw back his head and laughed out loud. "After chasing skirts all these years it's only right that you have a little girl to worry about. Now you'll know what the fathers of all those women went through worrying about their daughters going out with you."

"Yeah, I thought about that." Nate groaned. "I'm pretty sure I'm already well on the way to developing an ulcer just thinking about some skinny-assed kid trying to get her into the back of his daddy's pickup truck for some star gazing."

"Karma's a bitch," Jaron said, grinning. The most serious one of his brothers, it was good to see the man enjoying himself, even if it was at Nate's expense.

"Don't laugh too hard, bro," Nate advised. "You know what Hank always told us about laughing at each other. The very thing you make fun of has a damned good chance of coming back to bite you in the butt." Nate grinned back at his brother. "Like you said. Karma's a bitch."

"Yeah, but unlike you, I didn't try to date the entire Southwest female population," Jaron shot back good-naturedly.

"Hey, in the past two and a half years I've only been with one woman," Nate pointed out. The realization that what he said was true caused the breath to lodge in his lungs. Even when they had broken up he hadn't wanted to date anyone else.

"You should have married Jessie a long time ago," Jaron said, voicing what Nate was sure all of his brothers had been thinking. "She's the only one you ever went back to. That should have told you something."

Nate nodded. "I had my reasons, the same as you have yours for trying to keep Mariah at arm's length."

"Yeah," Jaron agreed as they walked back to Nate's

truck. "I've got too much respect for her to saddle Mariah with that kind of baggage."

Nate knew what his brother meant. They had not only become brothers during their time at the Last Chance Ranch, they had become best friends. Nate was the only one who knew the whole truth about what Jaron had gone through as a kid and the crushing guilt the man carried because of it to this day.

When they returned to the ranch house, Nate followed Jaron as he walked over to get into his truck to leave. "If you don't mind, keep the news about the baby's gender under your hat for a while."

"Hey, it's your news to tell." Jaron chuckled. "Besides, I figure you probably want to avoid the rest of the brothers giving you what for when they find out you and Jessie are having a girl. At least for a while."

"Yeah, I'm going to be a major source of entertainment for you guys for quite some time to come," Nate said, laughing. "But look at it this way. If they're picking on me, they're leaving you alone."

That earned him a big grin from Jaron. "That's what I'm counting on, bro."

Two days after Jaron stopped by the ranch, Nate found himself strolling through the furniture department at one of the baby boutiques in Waco. He felt like a fish out of water looking at all the gadgets and things a baby needed. How could something that tiny need so much stuff?

"I never realized there were so many different styles

of baby beds," he said, stopping to look at a white crib and the one just like it in light oak. "Or colors."

Jessie nodded as she used the scanner the manager had given her to scan the UPC code for the gift registry she was setting up. "I think I'm going with the white furniture. I don't know why, but it seems more girlish than the natural wood."

"Yeah, that oak is about the same color as a baseball bat I used to have as a kid," he agreed. He mentally noted the color and style she liked. He knew a master furniture craftsman and fully intended to surprise her by having the entire ensemble custom made for the nursery.

"Funny you should mention that," she commented as she checked out a rocking chair that matched the white crib. "I had decided to decorate the nursery in a baseball theme if I found out I was having a boy."

"What are you going to use for the theme now that you know we're having a girl?" he asked, picking up a purple unicorn with a rainbow-colored horn.

"I can't decide between ponies or ballerinas," she answered. "Why?"

"I was just wondering if this is something that would go in the nursery and if you think the baby would like it," he said, holding up the stuffed toy for her inspection. "I've never been a unicorn type of guy, but this one kind of grows on you."

Jessie laughed. "I don't think we'll know for a while what she likes."

"I think I'll go ahead and get it," Nate said, tucking it under his arm. When Jessie gave him an indulgent smile, he felt a little self-conscious. "You know, just in case it turns out that she does like unicorns." He wasn't sure why, but he wanted to be the first one to buy something for his little girl.

"I'm sure she'll love anything you get for her," Jessie said, placing her hand on his arm. She stared at the stuffed toy for a moment before she smiled. "You know, I hadn't thought about a unicorn theme for the nursery. But I really like it. Thank you for that."

Nate grinned. "Nice to know I'm good for something besides making you pregnant."

Her expression was thoughtful when she looked up at him and he briefly wondered if he'd said something she took offense to. The websites he visited during his research said that a pregnant woman could be overly sensitive at times and about things that normally wouldn't matter.

"It's kind of rough for dads, isn't it?" she asked, suddenly putting her arms around him to give him a hug. "In a way, I'm sure you feel a little like you're on the outside looking in. All of the changes are happening to me and all you get to do is watch."

He automatically closed his arms around her and thanked the powers that be that he hadn't upset her. "I don't mind too much as long as I get to watch you." Kissing her forehead, he smiled. "It's my favorite pastime."

"I love watching you, too, cowboy." When she stepped away from him, her sweet smile sent his blood pressure soaring. "We'd better get this finished and drive back to your ranch."

"Is there a reason we need to hurry back home?" he asked, watching her scan a car seat and stroller combination before moving on to add a high chair to the items on the registry.

Grinning, she nodded. "I think we need to take a nap."

Confused, he stood in the middle of the baby-mattress aisle for a minute before it dawned on him what she meant. He had also noticed the websites mentioning that during the second trimester some women noticed a decisive increase in their libido because of all the extra hormones. It certainly seemed to be the case with Jessie. She had suggested an afternoon "nap" the past couple of days.

He couldn't seem to stop grinning. He didn't mind at all that she wanted him to take naps with her. Come to think of it, he was feeling a little "sleepy" himself.

An hour and a half later, Nate smiled as they entered the master bedroom and he removed his boots. "Thanks for letting me tag along while you scanned all that stuff at the baby store."

She reached up to put her arms around his neck and he automatically wrapped his around her waist. "I love that you want to be so involved, Nate."

"I wouldn't think to be anything else but involved," he admitted, realizing it was true. "Even if we didn't plan on it happening, we created this baby together. I'm not going to just sit back and let you go through any of this alone. It's a joint effort, darlin'. And like Lane would say in one of his poker games, I'm all in."

"That means so much to me, Nate." The expression

on her pretty face robbed him of breath and he knew without a shadow of doubt that he wanted to be the only man she ever looked at that way.

Before he could process what that might mean, she raised up on tiptoe and gave him a kiss that registered a solid ten on his internal Richter scale. As her soft lips caressed his, her nails lightly grazed the back of his neck and sent a shockwave of heat racing straight to the most vulnerable part of him. Jessie had always had that effect on him and he knew for certain she always would.

"I need you," he said, kissing her lips, her chin and along her jaw to her temple. His voice sounded a lot like a rusty hinge and he was surprised he was able to form a coherent thought, let alone verbalize it.

"I need you, too," she said, sending another wave of heat through him when she kissed the pulse at the base of his throat. She reached to unfasten the snaps on his shirt. "You made me a promise the other night and I'm going to collect on it."

"What was that?" It didn't matter what she wanted. Right at that minute, he'd jump off a cliff if she asked him to.

"You told me that I could take your clothes off of you," she said, grinning.

Nate laughed. "Well, never let it be said that I went back on my word. Have at it, darlin'."

When she tugged the tail of his shirt from his jeans, Nate loved the playful look that crossed her face. Unless he missed his guess, she was going to treat him to a little sensual foreplay and a whole hell of a lot of torment before they made love.

Pushing the shirt from his shoulders and down his arms, he couldn't wait to see what she had in store for him next as she tossed it aside and reached for his belt buckle. He was thankful she made quick work of the leather strap and the button at his waistband. His jeans had become way tighter than what was comfortable and he couldn't wait to get out of them.

But apparently Jessie had other ideas. She toyed with the tab of his zipper a moment before she abandoned it in favor of running her index finger down the metal teeth and back up over his arousal.

He groaned. "You're trying to make me crazy, aren't you?"

"Is it working?" she asked, her smile promising.

Unable to get his vocal cords to work, he nodded.

"You seem to have a problem," she commented as she eased the zipper down a fraction of an inch. "Do you want me to check it out for you?"

Nate forced himself to breathe. "If you don't, I'll be crawling the walls in another minute or two."

Her delightful laughter was like a balm to his soul. "I certainly don't want to be the cause of that," she said, taking the zipper down a little farther. By the time she finally lowered it completely, Nate felt as if every bit of air had been sucked from the room.

But if he had thought she was finished teasing him, he was dead wrong. When she shoved his jeans down his legs and he stepped out of them, instead of taking off his boxer briefs right away, Jessie ran her finger along the top of the elastic waistband, then down the seams of the fly.

Closing his eyes, Nate let his head fall back as he tried to draw in enough oxygen. He wanted to let her take her time and have her fun, but he wasn't sure how much more he could stand.

"Jessie…don't get me wrong…I'm loving everything you're doing to me," he managed to get out as he opened his eyes and his gaze met hers. "But…if you keep that up much longer…I'm going to disappoint both of us."

"Then I suppose I'd better get you out of these," she said, slipping her fingers beneath the elastic band.

Just the feel of her fingertips on his skin was like a lightning strike to his system. In all of his thirty-three years he could never remember being hotter or harder than he was at that moment. His engine was definitely revved and firing on all cylinders. Much more and he was going to explode.

"I really don't know how much more of this I can take," he said, feeling perspiration pop out on his forehead and upper lip.

When she carefully freed him from the black cotton boxer briefs, Nate had had enough. He'd kept his end of the bargain and allowed her to take off his clothes. Now it was time for him to take control.

"Playtime is over, darlin'," he said, whisking her maternity top over her head in one smooth motion. Dropping it on top of his clothes, he unfastened her bra with one flick of his fingers.

"How do you do that?" she asked, sounding as breathless as he did.

"Do what?" he asked, adding the scrap of lace to the pile, then helping her out of her jeans and panties.

"It takes me longer to fasten my bra than it takes you to unfasten it," she said, bracing her hands on his chest as she stepped out of the rest of her clothes.

"Talent, darlin'." He laughed, releasing some of the tension gripping him. "I have a lot of hidden talents."

She glanced down at his aroused body and smiled. "And some that are hard to hide."

Taking her in his arms, he grinned. "Well, you got the hard part right. And no, I don't intend to hide how much I want you." He kissed her as he picked her up. "I don't even want to try. Now, put your legs around my waist, Jessie. We're going to do something you suggested."

She rested her forehead against his as he carried her over to the bed. "We're going to be a little creative?"

He nodded as he sat on the edge of the mattress and settled her on his lap. "This way I get to be closer to you. I can kiss you and hold you to me."

Nate lifted her and felt like he might pass out from the mind-blowing feel of her body consuming his. It was always this way with Jessie. When she held his body inside hers, he felt like he was part of everything that would ever matter to him.

Once she was completely settled over him, he placed his hands on her hips and helped her set a slow, gentle pace. Sooner than he wanted, his focus began to narrow and a red haze clouded his mind. He needed to complete the act of loving her, needed to once again leave a part of himself in her safekeeping. But not without assuring her pleasure before his own.

When he felt her body tighten around him, Nate knew that Jessie was close to finding her satisfaction, and sliding his hand between them, touched the tiny hidden nub of intense sensations. Her feminine muscles immediately began to gently caress him as she found her release. Only then did he give in to his own need and, tightening his arms around her, found the fulfillment of loving her.

As his strength began to return, Nate lifted her to the center of the bed, then lay down beside her. Gathering her into his arms, he reached down to pull the navy blue satin sheet over them as their bodies cooled.

Kissing the top of her head, he asked, "Are you all right, darlin'?"

"I'm wonderful," she said, snuggling into him.

"And incredible," he added. "And amazing. And—"

"I get the idea," she interrupted, laughing. "I feel the same way about you."

They were silent for a few minutes before Nate thought to ask, "Have you decided what you're going to name the baby?"

Jessie shook her head. "I thought we could do that together. Do you have a name that you're particularly fond of?"

"Not really," he admitted. He'd noticed that several of the websites he'd visited had lists of names for babies, but he hadn't even considered that she would let him help her choose a name for their daughter. "I'll start thinking about it and let you know if I come up with one I like."

"When we decide what to name her, I'd like to keep it a secret until she's born," Jessie said, hiding a yawn behind her delicate hand. "Besides not wanting people to try to talk us out of the name we choose, I want to introduce her to everyone by name."

"That works for me," he agreed. Chuckling, he asked, "I don't guess we can keep my brothers in the dark about her being a girl until then, can we?" He knew they couldn't, but if Jaron's reaction was any indication, the rest of his brothers were going to be merciless in their good-natured ribbing.

Jessie smiled tiredly and shook her head. "I promised to let your sisters-in-law know what we're having so they can choose appropriate decorations for the shower." Yawning again, her eyes drifted shut. "I'll call Bria after I get up from...our nap."

Her last couple of words were slurred and Nate knew without looking that Jessie was sound asleep. Smiling, he kissed the top of her head, arranged a pillow to support her back and eased out of bed. After a quick shower, he got dressed and, folding her discarded clothes, placed them on the bench at the end of the bed.

Heading downstairs, he walked into his office to turn on his computer. He had more research to do—this time to find names he liked for the baby.

Nate couldn't help but grin. For someone who could care less about technology, he sure had spent a lot of his time lately searching for things on the computer.

But as he read through list after list of baby names,

he found his mind wandering to the woman upstairs in his bed. How had he gotten so lucky that Jessie wanted to be with him—loved him? And there wasn't a doubt in his mind that she did. He had seen it in her eyes and felt it in her soft touch. And he'd lost count of the number of times she had said she loved something that he'd said or that it meant so much to her.

He took a deep breath and admitted to himself what he had suspected had been behind breaking up with her so many times—he had been falling for her. Every time he felt himself starting to care for Jessie more than he was comfortable with, he had cut and run in a lame attempt to avoid what he now knew had been the inevitable. He was in love with Jessie and probably had been from the moment they met.

His heart stalled and his stomach clenched almost painfully. What did he know about love?

He loved his family, but that was different. His brothers and sisters-in-law loved him and accepted him unconditionally. They weren't going to condemn him for past mistakes and the run-ins he'd had with the law when he was younger. Would Jessie be able to overlook his shortcomings and love him anyway?

Then there was his fear of reverting to the earliest example he'd had of what a husband and father was supposed to be. His biggest fear had always been that he would turn out to be like his shiftless biological father. To his knowledge Joe Rafferty had never held a job longer than it took him to show up and quit. He'd been content to spend his days sitting in front of the television with a bottle of whiskey in one hand and cigar in the other while Nate and Sam's mother worked herself to death to support all of them. After her death, Joe had abandoned his two adolescent sons to fend for themselves and went in search of another meal ticket elsewhere. They hadn't seen or heard from him again. And that was just fine with his sons. Even when the bastard was around all he had ever done was criticize and demean them.

Nate knew he wasn't anything like his old man in most ways. Unlike his father, Nate wasn't afraid to work for the things he wanted. He had put in the time and effort to get a college education, wisely invested the money that he'd earned from rodeo and amassed a sizable fortune. He had a huge ranch, a house that some might consider a mansion and enough money in the bank that he never had to work another day in his life if he didn't want to. But those were all material things. What about meeting the emotional needs of a wife and child? Could he be everything Jessie and his little girl needed him to be?

Sitting back in his desk chair, he stared at the computer screen without seeing it. Although it scared the hell out of him that he might let them down in some way, he knew he loved them and would do everything humanly possible to protect them from any kind of harm—both physical and emotional.

His biggest concern now was telling Jessie about his past and the reason he had never really considered himself husband and father material. He wasn't proud of it and would rather climb a barbed-wire fence buck naked than to have to tell her about it. But she deserved to know the truth—that the father of her baby was a convicted felon.

Could she accept being with a man who had a criminal record, even if it had been sealed by the courts because he'd been a juvenile when he committed the crimes? He was pretty sure she would understand the reasons he and Sam had resorted to breaking the law. But would she be able to trust and still love him once he laid it all on the line and told her about his childhood and the concern he had always had that he would somehow turn out to be like his worthless father? What would he do if it led her to leave him?

Nate wasn't sure. He only hoped that once he told her, she would understand and love him anyway.

Eight

When Jessie woke up from her nap, she wasn't surprised to find herself in bed alone. Nate had probably gone downstairs to his office to work on his computer. She had no idea what the project was, but it seemed that every spare minute he had, he was researching something.

Stretching, she felt a twinge in her right side and decided that she might need to invest in one of the bigger pregnancy pillows. Of course, she wouldn't need one except for naps. At night, Nate was all the support she needed.

She smiled as she got out of bed and walked into the bathroom for a quick shower. Nate had been amazing the past few weeks. He had been attentive, supportive and erased all doubt that he would be a good father. But what about her?

Her smile faded. She loved him with every fiber of her being and knew without question that she would for the rest of her life. But she wasn't sure he loved her. She knew he cared deeply for her. No man would have been as tender or as understanding of her insecurities about her pregnant body if he didn't. But he had never told her he loved her and he'd stopped mentioning that he wanted them to get married. Did that mean he had changed his mind? Could he want the baby, but not her?

She knew she could be reading more into the situation than what was there. Her hormones had been anything but stable lately and she could very well be misinterpreting things. But with no answers there was only one way to find out what was happening in their relationship. As she got dressed, she decided it was time that they sat down and had a talk about what the future held for them.

She rubbed her right side. The nagging twinge had turned to a constant dull ache. The baby was probably pressing against a nerve, she decided as she started downstairs. As active as her daughter had been lately, it felt as if she was practicing to be an Olympic gymnast.

"What do you think of Hope or Faith for the baby's name?" Nate asked, walking out of his office as she reached the bottom of the stairs.

"Hope and Faith are very nice names," she said, wondering why she suddenly felt hot and a bit weak. "Why don't we start a list of names and then choose the one we both like best?"

"It sounds like we have a plan," he said, grinning as he walked over to kiss her. Leaning back, he frowned. "Are you feeling all right? You feel pretty warm."

"I-I'm...not sure," she said haltingly when the ache in her side turned to actual pain.

"Jessie, what's wrong?" he demanded, holding her up when her knees started to buckle.

"Nate...something's...wrong," she said, holding on to the front of his shirt when another wave of weakness washed over her.

He quickly swept her up into his arms and instead of climbing the stairs, hurried to place her on the couch in the family room. "I'm calling Life Flight," he said, taking his cell phone from the holder on his belt.

While Nate made the call to the emergency service, Jessie's nurse's training kicked in and, assessing her symptoms, she was fairly certain she had a hot appendix. If that was the case, she was going to need surgery. That was a significant risk to the baby and she wanted the best care possible.

"Tell them I'm twenty-one weeks pregnant and showing symptoms of appendicitis," she instructed, trying to keep her growing panic at bay. "I need to go to the hospital where I work. It's a Level 1 Trauma Center and they'll be better able to deal with whatever I need to have done."

After giving the air-ambulance service the information and their location, Nate knelt down beside her and held her hand. "Stephenville Hospital is closer, darlin'. We could see a doctor sooner if you go there."

She shook her head. "If I have to have surgery it

might cause me...to go into labor," she tried to explain. Breathless from the pain, she finished, "The hospital where I work has one of the...best neonatology units... in the state. It's where our baby would have...the best chance of survival if she's born because of this."

"I give you my word that's where I'll make them take you," he stated.

Jessie could tell by the determined look on Nate's handsome face that if the paramedics tried to talk him into letting them take her to the nearest hospital in Stephenville, they would have a fight on their hands. And although that was normal medical protocol, she knew what she needed and didn't want to waste the time being assessed by the medical staff in Stephenville only to be sent to Waco later anyway. That would be a huge waste of precious time and might prove to be too late for her or the baby—or both.

As soon as the helicopter took off with Jessie on board, Nate jumped into his truck and drove like a bat out of hell toward Waco. When he asked if he could go with them, he was told there wasn't enough room. Although he hated being away from her, he understood. He wanted them to be able to do whatever needed to be done for Jessie and if that meant leaving him to get to the hospital on his own, then so be it. Fortunately, he had a friend who was a member of the Texas Highway Patrol and with one phone call to explain the situation and what he needed, Nate had a police escort from Beaver Dam all the way to the hospital's parking lot.

Even though he made the drive in record time, when

he ran into the hospital and up to the desk in the ER, he felt like it had been an eternity since he had watched the helicopter lift off from his ranch yard. "My...wife, Jessica Farrell was brought in a little while ago by helicopter," he informed the older woman behind the desk. "She's five and a half months pregnant and thinks she might have appendicitis."

The woman nodded. "She's in triage now and the trauma surgeon on call is with her. If you'll please have a seat in the waiting area, the doctor will come out and talk to you as soon as he's finished assessing your wife."

Too keyed up to sit still, Nate stepped outside to make a quick call to his brother Sam to let the family know what was going on, then went back inside to stand just outside the double doors leading back to the examination rooms. He had lied to the receptionist about being married to Jessie, but he didn't give a damn. Jessie was his woman, pregnant with his baby and he didn't want to take the chance of them refusing to give him any information about her condition or allowing him to see her.

"Sir, I'm afraid you'll have to go to the waiting room," the older woman insisted when she noticed him stationed by the doors.

Walking back to the desk where she sat, he shook his head. "Ma'am, I'm sorry, but I can't do that. My whole world is just beyond those doors and if I can't be with her, then I want to be as close to her as I can get."

The woman stared at him for a moment before she pointed to a spot close to where he had been standing.

"Stand over there, son. You'll be out of the way and as close as I can let you get right now." She gave him a reassuring smile. "I'm sure the doctor will be out soon to tell you what her diagnosis is and what they need to do to treat her."

"Thank you," Nate said, walking over to where the woman had indicated.

He could see through the small narrow windows on the doors, but he had no idea where Jessie was and his view was obscured by the drawn curtains of the cubicles. Glancing at the clock on the wall, he wondered what the hell could be taking so long. They needed to do something and soon.

Nate's stomach drew up into a tight knot when he watched a man in blue scrubs and a white lab coat leave one of the cubicles and start walking toward the doors. Opening one of them, he asked, "Mr. Farrell?"

"The name's Rafferty," Nate said. "Jessica Farrell is my wife." That was twice he'd lied in the past twenty minutes and two times more than he had in the past twenty years. But he wasn't taking any chances of them not letting him know what was going on.

He briefly thought the doctor might question them having different last names. But the man didn't even bat an eye. Of course, a lot of married women chose to keep their own surnames these days, so he probably didn't think there was anything unusual about it.

"I'm Dr. Chavez," he introduced himself. "I'm the trauma surgeon who will be doing your wife's appendectomy. She was right about having appendicitis and we need to get her into surgery right away to keep the appendix from rupturing. Under normal circumstances it would be a routine surgery. But because of her pregnancy it raises the risk to both her and the fetus. I've called in a team of specialists to stand by in case the surgery throws your wife into labor and we have to take the baby by C-section."

"Can I see her before the surgery?" Nate asked, needing to let her know he was there for her. If they'd let him, he'd go into surgery with her. He knew they wouldn't allow that, but he would gladly go if he could.

The doctor motioned for Nate to follow him. "Some of the surgical team will be coming anytime to take her upstairs to surgery and we've already administered a preop sedative, so I doubt you'll be able to talk to her." He stopped Nate just outside the curtained-off cubicle. "I want to assure you that we'll do everything we can for both her and the baby, Mr. Rafferty. But as I said before, there are risks for both of them."

Nate felt as if his entire world was falling apart around him. With a lump the size of his fist clogging his throat, he did his best to clear it and get the words out that no man ever wanted to have to say. "If it comes down to saving her or the baby, please save Jessie."

Dr. Chavez nodded. "We'll do all we can."

While the doctor hurried off to scrub for surgery, Nate stepped into the cubicle and walked up to the bed where Jessie lay with her eyes closed. Taking her hand in his, he gave it a gentle squeeze. "Jessie, I'm here for you now and always will be, darlin'," he said, feeling about as helpless as he could ever remember.

What had kept him from telling her he loved her

when deep down he was sure that's all she'd ever wanted from him? Why had he waited, instead of truly giving her his all? Jessie deserved to know everything about him and he wanted nothing more than to tell her and beg her to love him in spite of it. But had he waited too long? Dear God, would he even have another chance?

Before he could tell her how much he loved her and needed her more than the air he breathed, two members of the surgical team opened the curtain. "We're going to take your wife upstairs now, Mr. Rafferty," one of them said. "You can go up to the surgical waiting room on the fourth floor. The doctor will see you up there after the surgery is over to let you know how everything went."

Nate leaned over the rail to kiss Jessie's forehead and reluctantly let go of her hand as the two nurses moved the bed out into the hall. As he stood there watching them roll her away from him, he would have given anything to trade places with her—to go through this crisis so she didn't have to. When they moved the bed through a set of doors at the end of the hall and out of his sight, Nate took several shuddering breaths. Feeling a drop of moisture on his cheek, he impatiently swiped it away and headed for the elevators. He hadn't cried since he was fifteen years old, but he found himself fighting with everything he had in him to keep his emotions in check as he rode the elevator alone to the fourth floor, got off and walked into the waiting area.

Finding a corner of the big room that was relatively deserted, he sat down and stared at his boot tops. There weren't a lot of things he was afraid of. He could climb on the back of one of the biggest, rankest bulls, get thrown off and stare death in the face when the ornery animal came after him and never think a thing about it. But right now he was scared to death.

What if he lost Jessie? Or what if something happened to the baby? They hadn't even had the chance to give their little girl a name.

Scrubbing his palms over his face to push away the emotion threatening to swamp him, he leaned forward to rest his forearms on his knees and stare down at his loosely clasped hands. Hank had always told him and his brothers that a positive attitude was half of any battle. But it was damned hard to have positive thoughts when all of the what-ifs were bombarding him from all sides.

"Have you heard anything, Nate?"

At the sound of Sam's voice, Nate looked up to see all five of his brothers walking across the waiting room toward him. He wasn't the least bit surprised that they had all dropped whatever they were doing to come to the hospital to lend their moral support. It had been that way for the six of them since their days at the Last Chance Ranch. They had each other's back no matter what and he'd never been more glad to see them than he was at that moment.

"They took her into surgery about an hour ago," he said, glancing at the clock over the waiting room doors.

"What did the doctor say?" Ryder asked, sitting down beside him.

Explaining what had taken place and the doctor's

diagnosis, Nate finished, "He has a team of specialists standing by in case something happens and they have to deliver the baby."

"Everything is going to work out, Nate," T.J. insisted. "Jessie and the baby are both going to come through this with flying colors."

The most optimistic of the band of brothers, T.J. was always the one they could count on to lift their spirits when they were down. But as much as Nate tried to believe his brother, he couldn't stop thinking about the look on the doctor's face when Chavez told him about the risks to Jessie's and the baby's lives.

"T.J.'s right," Sam said, nodding. He sat down in the chair across from Nate. "Jessie and the baby will both be fine. You have to believe that."

Nodding, Nate took a deep breath. "We just found out a few days ago that we're having a girl."

Giving him a reassuring smile, Ryder placed his hand on Nate's shoulders. "About sixteen years from now, when our girls start dating, we can trade what scare tactics we're using to keep the boys in line."

"The day of the ultrasound I decided it might not be a bad idea to get a couple more guns to clean," Nate said, praying that he had reason to do just that.

"T.J., why don't you and I run down to the cafeteria to get us all a cup of coffee," Lane suggested.

"Good idea," T.J. said, nodding. "Hang in there, Nate. We'll be right back."

Nate nodded as he watched them leave. The last time he sat in a hospital waiting room it was with Bria when they were waiting on word about Sam's concussion. That had been two and half years ago—the day he met Jessie.

While Ryder and Sam started talking about Bria and Summer getting babysitters so they could join the men at the hospital, Jaron lowered himself into the chair on the other side of Nate. He had always been the quiet one of the bunch, but he was more silent than usual.

"What's up, bro?" Nate asked, careful to keep his voice low.

Jaron shrugged. "I was just wondering if anyone thought to call Mariah and let her know what happened. You know how she gets her nose out of joint when something's going on with the family and she doesn't know about it."

Nate shook his head. "I'm not sure. Maybe you better give her a call and tell her."

Nate knew that Jaron was looking for an excuse to talk to Mariah and he couldn't help but wonder how much longer his brother was going to be able to resist what the rest of them had known for years. Jaron and Mariah were meant to be together.

Jaron hesitated for a minute before he stood up. "I probably better go outside for that. You know how the staff gets when somebody uses a cell phone inside the hospital."

Nate didn't bother pointing out that most hospitals had relaxed their rules about cell phone use. Jaron was trying to avoid the rest of their brothers ribbing him later about calling her.

When Jaron walked out of the room to make his call to Mariah, Lane and T.J. returned with the coffee and handed one of the cups to Jaron as they passed in the doorway. Nate watched them talk for a moment before Lane and T.J. continued across the room.

Accepting the cup Lane handed him and unable to sit still any longer, Nate stood up and walked over to the window overlooking the street below. What could be taking so long? It had been almost two hours since they took Jessie into surgery and every damn minute of it had been pure hell for him.

"You okay?" Sam asked, walking over to join him.

Nate gave a short nod. "I just couldn't sit still anymore. I feel like I need to be doing something, but there isn't a damned thing I can do to protect her and the baby from this."

"I understand." His brother hooked his thumb toward the door. "Do you need to go outside for some air?"

"No, I'm not leaving," Nate said firmly. He took a sip of the bitter coffee. "As far as that goes, I don't intend to leave until I take Jessie home with me."

Sam nodded. "I'd feel the same way if Bria was the one in the operating room."

The sound of his brothers rising to their feet to join him and Sam by the window in a gesture of support had Nate turning to see Dr. Chavez making his way over to him. Whether from dread of what the man might say, relief that the surgery was over or the emotion threatening his composure, Nate couldn't for the life of him find his voice to ask the man if Jessie was all right.

"Mr. Rafferty, your wife made it through the surgery with no problems," he said, reaching up to remove his surgical cap. "We were lucky and got the appendix out before it ruptured. Everything is fine and she should be able to go home in a couple of days."

"Thank God!" The relief flowing through Nate was so intense it caused him to feel a little light-headed. "What about the baby?"

"We're good there as well," the doctor said, smiling for the first time since Nate met him in the ER. "I had an ob-gyn who specializes in high-risk pregnancies monitor the fetus throughout the surgery and she'll continue to watch things while Jessie is in recovery."

"When can I see her?" Nate needed to see for himself that Jessie was all right.

Dr. Chavez checked his watch. "They should be moving her to a room in about an hour. You'll be able to see her then, but I doubt you'll be able to talk to her much. The remnants of the anesthesia are going to cause her to sleep and she probably won't be completely out from under that until morning."

For the first time since Jessie came downstairs after her nap that afternoon, Nate felt some of the gut-wrenching fear that had held him in its grip begin to ease. "I can't thank you enough, doc," Nate said, shaking the man's hand. As the doctor turned to leave, Nate suddenly felt like his knees might buckle and, making it over to one of the chairs, he sat down.

"What's this about 'your wife'?" Ryder asked, raising one dark eyebrow. "Do you have something you'd like to tell us, bro?"

Nate shook his head. "I lied and told them Jessie was my wife. Hank might be spinning in his grave right about now because one of his boys wasn't completely honest, but I didn't want to take a chance that they wouldn't let me see her or let me know what was happening."

"If we'd been in your shoes, any one of us would have done the same thing," Lane stated. All of his brothers nodded in unison.

"How's that going for you?" T.J. asked. "Any progress toward changing her mind about getting married?"

"To tell you the truth, we haven't got around to talking about it lately," Nate admitted. "But that's going to change as soon as she gets out of the hospital and I take her home. I don't care if I have to wear out the knees on a new pair of jeans from begging. I'm going to do whatever it takes to make Jessie my wife."

Nine

When Jessie roused the room was dark and for a brief moment she wondered where she was and why the right side of her stomach was extremely sore. Looking around, she realized she was in a hospital room and vaguely remembered being airlifted from Nate's ranch to the hospital where she worked because she had appendicitis.

Suddenly frightened by what that could mean, she immediately placed her hand on her stomach. "My baby," she whispered.

As if responding to her mother's voice, Jessie's little girl moved, then gave her a definite poke. Tears of joy filled Jessie's eyes and her breath caught on a sob. Her baby was all right.

Saying a silent prayer of thanks, she became aware

of another person in the room and turning her head she found Nate sitting in a chair beside the bed. With his head leaned back at an odd angle, his arms folded across his chest and his long legs extended out in front of him and crossed at the ankles, she could tell he was sound asleep. He looked uncomfortable and she started to wake him, but her eyelids were so heavy and, unable to stop herself, she let them drift shut.

Sometime before dawn, a lab worker woke Jessie to draw blood for testing and she noticed that the chair beside her hospital bed was empty. Where was Nate? Why hadn't he stayed with her? For a brief moment she thought she heard his voice as the lab worker left the room, but the shadows began to close in on her and she once again fell back to sleep.

"It's time to wake up and eat your breakfast, darlin'."

At the sound of Nate's deep baritone, Jessie opened her eyes and for the first time since she was given a preop sedative in the ER she didn't feel like she was struggling to get through a thick fog. "Were you here all night?" she asked, knowing by the shadow of beard on his lean cheeks that he had been.

"I wouldn't think of being anywhere else." He pointed to the tray of food on the overbed table. "The nurse told me I could raise the head of the bed so you can eat."

She eyed the bowl of Cream of Wheat. Just the sight of it caused her to shudder. "I'm not all that hungry. But I will eat the yogurt and drink the milk."

"Not a fan of the cereal?" he asked, pushing the

button on the side of the bed to raise it until she was a little more upright.

"No." When he took the foil top off the yogurt and handed it to her along with a spoon, she asked, "Did they say when I'll be discharged?"

"I talked to the hospitalist just a little while ago and he said you might be going home as early as tomorrow morning." He shook his head. "They sure don't keep patients in the hospital as long as they used to."

She ate most of the yogurt, then took a drink of the milk. "How did you get them to let you stay here in the room with me last night? Hospital policy discourages after-hours visitors."

He shrugged. "I refused to leave."

"And they didn't call security?" she asked, unable to believe he'd gotten away with it.

"They did, but I knew the guard." Grinning, he took the empty yogurt carton and spoon from her. "For the past couple of years he's been one of the Justin Heelers attending to injuries during the annual rodeo my brothers and I put on in honor of our foster dad. He convinced the nurses that I'm relatively harmless."

Moving the overbed table out of the way, he lowered the rail on the bed and sat on the edge of the mattress beside her. "I need to tell you something."

"What is it?" she asked. "Is it the baby? I think I remember feeling her move sometime during the night. She's okay, isn't she?"

"Everything is fine with the baby," he reassured her. "It's something I did yesterday when I first arrived at the hospital that you might not like too much."

Relieved that the baby was indeed all right, she breathed a little easier. "What did you do?"

He gave her a sheepish grin. "Don't be surprised if the nurses and doctor refer to me as your husband."

"Why?" She couldn't imagine why he would do that.

Taking her hands in his, he explained, "They had already given you a sedative and I wasn't sure they'd let me in the room to see you before they took you into surgery or give me any kind of information about your condition if I didn't tell them you were my wife."

As she thought about it, she had to admit he had a point. Privacy was a big issue and he might very well have been denied visitation as well as information.

"Okay, I won't correct them," she promised. "But when we get back to your place, we need to talk about some things."

He nodded. "I've been thinking the same thing, dar-lin'." His expression turned as serious as she had ever seen. "I'd talk to you here, but I want privacy for some of the things I have to tell you."

"All right," she agreed, wondering what he was going to say.

When he leaned forward, he gave her a gentle kiss. "If you don't mind, I think I'm going to go home for a shower and to change clothes. Is there anything you need me to bring to you this afternoon when I return?"

"I'll need some clothes to wear back to your place tomorrow." They had cut her clothes off her in the ER and she wasn't about to go back to his ranch in a hos-pital gown. "There's a denim dress in the closet that would be perfect." The elastic waistband on her maternity slacks might put pressure on her incision and she wanted to avoid the irritation if possible.

"Anything else?" he asked. "Do you want me to get in touch with your folks and let them know what happened?"

Jessie shook her head. "I'll call them after we go back to your place."

It wasn't like they would have taken the time away from their real estate business to make the drive up from Houston to see about her anyway. She'd have to explain her relationship with her parents and why Nate had never met them. But that could wait until they returned to Nate's ranch. She was more curious about what Nate had to tell her that he wanted kept private.

When Nate pulled the Mercedes he rarely drove into the garage, Jessie waited until he came around to help her out of the car. He knew she was sore and moving slower than normal, but it was good to have her back at the Twin Oaks Ranch. Working at a hospital was one thing, but being a patient there was another matter entirely and he knew she was glad to leave. The two times he had to be hospitalized because of a rodeo injury, he had come to understand why so many people complained about needing to go home just to get some rest. It seemed that every hour someone came into the room to draw blood or take vital signs. And just as sure as he went to sleep, a nurse would wake him up to ask if he needed something.

"I'm so glad to be back here," Jessie commented as he helped her into the house.

"I had Rosemary make up the downstairs guest room because I thought steps might not be a good idea this soon after surgery," he said as they walked down the hall.

"That's probably a good idea." She smiled. "As slow as I'm moving it would probably take all night just to get up the stairs."

"Would you like to change into one of your night-shirts and lie down for a while?" Nate asked, wondering if she was tired from the hour's drive.

"No, I've been in bed for the past two days and I'd really like to be up for a while," she said, turning toward the family room.

"Do you want something to eat or drink?" he asked, trying to think if there was something else she might need.

She smiled. "You aren't going to hover, are you?"

"I'm just trying to make sure you're comfortable." He frowned. "Why do you ask?"

"Summer and Bria stopped by the hospital yesterday afternoon and they were telling me about Ryder's propensity to hover over Summer whenever she's ill," Jessie said, grinning. "I just wondered if you were going to be like him."

"Yeah, he does have a tendency to be an old mother hen where Summer and little Katie are concerned." Nate was beginning to understand how his brother felt about taking care of the woman and child he loved more than life itself. "Is there anything else you need?"

"Yes," she said as she sat down on the couch. "I'd

like to have that talk we discussed in the hospital yesterday."

What he had to tell her was going to take some time and was without question the most important conversation of his entire life, not to mention the most difficult. He was going to be laying his soul bare to her and once started it wasn't something that could be interrupted and picked up later. He could only hope she understood and loved him anyway.

"Are you sure you're up to it?" he asked.

She stared at him for a moment before she nodded. "Whether I'm going to like hearing what you want to tell me or not, things can't go on between us the way they've been, Nate."

"I agree," he said, praying she would understand and forgive him. Deciding there was no easy way to tell her about his past, he took a deep breath. "I'm a convicted felon."

Nate could tell by her shocked expression that was the last thing she expected. "When did that happen?"

"I told you up front that my brothers and I were foster kids and met when we all ended up being sent to the Last Chance Ranch," he said, reaching up to rub the growing tension at the back of his neck. "Believe me, we weren't sent there because we were little angels."

"I always assumed it was just a name," she said, shaking her head. "I didn't realize it had a literal meaning."

"Yeah, it was our last shot at keeping ourselves from being incarcerated," he stated flatly. "It was either finish growing up there or behind bars in a juvenile detention facility."

"What did you do that you were arrested?" she asked, her tone quiet.

"Sam and I started out stealing food and then graduated to robbing stores at gunpoint for cash." Unable to look at her for fear of seeing the condemnation on her pretty face, he walked over to gaze out the window at the land that represented how far he'd come in life.

She frowned. "What caused you to start stealing food?"

He shrugged. "Why does any kid start shoplifting food? We were hungry."

"Didn't your previous foster parents see that you had enough to eat?" He appreciated the indignation in her voice, but she had it wrong.

"Darlin', we didn't land in foster care until after we got caught robbing a convenience store," he admitted. "That was after our mom passed away and our dad abandoned us."

She gasped. "Oh, Nate, I'm so sorry."

"Don't be. The day our dad walked out and disappeared for good was the luckiest day of our lives," Nate said, unable to keep the bitterness from his voice. "He sat on his ass and let our mom work herself to death to support the four of us because he was too lazy to keep a job. And that wasn't his only flaw. He liked making us feel like it was our fault for everything that went wrong in his life. He had a way of talking to us that undermined any self-esteem or confidence we had."

"He was abusive?" she asked, sounding angry.

"Not physically. That would have required him to set down the bottle of whiskey he was nursing and get out of his recliner." Turning to face her, he shook his head. "Joe Rafferty preferred the mental abuse of telling us how worthless and pathetic we were."

"It sounds like it *was* the luckiest day of your lives," Jessie agreed. "How old were you when he left?"

"I was thirteen and Sam was fifteen when he cut out for good," Nate admitted. "We had been shoplifting food for a year or so, but it wasn't until he left that we found a gun he left behind in the hall closet. That's when we started holding up stores at gunpoint for the cash." He shook his head as he turned back to the window. "We had the idea that if we kept the bills paid, we'd be able to stay in the house and not end up sleeping in a back alley somewhere or put into the foster care system."

"How long were you able to keep up the ruse that you and Sam weren't on your own?" she asked, frowning. "I wouldn't think it would be all that easy."

"I can't remember exactly, but it wasn't too long," he admitted. "Probably a few months."

"How did you get caught?" He detected sympathy in her voice that he neither wanted nor deserved.

Looking back he couldn't believe how naive he'd been. "Sam was gone somewhere and I decided to hit a convenience store by myself because a final notice for the rent was posted on the door when I got home from school. I thought I would get the money we needed and everything would be fine."

"You continued to go to school?" She sounded surprised. "Most children wouldn't have tried to continue their education."

"We thought that if we kept going to school and made sure all the bills got paid, no one would be the wiser about the old man leaving and we would avoid being separated in the foster-care system." He shook his head. "I honestly don't know how we figured we would get away with it, but we tried."

"Children don't think things through like adults," Jessie said softly.

Nate walked over to sit on the coffee table in front of her. "That was apparent when Sam tried to take the blame and keep me out of trouble." He shook his head. "We didn't know it, but the police had been watching us and suspected we were the pair of kids robbing the stores around our neighborhood."

"You were only trying to survive and stay together," she said, reaching out to place her hand on his arm. "You were all the other had."

"That didn't make what we did right," he insisted. He needed her to understand that he wasn't telling her about his past to garner her sympathy. He was trying to explain why he had avoided making commitments and his fear of turning out to be like his father. "The bottom line is that I broke the law and even though the court records were sealed because we were underage, I'm still a convicted felon." He took a deep breath. "The main reason I kept breaking off our relationship when things started getting too serious was the fear I have that I would somehow turn out to be like our worthless old man."

She looked confused. "I'm afraid I don't see what that has to do with—"

"Until our dad took off and left me and Sam to fend for ourselves, all I heard was how useless I was. Then when I got in trouble and ended up with a record, I started to believe I was going to turn out just like the son of bitch who sired me." He took both of her hands in his. "All of my adult life, I've run from making a commitment because I didn't want to saddle a woman with a man like that. I didn't want my kids to suffer that kind of mental abuse. I don't intend to be that kind of man, but there are no guarantees, darlin'. All I can do is promise that I'll do everything in my power to be the best husband and father I can be."

"But you're nothing like your father," she insisted. She reached up to cup his cheek with her palm, sending hope coursing through him. "You're a good man, Nate. You've worked hard and earned everything you have. It sounds to me like that's something your father would have never thought of doing."

"I'm still a criminal," he said, wishing he could go back in time and change that part of his life. "You deserve better than that, Jessie."

"Stop it right now!" she said forcefully. "You had problems as a boy and a misguided belief that you could somehow make it all right. But you learned from your mistakes and thanks to Hank Calvert and his unique approach to teaching you right from wrong, you and your brothers have all turned your lives around. Any woman would be proud to call you her man."

"What about you, Jessie?" he asked. "Would you be

proud to call me your man?" He held his breath as he waited for her answer.

When she continued to stare at him, his heart felt like it had stopped beating. "What are you saying, Nate?" she finally asked.

He was pretty sure he knew what she wanted from him and for the first time in his life, he was ready to say it. "I love you, Jessie. Do you think you can overlook what I was before and be proud to be with the man I am now?"

Tears flooded her eyes and rolled down her cheeks. "Y-yes, Nate. All I've ever wanted is for you to love me."

Nate immediately dropped to one knee and, reaching into his front jeans pocket, removed the small black velvet box he'd been carrying around since stopping by the jewelers on his way back to the hospital yesterday afternoon. Taking her hand in his, he asked, "Will you marry me, Jessie? Will you let me make you proud to call me your husband for the rest of our lives?"

"Yes," she whispered. "I love you so much. I've always loved you."

He took the two-carat marquise-shaped diamond ring from the box and slipped it on the third finger of her left hand. When she started to lean forward to put her arms around his neck, he stopped her. "You just had surgery," he said, scooping her up in his arms. He sat down on the couch and gently placed her on his lap. "I don't want you hurting yourself."

Content to have her in his arms, they were silent for

a few minutes before he asked, "When do you want to get married, darlin'?"

She kissed him. "I know you have the National Finals the first part of December—"

"Do you think you'll be able to watch me make my last rides in Vegas?" he asked.

"You're going to stop riding?" she asked, looking hopeful.

He nodded. "Part of my job as your husband will be to eliminate as much of your stress and worry as I possibly can."

"I don't want you giving up your career because of my fears," she said, frowning.

"I'm not." He kissed the tip of her nose. "Jaron and I have both talked about retiring while we're still on top."

"Are you sure?"

"Positive."

"I'm not going to say that I won't resume my nursing career at some point in time, but I think I'd like to be a stay-at-home mom," she said thoughtfully. "At least, until our daughter starts school."

"Whatever you want to do is fine with me, darlin'." He held her close. "Now when do you want to get married?"

"Is Christmas too soon?" she asked, snuggling against him.

"Hell, no." He laughed. "The sooner the better."

"Are you going to ask Sam to be your best man?" Jessie asked, her smile radiant.

"Yeah, he's been my partner in crime all my life,"

Nate said, grinning. "I don't see any reason to change that now."

Jessie rolled her eyes. "You're impossible." Kissing him again, she smiled. "I thought I would ask Bria to be my matron of honor."

"Well, now that we have the wedding planned, we can move up the date," he teased. He'd never felt happier or more lighthearted in his entire life. "Darlin', you mentioned earlier that you had something you wanted to talk to me about. What was it?"

He watched her worry her lower lip for a moment before she admitted, "Just before I had the appendicitis attack, I was going to ask you if you had changed your mind about wanting us to get married."

"Why would you think that?" he asked, holding her close.

She laughed and it was the most delightful sound he'd ever heard. "You hadn't mentioned it and I thought you had lost interest in our relationship again."

"I made you a promise," he said, tipping her chin up to give her a kiss that rocked him to his core. "I gave you my word I wouldn't pressure you about getting married. And believe me, that wasn't easy when it was just about all I could think of."

"You could have hinted at it," she said, smiling.

"That would have broken my promise to you and that's something I will never do," he said honestly.

She stared at him a moment before she spoke again. "I have a confession to make."

"What's that, darlin'?" he asked, wondering what her secret could possibly be.

"You aren't the only one who has a parent they aren't particularly happy with," she admitted. "I have two that could improve in a lot of areas."

Nate listened to her explain about her parents having more interest in someone's net worth than the person. "I didn't want you having to go through the third degree about your bank account when it's none of their business," she finished.

Grinning, he whispered a number in her ear. "Do you think that would impress them?"

Her eyes were wide when she nodded. "Is that…"

"What I was worth a couple of years ago." He laughed. "My investment banker says I have a lot more now."

"I knew you spent a lot of time on the internet, but I had no idea you were watching the stock market," she said, shaking her head.

"Hell, I don't pay attention to the market," he said, laughing. "That stuff will make you crazy in a hurry."

"Then what were you researching if not stocks to invest in?" she asked, clearly confused.

"I wanted to learn all I could about pregnancy and what you were going through." He gave her a sheepish grin. "I was looking to see how I could make the next few months easier for you." He placed his hand on her stomach. "And I wanted to find out what was going on with our little girl."

When he felt the light movement within, his heart stalled. "Wow! She's moving, isn't she?"

Jessie nodded. "She's really active and I think she might be training to be a gymnast."

Nate knew he had to be grinning like a damned fool. "Thank you, Jessie."

"For what?" she asked, looking puzzled.

"You've given me everything I didn't even know I wanted," he said, kissing her with all the love he'd never dreamed would be his.

When he stared into her pretty violet eyes, he could see his haven—his safe place to land when life got to be more than he could handle on his own. And he fully intended to be the same for her.

"I love you, darlin'," he said, never wanting her to doubt it. "You and the baby are my world."

"And you're ours, cowboy," she said, pressing her soft, perfect lips to his. "Now and always."

Epilogue

On Christmas Eve as Nate waited by the fireplace in the Twin Oaks ranch house with Sam and the preacher from the church in Beaver Dam, he checked his watch. Within the next ten minutes or so, Jessie would be his wife and he was getting impatient. It seemed as though he had already spent a lifetime waiting for her. He couldn't wait to get started on the rest of his life with her.

"You aren't getting cold feet, are you?" Sam asked when Nate checked his watch again.

"No, I'd like to seal the deal before she changes *her* mind," Nate answered.

His brother laughed. "I never thought I'd see the day you'd be impatient to settle down."

"Yeah, it shocked the hell out of me, too," Nate said, grinning.

When the organist he had hired to play for the wedding broke into the first few notes of "Here Comes the Bride," Nate straightened his shoulders and looked toward the double doorway leading from the foyer into the family room. As he watched his sister-in-law Bria start to walk toward them, he held his breath and waited for Jessie and her father to step into view.

When he and Jessie went down to Houston right after Thanksgiving to tell the Farrells they were about to gain a soon-to-be retired rodeo cowboy for a son-in-law over Christmas and become the grandparents of a granddaughter in the spring, they had been anything but happy. But when Nate took Andrew Farrell aside and assured him that he loved Jessie, told him there wouldn't be a prenuptial agreement and had the man call Nate's investment banker to verify that Nate had more than enough to pay cash for any of the overpriced properties their real estate agency represented, they couldn't have been more enthusiastic. Nate didn't give a damn what they thought of him or how welcoming they were. All he wanted from them was a change in the way they treated Jessie, even if it did hinge on his, and now their daughter's, net worth. He loved her more than enough to make up for their shallow affections and that was something that would never come with a price tag attached.

The moment Jessie and her dad came into view and he saw her beautiful face, Nate's heart beat double time. She was absolutely gorgeous in her long white wedding gown and he knew for certain he would remember the moment for the rest of his days. He still had a hard time believing that in just a few minutes she would be his forever.

Waiting impatiently for them to reach him, when her father placed her hand in his, Nate felt as though he had been handed a rare and precious gift. "Are you ready to become Mrs. Nate Rafferty?" he asked, smiling at the only woman he would ever love.

Her smile lit his soul when she whispered, "I've been ready for this my entire life."

"Welcome to the ranks of the blissfully hitched," Ryder said, raising his beer bottle to toast Nate.

"I didn't think I'd ever say this, but I couldn't be happier about becoming a member of the club," Nate said, meaning it.

"Yeah, membership is damned nice," T.J. said, grinning as he looked over at his wife. They had announced at Thanksgiving that they were expecting to add another family member sometime in the summer and from what Heather told Jessie, T.J. had started hovering over her like Ryder did over his wife, Summer.

"So who won the pool?" Nate asked, taking a swig of his beer. "Didn't T.J. say we would be married by Christmas?"

Lane nodded. "I think he's won a couple of our betting pools lately."

"So what are we going to bet on now?" Sam asked.

Their gazes all swung toward Jaron.

"Oh, *hell* no," Jaron said, shaking his head vehemently. "I'm just fine on my own."

"I say Jaron and Mariah will be hitched by next fall," T.J. said, plunking down a hundred dollars on the bar.

"I've got Easter," Ryder spoke up, putting a hundred on top of T.J.'s.

"I'm going with Valentine's Day," Lane said, adding his money to the growing pile of bills.

"I've got the 4th of July." Sam added his bet. "What about you, Nate?"

"I'll take May," Nate said, topping off the pile of money with his hundred. He looked at his best friend, who was quietly fuming at being the subject of the betting frenzy. "Sorry, bro. But I have to agree with the others. Whenever you and Mariah are within twenty feet of each other, you could cut the tension with a knife."

"Probably because she wants to tear my head off and shout down the hole," Jaron shot back. "She still hasn't gotten over me being right about Sam and Lane both having boys when Bria and Taylor got pregnant."

"But she was right about me and Summer having a girl," Ryder interjected. "That should have made her happy."

"It did, right up until Lane and Taylor had a boy," Jaron said, shaking his head. "She took exception to me pointing out that I'd called it right two thirds of the time and she had only been right once."

"Yeah, women take a dim view of a man making comments like that," Sam said, laughing.

As the brothers continued to try to convince Jaron

that he and Mariah were destined to be together, Nate looked up to see Jessie smiling at him. It was the same smile she wore the night he had won the bull riding event at the National Finals rodeo—the night he had announced his retirement. Setting his beer bottle on the bar, he walked across the dance floor to take her in his arms.

"As nice as this reception is, I'm ready to start the honeymoon," he whispered. "How about you, Mrs. Rafferty?"

She nodded. "I love everyone and I couldn't be happier about becoming a member of the family, but I'd like to spend some time alone with my new husband."

Nate nodded toward her parents. "Do you think they'll be all right on their own?"

Jessie rolled her eyes. "Don't worry about them. I saw my dad pass out a couple of business cards to some of your rodeo friends."

He laughed. "Yeah, he never dreamed that rodeo cowboys could make damned good money riding a dusty old bull."

"Not until the most handsome retired cowboy I know enlightened him," she said, raising up on tiptoe to kiss his chin.

When the baby landed a kick to his navel, Nate chuckled. "I think she agrees with you."

"I think so," Jessie said, her beautiful smile sending his blood pressure sky high.

"Let's go get started on our life together," he said, taking her hand to lead her toward the door.

"I love you, cowboy," she said, looking up at him with more love in her eyes than he would ever deserve.

"And I love you, darlin'," he said, feeling like the luckiest man alive. "Forever and always."

* * * * *

THE GOOD, THE BAD AND THE TEXAN:
*Running with these billionaires
will be one wild ride.
Don't miss a single novel in this
bestselling series from*
USA TODAY *bestselling author Kathie DeNosky!*

*HIS MARRIAGE TO REMEMBER
A BABY BETWEEN FRIENDS
YOUR RANCH...OR MINE?
THE COWBOY'S WAY
PREGNANT WITH THE RANCHER'S BABY*

MILLS & BOON®
Desire™

PASSIONATE AND DRAMATIC LOVE STORIES

A sneak peek at next month's titles...

In stores from 20th November 2015:

- **Bane** – Brenda Jackson *and*
  Triplets Under the Tree – Kat Cantrell

- **Lone Star Holiday Proposal** – Yvonne Lindsay *and*
  A White Wedding Christmas – Andrea Laurence

- **The Rancher's Secret Son** – Sara Orwig *and*
  Taking the Boss to Bed – Joss Wood

Available at WHSmith, Tesco, Asda, Eason, Amazon and Apple

Just can't wait?
Buy our books online a month before they hit the shops!
visit www.millsandboon.co.uk

These books are also available in eBook format!